I0725743

<u>**Other Novels by Kristy Morgan Include:**</u>

The Adventures of Rocky and Skeeter: Rocky Goes to Jail

The Legend of Garrison Falls

Black Heart Revenge

Black Heart Retaliation

BLACK HEART
REDEMPTION

KRISTY MORGAN

Copyright © 2019 by Kristy Morgan.

ISBN   Softcover   978-1-950580-17-0

All rights reserved. No part of this book may be reproduced or transmitted in any form or by any means, electronic or mechanical, including photocopying, recording, or by any information storage and retrieval system without express written permission from the author, except in the case of brief quotations embodied in critical reviews and certain other non-commercial uses permitted by copyright law.

Printed in the United States of America.

To order additional copies of this book, contact:
Bookwhip
1-855-339-3589
https://www.bookwhip.com

ACKNOWLEDGEMENTS

First and foremost, always, I would like to thank my Lord and Savior, Jesus Christ for all of the things that He has made possible in my life. Without His love and guidance nothing would be possible. I love you Father! Thank you for everything, literally!

To my husband who has pushed for every goal with the intensity of someone pushing for his own dreams. He is the most wonderful manager. I am grateful for his love and assistance in all of my endeavors. I love you. You are the mate to my soul!

To my editors, Melissa Royster and Paris Ruddock, I thank you for the time and dedication that you have both put into every project. Without your wonderful insight I would truly be lost. I love you both.

To my daughter and extreme secretary, Jessica Kirkland, I thank you for all of the things you do to make my books possible. From corrections to the manuscript to scanning in jpegs, you are an office diva. Love you baby girl!

To my mother who listens to every new idea, without a peep, I thank you and love you very much. Thank you for all the support!

To my friend and coworker Clay cook, thank you for all the times that you let me pick your brain at work for geographical anomalies or fatalities.

To my friend and coworker that wishes to remain anonymous, you know who you are, Mr. Ed. Thank you for allowing me to pick your brain for geographical anomalies or fatalities.

To my son and computer specialist, Jesse O'Neal, I thank you for all of the things you do to make my books possible. From hooking up internet connections to bringing back computers from the blue desktop of death, you are the computer king. Love you baby boy!

To my sister, Katherine Threlkeld Huff, thank you for the time that you spent on this earth listening to me. You will forever be a part of what makes my life whole. Enjoy your mansion in the sky, my sweet angel-sister. I will love you forever!

DEDICATION

To my sweet husband, James Morgan. My best friend; my soul mate; I thank God for allowing me to have you by my side, as I walk through this life. Just knowing that all of my tomorrows will be faced with you by my side, fills my heart with peace. I cannot wait to walk into the future holding your hand, as we watch our grandchildren grow. I love you my darling. I will pray for you and lift you up through the years, as you have done for me.

My long-time family friend, Julie Morgan. May Heaven enjoy the beauty of your smile, the sweetness of your soul and the tenderness in your eyes. It was my privilege to have known you and shared in your life. I will think of you always. Our families will forever be intertwined. I pray all of our tomorrows will find you looking down, and watching over each of us.

CHAPTER

1

Morning dawned like any other: the hoots of animal calls dying on the wind, and the sound of the children's quiet whispers, as they tried not to wake their parents.

Jordan scooted closer to Lane. The chill in the air was undeniable. It was as if overnight, winter was upon them.

Though she grew tired of the drums in the distance, everything felt perfect. Jordan ignored the tireless efforts of the unknown tribe; they were probably just readying themselves for the hunt. Some of the tribes, Lane had explained, were still immersed in the traditions of their forefathers. The drums were played in celebration of the impending hunt. Nothing more.

"I love you." Her voice seemed to betray her thoughts before her mind could rationalize them.

"I love you, too." Lane admitted as he rolled over and pulled her body closer to his. Laughter erupted in hushed tones, from the other side of the tent.

"I think we have an audience." Jordan teased.

"You might be right, but I think I should go investigate." Lane sent out the warning.

A squeal split the air as both children fought for safety under their pallet of furs.

"No use hiding. I'll find you!" Lane moved across the tent with an exaggerated slow-gate. The menacing glare he must have held in his eyes was mirrored back in the feigned fear of Amelia's and Tristan's countenances.

Snatching the cover away, Lane roared like a beast, crazed with murderous intent. Amelia and Tristan screamed, as they ran pointedly to Jordan.

"She won't save you!" Lane carried on, weaving and bobbing as he crouched even lower. He made giant-exaggerated steps across the tent that seemed completely in place with his foreboding six-foot five stature.

Jordan choked back the laughter that was bubbling up inside of her.

"Yes she will!" Jordan hoisted the declaration. As a child stood behind each of her legs, peering out to see if their mother's assertion had made a difference in the intent of the viscous predator their father pretended to be. Giggles reigned supreme as the children hid further behind Jordan's legs, waiting for the verdict they knew would soon come: Would their father quiet his ranting? Would the savage beast he pretended to be, still under the command of their mother, or would he pursue them all?

Jordan knew too, that it could go either way. She stood ready for him to pounce. The adrenaline soaked through her veins as she stood at the helm of her feigned fort. She loved this game. It reminded her of her days with Black Heart, without the ugliness of death's dark shadow looming around every corner; calling her name.

She had been an agent for Black Heart, and like other agents, she was brought into the agency under false pretenses. Through a collective effort, Jordan, Lane, and some of their friends had been able to bring the dark dealings of Black Heart out into the light of truth.

Mr. Stanton, the Head of the Department, lay in a coma, still fighting for his life after a suicide attempt. Kirsten, one of the child-agents that Stanton had organized in an attempt to dull Jordan's senses and end her life, had been prompted by Garrison, Jordan's former partner to make a phone call. During the call, Kirsten used a voice distorter. She implied that every dark secret and every cruel deed Stanton had ever committed was known. Then Kirsten encouraged Mr. Stanton to turn to channel nine for the evening news report.

Lane had taken the story about Black Heart to a news reporter he knew well, Jerrod Fuller. Lane met Jerrod while on a mission trip in Honduras. Lane had immediately liked Jerrod. Though he was a reporter, Jerrod had always been candid in his reports of the news.

Though Jerrod had not been the actual reporter to divulge the truth on the eleven o'clock news showing, it had been his script that was read.

Jordan smiled slyly at Lane's still menacing, feigned-monster attempt. He was so into the character that it was almost believable. Amelia and Tristan alternated between giggling, and clutching the back of her legs. In moments like these, she found it easy to forget about the impending separation that they would soon endure.

It would be so easy to let her guard down, but she did not want him to see the fear and sadness that she felt. She tried to keep thoughts of his leaving, and how terribly she would miss him, from belying the truth in her eyes. Theirs was a special bond, forged by God. A love that had been ordained by the Creator of life, before they were born. Though the attempt was probably in vein, Jordan would make every effort to keep her anguish of his leaving from Lane's knowledge.

The serenity that she felt while nestled safely in his embrace would soon be forfeit. Lane would be headed back to the states to take Kirsten home in only a few short hours. Jordan would be left to face a world that she had only just begun to understand. In so many ways she could understand Amelia's and Tristan's need for security in the face of an imagined foe. Just as Lane loved their children, the people of the Cadotion village loved their family. Still, Jordan found herself quaking in the sight of their imagined threat. Opening up to others had never been one of her strong suits, but with Lane's ever-present example to draw upon she was able to manage.

After he was gone… Jordan couldn't finish the contemplation. She didn't want to imagine the bumbling mess she was bound to make of things in his absence.

Jordan was still lost in the revere of what ifs when Lane abruptly straightened from the menacing crouch he had adopted. Fear registered in his eyes, but only for an instant. Rocking back on his heels, Lane stared intently at the back wall of the tent. At first Jordan laughed. It seemed out of place for Lane to exhibit fear while trying to elicit fear, but just as quickly the thought passed. Jordan turned her attention to the back of the tent. She studied the furs that lined the wall: different shades of browns stood out in stark comparison to the red undertones. Some of the furs were rabbit, while other of the hides were dear…

Jordan searched with a deeper attention to detail, but still nothing about the wall, as far as she could tell, would cause such a reaction. Then suddenly, as if the wall faded out of existence the sound of drums finally made it into their haven.

Jordan hadn't noticed the drums before, or more to the point she had become desensitized to their presence, because they had been a part of the atmosphere for the better part of the week. Now though, as she listened, the sound of the distant drums grew, filling the air with an insistent hunger that seemed foreign, and yet personal in the same moment.

"Is that the same drums that we heard from the cove two days ago?" Jordan turned her intent emerald gaze back to the rear of the tent. She half expected the material to fade, and the distant drummers to materialize.

"It's the Manerky." Lane explained calmly, though something about the ready stance he adopted seemed… Jordan studied him, while trying to fill in the word that best described what she saw. His shoulders squared as his fist tightened at his side. His beautiful blue eyes had lost the angelic kindness, and had taken on the menacing intent of an eagle, searching the prairie floor for prey. Her six-foot five, light brown hair with blond streaks, blue eyed half angel, stood glaring at the back of the tent; not a trace of love caressed his heavenly visage. He was now the intent hunter with a foe in his sights. He would track and kill the threat to his family!

A thought occurred to Jordan as she watched her husband evolve into the ready hunter. "Why do the drums sound closer?" Jordan turned her attention back to the far wall of the tent.

"Because they are." Again, Lane sounded too calm.

Jordan looked then at the golden brown face of her daughter. It had been through a brutal attack on the Cadotion tribe that Amelia had come to be adopted into their family. Her mother had died during childbirth. Her father, while protecting the Cadotion village against the onslaught of the raiders, had met with an early death as well. It had been the Manerky tribe that had been responsible for that death, and destruction. Now, as she listened to their drums filter through the air, Jordan knew that the past was upon them.

Amelia's caramel eyes peered out from her angelic face. In that moment, Jordan was helplessly aware of the onslaught of terror that would befall them. The Manerky was an opportunistic tribe that fed off the weakness of the surrounding villages.

The Cadotions, the tribe that their family now lived in, were not a warring village. Their survival had hinged on two very important components: their all-consuming love for one another, and their keen intellect. The Cadotions were experts in survival. Each member of the tribe had a specific title. The title was indicative of the abilities that each particular tribesman possessed. None of those titles would paint any of the tribesmen as an avid hunter. None of the Cadotion villagers were killers. Their survival skills were grounded in everyday living, not the victory of the hunt.

For a long time, the threat that the Manerky represented had been silenced. Several of the surrounding tribes had issued a threat: if the Manerky raided any of the surrounding villages, each member of their tribe would be annihilated; every man, woman, and child.

"But the treaty?" Jordan threw the desperate plea out, though she knew it was pointless.

"Winter approaches." Lane said simply. "Most of the surrounding tribes have moved on in search of a warmer climate." Lane studied her eyes for a moment. She knew he would shield her from the truth, if it would help, but a lie was no shield. It would leave her unprepared to deal with the horrors to come.

Jordan turned then, to their three-year-old son, Tristan. His huge blue eyes were still filled with the anticipation of the attack. She gulped back the panic that filled her throat, and threatened to cut off her life's breath. Little did her sweet boy know, there was an attack on the horizon, and it would leave his untainted existence soiled, forever in the destruction of its foreboding aftermath…

CHAPTER

2

Edward Stanton pushed for the surface. He felt as though he were buried beneath tons of something… but what? His mind searched for a concrete—tangible, reality to hold on to; something that he could use to find his way out. Then finally, as if his hopes were a summons for the help he longed for, it reached down into the desolate, darkness. He struggled harder to make out the pulsing tick. He measured the sound against the last memory he had of the noises in his office. It was not the same. As he tested the noise another sound meshed with the first. He strained against the walls of his darkened prison, to make out the sound. It was a huffing sound, like labored breathing.

Edward was sure, he would be lying on the plush carpet, of his office, in a pool of his own blood. Dead. There should have been no other outcome. The incident with the long shard of crystal was no doubt, enough to have finished him off. As he listened to the ticking and huffing sounds, he knew with certainty that he was no longer in his office.

He tested his eyes, but something was obstructing his ability to open them. Panic filtered through his veins. He had finally done it! He was in a vegetative state! But where was he; where was his physical body? Edward concentrated. Stilling himself, he began trying to solve the mystery of his whereabouts. He squeezed his eyes shut. That worked! He felt exhilarated by the simple accomplishment. Okay… he thought. A vegetable would not be capable of cognitive thought. Right?

Edward decided to test the theory. As soon as the decision was made adrenaline raced through his body. This was it! This was the moment

of truth. If his brain told his hand to move, but nothing happened…
Edward cringed away from the unwanted thought. He knew that
the possibility could be for only one of two reasons: he was indeed a
vegetable, or he was paralyzed. He tried to imagine the shard of crystal
he had shoved into his neck. Surely, it could have deprived his brain
of oxygen, but paralysis? Could he have landed in such a way that the
crystal compromised his spinal cord?

Still, Edward knew who he was… He was Edward Stanton, Head
of department, for Black Heart, a secret organization, facilitated by
the government. He had ordered the deaths of many a murderer, child
molester, rapist, and thief that had escaped the clutches of justice.
Wasn't that the baseline? *Yes!* He thought. His mind grasped for the
smallest nugget of hope. If he knew who he was, that was the measure—
the definition of cognitive thought. It didn't matter whether he was able
to move an extremity on command or not; just that he could think, but
was that enough?

Edward summoned all of his courage as he twitched the fingers
on his right hand. His mind soared with the possibilities. He was
sure everything would be fine. He could do so much more, but at the
moment he was satisfied with the small token. He would test the rest
of his abilities later.

Satisfied that his mind was present, and at least some of his motor
skills were intact, Edward tried to assess other aspects about his
condition. He felt as though he had slept forever, and yet had only just
fallen asleep. It was a familiar, yet foreign sensation. As the HOD,
of a multi-million-dollar conglomerate, Edward did not have many
opportunities to sleep in. There were times in the past, as a college
student that he had fallen asleep, and did not wake until nine to twelve
hours later. He felt exhausted, and rested all at the same time. That
is the way he felt now. Another thing was his throat hurt. He noticed
that the pain was not what he would have expected. The burning,
tearing, and searing pain that he had felt when he had first thrust the
long crystal piece into his neck, was no longer present. This pain was
more of an obstructed, discomfort. It was like being in a seatbelt that
was too tight.

He allowed his mind at first to calmly investigate the obstruction. As he did he realized that something was forcing air into his lungs. He noticed, also that the air being forced into his lungs, was perfectly matched to the annoying huffing sound.

He had been in many compromising situations during his time as a field agent; some were even torturous. This was like nothing he had ever felt. This elicited panic like he had never experienced. It was then that he lost his grip on the calm. He tried to raise his arm, but there was something wrapped around his wrist; his anxiety doubled. Wherever he was, he was obviously not dead. Worse he seemed to be a prisoner. He had no control.

He tried to slow his breathing, however, at the moment even that was not in his control. He needed to calm down so he could think. He would recount his last moments, before slipping into oblivion on his office floor.

Buzzing, whirring, ticking. Buzzing, whirring, ticking. The sounds were maddening. Edward Stanton stared at the clock. The second hand pounded relentlessly, announcing every moment lost with a resounding: Tick! Tick! Tick!

He had sent Marshall and Denton, two of his best agents to the hospital hours ago. There should have already been word on their progress.

Edward eyed the door suspiciously; there had never been so many maddening sounds coming from beyond his office. What was the staff doing? Clomp, Clomp, Clomp a pair of high-heel shoes tapped against the marble flooring. Drip, drip, drip, the coffee pot, or sink, or both, who knows, carved out their pound of flesh from his already frayed nerves.

Edward cradled his head in his hands. He was going to lose his mind. A shrill ringing broke into the series of noises causing him to push back in his chair. His arms swung wildly, and a slight scream erupted from his throat. He eyed the intercom. He had been very clear that Sarah, his receptionist, announce all of his calls before putting them through. He liked to reserve the right to screen and decline any unwanted callers. He had demanded all of his appointments be cancelled; even the Hayes appointment was rescheduled for Monday morning.

Victor Hayes was Black Heart's number one offender, top priority; his family had money to burn, and as New York's crime boss, that dirty money covered a multitude of Victor's sins. Even the Hayes' case would wait.

"Hello, Mr. Stanton here." Edward squeezed his temples as he waited for the person on the other end of the call to say what was on his mind. He would definitely reprimand Sarah, before returning to the treacherous waiting.

"Good to see you haven't lost your professionalism, Stanton." The line filled with the eerie double timbre of a voice that was obviously being disguised by some kind of an electronic device.

"Who is this?" Edward demanded. It wasn't unlike Black Heart to receive threatening phone calls, but in the unlikely event that they did, never had one made it passed the secretary. Edward again cast a dissatisfied glare in the direction of Sarah's office.

"All in due time." The voice taunted. "For now just know it's not those two buffoons you used as watch-dogs, Marshall and Denton."

Edward's mind raced. He couldn't breathe. Marshall and Denton? He needed time to prepare for this call, but he had none. That traitorous clock had ticked all of his moments, along with his nerves into oblivion.

"That's right… you think, I'll talk." The strange voice declared.

In a strange way Edward was relieved for the silence granted him. Though he had been thinking all morning, it had yet to afford him one satisfactory explanation for Marshall and Denton's silence. He had further been unable to think of a plan for corking the massive hole in the sinking ship that was his life.

"I know everything," the decidedly feminine, voice claimed. Edward hadn't been sure with the voice distortion device that was being used, but after a few minutes of listening there was definitely a feminine quality to the voice.

"I know about the child-agents. I know about the connection between you and Jordan Buckley. I know about the drug ring and the gun cartel. I know about the henchman, Tommy Hayden, hired to kill Jordan, and I know that he was her nephew. I know that that played a big role in why Hayden was chosen." The voice continued to spout off an endless supply of Edward's un-seedy transgressions. But so what? None of the things said were at this point anything more that hearsay. All of it was knowledge that any member of Black Heart, with a level three clearance could obtain, but be unable to prove. Edward had personally destroyed any information linking himself and all the key players in the crime syndicate. Also, the only witness able to give damaging evidence of his own personal involvement, thanks to Tommy Hayden, was now dead. Furthermore, thanks to Jordan Buckley's, husband, Tommy Hayden was dead.

Edward leaned back in his black-leather-high-back chair. His back was straighter now, as he squared his shoulders. He was feeling better, all the time. He thought about the agents, Marshall and Denton, who according to the voice were now dead as well. Edward laughed, and then covered his mouth as he realized the sentiment had been out loud.

"Are you laughing at me, Stanton?" The caller demanded.

"Oh… Of course not." Edward lied. He couldn't help, but see the humorous, irony of the whole mess. It was as if his enemies was working for him. Edward could not have planned it better. Every key player, tying him to any illegal conduct, was being killed off one participant at a time, and with them, the evidence of their damaging testimony perished as well. "I take these types of accusations, however misguided, and false, seriously." Edward had somehow managed to strip his tone of every ounce of the humor; a feat he was proud of. He also managed to add indignation to the tone. A nice touch… He thought.

"Before you develop a sense of humor, Stanton, you might want to turn that sixty-inch television, in that lavish, overstated office of yours, to channel nine." The voice held a certain mocking, satisfaction.

Edward stiffened. Channel nine? He only knew of one thing that he would view at this hour, on that channel. The action nine news at eleven. His blood turned to ice as his eyes lifted to the large television, housed on the full-wall-oak entertainment center. His attention floated cautiously to the crystal wine glasses, hanging from delicate stems. A large crystal container with a stopper made of crystal held the fifth of Brandy, Sarah had just filled it with only an hour earlier.

Edward crossed the room, after turning the speaker phone on. His hands trembled as he flicked the red button on the remote, and the television snapped once, and then a slender blond stood with a blue sweater, outside what appeared to be the Irish Pub. All of a sudden the screen split, and a demure, brunette stood outside a small farmhouse. Ambulances and patrol cars raced in and out of the long drive, in front of the reporter.

"Dozens of bodies have turned up on the grizzly scene, here in Morristown, New Jersey. Former residence of the Morristown Slasher, Harvey Maddox. Locals claim that the place is evil. It would seem that whatever afflicts this manner of mayhem, evil or otherwise, it's still calling the shots, as emergency workers, and the public examiner's office share space on what seems to be a hopeless case of young lives lost..." the woman continued to vent about the dozens of bodies that had been found dead. The other reporter standing outside the pub was all too happy to place the blame on the Head of Department of Black Heart, namely, Edward Stanton.

All at once it was as though someone had thrown back the curtains, and Edward's hiding place was revealed for all of the world to see.

"Across town, in a hospital that shall remain undisclosed, one of The Truth's own, and a former agent to Black Heart, is fighting for her sight, as she was nearly blinded by an explosion set by one or more of Mr. Stanton's child-agents, as they are being delved." The reporter outside the pub claimed as an image of a woman, with gauze shrouding her eyes, flashed, briefly across the screen. Parts of the picture were blurred, making it impossible to make a positive identification, but Edward knew that the picture was of Jordan Buckley.

Edward stumbled to the crystal container of Brandy. His knees felt like Jell-O holding up a mountain of cement blocks. Everything he had ever done to maintain both his and Black Heart's anonymity had been undone, in a single afternoon. The two reporters seemed proud of themselves as they shoveled mountains of lies off of the truth, and into his open grave; his life was over.

Edward's mind raced as he tried to imagine who would be willing to chance such a thing as bringing to the light a dark secret as big as Black Heart. There was only a handful of government officials that actually knew of the Black Heart project; not even the president was privy to the truth of Black Heart. Now a business that had been underground, literally, for nearly thirty years, was being ousted on live television.

Edward poured the Brandy into the wine glass. Some of the amber liquid sloshed onto the marble top, of the massive entertainment center. His hand shook, violently as he clamored, wildly to hold onto consciousness.

"So Edward, what do you think?" The voice pierced the silence with such a thunderous boom that the wine crystal, and the container of Brandy slipped awkwardly from his hand, and shattered on the marble surface below. Edward reached for both of the crystal pieces a moment too late. His hand and wrist scraped heavily over several shards of crystal. Immediately, three large gashes spread wide. All three ran from his hand to his wrist, and Edward could tell from years of combat experience that all three wounds would need stitches.

Edward watched as the dark marble surface filled with blood that mingled with the amber colored brandy, and dripped to the floor. For an instant, Edward reacted with caution as he snatched his hand free of the broken glass: maybe it was the burn of the liquor in the open wounds, or maybe it was basic self-preservation. Edward didn't know, but whatever the reason, it was short lived. He pushed his hand back toward the broken shards, and clumsily thrust his burning flesh into the razor-sharp-jagged edges of the broken crystal. Though the pain seemed to double with the effort, the blood loss was still too minimal for Edward's ominous desire. He reached for a larger shard, of crystal, and staggered to the window. His life's blood drizzling, profusely down his throbbing hand from the multiple of stab wounds. The blood trailed over the carpet in a dotted formation as he made his way to the window.

His life had been, horribly long without his beloved, Amorous, by his side. He had made Black Heart and the revenge for her death the whole of his existence. The ache of her loss filled his every heartbeat.

He stood near the window peering out onto a sea of desks. People loitered the room in a frenzy of horrified faces, and flailing hands that carried paperwork to boxes. Each box was being loaded onto the elevator, and probably taken to another government facility, where it would be destroyed, or brought further into the light of public awareness. Tears fell down his face as he gripped the crystal shard in his mutilated hand. A lifetime of devotion to a ghost, and a secret now somehow felt hollow. Was it worth it? In an instant Edward saw

Amorous's beautiful-smiling-face, she seemed to beckon him to her. So many regrets for his life, but she had never been in the midst of those regrets. He had pursued her from the very first, just as his heart pursued her now.

Edward could feel time slipping away as his legs began to wobble, and his eyes felt heavy, but still it was too long to wait. He needed to be with her, and yet he did not know if he could go where she was. His would probably be eternal torment, but it was deserved. Wherever this journey would end, he no longer wanted to be in a world where she did not exist. Though he did not know that she would be in the world that awaited him, he knew with desolating acuity that she no longer existed in this one.

He could hear the voice on the phone saying something, but it sounded muffled, and meant little to him now. He gripped the tool of his exit, the crystal shard as his other hand rested on the large picture window. With a violent thrust, of his hand he speared the shard of crystal deep into his neck. First pain, and then fear slammed into his mind as he realized he could not breathe. In truth he had not known that this would be a painful death. He had somehow believed that the faithful blow would end his suffering, the moment he had nicked the artery, but as he lay on the carpeted floor listening to the whirring, ticking, and mumbling that filled the room he was reminded of a suffering he had never knew existed. He felt a profound separation from someone more important than Amorous, He felt separated from a divine holy power that he had never given a second thought. He was separated forever from God.

Edward's mind moved away from the horrible moments in his office. Tears streamed down his face, could he hope for a second chance? Could he be in a hospital? Had help come, at the last minute? He lay there a moment longer listening to the sounds of the room, as another sound abruptly broke through the cacophony. Someone had entered the room. Edward's body stiffened. He would be finding out soon, enough. He gripped the sheet beneath him, waiting for the moment of truth. Would he be tortured further? Had the enemy been waiting for him to wake so that they could expound on his blundered efforts to end his life. Edward cringed back into the soft surface of the bed, still unable to open his eyes... the footfalls grew ever closer as his destiny followed with them.

CHAPTER

3

The ground shook with thunderous vibrations, so fierce it toppled several of the clay pots, filled with sage and lavender. The small fire that had all but blazed its last, came to life as the vibrations pitched a log to the right. Rustic-colored-pottery-dust and spice leaves littered the hearth cradling the small fire pit.

Kirsten froze in mid-stride. Her blue eyes darted to Aniahi. She gauged the older-woman's reaction, against the trouble that she perceived to be coming. Aniahi's dark eyes seemed unmoved by the vicious assault on the clay pots.

Kirsten appraised the woman's commanding-posture and her gray hair. A long scar marred the right side of her face, just to the side of her eye, but did little to deface her obvious beauty; Lane had tried to prepare Kirsten for the scar. He had told her it had happened while Aniahi was caring for a patient. He didn't go into details, but as Kirsten looked at what should have been a hideous scar, wasting a beautiful visage, she could not help but think that it somehow added to the image that was Aniahi. The combination of time, indicated by the slight wrinkles on her face and graying hair, and the scar that told of a dark lesson learned brought a sense of calm to Kirsten. She could tell that no matter the force to come, Aniahi would know what to do.

Kirsten relaxed her shoulders as she decided to busy herself with the task of cleaning the ruined pots.

"Leave it child." Aniahi, gently commanded. "Now, no time to clean. Come!" She commanded in a biting tone, while directing Kirsten toward the back of the tent. Aniahi looked through a length of deer hide, as she waved Kirsten over.

Pulling back the flap of animal hide, even further, Aniahi pointed to an opening in the mountain, just to the left of the pass. Kirsten stepped back for a moment. She took in the small opening of the tent. She was amazed at how well the camouflaging had been, but the hole in the mountain, was beyond astonishing. Had Aniahi not pointed it out, Kirsten would have never noticed it was there.

Kirsten had seen painted walls in museums that seemed to come to life as a person stepped out, or paintings that when looked at from another angle had dimensions that she had not yet noticed... The monochromatic, shading of the mountain, faded together so perfectly that the hole was all but nonexistent.

"You go." Aniahi insisted.

Kirsten paled, her mouth popped open. Surely this woman did not mean for her to venture into the uncharted territory of a hidden cave.

"No one find you." Aniahi assured her.

"Uh... yeah... That's what I'm afraid of." Kirsten fussed as she peered back out at the camouflaged hole.

With a solid whack on the back, Aniahi pushed Kristen out of the tent. She landed in a sprawl on the ground. Her blond hair splayed across her face, and shoulders. She pushed at it with frustration. She hated for her hair to be in her face. Most of the time she kept it in a pony-tale, but she had only just woken up, and hadn't had time to prepare for the day.

"Hey!" Kirsten complained as she looked back at the annoying, medicine woman.

"Go!" Aniahi demanded with a note of irritation.

Rolling her eyes, Aniahi continued. "I bring baby and girl." Aniahi pointed to the slight opening in the mountain. "You wait." "Uchlay! Uchlay!" The woman nearly shouted as she gestured toward the mouth of the cave.

Kirsten could tell by the urgency of the word spoken, and the body language used that Aniahi was insisting she hurry. Kirsten summoned all of her courage as she stood, and brushed the dust from her pale blue robe. She tucked a stray, lock of hair behind her right ear, and then turned her attention back to the wall of rock, she was meant to brave. Swallowing back the lump in her throat, she put one shaky foot in front of the other.

She turned back for a moment. Aniahi was still pointing to the hole in the mountain, but now she held shards from the broken clay pots in her hand. Kirsten gasped as the realization of what Aniahi intended to do with the clay pieces, washed over her. The thought no sooner filled her mind, as rustic-colored-clay zoomed passed her head, and showered the darkened rock. A spray of rust-colored-dust fanned down the face of the mountain.

"Uchlay!" Aniahi shouted as her brow knit with agitation.

Kirsten, not wanting to test the woman's aim, sprinted for the opening. Once inside, darkness settled around her like a wool blanket. Her heart slammed into her chest. The pitch blackness of the cave was so complete that it seemed to make breathing harder, as if the air was somehow changed by its presence. Not wanting to touch anything, fearing what might live in the crevices of the rock, she kept her hands as close to her body as possible. She shuffled her feet, mere increments at a time. She was thankful for the boots she had been allowed to keep. She pulled the blue robe, she was wearing closer around her shoulders; terrified to have any skin exposed. Her skin came to life, crawling with the possibility of bugs or spiders that could be nesting within the suffocating darkness.

Kirsten wanted to be brave. She wanted to know that no matter how unorthodox, Aniahi's methods may have been, getting her to the cave, was for her protection.

She thought of another time in which she wished she could have been brave. Her eyes misted with tears, as she was carried back to that time.

Her family had been executed in front of her; soon after she had been taken. She would later learn that she was meant to be one of the child-agents, orchestrated by Mr. Stanton, the HOD for Black Heart. At the time all of the agents had been led to believe that it was Jordan Buckley-Gates that had executed their families. After learning that Jordan was the cause of their families' deaths, each of the agents thought of nothing more than making her pay with her life, for her believed transgressions. Even in that Kirsten had been afraid.

It was the fear of facing such a foe, unprepared that had pushed her to gather Intel on Jordan and Mr. Stanton. Kirsten wanted more than anything to have her fear turn into something more than the paralyzing prison she was experiencing at the moment.

Still shuffling her feet, she fought back the urge to turn and run from the darkness. She had no clue what lay beyond the darkness, in the belly of the cave. She could, however, picture the Cadotion village in the direction from which she had come.

She imagined the small tents lining the valley floor, nestled up next to the base of each of the adjacent mountain walls. The mountains stood surrounding the village—hovering protectively like twin sentinels, stretched to the heavens, keeping an eye out for trouble. Children would be running here and there, playing games with their teenager-guardians. It was getting colder now, but Kirsten imagined that the sun would be riding high in the sky, with tiny wisps of white clouds dotting the horizon.

The imagined heat from the make-believe sun was doing the trick, she was already feeling warmer. A smile filled her face, in the darkness as she moved less reluctantly forward.

It seemed as if her eyes were adjusting to the darkened world of the cave. She could make out the faint jutting of the rock wall. She cautiously tried to see her feet. The silhouette, of the stone, outcropping came into focus. She had once gone on a trip to Ruby Falls, in Tennessee. On the way back home, she and her grandparents stopped at a tourist attraction. It was a cave. A small lake ran through the bottom of the mountain; The Lost Sea. While at the very last exhibit, the guide moved for the light switch. After a quick warning about the impending darkness, the thousands of twinkling lights that lined the ceiling, of the cave, were vanquished in a single instant. That darkness was a lot like this. It was almost tangible, but in no time during the guide's finished story, about ancient cats that had lived under the mountain, and hunted prey in the darkness, had Kirsten noted a change in her visual acuity.

Hope grew as bright as that imaginary-sun-illuminating the Cadotion village, as she pushed further into the cave. Abruptly, what had been a small path, filtered into a vast canyon. The hewed out room, was scarcely lit with torches sitting atop wooden pikes, and bathed in pitch. The faint light flickered in the four corners of the cave. Kirsten took in the center of the cave where a low burning fire was housed in a fire pit that resembled the one in Aniahi's tent.

Three dark tunnels exited from the center of the makeshift room, in the middle of the cave. She decided it best to keep her distance from the darkness beyond. She had after all, already been taken way beyond her comfort zone.

Each wall between the torches were filled with clay pots of varying sizes that sat on shelves carved into the wall of the cave. She felt better that she could see, but something about the darkened tunnels reminded her of a horror movie she had once seen. She thought about all the possibilities for trouble, and how to combat each scenario: wild animals tended to avoid fire, but some insects loved the light. Kirsten decided that creatures that would avoid the flame, would do her the most harm. She crossed to the hearth, and knelt down facing the three tunnels, and the mouth of the cave. She tucked her booted-feet up under her to avoid contact with the dusty-cave floor. She didn't mind getting dirty, but the idea of bugs crawling on her flesh amped up her fear, to a new level.

She sat transfixed on the four exits, for a while. Then, she started to wonder what could be taking Aniahi so long. Kirsten reviewed the last thing Aniahi had told her. She didn't want a misunderstanding to keep her tied to the cave, when she should be doing more. Another few minutes passed with Kirsten contemplating Aniahi's words. Other than being somewhat broken, Aniahi's English speaking skills were impeccable. Kirsten knew with certainty that she had instructed her to go to the cave and wait. Aniahi had been adamant. She had told Kirsten that she would bring the baby and the girl.

Though Kristen could not at the time imagine who Aniahi had meant, the more she perceived the meaning of her words, she was now sure that Aniahi had been talking about Amelia and Tristan. At first, the words had no meaning because Kirsten did not think of Tristan as a baby; by medical standards Tristan would be a toddler, in the states, but by social standards, he functioned more as a preschooler. Aside from his enormous stature, Tristan was well spoken. He was already bilingual;

expressing himself in both the English and Cadotion language. Though he had trouble pronouncing some words, Tristan rarely used baby talk.

Then there was Amelia, at six years old, she acted more like a young woman, than some of the girls at Kirsten's school. Amelia functioned as Tristan did, well above her years. Her understanding of herbal remedies, could far exceed that of some of the herbal-shop owners in Kirsten's neighborhood.

Kirsten thought the terminology, "baby and girl" used to describe Amelia and Tristan, could be more easily accepted by one that was used to seeing a toddler and six-year-old function at such elevated cognitive levels, but she lived in the states where child prodigies were rare...

She shook her head. She didn't want to think about how elevated cognitively, Amelia and Tristan were; it forced her to critique her own inadequacies. She was so immature before the raid of her family home. Her biggest worry was whether she would be forced to brush Chestnut, her pet horse before bed. She missed his gentle nay, and the butterscotch color of his main that stood out against the backdrop of his huge-soulful-brown eyes. Her eyes filled with tears, and spilled over as she imagined, Roo, her tiny Pomeranian-Chihuahua, trying to keep up with the powerful stride of her beloved, Chestnut.

It had all been stripped away by the two home invaders, sent by Mr. Stanton. Kirsten had been so filled with rage that she would have done anything to get even with the agent she had been told was responsible for killing her family, but week after week of hearing about Jordan Buckley-Gates had paralyzed her with fear. Jordan's accomplishments, her abilities... Kirsten knew that the weak training in watered-down self-defense just did not measure up to a seasoned killer like Jordan.

After finding out it wasn't Jordan, but Mr. Stanton that had killed her family, Kirsten had gladly accepted the voice distorter from Garrison, Jordan's old partner. She summoned all of the lessons she had received in acting through plays at church, as she unleashed her fury into the telephone.

At first, Kirsten had been proud of the efforts; especially when Mr. Stanton had started to verbally squirm, but then she could hear that something was wrong. She tried to call Mr. Stanton's name, but he would not answer. Soon a gagging noise filled the phone line.

Kirsten felt like a hypocrite. Everything she loved about life, she had stripped away from Mr. Stanton, in one afternoon, and everything she had hated about him, she had become in that same afternoon.

She sat convulsing with anguish. She no longer cared about the darkened tunnels, or what lurked beyond their borders; she was a coward and a murderer. Let whatever would come from the blackened depths of the tunnels, come. She deserved that, and more. So caught up in her self-loathing, was Kirsten that she did not hear the approach, but as she lifted her eyes the menacing intent was made clear, in the glowing-yellow-gaze. All that she had been thinking, took a backseat, as she crouched ever closer to the flame, waiting for the end to come.

4

Penny was just putting the finishing touches on her new hairstyle, when the phone rang. She took one last look at her shoulder length, dark auburn hair; the edges jutted out, and framed her face. The pixy-style suited her. Her hair bounced with her every move, giving the new carefree look she adopted a subtle boost.

She twisted her body to the side, as she winked at the smoldering beauty standing before her. She could barely believe that a haircut could so completely change the way she looked, or at least the way that she felt about how she looked.

She admired her emerald green eyes and bouncy-dark-locks for just an instant longer, and then reached for the cordless-phone sitting on the small-brown-and-white sink. Though space was limited in the college dorm, she loved her new life.

Ginger, her new roommate, was part of a sorority. She had been talking to Penny about joining. Penny considered the offer, but with the fast pace of her life, so far, she wasn't sure that adding another responsibility to an already full schedule was the right thing to do.

She had lived a life of abuse and uncertainty, before Black Heart had entered her world. First, with her Aunt Jordan eliminating her father, and then Mr. Stanton eliminating her mother. After Penny had moved in with John and Cynthia Benton, friends of her Aunt Jordan; Penny had graduated high school early, and gone on to a local two-year college, not far from the Benton's home in Morristown, New Jersey.

The sizable trust fund, from an insurance claim, her mother had taken out on her father, prior to his death not only helped with college expenses left unpaid by scholarships, but allowed for some perks, such as her new hairstyle.

Erica, Penny's mother, had secretly lived in hopes that the John-Slasher killing all of the abusive men, would kill Jr., Penny's father. The John-Slasher had turned out to be Penny's, Aunt Jordan. Erica's hopes had been realized, but at what expense.

Penny had moved onto campus hoping that life would somehow slowdown and possibly feel normal, whatever that meant.

"Hello." Penny answered with a giggle. She was still excited about her new hair. Still giddy about her new look. In so many ways, she was like a new babe, seeing the world for the first time.

Though she had been one of the child-agents, organized by Mr. Stanton, she had never truly believed that her Aunt Jordan had been responsible for her mother's death. Although her aunt did have ample opportunity to kill her mother; Penny knew that Jordan was not the kind of person to squander such a coveted opportunity. Her aunt, quite simply would have killed her mother the same day that she had killed her father. Leaving Erica alive was not something that Jordan Buckley-Gates would have done.

Penny had gone with the other child-agents, in order to bide her time. She did what she had to; preserving her life, though not her singular motivation, was definitely at the top of the list. She knew that if she were patient enough, in time, the true killer would be revealed, and then she would have her revenge for her mother's death.

"Hey, Penny. Have you heard anything from your Uncle Lane, or Aunt Jordan?" Cynthia Benton's voice filled the line. Penny noticed a tinge of urgency in Cynthia's tone that she was not used to hearing. Normally, both Cynthia and her husband, John were the picture of calm. Penny had joked with them about being the 'Cleavers', a married couple depicted on a television sitcom that was the epitome of the perfect family, with one exception, a spirited son who's curiosity often got him and others into trouble.

"No, Mrs. Benton. I haven't heard anything." Penny paused for a moment. Maybe she had missed a call that morning. She had stepped out for the hair dresser, so it was possible that someone had called.

Maybe she had missed it. "I did step out to go to the beauty shop this morning." Penny admitted. "Let me check my messages."

She moved to the main room, where her bed and desk were housed. She quickly punched the message button, but the indicator window flashed a large red zero.

"No messages, Mrs. Benton. Should I call the airport, and check Uncle Lane's flight?" Calling Lane 'Uncle', felt strange. She really liked him, and she wanted to be respectful, but she had only just met him.

Penny flopped on the bed, and pulled the drawer to her small nightstand open.

"No, sweetie. I'm sure it's nothing. You need to get to class. I'll call you with any news." Cynthia cleared her throat. "How's Trig' going?" Cynthia chirped.

"Ugh!" Penny grouched as she flung herself back on the small half bed. The comforter felt good. The air-conditioner cooled the fabric, making the bed all the more inviting. The mere mention of the dreaded class made Penny want to climb back in the pelts of cool fabric and hide. She wasn't sure if humans had kryptonite, but if they did, hers was definitely Trigonometry.

"I know, honey. Believe me, I do, but you'll get it." Cynthia encouraged before saying goodbye and hanging up.

Penny placed the cordless back on its cradle, to charge. She was ashamed that she hadn't pushed for more information, but she just couldn't take any worse news right now. She wanted to enjoy this new lease on life. Her heart longed to see Nick, he would be on the flight as well, but even that could not bring her back to the real world. She needed this... this break from her usual world of bad; always bad. It seemed at every turn she was being thrust into something that was changing an already dark existence into something worse.

There was a time when Penny would never have believed her life could be the picture of normal that it seemed to be morphing into. Alcoholism had nearly stolen any chance at a normal life that she could hope for.

Penny's father was as cruel as her grandfather had ever hoped to be.

Her mother, Erica, talked about her father as though he were a bad man that had kidnapped them during a home invasion. Her mother had assured her that one day the evil man that was her father would leave them to live their lives in peace. They had only to be patient, because his smart mouth would catch up with him. One day, he was bound to die in a bar fight, or a jealous husband would come for revenge. ... It would all come to an end. Junior Buckley would finally pay. Penny and her mother would live a life of peace and happiness. One day...

That one day had showed up alright, but the justice that had come calling was no angry husband, or even a frustrated drunk in a bar... justice had come in the form of a Black Heart agent that had for so long been a victim of the same cruelty, as Penny. The agent had lived in the same house. Justice had come in the form of an angry sister that believed she held the key to a better life for all womankind. Justice had arrived in the form of an avenging Aunt that refused to turn a blind eye, while Penny grew up in the same hell that she had. Justice had been served, and it had ripped Penny's family up by the roots, and left her mother's dreams of a new life broken in the carnage.

Penny considered Cynthia's offer. Should she sit on the side lines enjoying her new life, a life afforded her by her Aunt? Or skip class and do what she wanted?

She eyed the alarm clock on her nightstand. She only had twenty minutes to make it across campus to her Trigonometry class.

She hated Trig'.

Penny thought of Nick. His dark eyes and dark brown hair that hung to one side, just long enough to obscure his right eye. The obscurity gave him a dark-mysterious look. So much had happened between them, during their time in the child-agent academy. If left alone, she was sure things would have escalated quickly; they would have taken things too far.

She had once saw a movie during Study Hall, with Sandra Bullock and Keanu Reeves. A very powerful statement about relationships had been made in that movie. Though Penny doubted it had been the producer's intent. Sandra Bullock's character had claimed that relationships built on stress or something like that... Penny couldn't remember exactly... but she did remember that the character had insisted that the relationships did not last. Penny did not want that for her and Nick's relationship.

Keanu Reaves' character had then, jokingly stated, that they would base the relationship on sex. Penny had thought the statement clever and funny at the time, until she had watched the next movie. She didn't have to wonder if Keanu's character had a better plan for long, because the movie had begun with Sandra Bullock's character engaged to another man.

Penny touched the small diamond on her ring finger. The tiny stone was a symbol of the promise she had made to be engaged to Nick one day, when they were ready. Nick had worked around John's and Cynthia's cabin for two weeks to earn the money. He had presented her with the ring the day before he had left for the Cadotion village, with Lane and Jordan.

She remembered the time she had spent comparing her relationship with Nick to that of the characters on the blockbuster, Speed. Though they were characters, and she and Nick were real people, the circumstance was not much different. She and Nick had met under extreme duress; she and Nick were headed toward making some big decisions that could make or break their relationship. She wasn't sure if she was ready for either side of that scenario.

Though, she was sure she cared for Nick, Penny could not be certain just how much. She had lived her life under the direction of someone else's needs, wants and demands—whatever it was that pushed the dictator-leadership she had been forced to endure, did not matter, the outcome was the same; Penny had no clue who she was, and if that were true, then how could she know how she felt about Nick?

Tears filled her eyes as she thought about Nick. He deserved more, but it was all she could give. She scrutinized the small diamond a moment longer. He had been so sincere when he had presented her with the ring. She could tell by the robotic timbre that accompanied his speech that Nick had rehearsed the words for a long while; possibly the whole two weeks spent earning the money to buy the ring.

The ring symbolized a promise, not a demand. It was probably the first promise ever made to Penny. There was something so final in the way Nick had made the promise; something concrete, in his words. Penny knew that if she would allow him to do so, if it were the last thing he did, Nick would keep his promise.

She smiled. She may not know how deeply she cared for Nick, if she loved him or not, or even what that meant, in terms of a future, but she knew she would never willingly allow harm to come to him. He was her best friend.

He deserved more from every one of the people that had been in his life, but he had never felt sorry for himself, or used his past as a crutch. He had pushed her in the academy. Nick had also taught her some of the Karate that his grandfather had showed him before his death.

Nick's world, at times seemed to be a mirror image of Penny's. His father had been a tyrant that had brutally beaten his mother. Nick had gone to live with his grandfather when he was ten. His mother's father had taught him everything he knew about martial arts. That combined with the simple self-defense classes given at the academy, had kept Penny from being knocked around, by the Johnston brothers.

Penny thought of Nick again. She knew so much about him; a whole lot of facts. Another important fact that she knew was, he had never made any demands on her. Even the time she had walked out of the woods at the farmhouse. Nick had simply tried to stop her, but in the end, he had allowed her to make her decision, and then met her at the consequences.

She loved so many things about Nick: his patience, his kindness, his loyalty to a fault, his uncanny ability to know exactly what he wanted, in every circumstance, and the fact that he was nothing like her father, or his father for that matter… but did that mean she loved Nick? Did she love him in the way the tiny diamond on her finger symbolized? Could she give her heart and soul to Nick? Could she throw caution to the wind as he had so many countless times in the past, and meet him at the consequences?

She crossed the room to her desk. She grabbed her keys, and ignored her book bag. Her life was on the fast track; she was only seventeen years old. She didn't have to make any decisions about her future with Nick right now. All she knew was she cared about Nick, and he was missing. Besides hating Trig' that was the only ingredient needed to make her miss that class.

5

The kitchen table was in shambles with files and numbers, written down from the phonebook. Cynthia had been searching all of the files, John had taken from The Truth archives. Also, a friend at Black Heart had managed to procure some new files. She was making some great headway in connecting some pretty-obscure dots. She was sure that Mr. Stanton, along with a few other Black Heart, powers that be, would be very upset if they knew about some of her latest finds.

She had been determined to fill in some of the more shadowy blanks, when the phone chirped to life. John, her husband, had called at one o'clock, with the news that Lane and Nick had not gotten off their flight. He would call back with anything further. He planned to check later flights. He was sure that they had simply missed their flight like before, and would, merely be detained for a while.

John had assured Cynthia that he would be fine. After checking for any other flights that they may have boarded, or even later departure times, he would grab a book at one of the many airport shops, and a late lunch.

In an effort to be proactive, Cynthia had called Penny to see if maybe Jordan had checked in. That, too, had been a dead-end. Cynthia decided to make some phone calls to the airport. Though John was there, the airport could make for a very hectic environment, to obtain information.

She hung up the phone. No later flights had been made. She was frustrated. Looking at the table scattered with files, she thought of John's time at The Truth. It was overrun with agents stationed by Edward Stanton. It had been Mr. Stanton's goal to keep anyone interested in proving his guilt, out of the archives.

John had nearly died to bring her the files. She wanted so much to put a profile together, but so far, she was gaining nothing more than a huge headache. Edward Stanton had gone to great lengths to keep that from happening. She felt like her brain had as many holes as the files she had been sifting through.

Edward was the Head of Department, for Black Heart. He had also headed up a gun and drug cartel. It was through the key players in that cartel, as well as those that had happened across the cartel, and coincidently led to the bust—that Cynthia was sure she would prove Mr. Stanton's guilt. Unfortunately, Edward Stanton had erased the evidence linking each of those key players not only to himself, but to Jordan. Cynthia's task would be to prove why. Especially now that Stanton had awakened from the self-inflicted coma.

Cynthia eyed one of the new files on the table. She had never heard the name before. For that matter she had never heard any of the names depicted in the new files. Both files were stolen from Stanton's secret filing cabinet, in his office. Why would he go to such great lengths to erase key players in a gun and drug cartel, just to keep two files in his office? Every other file that John had managed to get from The Truth archives had some holes in them; not so, of the two that were taken from Stanton's office. These files were fully intact. If Edward were so bent on destroying evidence, why not destroy these two files? What about these files would make Stanton want to hold onto them, even at the expense of being caught? If he had wanted to keep the files, why not put them in a safety deposit box? It was almost like Stanton had wanted to keep the two files close, in case he wanted to take them out and view them; trophies… The thought sent shivers up Cynthia's spine. What had the two people, depicted in the files done to get that kind of attention from a man like Edward Stanton?

She opened the file marked Amorous Dawson. There was a photo on the inner cover of the file. An exotically, beautiful woman stared back with big pouting lips. Her long blonde hair billowed over her shoulders. Electric blue eyes peered out from a perfect canvas of tan skin. In spite every flawless detail, there was something very dangerous about the woman's appearance.

Cynthia closed the file, and opened the one beside it. Cecil Schooner… she traced the name with her thumb, before opening the cover. Where had she heard that name before? She pushed the thought to the back of her mind for the moment. Lots of names sounded the same. Cynthia had made many profiles for Black Heart, if she wasn't careful, she could allow those past profiles to muddy up her initial response to new files. It had happened before.

During her second profile for Black Heart, she had become overwhelmed with pictures of a gruesome murder spree committed by the suspect she was trying to help eliminate. Her mind had become so filled with the images of the victims that she was unable to put together a profile. The fallacy had ensured the killer maintain his freedom. Through that freedom he had raped and killed three more college students. Cynthia had been determined to make the profile, though it would not bring back the three victims that would have been alive had she made the profile sooner. That awful time had taught her a very valuable lesson about her job as a profiler. She would never take the job lightly. She knew the need for a timeout. She would step back if need be to have a fresh perspective.

Cynthia had been transferred to The Truth, a missionary outreach program, housed in Black Heart. The Truth helped the agents to maintain some level of humanity. New recruits were sent to the Garden, a beautifully decorated ecosystem of exotic plants, birds, and fountains.

Training could be grueling. Killing was an unfortunate, but necessary evil of the job. The recruits were encouraged to take part in one of the many religious organizations in order to maintain some level of control on their mental stability. All of the religious groups had access to the Garden, which was housed in the furthest region of Black Heart's underground compound.

Cynthia had already been recycled, and was about to be eliminated for her bumbling attempts as an agent. Garrison, Jordan's former partner had been the one to champion her transfer. Due to Garrison's immaculate record with the agency, the department heads had conceded the transfer with little argument, with one very important exception—though,

Cynthia had been a rotten assassin; she was unmatched as a profiler. She would have to maintain contact with Black Heart so that her skills as a profiler could be taken advantage of.

She hated having to maintain any sort of contact with Black Heart, but she would do whatever it took not to have to be responsible for the mark's death once the profile was made.

Though Cynthia knew that she was miles from making sense of the garbled up mess that Edward Stanton had left to be sifted through, she was proud to finally be using her skills to put an end to Black Heart's reign of terror.

She smiled as the thought passed through her awareness. It was true. If she could find something besides their testimony that would link Edward Stanton to more than his dealings with Black heart... If she could link him to the drug and gun cartel that Jordan, Lane, and Garrison had stumbled across in the park, then she was sure Black Heart would be forever vanquished from their lives.

She pushed the file open just as the phone chirped to life, again. She was so deep in her thoughts that the ringing phone had nearly sent her screaming from the room. She laughed, as she picked up the offending device. She stepped to the kitchen window. It was a beautiful, sun-filled day, and she could use some of that fresh perspective she had been thinking of. She nodded her conceit of the stray thought as she stepped to the front door, and answered the phone on the third ring.

"Hey, honey!" It was John's voice. Cynthia thought he sounded frantic. She pulled her cell phone back to see the time: Three forty-five. It had been two and a half hours since she had last spoken to him. She was having trouble figuring where the time had gone. Thinking back, she hadn't been a very good steward of the time.

"Hey, John. What did you find out?" Cynthia's voice still sounded far away. She adjusted her eyes to the brightness of the sunny day, as she moved to a nearby rocking chair. A rogue wind blew, lifting the ends of her hair, causing a few lose strands to play across her eyes.

"Hey, honey. Are you okay?" John sounded alarmed. He did that a lot now that she was pregnant.

"I'm just frustrated. I guess. Trying to make sense of all of this," Cynthia waved her hand through the air. She felt on the brink of tears. Come to think about it lately, she always seemed on the brink of tears. "Nonsense." She finished with an exaggerated huff. "I keep daydreaming, John. I just lost two and a half hours, and I have no clue where it went."

"Daydreaming is often conducive of the pregnant female, due to hormonal surges." John gave his analysis of the situation.

Cynthia rolled her eyes, as she listened to her husband's latest analytical jargon on pregnancy. She loved the man to pieces, but it seemed to her that she was more of a lab-rat than a wife to her spouse at times.

"John, please don't analyze me. You know it drives me crazy. I'm not some lab-rat that you can poke and prod at until you figure out how I tick." Cynthia pushed her hand through her hair. She didn't want to fight. It had been John's nerdy-analytical brain that had attracted her to him in the first place. She knew he was right. Though he had a very cut and dry way of painting a picture, his diagnosis had been right on. She played with a stray leaf on the arm of the rocking chair, as it fought, uselessly for its freedom from the small slit it was wedged into.

"I'm sorry. You're right. I'm cranky, sleepy, stinky, and dreamy, because I'm pregnant." Cynthia laughed. "I sound like a group of dwarfs."

"You do kind of sound like you should be hanging out with Snow White." John laughed. "Have you heard anything at all from Lane or Nick, from anyone?" John was the one sounding frustrated now.

"No, I did manage to make a few calls, before nodding off into dreamland, but it was all a dead end. No later flights were made. They just, for some reason did not make that flight." Cynthia looked up at the sky, and appraised a bird as it flew effortlessly across the horizon. "Maybe you should just come home, babe. We probably need to call the police or something." She listened for John's answer. Silence filled the line for a long moment, before he finally answered.

"Yeah, you're right. Hey, I'm going to stop by the police station. Okay?" John announced.

"Okay. I'm going back to the drawing board. One of the new files has to have something that could help us out." Cynthia stood, as she mindlessly freed the leaf from its prison.

"New files?" John asked. Cynthia could hear the wind coming through the line, as he was obviously heading toward the car.

"Yeah, an old friend dropped off these two files that were in Mr. Stanton's office. The names seem familiar in some way, but when I looked at the first file, of a woman, she looked like no one I had ever seen." Cynthia laughed. Her voice filled with obvious appreciation for the woman's exotic beauty.

"Maybe I should have a look at this picture." John teased.

"Yeah, you wish buddy, but don't bother, apparently the woman died in the line of duty." Cynthia said, as she thought about the woman's electric blue eyes.

"Died? Well, what about the file?" He asked. She could hear the car door shut, and then the car motor as it hummed to life.

"Yeah, she's dead, tiger." Cynthia laughed. Pushing the front door open, she moved to the kitchen sink to fill a glass. "The other file, I haven't had a chance to review yet. I just found it odd that the name sounded so familiar; the man's name. I mean" Cynthia admitted, and then swallowed down the water and placed the glass back on the counter. A small white towel with musical notes held two other glasses from earlier in the day. She and John had enjoyed a light breakfast of wheat toast and scrambled eggs.

"Well let's hear it, what's his name?" John's voice sounded tired. Cynthia knew that he was just humoring her.

"We'll talk about it when you get home. I know you're tired. Besides you still have to deal with the police station, and I have supper to start." She was proud of the way she had so artfully let him off the hook. He hated profiling. The gruesome pictures did not set well with his tender sensibilities. He had had a lot of things happen as a missionary for The Truth that would give a weaker man pause, but John was more of the medicinal-nerd that saved the world through TLC (tender love and care). He had a low tolerance for the darkness associated with Black Heart. Cynthia, too hated it, but it was her only means of freedom, and she would take what she could get.

"I love you, honey. I'll be home soon." John hung up, leaving Cynthia with her thoughts.

Back to the drawing board … Cynthia mused as she crossed to the table. Her eyes moved from the name on the file marked Amorous Dawson. "What made you so special?" Cynthia asked the file. Her eyes moved to the open file of Cecil Schooner. Dark auburn hair and a ruggedly handsome face shone back from the file. Cynthia appraised the picture as she sarcastically wondered if Edward Stanton had a hidden collection of the most beautiful people to work for Black Heart.

Jordan Buckley-Gates was a vision as well. Her file, too had come up missing. Cynthia laughed again at the absurdity of the thought. Surely, Edward Stanton had a greater more pressing reason for collecting files and making them disappear, than the agent's other-worldly beauty.

Cynthia started to read over Cecil's file, and suddenly she realized that he wasn't an agent at all. He had been a counselor for a church. More than that he was a pastor.

She thumbed through the file for a moment longer, it was padded with endless accounts of this ordinary, and yet quite extraordinary man's life. He had lived the dream. Cynthia's dream… a wife and child. Working in the mission field as a pastor of a growing church.

She looked through the file hoping there would be some pictures of the man's family. Maybe that would give some insight as to how the man had made Edward Stanton's most wanted list. Unfortunately, there had been no such pictures in the file.

She turned the pages back, so that she could get a better look at the man in the picture. "Talk to me Cecil." Cynthia rubbed the photo with her thumb. "Who are you?" She leaned in closer, and as she looked into the man's emerald green eyes, Jordan came to mind again.

Cynthia nearly fell out of her chair. "Oh my Lord! You are Jordan Buckley-Gates' grandfather, aren't you?" She studied the photo for a moment longer, and then opened the other file. She needed to look for anything that may link the two. She had just found a person that definitely linked Jordan to Edward, but how? Or why? Cynthia didn't know if the discovery made her job easier or harder, but what she did know is Jordan's grandfather had been a point of interest for Edward Stanton… so much so that he would chance the discovery of a link he had worked so desperately to conceal.

6

Nick eyed the ground suspiciously. Grains of sand danced up and down, as if the ground were a great drum being pounded. His heart raced with the thunderous roar. The intensity of the sound filled the calm, making it impossible to hear the animal calls. His breath caught, as he realized there were no calls to be heard. The animals had silenced in an instant.

He knew the sound well. His grandfather owned a ranch in Wichita Falls, Texas. He spent plenty of time caring for the cattle. The horses were his favorite.

His grandfather's passion had been wild horses. He took Nick on hunts in the foothills, to add to his grand collection. Nick had helped to green break some of the more spirited horses. That had been a challenge, one that Nick was willing to rise to.

During one of the hunting details, Nick had his first glimpse of a stampede. No movie he had ever seen did it justice. It was glorious and frightening, all at once.

Nick turned to Haywalo. "Stampede." It was more of a statement than a question. Nick was certain, he was right. Though the sound was coming right for them, Nick was amazed at the calm that for the moment, filtered through his senses.

Haywalo turned from the leather he had been tanning, and shook his head. "Manerky come."

Nick furrowed his brow. He looked as if Haywalo had just slapped him. He knew the sound of hundreds of hooves pounding on the earth when he heard it. Haywalo, obviously seeing his disapproving glare decided to explain.

"Manerky great enemy of Cadotion people." Haywalo gestured to the west. "They come fast, to make war."

'Come fast to make war', Nick ran the words through his mind, trying to make sense of them. Why would anyone make war with peaceful people, like the Cadotion tribe? Nick looked to the west, and then asked the question aloud… "Why would they want to make war with peaceful people? The Cadotion tribe is a peaceful clan, right?"

Nick knew the answer to that. He had watched in amazement, as the people went about their daily rituals. There was no guile amongst the clan, no hate toward each other. Only love filled the foothills of the great mountains.

"Open eyes, Nick." Haywalo spread his hands wide, as if to unveil the beautiful landscape before them.

Nick blanched, his mind could scarcely take in the majesty of the mountains on either side of him. The Karakoram mountain range had been home to the Cadotion tribe for more than twenty years. Raid upon raid, the Cadotion people had lost lives, but had stood their ground to protect the sanctity that their foot-land offered. In the past, the raids had been gruesome, but met with the forces of the neighboring tribes that had come to help the Cadotion fight off the attack of the Manerky.

There was something awe-inspiring about the snowcapped mountains. The magic was like some untold secret that spun a web of serenity in every direction; only those that lived in the calm and untroubled land could understand.

Nick had been told of the mountain's magic passes that disappeared into a camouflage of color. He wanted to venture into those places, and reap the treasures that such hidden coves could yield. Instead, he watched wide eyed, as invaders forced their way into the valley, destroying the serenity forged in their midst. Suddenly the moment of calm exploded into a cacophony of screams and hoof beats. The statement that had been a lazy comment was now a terrifying declaration.

Screams ripped through the air. Horses whinnied impatiently, pawing at the ground as if the battle was taking too long to suit their fancies. Arrows flew haphazardly through the air, claiming lives with little effort.

War cries erupted from the painted faces of the Manerky. Their shaved heads were covered with dark symbols that looked to Nick like nothing more than an unspoken promise of the slaughter to come. From the distance that he stood from the approaching Manerky, it appeared that there were eyes peering out from the dark swirls. The arching lines of the paint covered the entire skin of each of the warrior's faces leaving nothing, but the whites of their eyes to stand out in stark comparison. The collection of eyes sent chills up Nick's spine. His heart raced, as the Manerky raged on claiming as many lives as would step into their unrelenting path.

Each of the warriors donned little more than a strip of animal hide that covered the lower half of their bodies. The fabric lay against their legs in a lose-fitting skirt. The material rode up on their thighs revealing sinew, and thin but muscular legs, as they flowed through the encampment. Speers were flung into men, women and children alike as the riders darted through the village, killing everything in their paths.

Nick froze for an instant longer, and then seeing a small child sitting to the side of a dismembered body, he plunged ahead. Scooping the child's flailing body up, Nick darted between two tents. Haywalo ran behind, screaming commands. Nick tried to comply, for a few strides, but soon allowed Haywalo to take the lead.

Nick ran as fast as he could, with the floundering child in tow. Nothing he did seemed to reassure the anguished child. His heart pounded. The child was like a dinner bell, to a hungry lion; surely his wailing would alert the scouts of their whereabouts. If he was unable to sooth the crying child, the Manerky would be upon them no matter where they hid.

Nick's mind swam with the assault. So fast was the attack, that the invaders seemed more spirit than human. He thought of the woman that lay beside the child, he had saved. She had been cleaved into. By the time Nick had thought to see her attacker the village was left in a cloud of dust, as the invading tribe swept undaunted out of the other mountain pass to the east. Nick could not imagine that an attack leaving so many dead, could end this abruptly.

"Scavengers!" Haywalo spat the word as he came to a halt at the back of a tent. His chest heaved as water fell from his eyes, and cascaded down his chestnut cheeks. "They will not stand as men. They flee as cowards! They are scavengers!" Haywalo shouted the word to the heavens with his fist pumping in the air.

"So that's it? They are gone?" Nick held the child tightly, trying to keep him from getting down. He could imagine that the child would return to his dead mother. Nick felt a surge of guilt, as relief filled his mind. So, it was over? He hated that so many had died, and the child was obviously without his mother, but shouldn't they all be thankful to still be alive?

Haywalo looked as if Nick had asked if it were raining outside when the sun was clearly shining. "Manerky return, soon." Haywalo said flatly. He stood his shoulders squared, facing the distant mountain pass with a defiant gaze.

Nick turned then to a noise coming from behind him. Fear slammed into his mind, as his heart sped up. His mind stood between two decisions, simultaneously bathed in logic: let the child go, or take the chance that whoever was pulling him into the tent would dismember the child, as quickly as the young mother that laid bloodied on the trail. In the end, Nick held fast to the child. He had little knowledge of what waited in the tent, but he knew the child's fate, were he to release him. He would surely suffer the same fate, as his mother, or worse, he would starve to death, with no one to look after him. Thinking about the horrific sites that had played out before him, Nick knew that it was not likely the boy would live long enough to starve.

The scent of lavender, and hickory mingled on the air. A fire burned low in the center of the tent. Nick's eyes blinked, as he tried to focus on who was standing in front of him. Hands abruptly took the flailing child. Though the back of his mind screamed for him to tighten his grip, the idea seemed so futile. What was the use? They would both be dead soon. Maybe those that had claimed the small child would have mercy. After all, hadn't the child been left to weep at his mother's side?

Nick waited both his and the child's fate. But, instead there was a tender cooing, as a female voice tried to sooth the anguished child. Confusion filled Nick's mind. He realized, then that it was Jordan. The hand that had been firmly in place, to silence his screams fell away. Nick smiled at Jordan, and thanked Lane. His head snapped up suddenly. He turned to the back flap of the tent, and started for Haywalo. Lane slowed his pace with a massive arm across his chest.

"Hey… what about Haywalo? We can't just…" Nick was pushing against Lane. He was determined to get to his friend. How could they just leave him? Though, Nick pushed with all of his might, the iron grip of the giant man was no match for his one hundred and seventy-pound body.

"He's gone." Lane's voice cracked a little, as his blue eyes filled with tears.

"We need to find Kirsten and Aniahi." Jordan said, while bouncing the now sleeping boy.

Amelia stood close at hand, with one soothing hand on the child's foot, closest to her. Her head held high, a pride passed down to her, through generations, colored her visage. Though her biological parents had died, Lane and Jordan had clearly not allowed Amelia to forget where she had come from. Living in the Cadotion village had only been a minute part of what they had done to ensure the strength of her bloodline, be passed down. Lane and Jordan had gracefully stepped back, allowing Aniahi to take over the vigorous lessons needed to groom the child into the medicine woman she would someday be.

A horde of killers had invaded her home, and still Amelia remained the ever ready medicine woman to be. The stoic contours of her face, held fast against the coming raid. Nothing penetrated the armor, put into place by heritage and grace.

"He's not gone!" Nick insisted, as his brain tried to make sense of why Lane would say something so obviously untrue about Haywalo. He had just been standing beside his friend while he screamed at the invaders.

"Nick, listen to me." Jordan spoke clearly with authority now. She moved closer to Nick. Bending forward, Jordan cradled the child more closely to her pastel robes. As she leaned further in. A lock of auburn hair fell forward shading the child's head. Nick thought she looked so much like Penny. How he missed Penny. How he longed to be anywhere but here. His mind grasped for anything that could deliver him into the hands of a lesser fate.

"Before I say this to you. I need you to understand, I will do anything to protect my children. By that I mean their physical and mental safety. So, what you need to know is, your reaction to what I am about to say, is vital…" Jordan pulled back, and eyed Nick pointedly.

Nick felt there was something very out of sync with Jordan's words and actions. What he witnessed was a mother, lovingly caressing the head of a child. What he heard was the premeditated intent of a cold-blooded-killer.

Nick looked at each of the children in turn, and then swallowed any rebuttal, he might have thought to give. He conceded his understanding with a nod.

"Good." Jordan smiled, and then continued in a whisper meant to evade the children's hearing. "Haywalo is dead." Jordan proceeded flatly. She acknowledged his raised brows as a question, and then tenderly touching his shoulder, she leaned in closer. "Archers on the mountain side, to the North, and South." Jordan moved to lay the child on a pile of animal fur.

Amelia seemed to automatically fall into step. She stoked the fire, and then sitting down beside the child, she covered him carefully. She brushed his hair away from his brow, with a tender, but automatic hand.

Nick was struck by a thought… Amelia may be filled with the strength that transcended a bloodline, but if he could imagine a child as belonging to the giant of a man and statuesque woman, exuding strength, it would be Amelia. She was one-part strength, one-part care; she was the perfect example of what would transpire if these two unstoppable forces were to meet and bring forth offspring.

Jordan smiled at her daughter for a moment, and then abruptly turned to Nick. "Modilo, has been through a great deal of trauma; he should sleep for a while. If he wakes, he will be stressed." Jordan turned to Amelia. "Leave him to Amelia, she is a healer. She will know what to do."

Pride filled Amelia's eyes, as she held her head high. "I'll give him tea, mommy." Amelia conceded, as she crossed to a clay pot near her bed roll.

"Thanks, honey." Jordan said as she cleared her throat, and turned her intent green gaze on Nick. "You will stay with the children. Lane and I will collect weapons, and map out a route to the hidden cave. We will never take our eyes off of this tent. One of us will be watching it at all times." Jordan promised as she turned to Lane, who was already pulling various forged weapons, from hidden spots that were too high for the children to reach.

Nick appraised each hand-carved weapon; there was six total: two knives, about six inches in length, one was carved form stone. The blade was sharpened to a thin, razor edge, while the handle was as smooth as glass. The second knife was whittled from some kind of a wood. Again the edge was razor sharp. However, the handle was wrapped in animal hide that had also been dipped in a marble substance that Nick believed to be dried tree sap. The third weapon was far more intricate in its design. Pictures flowed down the length of the small axe. Each picture moved gracefully into the next, depicting a story about a young boy growing into a man. There were no defining features about the figure on the axe that would mark the boy as anyone in particular, but as Lane gingerly handed the axe to Nick, he could somehow tell the story was about Tristan.

The next three weapons were very crude, as if they had been started, but never completed. Nick could see, though, regardless, of the design these weapons were as lethal, if not more so, than the first three. All three of these weapons were about two feet long, and dipped in the same marble substance as the knives. About middle ways down each of the weapons, a grip space was beveled out. The end of each was razor sharp on both sides running down the length of the weapon to about two inches from the grip space. The other end was wrapped heavily with leather, and gravel. On the top of the blunt end was the same marble substance holding it together.

Nick could see that the glossy surface was two-fold: it could be used as a handle when stabbing or as a blunt object to bludgeon a foe too death.

Lane stepped out away from everyone, as he kept his eyes on Nick. The whole while he was twirling the crudely formed weapon, he talked.

Each time the device stopped swirling Lane indicated another way it could be used, against the enemy.

Nick watched, mouth agape, as each graceful twist of the weapon ended in a potentially fatal blow. It was mesmerizing to see the large man before him move with such easy grace.

"The Manerky will strike in a sequence. It has never failed them, so they will not abandon their battle tactics." Lane was now explaining. "The first, and most frightening, as you have already witnessed, is the blind raid." Lane flourished his arms, and frowned. "Well I guess, unfortunately, that is self-explanatory." Lane turned to Jordan. She nodded.

Nick thought Lane must be making sure he wasn't crossing some imaginary line, concerning their children. Nick was glad to see, so far, that Lane was okay.

"The second phase has already begun. Archers will be posted on different levels of the mountains. Anything that moves will be eliminated." Lane turned to Nick. His eyes softened. "Modilo made himself a very big target." Lane allowed a moment of silence for the loss, and then continued. "I'm sorry."

"Well, what's the other stage, or is there more?" Nick turned from Lane to Jordan. He wasn't sure who the answer would come from.

"The next phase of their battle strategy, in essence had already begun." Jordan surmised.

"Already begun?" Nick felt more confused than ever.

"That's right." Lane concurred, as he moved to Jordan's side. "The last and final stage is an ongoing stage that in essence begins from the first attack, for it is then that the Manerky are assessing the landscape for what the battle is truly about... the prize to be claimed."

"What is the prize?" Nick asked the question, though he wasn't sure he wanted to know.

"Everything!" Jordan whispered.

Nick blanched, as he turned to the look of finality registering on Jordan's face. He knew that she was trying to convey a deeper meaning without alerting the children to the real danger they were all facing.

Nick gauged the reactions of Amelia and Tristan. For the first time he realized they weren't' screaming, or cowering behind their parents in fear. They were going on about their day, although, deprived of the outdoor play time they had probably been used to having. Still, it was as though nothing had changed. There was no confusion at all registering in the children's eyes. Nick saw then the raw fear of a mother desperate to shelter her children from a truth that would taint the very fabric of their being. Jordan had meant every word. She would do anything to shelter them, even if that meant killing him.

CHAPTER

7

Garrison checked his eyes in the mirror. Red-road-map striations covered the sclera, almost completely. The iris, of his eyes, a dark brown—normally stood out in stark comparison to that of the white, of his sclera—now the dark red combined with the dark circles, under his eyes from too much drinking, fused all of the colors into an unflattering shade of muddy-browns.

The color under his eyes and the color in his eyes, though were the only thing about him that seemed to be in harmony. His life had been a mess since the incident with Mr. Stanton. His hair was getting too long, and a slight stubble had started to fill in around his mouth. He looked like warmed-over-death. His grandmother had always said the words to his father when they visited for Christmas. As a child, Garrison never understood the words, but as a grown man, dealing with his messy existence, he understood, completely. Nothing about the image that stared back at him, would suggest life dwelled within. Peering back at him, was a shell of the former man he had once been. He was the epitome of death-warmed-over.

Garrison had played it cool, making Kirsten feel like some childish-brat, but the truth was he felt every ounce of the guilt that he had tried to put on that little girl. He had tried to use the guilt to shame Kirsten into making the call that had almost ended Edward's life. But now, as he pushed himself robotically from one room to the next he knew that the full brunt of the guilt belonged solely to him; not Kirsten.

Garrison checked his hair, again. Normally, he liked to keep it in a short style, of finger waves, but lately he had been neglecting that, as well. He turned to the living room portion of his open-floor-plan-apartment: beer cans lined the simple-cherry-wood coffee table and floor. Amber liquid was sloshed haphazardly across all of the things that he had once protected, as though they held the secret to life's only happiness. He cast a dismissive glance at the alarm clock next to his queen-size-four-poster-bed… what was the use?

He was glad he had brought Black Heart down, but where did that leave him? He had no job. Sure, he had tucked away a few grand, but that wouldn't last forever. His only skill was being a hit man and organizing hits; where would he get a job doing that? There was a market for underground death dealers, but that was not Garrison's thing. Most of the kills were set up by spoiled rich men and women that believed to erase all their enemies would ensure their every happiness and success. He would not be a part of that. He could certainly understand the need to alleviate the planet of those types of people, but who would pay him to do that? He was starting to sound like a whiny-child, and that ticked him off too.

He eyed his small apartment. He needed a plan; something to keep his mind off of Stanton, or the fact that he had traumatized Kirsten, just to vindicate his own need for revenge. He wanted to stop thinking, most of all, he wanted to forget that his best friend, his old partner, had skipped the country, again! Anger welled up in him, as the errant thought grew root, and once more tried to claim his every thought.

Garrison turned back to the mirror. He looked awful. It was time to get his act together. He glanced at the clock again. Grady's Barber shop would be open for another two hours. He could go to the one up the street, but the hairstylist just didn't have the same knack for doing a black man's hair.

"Dang white ladies, don't know a low fade from a box cut!" Garrison fussed.

The last time he went to the large beauty shop with elegant hanging curtains and priceless paintings cluttering the walls, it had ended in catastrophe. The woman tried to do a box cut on him. Garrison could tell by the nervous-mask coloring her visage, that things weren't going well.

Jordan had laughed for a week. She said his head looked like Frankenstein. The woman had cut his edges too far back on his head.

He had to wear a hat until his hair could grow out enough to undo the damage. He wasn't about to make that mistake again.

Garrison climbed into the shower making a promise to clean up later. He dressed quickly, and left for Grady's.

Garrison stopped by Wal-Mart to grab some eye drops; the traffic hadn't been too bad. He was surprised. He hated to shop. Shopping without a specific goal in mind at least, was useless in his opinion, and often ended in too much money spent on side items that he had no use for. But eye drops were a must. His eyes looked like death, and he didn't want to scare Penny. He had promised Jordan that he would check on the kid from time to time. Besides, anything beat hanging around the apartment like some drunken-ghost... He quickly dialed Penny's cell. It went straight to voicemail.

"Must be in class." he said to no one in particular.

"Hey, kid. Call me back." Garrison left the message, and then decided he needed to do something until Penny got out of class. He would take her for a quick Burger. Maybe if he got her to chatting about Nick, or whatever he would know that she was alright, and Penny would not feel threatened. He hated that when he was a kid. Adults always seemed to have nothing better to do than give him the twenty-question-grand-inquisition; he didn't want to be cornered up, and have to talk about things that he didn't truly understand himself. He just wanted to live his life, and make his own decisions. But from birth his father, along with all of the other adults in his life had plotted out his every moment.

Then there was Black Heart; just another kind of adult making the rules, but at least with the agency he could vent his frustration on the unholy-underbelly of society: the hits that he was assigned had been murderers, rapists, thieves, or whatever group that somehow continued to slip through the system. That's what he and Jordan, along with the other recruited agents had been; a means to an end. They were the answer to the unwanted members of society; those that could not conform to societal rule, but had the relationship or the money that would keep them from paying the price for their crimes.

Black Heart agents ended it; once and for all! But it was over; Black Heart was no more. He and his friends had made sure of that. Now as he stepped out of the car, and headed into the local Wal-Mart to cover the evidence of his wasted life, Garrison was reminded of just how hopeless he felt; just how disconnected with the rest of the world he had become. He missed Jordan. He missed the life. It was awful he knew that. Why would he miss the thrill of ending someone's life? But he did. He missed the hunt. He missed the comradery with his then best friend and partner, Jordan Buckley-Gates. He missed having something to do with himself, besides wasting away on his couch, and waking up in a sea of beer cans on a Sunday morning. He wanted to have his friend back. He wanted to have a life again. He wanted something, anything that was more than the useless blank page that had started this new chapter of his life.

He could remember his father's constant intrusion into his life. It made him feel smothered, but now he missed the interference. What he would not do to have his father ask if he had good grades, if he had completed an assignment, if he had found a job… anything would be great. He longed for the simple times, as a young college kid that had his whole life figured out.

The Visine felt good. He peered at his eyes again, as he came to a stop at the four-way. He needed some gas, so he pulled into the small 'mom and pop' gas station. Cruising his '69' Dodge charger into the space between the pumps and the store. He scrutinized both the pumps and the store.

There were two gas pumps, both were short, and squared off. Silver covered the entire length of them, but they were aged in such a way that made them appear all the more antique. His car looked to be right at home next to the cement island that stood bluntly underneath the two pumps. The store, like the tanks, seemed to have stepped out of the past. Old mahogany rocking chairs lined the porch, while a length of chicken pen shrouded a small alcove filled with fishing poles. A sign in the middle of the fencing boasted of bate and lures. Garrison shook his head.

"She's a beauty."

Garrison turned to the sound of a wolf whistle.

John stood admiring Garrison's baby, that's what he called his car; his baby.

"Just a little something I bought with my Black Heart scholarship." Garrison mocked his situation. He barely had enough money to survive the next two years. He had already had to down-size his living arrangement; moving from the lavish apartment afforded him by Black Heart to the small apartment with barely enough room to turn around. He at least deserved a nice ride.

"What brings you to this neck of the woods?" John asked as he moved to the car, and started to caress the passenger door.

Insanity… Garrison thought. "Checking on Penny." Garrison shrugged as he replaced the gas cap, and then hung the nozzle back on the ancient gas tank.

"I haven't been to your place. I knew it was close by, but I didn't realize it was close enough for this to be a place that you would shop." Garrison immediately regretted the comment. He was aggravated that Jordan seemed to be pushing him further out of her life, but was it John's fault? After all, he was a friend to Jordan as well.

John snapped his fingers. "Hey that reminds me, have you heard from Lane or Jordan?"

Garrison was relieved that John had ignored the obvious dissatisfaction in his comment.

"Why? Should I?" Garrison was irritated now. The question had blindsided him. He knew nothing about their situation.

"Well, Lane and Nick were supposed to be in town…"

"What do you mean… supposed to be?" Garrison interrupted with a suspicious twitch of his brow.

"Well it was a last minute decision. Lane called a week ago, asking if I'd pick them up from the airport." John stopped in the middle of his explanation. "Hey man, are you okay?"

Garrison turned to the door of the small store as he prepared to lie. "Yeah, I'm good." he was nowhere near 'good'. He was angry. His life was falling apart, and his best friend was on another continent. Now he was finding out that her husband was coming into town. He would be landing at the New York airport, which he lived three miles from, but instead of calling him, they had called someone thirty minutes away.

Garrison had thought that Jordan was able to forgive all of the lies that he had told, all of the manipulations that had helped to manifest her recruitment into Black Heart. He had believed that she had risen above all of it, but as he listened to John Benton, he knew that he had been fooling himself. Christianity was a nice place to hang pretty ideas about who you wanted to be, but at the end of the day, it left her just as screwed up as the rest of the world. Forgiveness must be really divine, because it existed nowhere near him or the rest of the world for that matter.

John discontinued his open appreciation of the car: Garrison's Burnt-Orange-Charger with the black racing stripes, and matching hood scoop, not to mention the tinted windows… the car sort of took on a life of its own; it was hard to ignore. Garrison had been stopped on many occasions. Some people didn't like that Garrison had kept large in part to the original version of the vehicle depicted in the Dukes of Hazard, but most people would just gawk at the machine; much like John was doing now.

John turned to the small blue Versa he was driving. Garrison watched as the usual disgust colored John's eyes. Normally, Garrison found it humorous, but today he was too annoyed to care.

"What about Jordan, why wasn't she coming home?" Garrison hated that he had asked the question. He wished he could recall it the moment it was out of his mouth, but it was too late. No wonder people had always believed him to be in love with Jordan. Could he sound any more pathetic?

"I don't know man. All I know is Lane was bringing Kirsten back to face Mr. Stanton, and Nick was tagging along to get a ride back to the states." John tossed his hands in the air. "We tried for later flights, but there was none. I stopped by the police station to file a missing person's report…"

"Wait… a missing person's report? Is it that serious?" Garrison's brow furrowed.

"I really don't know. The police don't seem to think so." John admitted.

"What do you mean?" Garrison asked as he moved back to the car.

"Well, like I said; I went by the station, but the officer in charge of missing persons said that they had probably missed their flight. That in normal cases they don't usually start suspecting foul play until twenty-four hours after the person of interest is supposedly missing." John shrugged.

Garrison could detect the frustration in his tone. John had made every effort to find out what was going on with his friends, and every avenue had ended in a slamming door.

"You said in normal cases?" Garrison prompted as he lay a hand on the roof of his car.

"Wow! Jordan was right. You don't miss a thing do you?" John laughed as he scratched the bits of stubble that was filling in around his chin.

"Not usually." Garrison conceded. "What makes this case abnormal?" Garrison hoisted his original question at John again.

"Exactly!" John snapped, obviously, frustration wasn't all that John felt about the day's events. "That's what I asked."

"Well?" Garrison pushed.

"Well… they claim that because they skipped town that they made a conscious decision to not be found at least not by the American Government." Garrison could see that defeat was starting to have the last word. Even as John relived the conversation his eyes begged for answers.

"What!" Garrison nearly shouted. "What kind of bull-crap hick-nonsense?" Garrison was livid. He knew better. He had been privy to the most final of U.S. laws over the past fifteen years, and nowhere had he read or heard such a load of crap. Garrison was moving now.

"Hey, what are you planning?" John called after Garrison.

"First I'm planning on paying for the gas, and then I plan to educate your local police department; I'm going to make an impromptu visit to the American embassy. I have a couple of friends in that office. I plan to drop a name… I think lighting a fire under our local 'pigs' would make for a pretty good roast. Then, I was thinking of doing some traveling." Garrison flashed John a wicked grin as he made his way to the front door of the small store.

"Some traveling?" John rushed into the store behind Garrison, and waited for him to pay the attendant.

After paying for the gas, Garrison climbed into his car. "Just be ready for my phone call. I may need some help state side."

"What about your friends at the embassy?" John frowned.

"Not that kind of help, pretty boy. You may have to get your hands dirty; think you can manage that?" Garrison laughed as he drove away. He finally had something to do with his day.

CHAPTER

8

Kirsten gulped as the eyes narrowed, and then dipped low as if preparing for the attack. She had moved as close to the fire as she could. Already, she could feel the heat radiating through the silk fabric of her robes. She pulled the fabric away from her legs trying to ward off the heat while she kept her eyes trained on the creature.

Her mind grappled for anything that she might have learned that would help her to overcome this moment. She grew up on a small five-acre lot with two horses and a dog. Her knowledge of animals, especially wild animals was very limited. Her father had always told her to never show fear to her horse, Butterscotch, but that was easy. Butterscotch had been a gentle spirit from the beginning.

Kirsten remembered some of the episodes on her favorite channel, The Animal Planet… she knew to run, would be a mistake. Running was no option, anyway, because she was frozen with the fear, which she should not be showing.

She knew her options were becoming as limited as her knowledge of animals. Her leg was burning, a wild animal with menacing yellow eyes crouched in the shadows ready to attack, and outside of the cave she could hear the anguished cries of the Cadotion people as they were being mercilessly slaughtered.

Her eyes watered. Her legs felt as hot as the fire from which she sought refuge. Her hands shook. She wanted to get away. She wanted so much to be home with her family, but they were gone.

A low rumbling-growl emitted from the animal as it crept forward.

"Leave me alone!" Kirsten hissed. In desperation she scooted closer to the blazing fire. Her hands frantically beat at the blistering heat on her leg. Tears streamed down her face, she was terrified to take her eyes off of the creature. She knew if she did not maintain eye contact, the creature would pounce, and she would be ripped apart. Reaching down deep, Kirsten summoned all of her courage. She finally took her eyes from the creature's yellow gaze. Her heart felt as though it would jump out of her chest. It was taking every ounce of her courage to not keep her eyes trained on the hideous-monstrous eyes. The pounding in her chest quickened, as she scanned the ground for some kind of a weapon.

She had almost given up the search, when a piece of hickory about a foot in length caught her attention. Several burned pieces lay haphazardly concealing the piece of wood. She pulled the slender log from under the pile, and quickly took inventory of the burning end. A slanted piece of the timber, about an inch thick had burned down leaving nothing but ash. She thumped the end of the wood on the burning pile, causing the ashy-debris to sloth away. A wedged end remained. The piece of wood looked like a stake.

She felt instantly stronger with the makeshift weapon in her hand. She again summoned her courage as she shifted her eyes, looking for the beast. Fear slammed into her chest, stealing her breath. The monstrous eyes were no longer there.

Moving away from the flames so that she would not catch her robes on fire, Kirsten waved the still flaming wood in an arch through the air. Shadows retreated as the flame arched across in front of her. The fierce red glow of the burning wood made streaks in the air, leaving in its wake an after image of red light.

The inner chamber appeared empty. Kirsten could not see beyond the darkened-hallways, but she wasn't about to go investigate. She thought about the loud cracking noise that the piece of wood had made as she slammed it against one of the other smoldering pieces of log… the sound had echoed so loudly throughout the chamber walls that she had nearly flung the wooden stake, and ran for the exit. Surely, the sound had scared the hungry beast away. It was as the echo had died out that she could again hear the pitiful screams. She had changed her mind, feeling her chances against a hungry beast, were much better than what she would face in the Cadotion village.

She pushed the end of the stake into the fire pit. She needed to stoke up the fire, now that the beast was gone, and she could really focus on the task. It would be easier to get the fire blazing. As she lifted the bottom log, fire covered sparks filtered into the air. The simple scenery filled her with calm. It reminded her of the bonfires at church camp.

Mrs. Harold, the GA (Girls in Action) leader was dedicated to getting the youth off of the streets. To that end, she had enlisted her husband's help. The two had plotted to scare the girls. Kirsten would never forget the screams that filled the camp as Mr. Harold exploded from the bushes like an avenging angel, and claimed a floundering Mrs. Harold, who had incidentally forgotten, at least for the moment that her husband was going to attack… making the pseudo attack all the more convincing a performance.

Kirsten snickered as the scene of that day filled her mind. Unfortunately, for the Harold's the attempt had worked better than they had initially hoped. Each one of the young women ran screaming from the campsite. Mrs. Harold had to explain everything to the police. Two of the girls, Meagan and Tabatha had run to a nearby neighbor's house, and called law enforcement. The Harold's had narrowly escaped a disturbing the peace charge.

Kirsten sniffed. How could her life be filled with this much chaos? She was only thirteen years old. She had already witnessed the execution of her parents, and now she was in the middle of a tribal war. She longed for a simpler time.

She was still reliving the magical time when she first heard the slight foot falls. The hair stood on the back of her neck. She had misjudged her safety, and now she would pay the ultimate price; she would pay with her life. Kirsten whirled around with the flaming stake in time to see the menacing yellow eyes launching through the air. While she had been claiming the wooden stake from the fire pit, the creature had been repositioning itself for a better attack.

A low hissing sound emitted with a snarl as the thing flung itself through the air.

"Shakia!" Aniahi growled as she slapped the creature away with her bare hand. It was then as the animal sulked back into the darkness that Kirsten had finally gotten her first glimpse of her would be attacker.

"A cat!" Kirsten hissed. "Are you kidding me?" Kristen jumped to her feet. She was so angry that she was vibrating. She had been held hostage by her terror, because of a common alley cat.

Aniahi stepped forward, claiming the flaming-stake from Kirsten's hand. "Come." Aniahi said simply as she led Kirsten down the middle tunnel. Coming to an abrupt halt, the old medicine woman pushed the torch forward illuminating something in a hollowed section in the cave wall.

The large-yellow-eyed cat lay protectively encircling two tiny black and white kittens. The tiny balls of fur eagerly nuzzled their mother, while kneading her stomach with tiny paws. A soft purring emitted from the pile of furry animals, as the two claimed what their mother offered.

"They're so tiny." Kirsten said as she started to kneel.

"Do you so soon forget?" Aniahi asked with a warning glare. "These two are all that is left of five." Aniahi studied the animals for a moment longer. "Come!" She commanded as she started to turn back for the inner chamber.

"But I want…"

"Not so long ago you believed her a dangerous foe, now because she is a small cat you dismiss the threat she truly imposes." Aniahi's face was a mask of disapproval. "Shakia is mother. She will protect what is left of her legacy. It is the way of life. She will not care about what you want." Aniahi turned to Kirsten. "Do not be so quick to underestimate your enemy based on size, or idea you have in mind, about enemy… Not all cat is same. Shakia means you harm, because she wishes to protect her young. The threat is just as real as it was before you were made aware of what Shakia's true form is." Aniahi pointed to the blazing eyes of the black cat.

"The threat to you more, because you have filled your mind with the pet you have. It is that belief that Shakia is something she is not that will give her a vantage point over you." Aniahi said with an abrupt turn. "Come!" Aniahi commanded with more finality than before.

"Well spoken." A familiar voice penetrated the silence. Kirsten's eyes grew wide she pushed off of her heals, with all of her strength as she flung her arms around Jordan.

"Worse still," Jordan said as she pushed back from Kirsten, and adjusted a tuft of hair back over Kirsten's shoulder. "Is the damage done, when you underestimate you?" Jordan kissed Kirsten on the forehead. "You are strong and wise. You have to learn to trust yourself; especially now. I need you to draw from the courage of the girl that stormed the archives of the Truth in search of any information that would keep her alive." Jordan leaned in closer making sure that Kirsten was paying attention. She was. She was so happy to see Jordan, but that had not stopped her from listening. She was so scared of the situation that she was soaking up any information that could keep her alive. Kirsten was a survivor, and information meant life.

"I need the girl that refuses to be blindly led around by what someone else demands her to do." Jordan cupped Kirsten's chin. She loved the feel of Jordan's hand. She felt safe with her around. "You need to trust your instincts; they will keep you alive. You were the only agent enlisted by Mr. Stanton that refused to believe you could defeat a seasoned agent with the bare essentials of combat. You were wise." Jordan tapped Kirsten's temple. "It was your common sense, your curious nature, and your determination that kept you alive then… trust it to do the same now."

Kirsten could not speak. Tears ran in torrents down her cheeks. She nodded her understanding.

Jordan turned to Aniahi then. "There are archers all over the mountains. Lane and I had to map out a trail to here, before we could bring the children." Jordan touched Aniahi's arm as she went on. "Haywalo is dead."

Kirsten watched as the steely glare closed in on Aniahi's warm brown eyes. It was something Kirsten had witnessed her grandmother do, when her grandfather had died.

Kirsten had thought her grandmother cold, and indifferent to the death of her grandfather. She had later found her grandmother crying in her bedroom. When she had questioned her grandmother's actions her grandmother had told her something that would stay with her always.

"Kirsten when something happens, there are things that must be done; there is no time to fall apart. Once you have everything that you need to do to take care of the problem, then you can fall apart."

Kirsten could see that Aniahi was preparing herself for what needed to be done to take care of the problem. Kirsten knew, just as the walls of preparation steeled over Aniahi, so too must she prepare for the problem. If she did not, Kirsten knew there could be only one outcome... she would die. People she had grown to love and depend on would die.

9

Three rows of cushioned, first class, reclining seats mocked Garrison as he marched down the isle of the plane to his dreaded middle seat. A line of three absurdly small captain chairs and his was smack-dab in the middle. He was having to cut costs. The money he had left would not last if he splurged on the finer things, like first class tickets, just to accommodate his craving for the high life. He was thankful for the frequent flyer miles that he had accumulated during his time as an agent, but even that would not last if at every opportunity he traded up to first class.

Tucking his carry-on luggage, which was his only luggage, into the overhead compartment, Garrison said, "Excuse me." to a heavy set gentleman in a blue jogging suit, and then squeezed himself into the middle chair. He had fourteen hours to catch up on his sleep, and prepare a strategy for locating his best friend and her family.

Garrison knew little about the Cadotion village; what he did know had been learned through excited conversations with Jordan and her daughter, Amelia. Armed with a vague knowledge of the village's location, he intended to call upon his dormant skills as an agent to rescue those he loved.

Though he had been drinking heavily since the incident with Kirsten and Mr. Stanton, Garrison had started a grueling boot camp-headed up by a very Tall-Amazonian-looking woman, named Jodi Dunn. Jodi was as beautiful as she was lethal. Her tactics bordered on insanity. Garrison, like all of Jodi's hapless victims, loved to hate her.

Jodi had a no-non-sense straight forward commanding presence that often made the members of her class want to choke her, but the results were undeniable… so he continued to go to the small, unkempt gym, where she trained, and follow her direction.

Garrison laid his head back on the barely reclined captain chair. He had a long way to go. Thinking about his tyrant-trainer would not gain him much needed rest. With that he closed his eyes; with an exaggerated sigh of defeat, he was soon asleep.

Two donkeys, a small crop duster, and a boat ride later, and Garrison was thirty minutes from the Karakoram Mountains, home of the Cadotion tribe. The small boat he had chartered, was equipped with nothing but oars to propel it forward. As Garrison drifted closer to his destination, he was thankful for his trainer's demanding workouts.

He thought of the small vendor by the water's edge. Purple and blue awnings stood out in stark comparison to the dull brown robes of the vendors. Each of the vendors stood near the small patch of earth, cradling the water's edge, holding their goods, calling to the tourists that meandered through the market. Garrison ignored the hanging slabs of meet, teaming with winged assailants—flies and other pests claiming bits of flesh—and fur that lined most of the small vendor camps, and made his way to the vendor that was selling the only thing that he had need of at this moment: a boat. The only access to be granted to the Cadotion village would be gained via the river. He would have to cross from the vendor's site, and float some forty minutes downstream to the smallest pass in the Karakoram Mountains.

The Cadotion tribe had used the small encampment to their advantage. They would be able to knit the passes closed during the winter, and the small passes would allow a breezeway in the summer; this made the land that the Cadotion tribe had claimed a prized commodity, thus the attempts made by the Manerky in the past to claim rights to the land.

Something about the worried look in the vendor's eyes, when he had asked for directions to the village, had sent up red flags for Garrison. The man had also mentioned the Manerky. Though, Garrison could not understand the language, he did know the reputation of the Manerky.

Jordan's and Lane's last trip to the states had been to petition The Truth for the right to take the word to the Manerky. It was during the trip that Tommy Hayden, Jordan's nephew had plotted to kill Jordan and her entire family. Tommy had fervently believed that Jordan killing his father, Jr. Buckley, had deprived him of a fantasy life. Tommy had built a world within his mind. Jr. Buckley, his biological father, Jordan's brother, was the key that could unlock every door of happiness in his life. Jr. Buckley in reality was a cruel man. He beat his wife and daughter. He chained them, helplessly to his will.

During an attempt to free Jordan from Tommy's evil clutches, Garrison and Lane had been captured, and nearly killed.

Garrison thought about the child-agents that had been recruited; each of their families had been executed, and they had all in truth been told that Jordan was the one responsible. One of those agents had been Kirsten Edwards. Garrison had encouraged her to call Edward Stanton, and pretend to be someone she wasn't. The idea was to scare Stanton into making a mistake. Stanton had destroyed every piece of evidence in The Truth and Black Heart archives, linking Jordan to himself and all the key players in a drug and gun cartel that he had personally headed up. The child agents had been poorly trained, and were never meant to survive the battle against Jordan. They were merely a diversion.

After several of the child-agents had rigged the bunker door that Garrison had been recovering behind, with explosives, the door had exploded prematurely, killing all of the agents on impact. Garrison had opened fire on the would-be intruders, with a machine gun.

Garrison's excitement for having gotten his 'groove' back was short lived. There was something very sobering about seeing the ground littered with the dead bodies of children. While the children were attempting to rig the door with plastic explosives, the other agents, Garrison had his suspicions of who it had been, ignited the explosives. The agents lining the door with explosives never had a chance.

Garrison was so filled with anger that he had manipulated Kirsten into doing something that she should have never done. He had convinced her to make that call. Stanton had tried to end his life while Kirsten was on the phone with him. All of Stanton's transgressions had been aired on the evening news. He would surely go to prison; death was better.

Garrison, try as he might could not think of any circumstance that would validate taking his life, so Stanton's reaction had been a completely foreign concept.

His thoughts spiraled from one to the next, but none of the issues that had plagued him back in his apartment seemed to matter now. Even the worst of his problems now floated up into the heavens and took their place amongst the weightless clouds, lining the liquid blue sky. Everything about the lush greens and rolling hills whispered of serenity. All at once he understood the call; the need that Jordan had to escape into its beauty.

The river, a wide-lazy snake of crystal blue wrapped endlessly around the snow-capped mountains. Just as all of his worries melted into the scenery, Garrison neared the Cadotion village. The landscape called to him like a siren, masking the concerns that he had about Jordan coming to the village; concerns about the Manerky seem pointless. But as he moved closer the beauty faded.

He watched in wide-eyed horror as painted horses stood tethered to tree limbs, but it was the symbols painted on each of the animals that ignited the most terror in his heart. Each of the horses was marked with red and black. The swirling pictures, depicted images of battle… Men raced in and out of the mountain pass. Dark-disturbing images of pure hate and futility stared back at him. Though Garrison could not make out the exact nature of the tattoos, he could feel the evil radiate from each symbol, each face.

He knew with certainty that this was the Manerky. They dotted the mountain pass like worker ants. Some holding spears, while others were filtering higher up on the snowcapped mountains to either side of the pass. What seemed like a serene picture of peace, had been disintegrated-instantly, by the obvious-evil intent of the invaders settling in for what appeared to be a long, vicious attack.

CHAPTER

10

Lane studied the majestic snowcapped mountain stretching high above the Cadotion village. It seemed to bend to the will of the aqua-blue horizon. Only a few clouds dotted the liquid-blue skyline, it was the perfect day for a family gathering by the lazy shore of the Cadotion river, but as Lane scrutinized the dozens of archers littering the mountain side, he knew there would be no serene moments; his family would each be doing their part to ensure the survival of not only their unit, but of those that remained, of the Cadotion tribe.

He felt the weight of those beautiful mountains on the shoulders of his family. Jordan was pregnant, and had thus far been overloaded with ridiculous amounts of stress. Amelia was only six years old, and would be responsible for a distraught child's wellbeing. Tristan, at three, was already the picture of a little man. His responsibility to maintain a cognitive level well above his years, seemed somehow the most unbearable… he would not be able to run and play; any amount of noise coming from the tents could lead to the archers releasing a deadly spray of arrows.

Lane prayed silently for a miracle. He did not want to think of his children ending up like Modilo, or even himself—with no parents to show them the way. Though Amelia had suffered the same tragedy, in the loss of her biological parents, her only memory was of Lane and Jordan; so in the end she had for the most part felt whole.

He could imagine Modilo's memory would be a little different. The child was nearly the same age as Tristan. How far back a child's memory could go was different in each individual circumstance. Lane could remember times from before his adopted parent's plane crashed. Some of his memories dated back to when he was around Tristan and Modilo's age, but in none of those memories could he recall his biological father.

His father had taken his own life, not long after his birth, though Lane wasn't sure of the exact time-frame. He had resented his father's memory after finding out during a near death experience that his father too had been a Nephilim, a descendant of the fallen angels.

He knew the story well in the book of Genesis, of the bible... Genesis six. He had read of the selfish-lust, the greed, of the Nephilim, as they took young human women, forfeiting their lives, through the birth of their offspring. Lane had believed his father guilty of the same selfish-lust.

It wasn't until Jordan had become pregnant with Tristan that he had realized how misguided his anger had been. Though, the Nephilim had sired children, and forfeit the lives of those women that had never been the intentions of Lane's father. His father had met and fallen in love with his mother. It was through their union that his mother had become pregnant, and subsequently died. Lane's father was so grief stricken over the loss of his true love that he had taken his own life.

He studied the archers on the plateaus of the mountain side. He knew that mapping out a trail from their tent to the hidden cave would take that miracle he had been praying for. The Manerky tribe was expert marksmen. Any movement on the valley floor would elicit a deadly response, of arrows blackening the sky.

Jordan had been trained in combat, but never had her training included a threat such as the Manerky.

Lane was a missionary for The Truth. It was his job to educate himself about the habits of the indigenous tribe populations of the Karakoram Mountain range. Through that study, Lane had gained vital Intel concerning the Manerky.

He knew all too well that the Manerky tribe was not governed by fear; death meant nothing to the Manerky, because they believed that their spirit would take on another form, such as reincarnation would suggest. The Manerky were especially dangerous for their ability to disconnect from their bodies during pain. The tribesmen practiced an ancient form of meditation, known as Ma-no-hi-lo, the trance walk. The

Manerky could go into a sort of trance that would compartmentalize the different centers of the brain, associated with pain and emotion.

Lane shivered as he imagined the savagery that could be inflicted by those not governed by emotion, or limited by pain. His family was at the mercy of that people.

"What's it look like out there?" Jordan's voice drifted from deeper in the tunnel as she approached from the darkness. Lane knew more than anything she was announcing her impending approach; now was not the time to surprise him. Any noises, including a shrill squeal of alarm, would alert the Manerky to their whereabouts.

He took her hand as he answered the rhetorical query. "The same." he smiled weakly into the darkness, though he knew she would not see the gesture, she would, however sense it.

"You know this mountain better than I, Lane..." Jordan squeezed his hand. "Any ideas on how we can gain the element of surprise?"

He considered the question as he played with her fingers. He hadn't really given the element of surprise much thought. He had believed the advantage gone the moment the Manerky had stormed, undaunted through their home. But as he considered her question, he knew that the Manerky were a proud people. Though they did not have many weaknesses, their pride would surely be a vantage point—he knew that the tribesmen would believe the victory theirs—the bodies littering the floor... Lane cringed back from the ugly truth. His family, precious members of the Cadotion people, lay slaughtered on the valley floor. As ugly a truth as it may be, he had to consider the deeper truth; the truth that would, hopefully give his family a much-needed chance.

"I'm sorry to say I didn't think it an option anymore." Lane finally admitted. "So I haven't really been giving much thought to the secrets of the mountains."

"During a battle, the element of surprise can always be called on to even the odds, as long as the cloak of invisibility is sustained." Jordan recited the rules of engagement form the Black Heart manual. She had graduated at the top of her recruited class. A virtual killing machine, she basked in the kill. The love of spilling enemy blood had nourished the appetite of another enemy in which Jordan had not been aware of, until it was almost too late: Hate, Lane knew all too well the fury of the demonic presence that had overcome Jordan's will... He could still see the shadow of that pain as it sometimes haunted her emerald eyes.

Jordan had experienced horrifying nightmares in which the scenes would change, but the underlying threat had remained the same. They had both believed the encroaching fog of her nightmares was the demonic presence, Hate, trying to gain a foothold in her psyche once more. While they had been wrong about the host, they had been right about the demonic parasite's impending return. Lane thought of the four demonic spirits lurking near Jordan as she lay helplessly tied up in the corner of the room, at the old farmhouse. Those spirits had been released, and given reign in the real world, in much the same way Jordan had opened doors for Hate to reign over her senses; Tommy, Jordan's nephew had entertained the same evil presence as Jordan, but in a more direct way.

Tommy had filled the farmhouse with artifacts, and props that would engender a certain demonic appeal, and elicit a reaction of fear. Doing so, he had opened doors to the demons of hell, and given them free reign of not only the world surrounding him, but his will as well.

Lane thought of how that time could relate to what they were presently going through. It had in essence been the element of surprise that had thwarted the enemy. Lane had been surrounded by the enemy, just as he was now: tied to a metal table with hundreds of steel shards surrounding his body, pressing into his skin. With every move, he was crippled with excruciating pain. In that room, Lane felt utterly abandoned by the Holy Spirit. The presence of evil was so tangible, it seemed to drain not only light, but life out of everything in its path... but even in the depths of that evil God had been there, waiting for Lane to call upon Him. It was in that moment, of clarity that he had felt the first spark of the Spirit's light. That spark had grown as Lane's faith blossomed, and the holy light of Christ had been so bright and hot, it had melted away the steel shards, and released Lane to fight the enemy.

Lane knew in that moment; Jordan had been right. The element of surprise was not lost, and he knew exactly what to do.

11

Penny froze in mid-stride. The scenes of horrified brown faces covered with muddy tears flashed across the screen of an overhanging, flat screen television in the middle of the Denali airport. She might not have paid any attention to the news report, but the words 'War Between Tribes' flashing across the top of the pictures depicting wounded and frightened tribesmen of the Cadotion village that had narrowly escaped into the river, and swam to the adjacent shore, had caught her attention.

She stepped out of the flow of people rushing to their expected boarding areas. She wanted to be able to hear what the reporter on the scene of a small marketplace, was saying about the situation. The frantic-demure-attractive-mahogany skinned young woman, explained in frantic undertones, the massacre playing out in the Karakorum Mountains. Penny knew all too well those mountains. She had heard her Aunt Jordan talk about the home of the Cadotion villagers many times.

Outside the picture windows of the airport Penny could see that dawn was just breaking. She had hoped to reach the village before sun down the day before, but she knew that was an impossible dream. It was a fourteen hour flight. As she watched the macabre scene playing out, she could see the error of that desire. It would be best to be in the village during the day.

The Manerky tribe had been a point of interest for Penny, ever since she had been made aware of her Aunt Jordan's desire to go to the people with the truth. The Manerky were one of the only tribes that had trained in complete darkness.

It was said that the Manerky believed their people to be lords of the underworld. They worshipped the night, and practiced black magic. To become a warrior, a tribesman would need to rely solely on his instincts. It was through those animalistic instincts that the Manerky believed that their other five senses could be honed to a razor's edge. To face the Manerky at night, would mean death to any opponent. Penny knew that her Aunt Jordan would want the cloak of night to shroud her and those that fought at her side.

Penny swallowed back the bile, threatening to choke her. Fighting the Manerky at night, would be like fighting a bat at night. They would be completely in their element. It would be a mistake that Penny knew Jordan may not live to regret. She gulped air, and batted her eyes. She may already be too late. She had not been able to get word to her aunt in time. She had already lost too much of the battle. The night spent in the village, could have been no less than a horrific nightmare, come to life.

She regretted not being able to speak with Jordan, but so much had happened that it had slipped her mind; now it was all she thought about.

She had even done a paper on the Manerky in one of her college classes, Modern History. The paper had started out being about the Cadotion, but after Penny had found out about Jordan and Lane's desire to bring the word to the Manerky, Penny had decided to change the subject matter. Her teacher had agreed. The paper had given Penny crucial insight about the dangerous habits of the Manerky, and increased her GPA (grade point average), at the same time.

Her heart was racing. She had just gotten her Aunt Jordan back, she wasn't prepared to lose her so soon.

Penny had learned many things through her research, but none as frightening as Direignbang, the belief that the Manerky people could dig down into the earth's surface deep enough to find the ruler of the underworld. If the people reached the ruler of the underworld, Direign—He would then grant them eternal life for helping to release him into the realm of the living. The amount of years granted to the Manerky in the afterlife would be based on the human souls they had taken—this was achieved by ingesting human flesh.

Shivers ran down her spine as she thought of what her aunt would have to face. Then Penny thought of Amelia and Tristan… how could Jordan, Lane, and Nick be efficient fighters when charged with the welfare of ones so young. Penny was not a mother, but she knew what it meant to fight while being distracted. It mattered not what the distraction, good or bad, the outcome would be the same; lack of focus meant lives lost.

She tried to collect herself amid the meandering crowd. She needed to make a plan. She was racing the clock. She needed to get to Jordan, before another night could settle over the Cadotion village, assuming it was not already too late. She needed to get to Jordan before she had the chance to underestimate the enemy. She knew her aunt's knowledge would be limited to all that the Cadotion knew of the Manerky. Unfortunately, that was a very dim understanding, based solely on past raids. The Cadotion, unlike the Manerky, were not a battle-hardened tribe that knew the importance of profiling the enemy. To underestimate the enemy, meant death.

During her research, Penny had searched Google for legends on the Manerky. That search had led to ancient writings. Penny had gone to the small book store, in New Jersey. A woman with golden brown skin, and caramel eyes, had given Penny more than the book of watered-down-tribal history… Karen, like Amelia had been adopted after a raid on the Nyguawia, a village that lived to the west of the Cadotion. The woman was clearly very old. She had extreme signs of aging: deep grooves lined her tan features. White hair gracefully shrouded her head, and was pulled back into an upsweep of intricate braiding. It was from the aged Nyguawia woman that Penny had learned the darkest of the Manerky secrets…the more years stolen from a human's life, through ingestion of the flesh, the longer years received in the afterlife.

The Manerky would not kill a child in battle. To do so would be a waste. Instead, children would be collected, and served for the feast of Direignbang.

CHAPTER

12

John was still frustrated that he had not been able to see Max at the corner grocery store. Max had helped John through many a rough patch. He had gotten Cynthia, as well as Jordan's children to the safety of the log cabin—that coincidently he had also helped to locate the land that it had been built on. Come to think about it Max was always there, in the background, navigating their lives to a better place. He was like an angel that was sent solely to guide them on their way, as they traverse the harsh realities of life. John felt as though he could talk to Max about anything, Max was John's best friend.

John was going to ask Max's father; the owner of the small country store about Max's absence. Unfortunately, he had been distracted by Garrison. Seeing Garrison had allowed John the much needed help in locating his friends, but had also cost him the opportunity to enquire after another friend. Now as John rounded the last curve that opened up to the straight length of highway, ending at the drive leading to his cabin, John had suddenly remembered. He was still too distracted by the last thing Garrison had said to commit any real thought to his friend's sudden and complete disappearance from his life… besides, Max was a grown man. Calling him constantly, or sending him an obscene amount of text messages would be completely inappropriate. But if John were being honest, it was exactly what he wanted to do. Max had seemed to drop off of the grid of his life, the moment that he and Cynthia had moved into the cabin. Sure there was a time or two here and there that John had seen him fixing up the old car in the back of the store, but hearing from Max had been a weekly, if not daily event for nearly five years. John thought back, it had almost dated back to Jordan's first appearance in their lives.

One-day John had received an e-mail from someone claiming to have met him on a mission trip. The e-mail went on to say that too much time had passed. It further stated that he and John should get back together soon and recount the past, while filling in the gaps in their lives up until the present. John had simply replied with a sure thing, and then gave a quick warm regards. His e-mail was sent, and no other thought was given to the e-mail. It was the next day that Max had started e-mailing him more frequently. Max had explained that he was in town and wanted to meet for a quick lunch. From there, he and Max would meet two towns over every week. John found the whole Cloak and Dagger lunching to be a bit quirky, but had thought nothing more of it after listening to Max talk about his time in the field. Max had been running from some very bad criminal elements, because he had testified in open court against the militia forces that had taken the lives of the missionaries and locals in Honduras. John had thought it odd that he had been a witness to the same murders, but had never been called to testify, but he had never voiced his apprehension.

John reached across the console to the passenger seat, after parking the small blue Versa, and claimed the flight manifest for flight 384. He had also been able to use his clearance gained by the CIA badge Garrison had made for him, to obtain the flight manifest for all twenty of the flights arriving that day, and the next day. John had sifted through all of the pages, and still not managed to find Lane's name on any of them. He intended to get Cynthia to look through each of the manifest. He could use a fresh perspective.

Sweet potato Soufflé wafted through the door as John stepped inside, and hung his coat on the wooden-peg. His stomach immediately growled its protest, while his nerves relaxed. He loved this about Cynthia. She had inherited her love of cooking from her mother, who had gotten it from her mother. It was that love of cooking that had sustained her during the nightmare inflicted on her life by Black Heart.

Forced into a life of murder, Cynthia had purged her anger for the breach of her perfect life in the lavish kitchen of the apartment afforded her by Black Heart. Soon, she had moved that love of cooking to The Garden after being sent there to be recycled. The missionaries responsible for helping the misguided souls, sent to them by Black Heart, encouraged the lost agents to indulge, within reason in those things that brought them the most peace… it was there that The Truth believed, one could find their calling.

"Smells good, honey." John announced.

"Good, then you won't mind joining us."

John stiffened for a moment. He knew the voice; it was Max. But why was Max here? More importantly, John thought, why did he sound so menacing? John disregarded the last thought. His nerves were on edge; he was bound to read things into situations that weren't there. Truth be known he was still harboring a few hurt feelings about Max disappearing on him.

"Max." John called cheerfully. "I was wondering…" John could feel all of the color drain from his face as he rounded the corner from the mud-room into the kitchen. Cynthia's eyes spilled over with tears, a piece of duct-tape was haphazardly slapped over her mouth, and her hands were tied behind her. John lunged forward.

"That's far enough John." Max warned in a low growl. He placed the black pistol to Cynthia's head. Terror immediately filled her liquid-brown eyes. Tightly closing her eyes, Cynthia cringed helplessly away from the weapon.

"What the hell is all of this about Max?" John demanded.

"Language, John. Be careful, Christian boy… remember, 'be angry, but sin not'."

"Cut the crap Max!" John warned. "We both know you're not here for a bible lesson, so why don't you tell me what this is really about." John was angry, he wanted to show Max how good he had been at sinning, before being set free. But more than that he was confused. Max was after all the closest person to him, besides Cynthia. What could have possibly happened between the two of them that John had missed; what could be so bad as to warrant something as unforgivable as this?

Max clucked his tongue, while rubbing his temple with the barrel of the gun. John scrutinized the man he had believed to be his friend, as he shamefully hoped the gun would malfunction and blow the guy he had called best friend into oblivion.

John had never seen Max dressed in anything more than hole-filled jeans, and a t-shirt. His black hair was usually slick with sweat, and oil from whatever car he was working on at the time. Now, though, Max looked like a corporate-clone of his former self.

Max's jet-black hair was cut, and combed neatly to the side. He wore a gray-pin-striped suit with a dark gray tie—pinned pristinely to the front of a freshly ironed white shirt. Max looked like new money, very new money.

"You still haven't figured it out, have you John?" Max asked with a sardonic grin.

"Figured out what? I'm still trying to understand why the guy I believed to be my best friend is standing in my kitchen, holding a gun to my wife's head, who incidentally, he has also tied up!" John roared.

"Poor John Benton… Everything is always about you, isn't it?" Max hissed while waving the gun around to indicate the elaborate fixtures, decorating the beautifully adorned cabin.

John studied the cabin for a moment. It was truly a masterful work of art. Every thought that had went into the blueprints of the cabin, had been with their extreme love of music, and their devotion, and yes love for the Lord. The cabin was a sanctuary of shrines lending themselves to the single concept of what it meant to be John and Cynthia. The kitchen cabinets were mahogany wood with handles made in the shape of musical notes and instruments. While the living room was lavished in intricate pieces of crystal that were painstakingly, etched pictures, depicting hands outstretched in supplication to the only One that could grant grace. A beautifully painted picture depicting the same image as the lamps, held center stage over the fireplace that was also a raw shade mahogany—honesty, no pretense. John and Cynthia preferred the unfinished hue of wood in its natural form. God made no mistakes. There were more intricacies lining the room, which paid homage to specific things that the two might hold value in… All of which had been made possible by God, and the man standing before him, holding a gun to his wife's head.

"If you weren't so self-centered, then maybe you could have seen all of this coming." Max admonished. "Come to think about it sugar, I should do you a favor, and put him out of your misery." Max growled, as he lay one of his hands on Cynthia's shoulder.

Cynthia whimpered pitifully through the tape. She shook her head, vehemently begging for John's life. John wanted to end this for her sake, but he needed to know what had set Max off.

"Why are you doing this Max? Tell me… what did I do?" John was nearly begging. He didn't care; pride was the farthest thing from his mind. He wanted Cynthia to be safe; their child to be safe. He wanted her to be lying down, or at the very least humming in front of the oven as she did what she loved best.

Max stepped away from Cynthia. He faced the mahogany cabinets. "I really like the musical notes, John." Max claimed offhandedly, while wielding a simple smile.

John resisted the urge to peer at the handles that were in the shape of various musical notes and instruments. His house décor was another subject at the bottom of his list of concerns. John wanted to tell Max that, but at the moment he was calm, even though the subject matter was obviously not getting them anywhere.

"Has it never occurred to you, to wonder why I would be so willing to do anything for you, John?" Max suddenly asked.

"Of course it has, Max. I appreciate all that you have done; I've tried to pay you for it. I asked you if the payments were not enough." John insisted.

"Payment!" Max scoffed. "Not enough!" Max closed the distance between him and John. Grabbing John by the arm, Max shoved him into the living room.

Losing his balance, John wobbled unable to stop into Cynthia's hand-sketched Crystal lamp. The beautiful piece made to match the painting over the fireplace, wobbled—as it seemed to be as desperate as John to gain balance. But just as quickly as John was seeming to lose ground, the lamp was plummeting to its destruction. It shattered on the floor.

John bent to collect some of the pieces. His heart was breaking for Cynthia. She had gone through so much to have the pieces match perfectly. She had waited patiently as the shop keeper had painstakingly, etched the design into the crystal lamps, to match that of the painting that he had also created.

John flinched as an explosion ripped through the silence. He looked up in time to see the crystal lamp on the opposite end-table shatter, and explode outwardly as the bullet passed through the middle of the lamp undaunted.

"Sit down John!" Max warned in a murderous tone. Then he walked back to the kitchen, and lay a hand on Cynthia's shoulder. She pulled away. "See, now they're a set again." Max quipped, as he gave an affectionate pat to Cynthia's shoulder, and then started to the couch where John was now sitting.

John felt helpless. What was he going to do?

"As I was saying, before you rudely interrupted me." Max turned to Cynthia. "Thanks to your little scholar…" Max said through gritted teeth. "All of this…" Max waved the gun at the cabin again. "Goes away. I'm what's known as the silent partner, John." Max laughed. "Well, I guess you could say we were all, to a degree supposed to be silent partners… that's until Miss Goody-Two-Shoes, had her little friend get those files from Stanton's office." Max turned back to Cynthia for a moment.

John wanted to keep Max's attention off of Cynthia. "How do you know all of this?" John asked.

"Well, if wifey here was as good an agent, as she is a tattletale…"

"Profiler." John corrected, without thinking.

"Profiler… six of one; half a dozen of another." Max frowned, and then shrugged. "It matters not what her title is; just what she is about to do." Max turned back to Cynthia as he clucked his tongue, and wagged a finger at her. "Bad girl…"

John needed an opening. He needed to stop this, before Max killed Cynthia. He needed to keep him talking too, so he could find out all of the missing puzzle pieces that Cynthia had not yet been able to obtain, through the files.

"What is she about to do, Max?" John tried to be as casual as possible when asking the question. He didn't want his attempt at disarming Max, while he thought of a way to retaliate, to backfire and ignite Max's anger; resulting in him hurting, or even killing her.

"What is she about to do?" Max was shaking his head. "Now John you can't be this naïve." Max laughed without humor.

John's eyes darted quickly to Cynthia, and then back to Max. Cynthia's eyes filled with tears as her head shook, feebly from side to side. What had she been trying to tell him, in that brief instant? Did she not want him to continue on this line of questioning? John was so frustrated. Lately, he had been expected to shine in some avenues that were very unfamiliar to him: first, with Cynthia expecting him to act as an agent, while he retrieved the files from The Truth archives, and now with Max expecting him to put the pieces to a very vague puzzle together; that was Cynthia's field of expertise, not John's. John felt sad, because it was obviously that ability that had brought her to this.

Anger flooded through John's senses. Max's trivial actions was more than John could take. Max was treating this as a game... John's eyes flashed quickly to Cynthia, she almost seemed to beg him not to answer.

John turned to Max, and there he saw the truth. Max was playing a game. There would be only one outcome, if John stumbled across the truth, and connected the pieces of that puzzle, he would die. John turned to Cynthia then, if he didn't find a way out of this it was already too late for her. Cynthia had made the profile, and Max had planned from the start of this dangerous game to kill her. He was merely using her as bait, dangling her over John's head as he sifted through his mind trying to find out how much he really knew. John studied his wife for a moment longer... he had to keep the questions coming. Time was all she had, and he was desperate to grant her more.

13

Julie held the small mirror up. "See, Edward. I told you, it's not that bad." She fluffed his pillow, and placed the mirror back on the rolling table. Then, she collected the plastic cup of water. Offering him another drink, she prayed that the casual-indifference on his face would soon be replaced with something; anything…

She had a point. The scar was ugly, but it did look better each time he saw it. Edward didn't like Julie, though. She reminded him of all the things he couldn't have. Julie wasn't the exotic beauty that Amorous had been, nor was she at all adventurous. Julie was a fifty-five-year-old, nurse with three grandchildren she loved dearly. Her husband was deceased, after thirty years of marriage; he had been dead for four years now. She lived alone, in a single wide trailer, she had bought after selling their family home, and paying off all of her deceased husband's medical bills.

Julie's beauty was subtler, with her corn-flower blue eyes and blond hair kissed with time, giving her an almost angelic crown of soft white around the perimeter of her pristine face. She had a jubilance about her that captured Edward's attention and irritated him in the same instance. It pulled him along in its vivacious-current, refusing him the mundane existence that had become his sanctuary. The isolation of nothingness wrapped his heart in its steely armor and protected him from the unwanted tumult of feelings that ravished his thoughts every moment.

There was no point in hoping for a future that wouldn't come. He had long since stopped feeling sorry for himself. He deserved what was coming. He was just thankful for the near-death experience that had showed him the true loss he was about to experience. Edward couldn't breathe, when he imagined how utterly lonely it had been in that dark-outer-place without God. Though he was not a Christian, or whatever it took to be as high on life as Julie seemed to be all the time, he could feel a tugging of sorts on his heart.

In that place, that void where he had gone during his near death experience, there was nothing. It was completely without the sweet-nudging that had started since the day he had met Julie. She talked about her Savior constantly.

Julie always exuded a love for Christ that Edward didn't quite understand. He knew all too well that he never wanted to be in that dark place without Him again, but what Julie exhibited—daily... Well, Edward thought, it was a kind of awareness; she seemed to literally experience something, and more to the point, she loved God. He was her entire reason for being. Her job, her home, a great car, and no, not even her family could fill the shoes of her God. He was quite simply her everything.

It bothered Edward. He was confused about Julie, and he was confused about her relationship, as she called it, with Christ. He would have to leave the hospital soon, he didn't think he had anymore reconstructive surgeries to replace his trachea, and the surrounding structures in his throat, though he hoped he did. Being in the hospital, being cared for by Julie, was a thousand percent better than the alternative.

Edward knew that as soon as he was better, he would be remanded to the custody of state officials. From there, he would go to trial for numerous counts of murder, attempted murder, and kidnapping... not to mention the drug cartel he had been involved in. He had decided that he would throw himself on the mercy of the court. It was what he deserved; besides there would be no one to grant him immunity. He had granted countless recycling details for agents under his authority, rather than death. Edward had allowed recruits to be cycled out to The Truth rather than erasing them and all that they loved, but for him, Edward Stanton, there would only be what he so richly deserved. He would rot away in prison until he died. Then he would travel, again to that dark place, devoid of the one thing he knew he could not live without: God's love, His presence. And though Edward knew it to be true, he had no clue how to get to where Julie was. How could he expect that same loving God that put a smile on Julie's beautiful face to forgive a man as vile as he?

He had but one alternative; he would bide his time in whatever cell they gave him and be thankful for even the smallest of space—time, physical room, as long as it was not the dark place. Maybe one day soon, the gentle nudging would find a way to reveal a deeper understanding of what it meant. John closed his eyes. He dare not allow himself to hope for things so far out of his grasp. His time would come. He was due an avalanche of payback, and even as the thought made its way through his tortured psyche, John knew just how much that payback would cost him... Complete separation from Julie's Savior.

14

Jordan pushed back her fear for Lane's safety as she watched the dried clay spray and pebble down behind him. The darkness enveloped his fading silhouette, as he followed the tight-fitting tunnel that opened a few feet above where the first file of archers was stationed. She had wanted so badly to be the first to go, but she was not familiar with the terrain. It made sense for Lane to ascend the tight space of the tunnel, and then explain the route to her.

Lane had said that he had easily maneuvered through the passageway as a small child. Jordan feared his hulking size would hinder his ability to advance, and may even be the cause of him being trapped in the darkness. There would be no tools to pull him free of the small space; he would be entombed, buried alive. He had promised to turn back if the passage had narrowed to even the slightest degree. Jordan knew all too well how quickly one could become trapped in an unfavorable condition such as a tunnel. She had been trapped in a chimney that she had misjudged the width, once long ago. The time still brought sweat to her brow. Jordan had finally been able to relax enough to slip through the opening, but there had been a time in the midst of that terror that she had almost cried out. As an agent, that would have meant her capture at the very least, and her death at most.

She stood her ground, though she wanted to rush up the tunnel. Everything in her screamed for confirmation that Lane was unharmed. Having them both lodged, helplessly in the narrow space would not help their situation. Besides, she could tell by the constantly descending debris that he was still moving upward.

She moved back as a copious spray of dried clay filled the space in front of her. Her brows knit as she waited to see what the extra debris could mean. Her heart raced with the moments that seemed to stretch, relentlessly, mocking her fear.

Jordan's breath caught as one of Lane's feet, and then the other exited the tunnel. With a resounding thud he dropped to the cave floor.

"I went as far as I could. The passage gets narrower up above." Lane dusted some of the red clay off of the black pants he had changed into. A bitter scowl etched the contours of his beautiful face. Jordan noticed bits of rock that reluctantly clung to the dark fabric of his jeans. She too had maintained a healthy portion of dust, but nothing like Lane's now white-dusty-mattered-rock attire.

They had both changed into the garments packed for traveling to and from the Cadotion village. They were both thankful to not have to traverse the terrain, while doing battle with the Manerky in robes. Even the bits of dust and rock could not infringe on their happiness for the comfort of the familiar fabric.

"I can't be sure how narrow, but I'm not going to chance it." Lane pointed a dusty hand to indicate the tunnel. "I recognize the area in the tunnel, because as a boy, I drew an emblem deep in the clay, and colored it with berry juice." Lane rolled his eyes. "Most of it has washed away, but still enough of the color remains that I was able to identify it. I wanted to reassure myself that it was close to the surface." Lane smiled sheepishly. "I guess I was a little afraid."

Jordan smiled at the admission, and then studied Lane for a moment. She could see that there was something he was not saying.

"What about me?" Jordan asked. A part of her hoped not, but there was more at stake. This wasn't about her and Lane's safety. They needed to end this for the children's sake.

"Maybe. It's hard to tell." Lane admitted. "You could..." His voice trailed off. He rubbed a hand through his dust-filled hair. Jordan stepped forward. She gently claimed his arm, pulling his hand down from his head.

"I don't like this anymore than you do." Jordan admitted as she rubbed her hands on his forearms. "But this isn't about us, Lane. " She cleared her throat, trying to ward off the tears. "Lift me up."

The moment Lane had lifted Jordan up into the tunnel, she was shrouded in complete darkness. Her hands searched for a grip, and was rewarded. Just as Lane had explained, there was a shelf of rock right on the inside of the tunnel. She pulled herself up into the darkness, and placed her feet on the shelf where her hands had been. As soon as she had her balance, Jordan pawed around for the slight bend to the right. An outcropping of rock just to the left of the bend served as an anchor to push her weight against so she could move into the bend. She then followed the meandering tunnel to the exit above. Soon she made it to the emblem sketched into the earth that Lane had told her about.

The emblem stood for harmony of spirit; it had flowing lines that appeared to be in a dance. Jordan could also see the faint rays of sunlight. She took in the narrow expanse beyond the emblem. The passage seemed to be somewhat wider than her bulk, but she could see where Lane's massive form would not have fit. She allowed a weak smile. Her husband had once been not much bigger than she.

She wondered how old Lane had been. Jordan imagined the word 'boy' could mean anything from a toddler to a teenager. The ceiling, though it did hang low in the cave, was still too high for her to reach the opening of the tunnel. Jordan surmised that would mean Lane was a teenager that was obviously taller than she.

Thinking of Lane as a boy, filled Jordan's mind with thoughts of Tristan. How tall would he be? Would he be a devastatingly handsome man like his father? She touched her stomach… a sob escaped as she thought of all she would face. There would be no way to protect this child from all that she would be forced to endure. She could not leave the child with Nick or Aniahi while she fought alongside Lane against the Manerky; the child's fate would match that of her own.

She peered into the last refrains of sunlight as she pulled clear of the tunnel, and crouched behind two archers. Arrows knocked behind an outcropping of rock, the archers sat poised for trouble below.

She and Lane had managed to scavenge several weapons off of a few of the Manerky warriors that they had killed on the way to the cave, but still the pickings were meager at best. They would need many more weapons if they expected to diminish the numbers of the Manerky forces.

Jordan thought about the warriors, something seemed off about the way they were fighting. It was almost as though they could not see well, as though the sunlight had obscured their vision. She had trained for two weeks blindfolded. Once she was allowed to have her sight back, she found it disorienting at first. The lights, no matter how dim seemed to seer straight through her retina. Her head ached behind her eyes, making the attempt to focus all the more difficult, and agonizing. As Jordan thought of the warriors she and Lane had killed she was suddenly aware of the most dangerous enemy of all, they had yet to realize they were up against; time. They were in a race against the setting sun.

CHAPTER

15

L ane stared nervously at the opening of the tunnel. It had been quite some time since Jordan had disappeared into its dark recesses. He wanted to go in after her, but he knew he would never fit. Jordan would call down if she needed help. Lane's heart raced. She must have already breached the surface. She would be out on the mountain's edge facing a fierce Manerky warrior alone.

He tried to think about all of the weapons Jordan had with her. He had given her one of the hand crafted knives. She had also taken one of the three crudely fashioned Bartons. Lane had named the weapons for their bar like appearance, and their twirling feature that reminded him of a baton being twirled. When the elders had convened to decide the structure of the weapons to be made, a name had not yet been given to the Barton. Jordan was a master at weapons, and she was trained in Tai-kwon-do, among other types of martial arts, such as Tai-chi and Karate. He needed to trust in her abilities, but he just couldn't seem to relax.

When Lane had met Jordan, he was impressed by her fighting skills, but not so much so with her lack of discipline. She was filled with hate back then, and would often allow her temper to predict her actions. Lane had trained her to listen to her inner-being. He had taught her that through meditation, to center herself, and block out all of the non-essential emotions that would often come up during a battle—such as fear, and anger; both were useless, and would do nothing to keep her alive—she could be the victor. Either emotion could only make one lose focus.

He scrutinized the hole; he would have to somehow trust that Jordan had taken in all that he had tried to teach her, and that she would use that training combined with her instincts. He prayed that she would combine the valuable elements with the things she had already been to make the right decisions.

Jordan scanned the area between her and the first two warriors for scree. She needed to be careful not to tip off the men that she was there. She noticed that two men were stationed every few yards apart. She needed to claim the bow and arrows of the two men closest to her location.

Satisfied that there was very little loose rock, she crouched as low as possible. She finally made her way to a sizable group of rock formations just above the men's location. Once she was sure she had traversed the space between her and the warriors without being detected, she reached for the knife that hung loosely at her side in its sheathe. Then, without a moment delay she stabbed the first man in the neck. Then twirling the Barton, she plunged the sharpened end into the other man's ear as he turned to investigate what had caused his friend to suddenly convulse in pain. The man's face was frozen forever in surprise. She pulled both men back against the boulder they had been hiding behind, making it appear that they were still scouting for the enemy. Her muscles ached with the effort of the men's weight. Though both men were reasonably small in stature, their bulk was more than that of her own five-foot-nine-inch physique.

She leaned over the boulder, between the two dead men, and claimed the two bows and quivers of arrows. As she started to move away, she caught site of their tent. No one seemed to be coming or going from the tent, and nothing seemed amiss. Jordan was hopeful that it would remain that way, but something did not seem quite right. She had already surmised from the Manerky's squinted eyes, though the sun was low in the sky that the warriors would be efficient night hunters. However, Jordan could not figure why they had not killed Modilo, when given the chance. For that matter it seemed all of the children were being spared, but why?

CHAPTER

16

An eerie silence filled the air as Garrison crouched low in the bushes lining the side of the river. He expected screaming, chanting, or anything that would mark the mountain pass as being over taken by invaders. Instead, he could hear a pin-drop. Even the animals seemed intent on driving him insane with their indifference to the obvious mayhem that spread throughout the village. The contented reverent chewing of the horses mocked the menacing truth.

He really didn't know the best strategy for thwarting off the enemy advances. He had watched movies and read many books, but even then, there had been battle cries and screams of tormented captives. He could only assume by the two archers in view from his vantage point that the tribes were at some sort of an impasse.

He looked to the painted horses. They were happily grazing on the grassy areas near the mountain where they were tethered. It irritated him that the animals were not betraying the true wealth of danger. Garrison felt as though he were in some Twilight Zone version of the old west. Even in the old movies of cowboys and Indians the horses and dogs would sound their nervous warning of the approaching enemy.

Finally, conceding that the best defense was a good offense, he squatted as low as possible to the ground. He moved quickly though the horses, cutting each of their reins. After the final horse was released, he moved quickly back to the river bank, and collected a handful of rocks and dirt. Flinging the debris at the horse closest to the pass, Garrison darted to the opposing mountain. He had seen an entrance while standing among the horses cutting them loose.

As the rocks and dirt met with furry flesh, a large-midnight-black horse with his mane chopped short like a Mohawk, reared back screaming in fright; the horse blasted through the other horses, but not before scraping his hoof on a fellow horse's rump. The assaulted horse, a golden tan with the same red and black swirls that looked like bottled rage, bit the horse in front of it. Garrison watched in wide-eyed horror as the horses fought amongst themselves, before mercifully making a run for it.

He disappeared stealthily into the small opening in the mountain. A torch was just on the inside of the tunnel. It was not yet lit. Garrison pulled out a Zippo, though he did not smoke, there was always a need for a liter. A strike of his thumb filled the darkened-tomb with a luminous glow.

The tunnel wound endlessly through the mountain. Garrison had for a while considered it a mistake, but then started to see a glowing light ahead. His heart raced. He knew it would either be the exiting tunnel, possibly leading him into the thick of the battle, or it could be tribesmen. As he moved closer to the flickering light, his mind swam with possibilities; would it be Cadotion, or the dreaded Manerky?

Penny stood by the bank thunder-struck as she watched Garrison disappear into the tunnel. She felt a sense of awe and relief flood her senses; so welcomed was the familiar face. Her head spun with warring emotions for a moment. She almost allowed herself to be swept away in the current and run to him, but thought of the enemy they faced. Though it was light out, and their chance of survival was better in the day, an emotional outburst tipping the enemy off as to their whereabouts could prove to be deadly. Underestimating the enemy was a deadly game she refused to play.

She watched the last of the painted-war horses as they scattered, and then moved to the cover of a tree-line just beside the river. Regardless of her game-plan, if she didn't make it, she would be killed. Though the Manerky, were for the most part, blinded by the sun, they were nowhere near deaf. The frightened horses were in a frenzied state of shock as they cried out, alerting their owners of the threat. Someone was bound to be sent to assess the situation, and Penny had no intention of being anywhere near the scene when they did.

She watched in astonishment as a single young warrior exited the pass to check on the frightened horses. She had read that the Manerky were a prideful people, believing themselves to be animal-like beings above the human race. However, as she watched the lone warrior, head shaved, with terrible markings that looked like death come from the underworld to destroy all of life, Penny stood dumbfounded at the idea that one man would be thought enough to stop the threat. She had considered that it could be a trap, but then the young boy ran after the frightened animals, shouting something in his native tongue.

Penny seized the opportunity. Stalking after the boy, she followed at a distance, hiding behind trees, and high patches of grass near the river's edge; always careful to remain silent. Then feeling better about her chances of survival, she threw the large knife she had bought at the small encampment of vendors. With a thwack the knife hit home, at the base of the boy's skull. The boy fell forward, his legs scooping awkwardly forward, and then fell lifeless as the rest of his body collapsed in the still settling dust.

She raced forward, ignoring the dead-still-eyes of the boy, and claimed the bow and quiver of arrows beside his body. A quick survey of his body, led to more hidden treasures. She claimed a wooden-stake; the end hewn to a razor's edge. The boy had a few sharpened rocks in a low hanging pouch around his neck that she imagined he would put in the string of his bow, and send them into enemy skulls; probably used if he were out of arrows.

She claimed the rocks for throwing, she would never figure out how to make them reach a desired target without first stabilizing them on the handle of the bow. She smiled, a weapon was a weapon, even if she didn't know the way the enemy used it, there was always the conventional way… they were rocks, after all, she could throw them.

Penny bent to the task of claiming her knife. Placing a booted-foot on the dead boy's head she gave a massive yank, and the knife was free. With the coolness of a seasoned hunter, she bent over the boy's form, and cleaned the blood on his animal hide thong. It was time to find out if the Manerky were really the dreaded creature of the night that they believed themselves to be, or if they like most bullies, had placed themselves on an elevated notch in the proverbial totem-pole of life that was undeserved.

CHAPTER

17

Cynthia kept her eyes straight ahead trying to seem as beaten as possible. She had been near the small table in the dining area, still putting the scattered pieces of the puzzle together when Max had entered with the gun. She instinctively grabbed the letter opener. It was lying near the pile of mail she had claimed from the mailbox earlier in the day, during a moment of frustration. Her body was blocking the view of her hand, so Max had not seen her neatly tuck the silver-opener up into the sleeve of her olive green blouse. She was thankful to have worn the sleeves that morning; normally due to the pregnancy hormones, she would have donned a tank top. As her pregnancy progressed she was certain she would be able to incinerate whatever she put her bare hands on in moments, but today she felt a little chilly.

Though, she wasn't sure when the opportunity to use the weapon would present itself, she knew it would come. A letter opener was not a good weapon to bring to a gun fight: light weight it made for a poor throwing weapon. The lack of serrated edges made cutting her enemy an impossibility. She would have to be close enough to Max to do any real damage with the device, but it was all she had at the time.

Her time in the field may not have taught her a lot about what to do, but the mistakes she had made definitely schooled her on what not to do.

She slipped the letter opener down into the palm of her hand, as she methodically sliced at the tape; she had been doing so since John had come into the house, and claimed Max's full attention.

Her first big break had come when Max had stepped passed the table to scold John. She had nearly dropped the letter opener the moment John had stumbled violently into the lamp. Her heart skipped a beat, as she waited for him to regain his footing. She searched frantically for any signs of blood; other than a few minor abrasions to his right hand, John was relatively unharmed.

Once Cynthia had been certain of John's wellbeing, she used the break in Max's attention to fitfully finish her work of removing the tape from her wrists. She felt the tension release on her arms. Her heart had only just calmed when Max pointed the gun, and pulled the trigger, igniting the twin lamp that was still standing on the opposite end table. A thousand shards of crystal debris sprayed the air. A gasp escaped her lips as she involuntarily threw her hands protectively over her face. Realizing her folly, she quickly tucked them safely behind her back, in time for Max to walk around the corner of the small table.

She braced herself for what was to come. Determined not to drop the letter opener, her only source of possible escape, she gripped it with all of her might. The pointy-blade bit into her wrist, but she held her ground. No matter what Max did she would not let on that her hands were free. She had but one chance to use the makeshift weapon, and she would not squander it on fear.

18

Julie had been off for three days, and she wasn't due back to the hospital for four more days. The nursing staff worked twelve hour shifts, four days a week. The other three they had off to be with family, or take care of bills, and such. Every three weeks they would have an entire week off. The hospital had incorporated the new time off after too many unexcused absences had left the staff shorthanded during a mass casualty event, which Julie had explained to him was any trauma related event that included more patients than the medical staff could reasonably care for.

It was Tuesday, and Edward was recovering from yet another surgery; a coughing fit had herniated some of the scar tissue near his trachea. The doctor put Edward on muscle relaxers, and cough medicine to ward off anymore bouts of coughing. It wasn't that he minded the relaxed state that he was in, he just didn't like not being able to think. He hated to admit it, but the thought of Julie not returning tomorrow bothered him.

Dr. Thompson had been in to see Edward earlier that morning. The squat man reminded Edward of a short version of Adam Sandler without the sense of humor. Dr. Thompson had informed Edward of the grueling months that lay ahead.

After the setback with the scar tissue, Dr. Thompson did not want Edward to be away from the care of a vigilant nursing staff. The moment Edward was healed to the doctor's satisfaction, he would be released to the rehabilitation center on the second floor of the hospital; there Edward would try to regain as much of his small motor skills as possible—the incident had cost him very little of his gross, or large motor skills: he could walk with help, wave his arms that sort of thing. It was the intricate movements, such as being able to hold a pencil, or pick up something small that evaded his ability.

He was growing restless in the small hospital room. He longed to be able to get out of the bed, to walk out the front door of the hospital; not to escape, he didn't feel he deserved that; he just wanted to feel the warm sunlight on his face… to feel all of the things he had never before taken the time to appreciate: he wanted to sit on a park bench, bask in the sound of bird's singing, and children's laugher. He wanted to ride to the ocean with the top down—A beat up convertible would do. He didn't care to have the finer things in life that had already brought him enough trouble. He just wanted to feel the wind in his hair. He wanted to stand beside the ocean, and once again feel small.

Tears filled Edward's eyes as he realized the rawest desire of his heart that for so long lay dormant: he wanted someone to share it with, but not just anyone; he wanted Julie.

Though he had only met Julie a week earlier, it seemed that he had known her his entire life. He felt as though he could tell Julie anything. That dream or any dream for that matter, seemed useless, unfulfilled without the presence of his new friend.

Amber Noel shrieked endlessly in her mother's arms. Katie was so spent, between work and school that exhaustion was starting to filter into her every action. Eric Jonson, Amber Noel's father had broken his promise of forever… it was all taking its toll on Katie. Julie hated to keep taking the baby, but Katie had to have help. The father hadn't stuck around, so Katie, Julie's youngest was on her own with the task of raising an infant, working and trying to keep her head above water in her college courses. Julie's heart broke for her baby girl. Though she didn't want to destroy the bond that should be created between mother and child, Julie couldn't leave her to the struggle without some sort of a support system. Still, Julie hated to see Amber thrash in Katie's arms, because there was something very broken, very wrong with the connection between her daughter and granddaughter.

Julie sat a few minutes longer, hoping that Katie would calm, but tears streamed down her face instead. With a sigh, Julie stood, and claimed the wailing babe.

"She hates me." Katie pouted pitifully.

Julie took in the earthy beauty of her daughter. She reminded Julie so much of Ronald, her deceased husband. Her big-cow-brown eyes, and light brown hair with generous amounts of curls only twisted the ache in Julie's heart for her daughter.

"She doesn't hate you baby, she just doesn't recognize you…"

"What?!" Katie's brow furrowed with an angry glare. Her eyes blazed with the fire of her Leland temper.

"Oh honey. You know what I mean. Amber Noel can't see very well right now, so she relies very heavily on her other senses." Julie sat on the couch next to Katie with the now quiet Amber Noel. She ruffled the ball on the top of Katie's head. "Why don't you take a bath, and get gussied up? Then call Marcy, and go see a movie with her."

"What about Amber Noel?" Katie brightened a little, and then slouched back on the couch as she reached a hand out to caress her daughter's tiny hand.

"Why don't you let Memaw take this sweet girl for a while, besides I'd like to introduce her to a friend? If you don't mind?" Julie sent a questioning look at her daughter that softened into a smile.

"Are you sure? I mean this is your week off." Katie asked with expectant hope coloring her big brown eyes.

"Of course, I am. As a matter of fact, why don't you just stay over at Marcy's house for the night, and let me take care of Amber Noel?"

"The night?!" Katie looked like Julie had just slapped her. "Amber Noel is only a week old, mom."

"Yes she is, and I believe I have had the occasion to do this before." Julie quipped. "You know this ain't my first rodeo, kid." Julie rolled her eyes playfully.

Katie laughed. "I guess."

"Look girl… you get out of here, before I change my mind, or come to my senses." Julie mumbled under her breath as Katie bounced happily to her bedroom. Katie had moved back in two days after Amber Noel had been born. Life with an infant was not going to be as easy as she had initially thought, especially not while nursing a broken heart.

Julie sat playing with Amber Noel's tiny fingers, before realizing how excited she was to be going to the hospital to see Edward.

She thought of Ronald; she missed him so much that at times the mere mention of his name could close off her throat and leave her gasping for air. She hadn't felt whole for a very long time; not until she had met Edward that is.

CHAPTER

19

Nick stood spell bound as Amelia tilted the cup up, and then in a matter of minutes after drinking, an inconsolable Modilo fell back onto the mat of furs into a restful slumber.

"What the…What's in that?" Nick finally managed.

"Just some herbs to help him sleep." Amelia said with an uninterested shrug.

"That stuff is like anesthesia… better… he didn't even count backwards from ten." Nick laughed.

"Huh?" Amelia's confused expression told Nick he had better change the subject.

"So, do you have any games you like to play?" Nick pepped up as he twisted his fingers together; the whole babysitting gig in the middle of a war zone was beyond nerve racking.

"Games?" Amelia gave Nick a frown of disapproval mixed with confusion.

"Yeah. You know Truth or dare, freeze tag, Uno… whatever, just anything to stay busy, and have fun." Nick was feeling more and more unsettled under the weight of Amelia's scrutiny. It was like talking to a tiny Jordan.

Amelia held up her hand. "Nick, games… fun" Amelia arched a small eyebrow, giving her even more of a Jordan allure. "Make people happy."

"Exactly!" Nick nodded. She was getting it now. He relaxed a little. He thought the tiny menace with the sleep meds would never calm down. The whole Jordan meets Aniahi thing was beginning to freak him out.

"Happy people laugh!" Amelia was raising her little girl eyebrows again as if she were waiting for Nick to arrive at some understanding that should be obvious to him. Amelia moved to the clay pot near the hearth, and sifted out a few drops of the sleeping agent, she crossed the short distance to where Tristan was sitting. The large three-year-old looked to be more like a five-year-old. His hands were folded peacefully in his lap; the picture of a little man. His fingers twined together as he played thumb war with himself. Nick had never before witnessed children, Amelia's and Tristan's age act so well behaved.

Amelia leaned down, and gently offered the concoction of herbs to her younger brother. Tristan drank it down greedily. At least it tastes good. Nick thought. Though it took a moment longer than it had with Modilo, Tristan was soon fast asleep.

Amelia again stood, after tucking the blanket around Tristan's shoulders. She straightened her pastel blue robes, and started for the hearth. Stoking the fire, she again sifted a few drops; this time a little more than before. She then turned and walked purposefully to Nick. What she intended dawned into Nick's awareness like a brick wall.

He abruptly stood, and retreated a few steps. "Okay, sandman. You can back up with the herb wagon. Not interested." Nick shook his head with the vehemence of his convictions.

Amelia's adamant glare bore into Nick with a sovereign authority. "Nick… you're tired. We need to sleep, and we have to be quiet." Amelia sounded tired, and filled with a spirit beyond her years as her gaze softened.

"Look Amelia, don't think I don't appreciate the offer. I do." Nick nodded. "But going to sleep when there are…well it's just not possible." Nick looked around as he thought of a way to side track his own argument. He couldn't tell the children what he knew. Jordan would flip.

"I am the next medicine woman in line for the Cadotion people." Amelia explained. "It is my job to know of such threats to the people of my village." Amelia said as she moved to lay a comforting hand on Nick's arm. "Aniahi says it is my job to maintain order in chaos."

Nick felt numb. "Who told you about the…"

Amelia pointed to the mat. Nick lay back woodenly on the makeshift bed.

"Aniahi told me of the many drums that sounded, before I came to live with mama and daddy." Amelia said with a sad smile. "Those drums like these, marked the coming of the Manerky. My father was killed in that raid." Amelia looked across the tent to Tristan. She seemed miles away in thought. Nick was struck by how well articulated, for a six-year-old Amelia was.

When Amelia's eyes turned back to Nick, she seemed older. "Look around Nick." Amelia finally whispered. "You have three children to care for in the middle of a war. Be thankful we survived the night." She handed the cup to Nick. "It won't keep you asleep, but it will help you to go to sleep." Amelia promised. "We need our rest, night approaches."

Nick took the drink, and finished it. He couldn't make out every flavor in the concoction, but he was fairly certain he tasted mint, and maybe cinnamon… as he tried without success to ascertain the different scents, and tastes, Nick drifted into oblivion.

Amelia had struggled for a long while with the decision to put everyone to sleep. Aniahi had been very clear about the job of a medicine woman. She needed to maintain order, and Nick was becoming increasingly, more anxious; not that she could blame him. The situation didn't exactly incite feelings of calm, but she could not allow Nick to continue to lose it. The Manerky would come, and they would kill them; all of them. So in the end the decision had been made: their ability to maintain invisible, coupled with her need to maintain order as the village medicine woman, had made the decision easy.

Amelia looked to each of her charges, and then crawling into the bed next to her brother, she took her own dose of the herbal sleep aid. Soon she was fast asleep.

CHAPTER

20

Loose scree glided down the side of the mountain. Jordan's heart lurched as the archer turned to the source of the disturbance. Gone was the opportunity to duck behind the large boulder jutting out from the smaller outcroppings, just in front of where she was standing. The large protrusion of rock inhibited any advance on her part. She had but one chance: the archer had already positioned the arrow into the nock. The bawled archer with angry-painted-red-and-black swirls stood seething; his cloudy brown eyes glazed with murderous intent. He was ready to release the arrow, aimed straight for her heart.

Jordan had spent the better part of the night clearing the side of the mountain of archers, while Lane guarded the inner chamber of the cave, where Aniahi and Kirsten were preparing for the children to be brought. Jordan didn't exactly understand the full brunt of what was coming, but she knew that their time grew short. They had only until the end of the day before an army of Manerky warriors, the like she had never seen invaded the land; an army of predators with the instincts of a bat, their only undoing was light. Jordan needed to clear the mountain so that she could safely escort her children into the sanctuary of the mountain chamber; there they would fill the chamber with as much light as possible so that the hunters would be limited in their abilities. Jordan and Lane planned to spend the night walking among the terrible foe, hoping to eliminate as much of the threat as possible; if the night was a success their children would walk away unharmed, even if they did not.

Jordan had even been back down the small tunnel to explain her suspicions concerning the Manerky's night abilities... though the

Manerky were hindered by the sunlight, or any kind of light for that matter, the tribe killed with deadly precision in the dark. All of her efforts stood on the precipice of this decision; how would she disarm, and subsequently kill the archer, without getting herself killed, or alerting any of the Manerky warriors scouting the village as to the trouble that walked among them? So far the Manerky believed that they were only dealing with peaceful Cadotion; they were not aware of the threat that ghosted among them.

She knew it wasn't as simple as throwing a knife while ducking for cover. If that were true, she would have long since taken the shot. She had up until this moment managed to eliminate the enemy forces without alerting the opposing archers on the side of the adjacent mountain, not to speak of those warriors that walked among the village, scouting for stragglers outside of their tents, looking to escape.

She couldn't imagine what it was that the Manerky really wanted; what was the real agenda here? Why not just kill every one of the Cadotion tribe, and take the land? None of it made sense to her. Why would a tribe that couldn't stand to be in the sunlight want a land that ran between to mountain passes, and was bathed in sunlight all day? For that matter, why were the Manerky allowing some of the tribe to live, but killing others with extreme prejudice? What did those that were being saved have in common?

Jordan could see that the warrior was young and inexperienced, or he too would have eliminated the threat that she imposed. His lack of experience had worked to her advantage. The issue that most confounded her was the position of the archer. The young warrior squinted painfully against the merciless rays of the rising sun. Jordan could also see, if just barely, the beginning of a pale film covering the brown iris of the young warrior's eyes. It seemed as though he were going blind. Jordan supposed it would be much like being underground, the lack of vision would cause the sight to perish, leaving a white film over the useless eye. Now Jordan stood face to face with a self-inflicted-devolved-creature that was dangerously close to the mountain's edge. If she made the wrong move, he would plummet to his death; in so doing the enemy forces would be alerted to their presence. Their last chance for anonymity, for the element of surprise would be lost.

A light glow filtered through the darkness, radiating forward, announcing the approach of someone. Lane moved to the wall of the tunnel as he pushed his six-foot-five bulk back against the wall, and quickly tossed the torch, fueled with pitch, not easily extinguished, in the opposite direction of the intruder. The move would probably cost him, but Lane had panicked. He had been in the tunnel waiting for Jordan for so long that he had grown comfortable listening to the soft purring of Shakia and her babies. The sound of the approaching footsteps had been an alarming jolt back to reality.

Shakia had, up until that point, been cleaning her two mischievous kittens. Now she stood, back arched, eyes narrowed to slits, a low growl emitting from her throat as she waited for the trouble to at last reveal itself.

The careless intruder, whoever it was, definitely was not a tribesman. Lane waited for the clumsy invader to make his or her way passed where he was standing. Lane feared it was a tourist walking among the caves hoping to make discoveries. Unfortunately, the hapless explorer had happened across a tribal war.

He didn't want to hurt the tourist, but he didn't want to be hurt because he had underestimated the possibility of an approaching threat. He had to believe that anyone ready to traverse the rugged terrain of the Himalayas had to know something about self-defense. With that in mind, Lane swung his right hand out hoping to make contact with the man, and pin him to the wall. Unfortunately, the man ducked, whirling around with a round house kick, connecting booted-foot to Lane's head. Lane grunted with the impact of the blow. His head pivoted to the side, but he quickly recovered. Bending low, Lane, with a wide arch of his right foot was able to sweep his opponent off of the foot he still had planted on the ground. Lane heard a low whoosh as the air left the man's lungs; he landed with a thump on the ground in front of Lane.

"I don't want to fight you." Lane warned.

"Yeah, I can see that." A familiar voice quipped angrily.

"Garrison!" Lane said in a loud whisper.

"Lane?" Garrison asked as he worked to right himself. "A nice hello, would have sufficed." Garrison complained.

Lane offered Garrison a hand. He took it easily. "We're sort of in the middle of something here." Lane laughed. "Wow! It's good to see you!" Lane added as he pulled Garrison into a hug, and then put him back on his feet.

Garrison teetered for a moment trying to gain his footing, and then turned to the torch on the ground that Lane had thrown. "What was that all about?"

"Trying to extinguish the light. I didn't want you to see me." Lane laughed at the impromptu moment that had thankfully not cost him his life.

"I can see the unmistakable logic…" Garrison eyed Lane for a second, and then continued. "It sucked!" Garrison laughed.

"What can I say? I'm new to this; I'm not Jordan." Lane admitted with a shrug. Lane knew that his ability to cloak himself was more or less pathetic… he was a six-foot-five giant; hiding that bulk took powers of camouflage that he did not possess. He was a toe to toe, face to face type fighter. He would have to leave the cloak and dagger stuff to Jordan.

"Amen!" Garrison teased. "Speaking of Jordan…" Garrison knit his brow, and lifted his hands. "Where is she?"

Lane pointed a finger toward the low hanging ceiling of the tunnel.

Garrison taking the cue, turned a puzzled glare on the spot where Lane had pointed. "On top of the mountain?" Garrison's voice cracked as shock filled his features.

"Not exactly." Lane corrected. "She's on the side of the mountain, to be more precise."

A look of understanding replaced the shock on Garrison's face. "Archers." Garrison nodded. "Okay. How do I get up there?"

Lane crossed over to the other wall, and pointed up into a hole as black as midnight. "Through here, but you may not fit…" Lane silenced his objections, because Garrison was already disappearing into the darkness.

21

Edward stared at the blank screen on the small twenty-one-inch television that was suspended from the wall near the ceiling by a metal swivel-arm. He had prided himself on staying abreast to current events, but ever since the day in his office with the voice… He couldn't finish the thought. The images flooded his mind, and the news was more of the same. It filled his head with visions of that dreadful day. But Edward was tired of being in the lonely hospital room waiting for the nurses that ghosted the corridors to pay him a visit. He was going stir-crazy. Like some guarded dark secret, he sat crouching in a hidden vault waiting to be discovered.

Pushing back the dreaded images, he flipped on the television. Boredom was definitely out-weighing the fear of what he may or may not see. Edward braced himself for the flashflood of images, but nothing happened. The television lit up with vibrant-dancing colors, as a cartoon came into focus. He ignored the multihued aquatic life of Nemo. He had little time to devote to cartoons or television in general, but since the office incident it seemed that his life had started to revolve around all things televised. More faces danced across the screen as he raced through the channels to Fox.

At first, it seemed like the same report that had filled the airways concerning a militia group in the Middle East… the things that had been the topic of discussion before his public debut. Then, Edward realized that it wasn't the tyrants at all, though some of the scenery seemed much the same. He was astonished by what he was seeing and hearing.

"Tribal war bleeds into local awareness as the American Embassy is flooded with calls, demanding to know if loved ones are well."

Edward adjusted the volume so he could hear the tall brunette announcing the recent events of what he thought would be more about the war in the Middle East. He almost turned the channel when the woman's hand pointed to an image that Edward was all too familiar with; Jordan.

"Sources say that an angry former member of the secret services, stormed the halls of a New Jersey police station early yesterday afternoon, flashing his badge, and demanding answers. The outraged former agent did not capture attention of local law enforcement so he made an impromptu visit to… you guessed it… the American Embassy." The cadence of the woman's voice that had until that moment kept to a lulling ebb and flow of disinterest, suddenly rose with the need to make her point.

Pointing again to the picture of Jordan, the woman continued. "A connection to this woman, may have been made concerning the war in the Himalayas. Recognize her? You should." The woman arched one neatly manicured eyebrow. "Mrs. Gates was recently in the news. It seems that she too was a former member of the CIA…"

Edward continued to listen as the reporter mapped out the grizzly details of how Jordan had been nearly blinded by a bomb that was meant to end her life. A twinge of guilt twisted his gut as he made himself endure the ugly truth. Finally, after long moments of the reporter drudging up the unbearable-sins of Edward's past, she mercifully returned to the original subject matter.

"It seems that Mrs. Gates may have jumped out of the proverbial frying pan and into the fire." The reporter claimed as she plastered a sympathetic frown on her lipstick-coated mouth. "Having left her roots in the CIA, Jordan is now a member of an organization housed in Black Heart; a mission-minded organization labeled The Truth. Apparently, Mrs. Gates left the U.S. for a mission trip in India. She has been living in the Karakorum Mountains with her husband and two children… the couple have apparently been bringing 'The Truth' of Christ to the villages surrounding the Himalayas." The reporter made air quotations around The Truth, as she allowed a doubtful expression to play on her pristinely made-up face.

Edward tried to straighten himself in the bed. The image of Jordan was the same one used by the news syndicate the day that he had tried to end his own life: bandages covered her eyes as strands of dark auburn hair, bunched in angry gnarls overlapping the gauze bandages, blew around seeming to struggle for freedom from their makeshift prison. The picture of Jordan sickened Edward. It seemed to solidify him as the monster he felt himself to be.

Tears burned at his eyes. He didn't want to feel sorry for himself. For that matter, he didn't want to feel at all. He felt as though life and death was crushing in like two halves of a prison, trapping him in this place of unrest... of dread. He felt prisoner, also to the past and the present: he missed the numbness of his once dark heart, and he craved the future he knew in his heart he had no right to hope for.

Edward heaved a sigh as he finally turned off the television, and pushed the remote away in bitter remorse for his transgressions: he wished he could go back. He wished he would have never longed for something better; he wished he had not openly watched Amorous as she killed the unwitting victim in the alley. He wished he had not wanted her to see him because he was so unsatisfied with his mundane existence; he wished he had not been recruited into Black Heart, or become the Head of Department. He wished he had not loved Amorous, and that he wouldn't have thrown away years of his life on revenge... he wished...

22

Julie hurried along the hospital corridor with Amber Noel in tow. Every few steps someone would stop her, and swoon over her granddaughter. She didn't want to seem ungracious; she was just anxious to see Edward, and introduce him to a very special part of her life, one of her grandchildren.

Julie supposed she really couldn't blame the other nurses. After all, Amber Noel was the exact image that had been conjured when she imagined a cherub: blue eyes, and pudgy cheeks that seemed to swallow up her tiny face. Her arms and legs were so fat that it looked as though she was wearing rubber bands on her wrists and ankles. Brownish blonde hair adorned her perfectly-circular head, and played around her exquisitely fair skin.

"Look at that juicy baby!" Cindy nearly shouted. At the same time Erica Winston, a short African American nurse with a beautifully made up face, and perfect figure all but jumped over the nurses' station to get her hands on Amber Noel.

"Come here big-ole-juicy baby!" Erica squeaked as she reached into the baby seat, and claimed her prize. In a snap she was headed off as if Amber Noel were her own grandchild.

Julie appraised the two women. Each woman was beautiful in her own way. Cindy, though leaner and visibly taller than her vibrant co-worker was no more or less attractive. Her red hair, cropped in a loose bun on her oval-shaped-head bounced gloriously, as springy-ringlets danced around long-silver hooped earrings. Julie suspected her granddaughter would soon stop at nothing to claim the silver treasures from the green-eyed-beauties ear.

Julie sighed. The wait was on. She sat the pink-floral-seat down next to the wrap-around mahogany desk, and placed her elbows on the top of its sleek surface, as she tried to maintain her cheery mood. She resisted the urge to go to the ladies' room, and check her look again. Already she had fluffed her hair ten times at least. She could practically feel the oil forming on her scalp, and preparing to drain down her hair. It would ruin the body that she had managed to salvage after too much time with the blow-dryer. She wondered why she was being so fidgety. It was just Edward; besides, she took care of him every day. Why was today any different? She supposed it was, because if she actually went through with the visit, then she could no longer lie to herself. She really did like Edward.

Julie sighed again. She should go home. Who was she fooling? She was a frumpy widow with three grandchildren. Edward was probably a business man that had allowed the pressures of life to get to him. More worries were the last thing the man needed, but Julie was under his spell.

He was just so handsome. His deep soulful brown eyes that searched the room as if always assessing some unseen threat, and his cloud of dark brown hair that was neatly managed around his ruggedly handsome face did little to sustain her common sense. Her heart raised with the enthusiasm that his presence infused in her world. Her mundane, every day, ordinary existence was somehow transformed into more when she was near her tall-dark-stranger.

"Shhh… okay little-big-girl." Maggie, a Caucasian nurse, about middle height with short-cropped brown hair, tried to sooth Amber Noel.

"Okay… time for Memaw." Julie chirped while rubbing her hands together. "They got enough of Memaw's sugar; didn't they?" Julie laughed as Amber Noel fell to silent, and nestled contentedly into the crook of her arm. Reaching down, she claimed the pink-frilly-handle of the baby bag, and pulled it up on her shoulder, and then grabbed the car seat. Without delay, she disappeared down the hall, and into Edwards's room, before she lost her nerve.

23

Her heart had never pounded so hard. Jordan didn't know if it was the danger she was placing her unborn child in, or if it was the real possibility she faced of alerting the whole of the Manerky tribe as to their whereabouts, whatever the problem she had to calm down. She had already managed earlier that night to pull off the deadliest of stunts. In all of her time with Black Heart, she had never had to go to such links to make a kill; with the archer standing inches from the mountain's edge, an arrow ready to sail on the wind, straight into her heart, Jordan had defied the odds.

The decline of the mountain side lent itself to her seemingly impossible task. She threw her knife as she dropped into a freefall down the edge of the mountain. Barton in hand, she jammed it into a wedge in the boulder, the archer had been using for cover. Then with a thunderous plant of her feet, against the large boulder, Jordan threw her body into the air. She grabbed hold of the middle of the Barton, pivoting around its sculpted-smooth frame, then slammed both feet hard into the already falling archer. The impact forced his body back toward the boulder. He ended in a lifeless heap face down on the giant outcropping.

She had braced herself for the impact with the warrior, but it had almost been a benign effort as her body sailed back the opposite direction, her hands clung wildly to the Barton. Jordan panted with the effort of gaining her footing. She felt the Barton pivot wildly. Her eyes grew wide, as she glimpsed the fate that awaited her at the bottom of the dizzying chasm. Panting with every desperate grab, mercifully her feet found purchase.

Now as she stood face to face with two warriors, she too had an arrow ready to fly. Both men stood with murderous intent coloring their visage, as they waited for her to make a mistake.

"Fancy meeting you here." A voice as sweet as an angel's singing broke through the horrific silence.

"Bout time you showed up." Jordan smiled while still staring down the two men in front of her that were now looking more confused than angry.

"Would've been here sooner. Guess the invitation got lost in the mail." Garrison threw back.

"Oh, yeah. Talk about that later. Until then… call it." Jordan said flatly.

"Okay. I'll take the ugly one." Garrison laughed.

"They're both ugly." Jordan growled.

"Right side; middle pocket." Garrison finally said.

"Count of three?" Jordan asked.

"It's your party." Garrison quipped.

"Three!" Jordan called as she sent first one, and then another arrow into the two confused men. Both arrows slammed into the left eye of both men.

"Hey! What was that?" Garrison complained as a silver handled knife slammed purposefully into the warrior on the right's chest.

"Nothing. Just wanted to see if you could hit a falling target." Jordan laughed as she turned to her friend.

"Do you have any idea how good it is to see you?" She asked as she raced to Garrison. The snow sounded like a giant animal eating as it crunched loudly under her boot-shod feet. "How did you… know… get here?" All of Jordan's questions ran together as she flung herself into his arms.

"I'll explain later." Garrison said as he pushed Jordan in the direction of the tunnel. "I think your husband is getting a little anxious." Garrison rubbed the back of his neck. "He's starting to attack the guests."

Jordan dipped her head with an apologetic cringe. "Oops…" She offered.

"Yeah… tell me about it." He countered.

As they headed back down the tunnel, Jordan first; Garrison cleared his throat. "So Jordan."

"Yeah?" Jordan asked.

"You took that shot because you thought I couldn't; didn't you?" Garrison pushed. Jordan could hear the badgering undertone of the question. This was going to turn into one of Garrison's famous speeches about teamwork; not to mention the bragging rights that he had over making a point blank shot on a falling target.

"No." She lied.

CHAPTER

24

Penny hung the bow around her neck, and looped her right arm through the string. She then tied the quiver of arrows around in much the same manner. After checking the knife at her side, she reached up, and grabbed hold on a small, but sturdy sapling jutting out of the side of the mountain. Fitting her boot-clad foot into a deep impression just below the young tree, with a mighty yank, she hoisted her body up to grab a finger-tip hold on a small outcropping of graying rock. Using the same technique, she made her way up to a level just above the highest archer-post.

She reasoned that she would need to stay out of the line of sight of the Manerky warriors; if she was going to be able to eliminate as many of them as possible without being caught. Anonymity would be her only ally. The task would be substantially more easy to accomplish if she could somehow put the sun between her and the archers, but the sun rose from the east and set in the west, of course… with a mountain on the north and south side of the village, the sun was making a perfect arc right down the center of the two massive landmarks, placing the archers to the side of the much needed sunlight.

She did at least think to wear white: her hair was tucked neatly into a white-cotton hat. She wore white leather pants, and a white leather long sleeve pull over. The fabric of her ensemble moved freely with her body, making the grueling task of climbing, and hiking seem a little less daunting.

She settled in a large outcropping of rock, as she scanned the lower lying regions of the mountain, for the enemy. It wasn't long before two archers sitting side by side, a few feet below, ghosted into sight. She looked further back toward the way she had come. She noticed that each post of archers consistently held two warriors at the ready. These were definitely the first two in a series of archers blanketing the side of the mountain. She needed to get lower, and further along the side of the mountain, so she could take out at least four of the archers at a time; with the right vantage point the archers would be dead before they were able to recognize the threat that existed among them. Penny knew from the moment the first arrow flew free from her bow string she would be on a very unforgiving schedule.

She had been readying her bow for the strike, when a commotion from the adjacent mountain caught her attention. Two figures clad in black stood embracing. After a few moments, the two figures then made their way toward the east end of the mountain. First one and then the other disappeared from sight. Penny could only imagine that they had descended into a tunnel of some sort.

The shorter of the two seemed feminine. So Penny had to assume it was her Aunt Jordan. The taller figure was probably Garrison; the bulk hadn't been large enough to be her Uncle Lane.

She wished she could know for sure that it was Jordan, but right now speculation was all she had. She didn't' have time to ponder the assumption any further. She needed to do what she had come here to do; besides she hadn't seen any of the Manerky tribe participate in any sort of warm moment. Every man on the side of the mountain seemed focused on the task at hand; nothing about the dark snarls of angry red and black paint covering their slim-muscular bodies suggested that there had been or would be any moments filled with affection for their fellowman.

Penny wasn't surprised to see the archers littering the mountain side that she was now scouting, unmoved by the open display of affection, in the midst of a battle. Though, the sun was still very low in the sky, it was enough light that it would hinder the pale eyes, of the almost blind archers. She too was not surprised to see the spray of bodies, littering the ground, surrounding the tents, on the valley floor. She imagined most of the damage had been launched in the predawn hours, the morning before. What did confuse her is how her Aunt Jordan knew about the enemies' limitation, as applies to light. Penny knew all too well that her aunt definitely knew… if not she would have never stood openly on the other mountain, like some dear caught in headlights. No, Jordan was an agent. Once and agent, always an agent. It didn't matter how many kids she had, or how many third world countries she visited to bring the truth; Jordan Buckley-Gates was a killer.

Penny knew that Jordan had changed, she did not doubt that, but she also knew that her instincts would never change. She would always have a razor-sharp mind, searching for threats, and identifying every object that could be used to remove those threats. She would also be able to recognize through the same powers of deduction, the weakness of her enemy.

Penny eased forward, peering at the archers to her right, and then to her left. She needed a diversion. In a perfect world the archers would have spotted the people, hugging on the opposite mountain, but she knew that wasn't going to happen. She also knew that if she wasn't quick to make a move, she would lose daylight, the most precious tool in her arsenal.

She considered that for a moment. The Manerky were blind for the most part, during the day, but not having use of their eyes would make their other senses all the more elevated.

She needed a way to make sure the archers to either side of her were distracted long enough to make the first two kills. In order to do that, she would not be able to allow the Manerky to see that the diversion had originated form where she was standing.

She was starting to rethink her initial strategy. Maybe trying to take out four Manerky archers wasn't the best plan. Then she remembered the rocks in her pocket. Penny reached in, and claimed two of the rocks. This better work… she thought. With all of her strength, she threw a rock in either direction, and then knocked her first arrow as the two sets of men instinctively looked in the direction of each respective rock; Penny wasted no time. She had none to waste. With a deadly precision, she sent the first arrow into the neck of the first man to her right. A three-sided-razor-sharp-broad head-arrow-tip exited out the warrior's neck, spraying blood on the face of his unwitting cohort. Then with lightning speed, the second arrow was away, tearing into the cheek of the man next to her first target. Blood exploded into the air and sprinkled its crimson testimony on the snow at the two men's feet.

Penny cried out as a searing pain tore through her left shoulder. As she was trying to regain her footing, and ready the next arrow; the farthest man on her left had sent an arrow in her direction. Her moment of over-correcting her stance had cost her an arrow to the shoulder, but at the same time, spinning to shoot her next target had mercifully, changed the trajectory from a direct hit to a glancing, graze. The painful wound sent chills through her body, as red oozed out from the tear in the white fabric of her shirt. The contrast of red on white was a bold reminder of the very real danger that she faced.

Penny didn't hesitate, her arm was fine. She sent the next arrow square into the man closest to her left. The arrow hit dead center of the man's chest. His arms swept wide, slamming into his partner. Both men fell from the mountain. The archer that was still alive never made a sound. A chill ran up her spine as she imagined the impossible drop, and how the man had removed himself from the moment. Even this, his final moment, had not been enough to penetrate his iron-concentration. He was Manerky.

She collected the weapons that were available. The two men that had fallen to the valley floor had obviously taken their weapons with them; they were useless to her now.

Turning to a sound, Penny saw that a few of the archers at the West end of the mountain had heard the commotion, and were coming to investigate. She gasped. She hadn't put enough thought into her attack. Though, she had killed four men, she had several more headed her direction. She felt the warm rays of the morning sun as she leapt into the air, and started the arduous descent of the mountain. She knew she had to hurry, though the Manerky could not see her, they would hear her steps, and possibly her breathing as she panted with the exertion of getting away.

Fear quickened her pulse as she reached up to assess the damage to her throbbing arm, and felt the warm sticky blood oozing out; she knew without a doubt like a predator seeking its prey, the Manerky may not be able to see her, but would definitely smell the inviting aroma of fallen prey.

25

Sleep had just claimed Edward when the door squeaked open. He was so frustrated. No wonder it took patients so long to get well in the hospital; if sleep was healing, then he was on the slow track to better days. The nursing staff gave medicine to go to sleep, and then just as soon as the patient fell asleep—the staff would wake them up to give more sleep meds. It was an unending vortex of opposite concepts, inhibiting a desired outcome.

Edward sighed. It was probably for the best. Every time he closed his eyes to go to sleep his mind was filled with the images of the earlier news cast. He mashed the button to raise the head of the bed. May as well be up for what was coming next. He didn't want to miss the sleep meds. Edward rolled his eyes.

"A hospital is no place to go if you want to rest." Edward heard the voice, but his mind wouldn't let him believe it could be true. His eyes focused on the spot near the door, where the light didn't quite reach. Finally, Julie materialized like an angel carrying an arm load of bags, a baby carrier, and a baby.

He batted his eyes, he must be seeing things. Julie walked over to the red recliner, and discarded all, but the baby. Then she carefully adjusted the new weight.

Something about Julie holding the tiny baby, made him want to retreat. She never looked more like an angel than she did clutching the tiny babe to her breast. She was the image of mother and child. Her blue sweater made the cornflower blue of her eyes shimmer and dance all the more. As she started to unwrap the child love filled those shimmering spheres of blue, in earnest. Edward had never seen a more tangible force than the bond, between this woman and her precious granddaughter.

"This is Amber Noel." Julie introduced the baby girl, and as if on cue, blue eyes, the color of Julie's, found his. Edward felt as though he was stripped bare in that moment. It was as though with one look the tiny girl had scaled the wall of his defenses, and plundered his darkest secrets, leaving them laid out for all to witness, on the altar of that unrelenting gaze.

Edward forced his eyes to return to Julie's. "She's beautiful." Edward finally managed while clearing his throat.

26

Something sounding like concussed wind, or a broken drum being struck, pulled Nick from his herb-induced sleep. He looked around the tent. All three of the children were still in various stages of sprawled slumber. He turned his attention to the hearth. He wasn't a big outdoors man, but his grandfather had taught him some simple ways to tell time if he didn't have a watch handy.

For one the sun high overhead in the middle of the sky, was noon, just as a clock suggested. Also, there were other more basic means of telling time, such as the amount of ash on a burning log.

Nick had witnessed Amelia place a log on the fire before giving them her sleeping-aid. Judging by the logs, it appeared to have been at least a few hours, maybe three or four, since they had fallen asleep.

He pushed up from the fur-pallet. He checked on each of the children; all three were breathing deeply. Tristan had a sweet-contented smile on his angelic face. Nick smiled back uncontrollably. Amelia lay next to Tristan; her arm lay over his middle as if to stake her claim. Even in sleep Amelia was protective of her younger brother. Nick thought the gesture seemed odd, because Tristan at three was already much bigger than his older sister.

Modilo, too was on his pallet. He looked content enough, but something seemed so lonely about the little boy sleeping alone, unclaimed, so Nick scooted some cover up under him to give the false sense of a human body lying next to him; something he had witnessed Jordan do with Tristan.

Nick moved to the back of the tent where he believed the noise, if it was a noise to have originated. Gently pushing the camel-fur-tent aside, he peered out. Nick froze. Two archers lay, bodies tangled together in a bloodied heap. One had a broken arrow protruding a few inches out of his chest.

Nick turned, reflexively from the gruesome, sight, but quickly summoned his courage. He had been left in charge of the children's safety. Hiding out in the tent with dead bodies falling all around, was not going to cut it. Someone had sent that arrow into the man on the top of the pile, and from the looks of it, he had fallen from the mountain side, but the man on the bottom had no arrows protruding from his body. He appeared to have obvious signs of a fall, of course, but nothing to suggest that he had been mortally wounded before the fall. Nick could only guess the man with the arrow in his chest had inadvertently caused the death of the second man.

Now Nick was really curious. Who had shot the first archer? He supposed it could have been Jordan or Lane, but it was highly unlikely. This had not been the first time Nick's curiosity had pulled him to one of the flaps to look out the tent.

He had waited for Lane and Jordan to exit the tent, and then after a moment he had checked to see which direction they were headed in. Both, Lane and Jordan had moved swiftly in the direction of Aniahi's tent. Nick had never seen the hidden cave outside of Aniahi's dwelling, but he knew from the stories that Haywalo had shared that it was there.

Nick wasn't the caliber of agent that Lane and Jordan were, but he figured common sense was not something one had to earn from an undercover agency. Lane and Jordan needed to end the threat that the archers posed, in order to do that they would need to gain access to a higher plateau on the mountain than that of the archer's post. Lane had grown up in the Cadotion village, he knew all of the mountain's secrets.

He knew that Jordan and Lane would be exact in their efforts to kill the Manerky. Dropping dead bodies from the mountain side did not seem like something a seasoned Black Heart agent would do.

Nick leaned his head back to look up at the dizzying height of the mountain. From this angle he could see nothing, but a straight up towering wall of green. He knew from this vantage point that no archer would see him, at least not from the southern facing mountain.

Finally, unable to deny his curiosity any longer, he stepped carefully from the tent, and pressed his back against the dry-itchy camel fur. Holding the Barton in his left hand, and the intricately carved axe in his right hand, Nick walked with extreme caution in the direction of the fallen bodies. He tried to keep his eyes from going to the two dead men, but the more he tried the less he was able to maintain his focus; finally, he just gave himself permission to look. The tangled mess of broken bones, and motionless eyes somehow made the moment that had only felt like moving from scene to scene in a dream-state, feel more real.

Satisfied that he had tortured his senses enough, Nick studied the mountain-side. Farther to the east the mountain seemed to level off. He couldn't see any signs of the enemy approaching, nor did he see the person responsible for the offending arrow protruding from the Manerky warrior's chest. Venturing any farther away from the tent wasn't an option.

He started back for the tent. Just as he passed the ruined bodies, he heard thundering footsteps as if someone were in a hurry... he turned to the sound, and raised the axe, readying himself for the attack.

"Do it!" a female shrouded in white leather screamed, as she dropped to the ground.

Nick wasted no time complying with the command. With all of his strength, he thrust the axe, releasing it to do his bidding. With a sickening crunch, metal parted flesh, as the axe slammed into the archer's chest leading the procession of attackers. Nick readied the Barton as he took a side defensive stance, to make himself a smaller target. The girl was already rolling to safety.

The warrior's eyes that had been impaled by the axe glazed over as if he were no longer present, but he was still walking.

"Snap out of it Nick!" The female screamed.

Nick's head shot up. He knew that voice, but it wasn't possible. His head spun with the reality of her standing there screaming for him to invest in the fight. Time stood still as Nick watched Penny release first one arrow, and then another. The man with the axe in his chest dropped to his knees as blood burst in a huff form his mouth. He fell face first into the grass-covered valley floor. Nick blinked wildly as he looked at the two arrows protruding from the archer's back and neck.

Witnessing the man's still form awakened a primal instinct. He started to spin the Barton as he sprinted for the two archers that had been closing the distance behind the warrior Penny had killed. He focused on the archer close to him. His mind intent on the moves Lane had demonstrated, Nick pressed ever onward. The second archer lunged for Penny. Both men had obviously used all of their arrows, and were down to hand to hand combat; seeing the animalistic warrior race toward Penny intensified their ability to incite fear.

In a small chamber of his mind, Nick acknowledged the fear gnawing at him. He had no way of knowing how these men would fight, or what their skill level was, and if he knew enough to accomplish what he needed to do. He had never been so sure that he would die than in that moment.

The man searched with his pale eyes, both men sniffed at the air, and growled like wild animals. Penny waved the bow she was holding in the air, shoving it at the Manerky warrior, she faced. A low growl emitted from his throat as he crouched waiting for the right opportunity to attack. His hands batted at the air like a hungry tiger.

A sudden ripping pain tore through Nick's arm. A bald archer with pale eyes, and angry red and black swirls covering his upper torso and back hissed. Nick comforted his side for a moment, and then jabbed the Barton furiously at the man-beast. Jumping back just in time, the warrior pulled his hands back, and curled the end of his fingers. Nick could see blood, and skin tissue under the jagged and broken edges of the archer's blackened finger nails.

"The sun Nick!" Penny called as Nick glimpsed her dancing her opponent around so that he was now facing the light. "The light hurts their eyes." Penny called.

For a while Penny had almost lost hope that Nick would heed her advice. Without the opposition of sunlight, the Manerky were a formidable enemy that fought like the deadly-wild animals that they had studied, and so desperately wanted to be.

The Manerky lived in the mountains. The Cadotion, along with the surrounding tribes that had left for a warmer climate, were under the mistaken belief that this battle was about land... it wasn't.

Penny believed the Manerky had journeyed deeper into the mountains in search of the ruler of the underworld, Direign. In that search the Manerky had made a discovery; the discovery was about themselves. They had realized without sunlight, or fire to light the way, they were given a kind of keen awareness. That awareness was merely the more refined capabilities of their other four senses. The Manerky had not realized that though their other senses were made more efficient in the darkness, their sight was failing, because in the darkened cave their eyes were useless. That oversight had been their undoing.

Penny knew, though that the Manerky were still hundreds strong, and they would soon be infiltrating the Cadotion village with that dreaded force, under the cloak of night. Her knees trembled with the vision of the animalistic beings covering the Cadotion land with one all-consuming desire; to find and ingest young human flesh at the feast of Direignbang. It was there that the Manerky believed Direign would return to the world of the living and grant his children the fruits of their labor... they would gain the years of life taken from the young through ingestion.

She knew that the feast would not just be some pleasantries over a nice dinner of human flesh; the Manerky believed themselves to be immortal beasts, above the frailties of their human prey... as such the warriors would fight to the death for the right to consume the youngest lives harvested during the raid. After that Penny didn't want to imagine what would befall the captives, but she did know animals have no mercy. Animals ripped and tore at their prey until they were dead, and then...

Penny turned to Nick. His side had finally stopped weeping blood from the angry scratches, left behind by the vicious warrior intent on murder. If Nick's side was any sign, and Penny could imagine that it was, they were in for a long horrifying night.

27

Lane watched as red clay filtered through the tunnel. He had stood watch all night while Jordan brought weapons back, and gave updates on her progress, but he hadn't heard anything since Garrison had disappeared through the tunnel. It was beginning to wear on his patience.

Kirsten and Aniahi had slept in the inner chamber on fur pallets by the fire. They had collected a few things upon Jordan's third report, soon exhaustion had won out.

Most of the archers were dead except a few at the north end of the mountain. It was impossible for any of the archers to see Aniahi and Kirsten from their position inside the cave, though, there would still be the chance of warrior's roaming the camp happening upon them, but that didn't generally happen until the second night of the raid. He had often wondered if the Manerky would keep those left behind after the battle, in order to turn them into slaves for the Manerky. But he knew that there had been no reported sightings of living captives. Word of something like an enemy tribe holding hostages would make it through the tribe's in no time. Then, of course the subsequent archer stake out; that time was upon them, and Lane was growing anxious. The Manerky were confident in their tactics, so the archers would be left to the task… that left the window very small. Lane and Jordan would have to eliminate the archers, and all possible warriors, if any were left, before night fall. They needed to get the children a safe distance from the village, before they became just another casualty in this tribal war.

Lane's pulse slowed as Jordan's black boot exited the dark hole at last. He reached up, and claimed his wife. He warned himself not to smother her, not to make a big deal, but the moment he held her warm, thriving body next to his, and peered into her soulful green eyes, he was lost.

"Okay, Lane." Jordan cleared her throat. "You can put me down now. Still in one piece…see?" She gave an innocent grin followed by a theatrical flourish of her hands.

"Sorry." Lane smiled.

"Get a room." Garrison cleared his throat. "I swear, even war doesn't slow you two down." He was dusting himself off now as he rolled his eyes.

"Lane was just worried." Jordan informed with another innocent smile sent in Lane's direction.

"He should be," Garrison grouched. "About me."

Lane was confused now. He forced his lingering gaze away from his wife to fit Garrison with an inquisitive glare.

"Why? What happened to you?" Lane finally managed.

"Nothing!" Garrison barked as he sent a murderous glare in Jordan's direction.

"Okay, but isn't that a good thing?" Lane asked as he lifted a hand, and arched his brow.

"No Lane… it's not my idea of okay… when GI-Barbie hogs all the kills." Garrison stopped pacing and faced Jordan. "What's your deal?"

"Nothing." Jordan pushed a lock of her dark-auburn hair that had escaped the braid back over her ear. "I just took that shot. It was instinct." Jordan insisted clearly aggravated by the third degree Garrison was launching at her.

"Because you thought I couldn't!" Garrison accused with his finger jabbing the air.

Jordan gasped.

"See, you can't deny it!" Garrison hurled the accusation.

"You made the shot Garrison. What is the big deal?" Jordan held both hands up with her palms flat pointed toward the ceiling of the cave.

"But you didn't think that I could." Garrison said flatly.

"Garrison we don't have time for this." Jordan breathed.

"Or anything else." Garrison whispered.

"Is that what this is about; me moving to India, to the Cadotion village?" Jordan's voice rose with the concern that colored each word. "Garrison, the move had nothing to do with you. It wasn't some plot to get even with my best friend for…" Jordan stopped.

"Exactly! Jordan say it…" Garrison thrust a hand across his head. "It's not that I think you moved thousands of miles away to get even with me, and you know it. It's that you don't trust me. You haven't forgiven me."

Lane watched as sorrow flashed in Jordan's emerald eyes. He waited, as Jordan remained silent.

"Jordan we have to trust each other, if we are going to make it out of this alive." Garrison stepped toward Jordan, and extended his hand.

Jordan took an involuntary step backwards in retreat. "I forgave you," Jordan said. Lane noted that the look on her face was of anything, but trust. She seemed to be more a small animal sidestepping the unwanted advances of a fierce predator, than the forgiving friend she claimed to be.

"But you don't trust me." Garrison finished.

"We don't have time for this!" Jordan growled as she turned to walk away.

"When then? We sure as hell can't take this out there!" Garrison pointed toward the Cadotion village. "You second guessing every move I make…" Garrison threw his hand in the air. "Making extra steps, because you can't be sure I would do what you thought I should have. Jordan this is not a mark. This is a war!" Garrison looked to Lane as though he was pleading, and yet another part of him seemed ready to do battle with the enemy alone. Lane had fought with Jordan before. He understood the feeling.

"There are probably going to be hundreds of the Manerky swarming this camp." Garrison threw the obvious reason down like a gauntlet he was exhibiting for evidence in the middle of a debate.

"Don't you think I know that?" Jordan nearly shouted. "My children are out there!" Jordan's voice cracked as her eyes swam in emerald pools of liquid anguish.

Garrison raised his hands, and started to step forward, but dropped them to his sides again. Lane felt so bad for him. Jordan's love was like a fortress that filled the one in its stronghold with such assurance; her disapproval was just as iron-clad, and felt as barren as her love felt full.

Guilt and hurt mingled, and then fought for center stage on Garrison's visage.

"I would never intentionally do anything that would bring harm to your family." Garrison whispered.

"I know that," Jordan said with a voice devoid of emotion. Her eyes lifted to his with icy-absolute-intent, it was the look of a judge about to issue her sentence. "It's your good intentions that scare me the most!"

Garrison pulled back, looking as though Jordan had slapped him. "What is that supposed to mean?" Garrison met her gaze with equal intent.

"Oh, is that the way that you want to play it? The innocent act!" Jordan thundered. "You say you want the truth, but run from it every time it gets near you!" Jordan spat. "You think you can tell half-truths, take chances with people's lives that are not yours to take; in the name of protecting them, but I say it's to protect yourself. You are a coward!" Jordan fumed. Her hands opened and closed in fists at her side. She leaned forward, her face now inches from his.

"You're right." Garrison dropped his head, and turned to walk away.

"Oh, no you don't!" Jordan screeched as she snatched Garrison around. "You are not running. You wanted to do this. Let's do it!"

Garrison had his hands in the air as if Jordan had pulled a gun. "I'm not here to fight with you Jordan. The fight is out there, but since you can't trust me… its best I take the fight somewhere else. This is your base camp. I'll find my own."

Jordan stood with her arms crossed, not offering to stop Garrison. Lane was fed up, he had all that he could stand. He had stood idly by watching as the two friends hashed out the issues of their past. He had hoped it would put an end to the feud between them, but instead it had simply fanned the flames of their rage and resentment.

"Stop!" Lane heaved a frustrated sigh.

"Stay out of this Lane!" Jordan warned.

"Stay out of this, Lane?" Lane turned his intent glare on his wife. "How do you suggest that I do that? Would it be when you keep me up at night reliving the hurtful things your best friend did to you while crying yourself to sleep?"

Lane watched as Jordan turned a haughty look on Garrison, and then turned away. He ignored the warning glare she fixed him with. He had been at the opposite end of that glare when Jordan would have killed him. It had somehow lost its effect on him.

"Or maybe the fact that my children are in the middle of a war while you two-year-olds hash out the past, while dancing around the truth!" Lane glared at both of them in turn.

Garrison laughed without humor as he nodded in Jordan's direction.

"I wouldn't be so pompous if I were you!" Lane warned. "She could have, and would have killed you if she hadn't given her life to Christ, and you would have deserved it!" Lane stormed.

Jordan was the one laughing now.

"And if you'd like to take time off from being a martyred-victim; we have a battle to get back to. And as far as you wanting to crucify Garrison every time you see him for the past—Jesus already died for his sins; so if you could politely put the stones you've been collecting to throw at him down, and pull your big-girl-panties up—I'd like to go save my children!" Lane stormed off toward the inner chamber.

"Lane..." Jordan called.

"No, Jordan." Lane said as he turned back to face them. "You need to fix this. Garrison is your friend; he would die for you, and almost did. You remember the farmhouse?" Lane turned to Garrison, and then back to Jordan. "Did he make the shot?"

"What?" Jordan raised her brow.

"The shot... you know up on the mountain side. The thing that started all of this." Lane explained with as much patience as he could manage given the knots in his shoulders.

Jordan turned to Garrison. When she again faced Lane, her eyes were brimming with tears. "Perfectly." She whispered.

With that Lane touched her face, and walked away.

28

Kirsten was tired of being afraid. So much of her life had been governed by fear, especially since Black Heart's unwanted intrusion into her life.

Ease-dropping had not been her intention. She had woken up suddenly that morning, and felt the need to check on Shakia's kittens. Aniahi had already explained that the cat would never allow her near the kittens, but Kirsten couldn't help herself. The kittens were so adorable, and she hoped if she could prove herself worthy of Shakia's trust, the cat would eventually warm up. She longed to lavish affection on the adorable balls of fur.

As Kirsten started down the tunnel toward where she knew the mother and kittens to be, she soon forgot her original plan. She could hear voices. She listened, and soon she was able to ascertain who the voices were coming from.

Garrison was there, but more than that, he and Jordan were arguing. Kirsten listened as the two disputed some wrong that Garrison had committed against Jordan. She couldn't make much sense out of all that was being said, but what she did understand was that Jordan and Lane's children were in danger.

Kirsten froze at first when Lane said he was leaving, but then she realized this was her opportunity. It was now or never. If Lane caught her, before she had a chance to leave the cave, the moment would be lost to her.

She ran as quietly as she could back to the inner chamber, where she had been sleeping. Aniahi was still asleep. She was glad. She could see that the covers were piled over the medicine-woman's sleeping form.

Kirsten couldn't see anything of Aniahi's head or body for that matter, but she knew that meant nothing; lots of people slept with their heads covered. Besides, that made what Kirsten needed to do easier.

She raced over to the pile of weapons that she and Aniahi had collected from her tent. There weren't many, and most were very crudely made. Kirsten settled on the weapon that looked most dangerous. It was called a Barton. Aniahi had said that all of the Cadotion people had one; some had more.

Though the tribe was a peaceful people there was always the threat of a raid. The Manerky were believed to be silenced forever, but in the last few winters the other tribes had chosen to move on. None of them were afforded the comfort of the mountain pass that the Cadotion people enjoyed. Aniahi had mentioned to one of the elders that many of the young of the other tribes had started to go missing. There was no real proof that it was the Manerky that had taken the children. However, the idea and the approaching winter had been enough to send the other tribes packing.

The Cadotion tribe on the other hand, held coveted land that lent its natural resources to the tribe's protection. It was that reality that had encouraged the elders to seek methods of making tools that could protect them from an enemy such as the Manerky.

Kirsten pulled a wooden knife that was covered in a hard-glossy substance, out of the pile, and placed it in a bag that she put around her neck, and draped to the side of her body. She tightened her grip around the center of the Barton, testing the weight of the weapon. It felt good. Something about the dangerous-looking weapon made Kirsten feel more alive; confident. She felt like she could face anything, even the Manerky.

She ran from the inner chamber into the darkness of the exiting tunnel. The dark meant nothing—it was empty and black, but there was nothing to harm her there. She was safe with her Barton by her side. Nothing could take her. She would go. She had to bring Lane and Jordan's children to safety. She would bring them back. She would not be afraid. She could feel the wonderful new-exhilarating assuredness as it coursed unbidden through her senses. Fear was no longer apart of who she was. She would walk passed that fear. She would be the one that made things happen. She would…

29

Max turned back from the shattered crystal to face John. Cynthia felt as though the speech he was giving would go on forever. Several times she had to thrust her hands behind her back as Max paced back and forth mulling over the last thirty years of his life.

She already knew everything. She had finally pieced together the parts of a very obscure puzzle. The photo of the blue-eyed-exotic beauty had been Amorous Dawson. After recruiting Edward Stanton, the two had eventually fallen in love.

An order had been given to take out a mark. That mark was Cecil Schooner, Jordan's grandfather. What Cynthia could not ascertain was the 'why'… why had Cecil Schooner, a Baptist preacher, a mission minded counselor, fallen under the radar of an undercover organization that existed for one reason… to rid the world of scum that escaped the clutches of the law?

She considered her own life. If one had met her before they would have never guessed that she had been an undercover agent, howbeit, an inefficient agent, working with the CIA to eliminate marks with a terrible history. As she considered the implications of that truth, Cynthia had to ask; had the process ever worked in reverse? That led her back to Jordan she was now a member of The Truth, a missionary.

She had been a cold-blooded killer; not just an agent set into motion. Jordan had vented her rage for an ugly past, in the worst possible way, she had killed innocent people that matched a set of criterion, a profile… people that embodied certain traits of her father; Jordan had been a serial killer, and now she was a redeemed, blood-washed Christian. Maybe the apple didn't fall far from the tree.

Cynthia had called Judge Harrison, the very same judge to cover up most of Black Heart's ugliest of transgressions. Judge Harrison had been the judge on Jordan's case as well. He had helped to place Jordan in the capable hands of Dr. Schoonhoven, a psychiatrist with a history of dealing with paranormal cases. The truth was Dr. Schoonhoven was a Christian that believed Jordan's claim of being possessed by a demon.

What Cynthia found was amazing. Cecil Schooner had defended himself against one of Black Heart's well placed prison inmates, but Cecil had lost. Black Heart had a choice to make. Their foolproof way of discerning-desirable recruits had backfired. Cecil had been put in a private medical facility with no memory of the event, but Black Heart could not take that chance. That over-zealous desire to tie up loose ends had been right on. Just a couple weeks after waking up Cecil had started to regain his memory of the event, but had tried to keep his memory quiet. H had hoped that hiding his memory would save his life, but he knew that living in the shadow of that hope would be no true solace. He had but one hope. He would have to be prepared.

Amorous had been sent to take out the useless recruit… what she found was a man that had trained vigorously for such an event. The attack by the inmate that had all but cost Cecil his life had lit a fire under him. Amorous had underestimated her mark, and had paid with her life.

One Jerrod Bennington, had changed his name to Cecil Schooner.

Edward Stanton had spent a lifetime searching for a man that no longer existed. By the time Edward had discovered his folly, Cecil Schooner had died after a long happy-life dedicated to God and family.

Edward had eventually turned his hate for Cecil on his family. Jordan was Cecil's pride and joy… his favorite grandchild. Edward would make her pay for Cecil's sins. That, Cynthia soon discovered is where Max came in.

Max was enlisted by Edward to befriend someone close to Jordan. Someone that Jordan would never suspect was giving vital information about her life to the enemy, because even John did not know of his betrayal.

Max was friend to no one, not even Edward Stanton. He had been selling secrets about Jordan's whereabouts to Stanton, while he was sealing the man's fate. It had been Max's idea to bring in the child-agents. He had assured Edward that the children would not be harmed, but that had been Max's intention from the start. What better way to mark Stanton as a monster than killing children, and pinning the blame on him?

Edward was a vengeful, evil man that allowed an even more evil man to call the shots, but he was no child killer.

Cynthia had to make sure that Max paid for what he had done, and she wanted Jordan to know her grandfather was innocent. He was a good God-fearing man that had been nearly killed by Black Heart... Cynthia feared that believing her beloved grandfather to be anything less than the God-fearing man that she had known and loved was enough to rock Jordan to her core.

Her eyes darted to John. He was thinking something. She could see it in his eyes. He looked terrified and angry all at once. He was bottled fury waiting to explode, but at the same time he was calculating his options. She didn't like his options. He could attack with what: a shard of crystal, wire, or the metal from the broken lamp? None of which were a match for a gun. No, John's options were not good... it was up to her. She would have no choice, when Max turned to pace the other direction, in that instant when the gun would no longer be pointed at John, Cynthia would have to make her move.

John gripped the shard of crystal. The serrated edges bit into his hand. He could feel the skin tearing where the jagged edges broke through, but he did not care. It was a scratch compared to what Max would do to him, to Cynthia. John knew they were dead. The longer he waited, the more bored Max would become with his game. The moment Max turned to pace the other direction, John would make his move.

30

Julie hadn't stayed long. She felt sort of letdown. As if she had built this grand illusion of a meeting up in her mind—only to have it fall pathetically short of her expectations. Edward's words had been that Amber Noel was beautiful, but Julie had seen the truth in his eyes. There, she had seen a mixture of fear and disgust. Edward had even physically retreated from Amber Noel.

If actions spoke louder than words, then Edward's actions were screaming… 'He hated kids.' Julie didn't need to know anything more about the man—she was armed with all the information she would ever need. Julie's children and grandchildren were a major part of her life, anyone that could not accept that, would not fit into her world. It was decided. She would call Paula Matthews, the administrator of nursing, and ask to be removed from Edward's case. She had allowed her emotions to call the shots long enough. She would put space between her and Edward Stanton, and in time she would forget him.

Julie got up early the next morning with Amber Noel. Still feeding every three to four hours made for a long night. Her daughter would be home around ten to get the baby. Julie prayed over Amber Noel each time she had to go to her in the night. She asked God to forge an unbreakable bond between her daughter and granddaughter. She knew from the babies, she had worked with in the nursery, during her time as a labor and delivery nurse that if the bond between mother and child was tainted in any way the child would react poorly.

Katie had had a very specific vision for her life, but when Amber Noel's father had rejected Katie, it had crushed her desire to thrive.

Every time she held Amber Noel that sadness was translated through every touch. Amber Noel remembered her mama, and this dejected shell of a human being was not who she remembered.

Julie finished her granddaughter's bath, and rubbed lotion all over her; making Amber Noel smell like Jonson and Jonson baby lotion. The aroma was so breathtakingly baby that Julie could do nothing, but smile and coo at her granddaughter for a few moments. She dressed her in a comfortable, but adorable pink cotton dress with white leggings and pink lacy socks. Tiny white flowers with dark pink centers filled the cotton dress. Julie had stopped at Dollar General on the way to the hospital. She was rewarded with a fifty percent off sale on children's apparel. She wanted to get something that fit within her budget, but was adorable for the mother and daughter reunion. If the Lord answered Julie's prayers, then Katie would be rested, and miss her daughter very much. That moment of jubilation would be enough to prove to her daughter that Amber Noel did love her; she just couldn't find her happy-go-lucky mother that had been giddy with a dream of the future.

Julie listened as the front door closed.

"Showtime." She smiled down at her tiny granddaughter. Her blue eyes searched for voices and noises that were still too far away for her to see.

"Hi, mom…" Katie stood in the doorway of Julie's bedroom with tears filling her eyes. "Oh my goodness. Look at her. She looks like a living doll, mom."

"She does." Julie admitted.

Katie reached for Amber Noel. Julie smiled, and handed her willingly; all the while praying.

"Hey, baby girl." Katie cooed as she placed her hand on the flower covered dress. Amber Noel's eyes filled with wonder as if she had finally gone home after years of being lost in the desert. Her tiny hand reached up, and claimed one of Katie's fingers.

Katie looked up then, at Julie. "She's so quiet, so content. What did you do mom?" She smiled.

"Not me…" Julie pointed at Katie. "You." Julie said as she placed a hand on Katie's cheek.

"I don't understand." Katie confessed as she looked down into her baby's face with wonder and then found her mother's eyes again.

"Amber Noel has finally found who she's been looking for." Julie said with a smile.

"But I've been here everyday mom." Katie frowned.

"Not to her sweetie. Remember when I told you that babies can't see very well, so they are driven by basic instincts: hunger, smell… that sort of thing?"

"I remember."

"Well you smell like her mommy, but her instincts have said until now that you aren't her mommy." Julie explained with compassion filling her eyes.

"But why?" Katie almost begged as she gazed down into Amber Noel's eyes, and caressed her tiny head.

"Sweetie, sit down." Julie said as she pointed to the end of her queen-sized bed. Julie waited for Katie to sit, and adjust the baby in her lap, before she continued.

"While you were pregnant with Amber Noel, you were happy: planning a life for the three of you. After she came into this world you changed, because her father left. He changed the dream. You lost someone very important to you." Julie waited for a moment as Katie wiped at some tears. "You've been grieving that loss." Julie placed a hand on her tiny granddaughter as tears filled her eyes. "What you haven't been able to understand is Amber Noel is grieving, too. She lost two people."

"Two people?" Katie knit her brow as confusion stole over her visage.

"Yes honey she lost her daddy and her mommy. Though you have been here every day, struggling, while he is gone… you have not been the mommy that Amber Noel remembers." Julie stood as she placed a comforting hand on her daughter's shoulder.

"Why don't I give you two a moment alone?" Julie smiled and patted her daughter lightly on the shoulder once more.

A worried look flashed in Katie's eyes.

"It's going to be okay. You are fine." Julie whispered.

As Julie left the room she heard the simple pledge that gave her all the assurance she needed to know what she had said to her daughter was true.

"I'm here, baby." Katie offered. "I'm never leaving you again." She promised. "I love you my Amber Noel." She confessed.

Julie had left the house not long after Katie had gotten home. Now that she was truly committed to her job as mother, and understood that God knew the plans He had for her (Jeremiah 29:11), Katie seemed almost joyful. Julie was thrilled to see that change in her daughter, more than once, she had given a tearful thank you to God for His much needed intervention.

Though she was excited about the monumental victory of her daughter reuniting with her granddaughter, she couldn't help but feel remorse for what she would now have to do. She had missed her husband for five long years, and each day she had slowly reconnected with what was left of her life. It wasn't really living, but she finally wasn't just waiting to die.

Edward had made Julie want for things that she had long since stopped believing she could have. She had felt connected to him on a level that transcended mere attraction. He made her feel alive, with the need to figure out his mysterious past… yes, but she would have gladly forfeit the knowledge to spend a lifetime discovering a future at his side.

Julie sighed, as she imagined a long-dreaded future without someone to spend it with. In that moment, she felt so connected to her daughter. She truly understood her loss. Her heart ached, and celebrated, because she knew that though she would feel hopeless, God would give her hope, just as He had her daughter.

31

Jordan stared at Shakia, refusing to meet Garrison's iron gaze. She wanted things to be like before, but they couldn't be…may never be. So many of the things that had built their relationship had been lies. If that were true, then their friendship was a lie as well. Garrison wanted her to pick up her shattered heart, and move forward as if everything were the same; as if nothing had ever happened. That wasn't going to happen. She couldn't. She wanted to, but she couldn't.

"You're wrong, you know?" Garrison finally broke the silence.

"About what?" Jordan's gaze remained on the black and white cat who was now grooming her kittens as they both meowed their complaint. The kittens brushed back and forth trying to ward off their mother's unwanted affections. Finally, realizing the error in her strategy, Shakia flipped on her side, allowing one kitten to rush in and claim the prize she offered while she stilled the other with her paws, and continued the bath.

Jordan allowed a small laugh. She had lived on the edge of madness as an agent for Black Heart, and still her most challenging objective had been wrangling her children for a bath.

"Can you look at me?" It was more a demand than a question.

Jordan turned her fury-filled gaze on Garrison. "Well?" She snapped.

"Are we back to that again?" Garrison huffed.

"Back to what, exactly?" Jordan glared. "We never had anything to get back to." Jordan hissed. "From the moment I met you, it was all a planned ruse. Every aspect of our so-called-friendship since that moment was a smokescreen, orchestrated by you for Black Heart, or your own selfish purposes." She pointed a finger as she took an involuntary step forward. "You have been manipulating me like some puppet master, pulling my strings. Well, I'm through. I refuse to be handled by you, or anyone else ever again!" Jordan lowered her voice into a menacing growl. "You do whatever it is you wish, but don't expect me to swing the door open for you to lead me and my family around by the noses, into whatever danger comes next, because you are too much of a coward to put your cards on the table; to let the chips fall where they may." Jordan's chest was heaving. She was so angry she wanted to rip something apart. She was blindsided by the rage. She had truly thought she had handled this, but the truth was staring her in the face—she had run from it—left it behind in New York. Unfortunately, here it was face to face with her, demanding answers.

"I deserve that." Garrison conceded without a fight.

"And a lot more!" Jordan amended. "But Lane is right, Christ died for your sins and mine. He has forgiven you, and so do I." Jordan crossed over to Garrison. She squared her shoulders as she met his gaze with, not anger, but the hurt that he had fostered.

"I do not trust you. Trust is earned, and you squandered your stores." Jordan swallowed, trying to ease the lump in her throat. "I will not second guess you in this, I trust you to make the shot." Her voice turned to ice. "But not as my friend. You lost that privilege."

Garrison dropped his head as she turned to walk away. His hand reached out, but then fell to his side again. "Agreed." He whispered.

Jordan stopped short as Lane materialized out of the darkness. His face was ashen.

"What's wrong?" Jordan could hear the alarm in her tone.

Garrison was at her side. A side glance revealed his level of concern was as high as her own.

"Kirsten..."

Jordan brushed passed Lane, running straight for the inner-chamber of the cave. As soon as she reached the dim lit chamber she knew what Lane had been about to say.

Kirsten was gone, but that was only part of it. Somewhere in the earlier part of the day, while Kirsten was sleeping, Aniahi had left the safety of the cave. Probably to go for the children.

Jordan paused over the undisturbed mass of covers, she had used this tactic to fool Garrison into believing she was still on the small cot in the observation room at The Garden. Garrison had taken her there to protect her from Black Heart. Jordan swallowed back the tears as the memory blindsided her senses. Garrison had not always been out for himself. Though his actions had more times than not, put her in harm's way, his intentions had been for the most part pure. It was his good intentions that managed to bring the most disaster upon her life—could she force him from her life for that? Hadn't her good intentions almost gotten Penny killed?

Jordan pushed the line of reasoning out of her head. There wasn't time. She turned to Kirsten's bed. It was left uncovered. Jordan knew that she would not have been able to leave the cave without waking Aniahi. There was a chill in the room that would have pulled one of them from their slumber to stoke the fire. Instead, a log laid half in, half out of the hearth, the stabilizing end had burned down to ash. The log hung in the balance, waiting for the final shred of weight that had been holding it in place, to fade away.

Jordan turned to Garrison.

"I see it." he confirmed.

"What?" Lane arched his brow.

"You see that log?" Garrison asked.

"Yeah," Lane nodded. "What of it?"

"It takes time for a log to burn down to that degree." Jordan explained.

"So?" Lane was looking a little frustrated.

Jordan understood. "Lane, it's cold in here." Jordan held his hands. "Someone would have woken, and stoked the fire. Aniahi has been gone longer than Kirsten. If she hadn't then..."

"Aniahi would have stopped her. She's a light sleeper." Lane finished.

"Exactly," Jordan concurred. "Also, Aniahi's bed has been fixed as if to fool someone. That someone would have to be Kirsten." Jordan pointed to Aniahi's mat of fur that lay in a large clump as if someone were still sleeping, soundly underneath. "But more than that, Lane. No one, especially not a thirteen-year-old girl would stay in a place this cold, and not do something to get warm. Had she been in here that log,"

Jordan pointed to the smoldering log. As if on cue, the log collapsed to the cave floor. "Would not still be in the same place." Jordan searched his eyes. "Lane she's alone." Jordan choked out the last words.

Lane rubbed Jordan's head as he held her to him. "We'll find her." He promised.

"But what would make them leave, and at separate times?" Jordan sounded pathetic even to herself. Kirsten simply did not have the skills needed to survive an attack by the Manerky, not even during the day. Simple self-defense tactics would not measure up to warriors trained to fight like wild animals in the night.

32

The wind whipped and howled as if laughing its evil taunt of Kirsten's predicament. She sat in the dead center of the small cage with her arms wrapped tightly around her knees. She could not stand, only sit, and even if she could she was not sure she had the courage.

The blackened nails and pale white eyes of the enemy enhanced the grotesque set of his blackened teeth. Angry animal noises escaped his haunting visage, as he danced around the cage he had trapped her in. His jubilance sang out in bitter reminder that all was lost to her.

Her attacker had spent most of the morning on a wild-goose-chase. She had roamed aimlessly through the village determined not to lead him to the children. Kirsten had been so afraid at that moment that she wanted to run, screaming back to the safety of the cave where her friends were at, but to do so would condemn them to the same fate as she.

She had been so stupid; leaving the sanctity of the warm cave, to go blindly out into a village blanketed with the Manerky tribe. For what? Her mind screamed demanding an answer even in the midst of this her darkest hour. She had wanted to prove she was brave. How ironic; now she sat in the middle of a cage more afraid than ever.

She had been looking through the bleached-white bars, never really caring to comprehend what her prison was made of. With nothing left to do, but await her eminent death, or rescue, Kirsten wiped the tears from her eyes, and decided to investigate her crude accommodations. A glimmer of hope was sparking to life; maybe she could free herself. Maybe her makeshift prison had not been as iron-clad as it seemed.

She trembled as she pulled herself timidly to the bars in front of her. At first her vision blurred, but then with all-consuming clarity she could now see the horrific truth. Bleached-white bones were tied together with leather thongs at each end, but not just any bones... they were the leg bones of humans. Kirsten looked past her makeshift prison. There were several more of the tiny bone-cells scattered across the grassy-plain.

She thought of all the dead bodies in different stages of mutilation lying throughout the Cadotion village. She had not thought about it, never seeing a reason to, but there was not one child among those dead. She couldn't help but wonder why she had found herself in a cage, awaiting an uncertain fate... was her fate to be far worse than that of the scattered dead on the valley floor?

Looking at all of the empty cages before her, Kirsten believed she knew. Obviously the Manerky did not think much of the Cadotion people, but that hatred was not limited to the Cadotion. She would probably become some cliché: a slave captured to cook and clean... she would live out her life, as would the other captured children, as malnutrition, filthy servants, running from one tent to the next, carrying food and water. What if they turned her into some baby machine: passing her from one Manerky warrior to the next ensuring the Manerky bloodline continue—she had to admit that idea made little sense. The women of their tribe would probably fill that need. She had to stop reading the half-bread novels by Nora Roberts. Her fate would have a far less romantic end than that of the women depicted in those books. Real life was usually worse than works of fiction.

Kirsten thought about the warrior that had captured her. His grotesque hazy brown eyes seemed to disapprove of her in some way. His lips curled into an angry snarl, revealing yellow-blackened teeth that were crooked and jagged. He laced his fingers into Kirsten's long blond hair, and dragged her with a fistful of it to her would be prison. As he leaned over and secured the door with a leather thong tied in tight knots, his breath filled Kirsten's nostrils, making her gag on the putrid smell of dried blood, mingled with decay. As he moved away she could see the hideous mouth curve into an inhuman-dangerous grin, as if he were for some reason pleased with himself.

She sat stone-still in her bone prison afraid to cry for help; afraid not to—what if the nightmare returned? What if he was no longer satisfied with his chirping calls of glee? What if dancing around her prison no longer satisfied him? What if he did the awful things that existed behind that ruthless grin? Kirsten shivered as the wind whipped through the bones. Somehow none of her imaginings seemed to fit with the monstrous-intent of that ominous grin—she knew he could do worse than what she could imagine. His hideous-dead eyes told of mayhem that her young mind would never be able to conjure.

33

Penny scooped Modilo into her arms as she waited for Nick to do the same with Tristan. Though both boys were around the same age, Tristan was nearly twice Modilo's size. Penny stared down at the small boy as he nestled deeper into her chest, seeking the warmth he would find there. She absently pulled the fur blanket up tighter around his beautifully-tan face. His golden brown features seemed to be deliberately etched by the hand of God; a painting come to life, rooting for warmth in her arms. His tiny lips a perfect shade of pink, were the shape of a heart. His lower lip dipped slightly inward as if to pout pitifully about his ruined life.

Penny's heart ached for the boy. Nick had briefed her on the events of the morning; his mother had been cleaved in half as the boy sat, helplessly begging her to hold him to her breast, and make the horror he had witnessed, retreat into the shadows.

She crushed the boy to her as tears slipped unbidden from her eyes. "I'll make them pay," she whispered her heart-felt oath into the soft fuzz that had escaped his tiny-elaborate braids. She felt like a kindred spirit to the Cadotion toddler. She too had lost her mother, while she wept helplessly on the floor.

The attackers sent by Edward Stanton had forced their way into their home, into their lives, and taken all that was left of Penny's innocence. In that moment, as the men executed her mother, while she knelt before them begging for her life, and for Penny's life, Penny knew that that mercy would not be granted. While the killers claimed that they were sent by Jordan-Buckley-Gates—Penny knew it was a lie—she was aware in that moment of another overwhelming truth… she had been wrong: she should have gone with her Aunt Jordan, instead of shying away. She should have heeded that call when she had the chance.

Jordan had it right then. Though her life had changed, and penny could see that it was certainly for the better; her aunt had been right. Women needed to be able to protect themselves. Penny had gone with the men that had killed her mother, without a fight. She pushed back the fear, disgust or any other emotion that tried to tie itself to the memory of her mother's murder. It was all worthless, fruitless emotion; one reason spurred her on; revenge! She held tightly to the desire to vindicate her mother. She would soon have her justice—no useless emotion would slow that fact!

The moment that Penny had been taken to Black Heart to be trained for a supposed revenge detail on Jordan Buckley-Gates, for her treachery, she would get up close to the man that had ordered her mother's death. She had played her captors like a fiddle. She allowed them to see the depth of her hate for her mother's killer, but placed a false name and face on the source of that hate. She had led them to believe that she hated her aunt with all of her being. The trainers were thrilled. They believed Penny could be more than just a mere distraction. She could be the one to actually destroy Jordan. Armed with that belief, the trainers shed every light they could on self-defense and weaponry. She became the prized pupil that was taught how to use a bow, to throw a knife. All of the trainer's time had been spent honing Penny's combat skills to the highest level possible in such a short window of time.

Penny knew she was not the match for Jordan, as did her trainers, but it was her trainer's hope that she could disarm Jordan with her presence, and in so doing, be her end.

Penny followed their every command; in the end it wasn't her aunt that had been fooled. It was the trainers.

Penny eyed Nick as she delved further into the memoirs of their time with the agency.

Nick had come to Black Heart before Penny—their connection had been immediate. A trust was built between the two that was unlike anything she had ever known. Soon she had confided all her truth in her new friend; he had believed Penny's stories about her aunt, and had committed himself to helping her. Together they would ensure she learn all she needed to not only survive, but be prepared to take out her mother's true murderers.

He had pushed her to stay the course when she wanted to end the charade and run away. He was driven by a singular, need… he needed to end the life of the one that killed his grandfather. That time seemed so long ago now, as they stood in the midst of a bloody-tribal-war.

Penny followed Nick out of the tent. She held tight to Amelia's hand. She was slowly starting to wake, but her hands were still pushing groggily at her drooping eyes. All of the archers were removed from their entry-points; there was little time before dark. Penny and Nick intended to move the children to the hidden cave, and cast as much light as possible in its center. They would wait for night to fall, and the Manerky to come for their pound of flesh. The Manerky would come, but the light in the midst of the cave would put them at a decided disadvantage.

Penny moved with determined intent toward the opening of the cave, all the while she and Nick never stopped searching for any sign of trouble. If the Manerky did come, no matter the manner in which they chose to fight, beast or man, she refused to join the menu without a fight.

34

The moment that Jordan said that they were no longer friends, Garrison felt the air leave his lungs. At first, he wanted to leave, but he knew he could never do that to Jordan, and her family; no matter how big a rift stood between them. Then as Jordan looked at him, almost as if she knew… no, expected him to understand the deeper meaning behind the incinerated log; Garrison saw in that moment that the connection may be broken, but it wasn't dead. He knew that though Jordan was not ready to admit it, she could feel that connection as well.

She was harsh in the way she had made plain, her feelings, but as much as it pained him to admit it, she had been right. Saving someone's feelings in the face of truth was not one of Jordan's strong suits, but it was one of the things that made Garrison the most comfortable around her—no matter what, he knew what she was thinking, and that was worth all the rough edges he had to brave, in order to be her friend.

He also knew that she had been right about him squandering his stores of trust. She had always said that meeting someone was a lot like opening a savings account. You put in what you will eventually take out, but when you first meet someone you are given a certain amount of trust: you could earn more or squander what you have already been given.

Garrison had at first completely disagreed with the logic, but then as he and Jordan were sitting on a park bench one afternoon, gathering Intel on a mark; where he lives, works, goes…etc.—Jordan had pointed to an elderly couple not far away.

"What is your first impression of the old couple at six o'clock?" Jordan asked as she threw another piece of bread to the pigeons meandering in front of where they sat.

"Why?" Garrison asked, apprehensively.

"Don't avoid the question. Just tell me. What's your first honest to God, gut feeling about the couple?" She pressed.

"Okay… I guess what everyone thinks when they see a couple that age." He shrugged as he too, threw a piece of bread to the birds he barely noticed.

"I'm not asking you what everyone else thinks Garrison. I'm telling you to tell me what you think." Jordan knit her brow.

"It just don't…"

"Garrison just answer the dang question!"

"Okay… okay… They look nice. I trust…" Garrison sat up straighter. "Wow!"

"Ah ha! See. You know nothing about them, yet based on what you've seen, you have given them a certain amount of trust. It may be that you simply trust them not to kill you, or steal your wallet, but you gave them that trust based solely on what you have seen. Everybody does that it's called stereotyping; someone in this park is watching us right now, and they're making an assessment based on what they see." Jordan waved her hands about theatrically, and then gave Garrison an innocent smile.

"Do you think their first impression would be an accurate depiction of who we really are? Do you think if someone gave the two of us our first trust stores it would be well spent?" Jordan again smiled at Garrison as she looked deeply into his eyes waiting for his answer.

He thought about the ruthless way in which they had killed people, and the items they had stolen to make some of their kills possible: cash, cars, and even personal ID cards for access…

"Wow!" He finally conceded, as he fell back against the wooden bench. His eyes studied the many couples and even loan walkers in the park. Suddenly, without warning he felt very vulnerable.

"Exactly!" Jordan exaggerated the word.

As the memory faded, Garrison realized that he hadn't squandered unearned trust, Jordan would never freely give it. He had squandered the trust that she had given based on an elaborate ruse. He had lied to her from the moment they had met. He had never done anything in their time together to truly gain the most valuable thing Jordan had to give; her trust.

CHAPTER

35

The room was quiet, except for the steady drip of the IV bag. Edward had finally dozed off sometime after lunch. He had jolted awake several times in the night, almost as if some unseen ethereal being hung close at hand, waiting for the command to torment him. He felt like the punch-line of a cosmic joke. His life was in shambles. He was falling for a woman that was the exact representation of what his ugly existence had never even had a chance at being.

He lay awake staring at the shadows dancing on the wall, cast by the dim overhead light, playing through the amber liquid of his IV bag. It was four in the afternoon, and a nurse would be in with another round of meds. Though it was not the nurse he wanted, Edward's mind grumbled the adolescent protest for things he wanted to be that were not only out of his control, but out of his league. Julie was out of his rights as a… Edward had no proper term that was degrading enough to describe what he had become.

He thought of her face the day before. She had been so beautiful in the modest-powder-blue sweater she wore. The color was like a beacon pointing to her cloudy blue eyes; making them sparkle as she cradled her beloved Amber Noel. He wanted so much to belong in that world—to be an easy stroke of an artist's brush as he thought of an addition to his masterpiece that made sense. Oh, that he had met her a day before his exotically beautiful Amorous. Maybe if he had happened across her in the supermarket, before allowing his hate for Cecil Schooner to fester into a mad search for revenge that had led him to Max.

Edward had known Max was dangerous, but he wanted so desperately to make Cecil feel the immense ache that had become a part of his everyday existence, since Amorous' death. He would have reached into the afterlife and ripped every good thing away from Cecil Schooner in order to stop the pain that crushed down upon him.

Things had gotten so far out of hand, but Max had assured Edward that he would take care of everything.

"You asked me to do the job, because you knew I could take care of things. Right?" Max had prompted, as he paced like a caged lion across the cement underpass. The road like Edward's life was in desperate disrepair. Vines snaked up the cement pillars holding up the overpass. Bubbly-letters of graffiti with its bright reds and blues, brought a vandalized-art to the desolate underpass; the savage-beauty, a forbidden aesthetic, somehow brightened the gloom. The rumble of tires filled the air, making it hard to understand the other without raising their voices. But Edward had wanted the location of their meeting to be precise. The location had to be somewhere not frequented by the cops, and somewhere that other prying ears would be unable to hear the conversation. The underpass on Thorp street was the perfect place.

"Yeah, but children?" Edward heard his voice squeak. He wanted to take the tone back but it was too late. The last thing he needed was to seem weak and out of control with the people he hired to do the dirty jobs. Sometimes it was necessary to hire people less scrupulous than he, but allowing them to see any hint of fear was a mistake; a break in his armor that he could not afford.

Edward straightened his black suit as he turned his attention to his cronies. He wanted to know that the men had his back, if for any reason Max were to lash out. Second guessing a man like Max just seemed like dangerous propaganda.

Edward stood a little taller as Marshall surreptitiously showed off the large-silenced revolver just behind his Tailored-Armani jacket. Edward smiled. He had taken very good care of Marshall and Denton. The two were as loyal as lap dogs.

"Listen Stanton... Mr. Stanton." Max amended.

Edward could feel the fake loyalty radiating off Max like a blazing space heater. He knew loyalty; he had plenty of people that would give their lives to do his bidding. Edward knew that Max was merely a means to an end. He was a necessary evil, but at the same time he was a dangerous dog that could not be bought, or trusted. Still, Edward had very few options. He needed Max.

"Go on." Edward commanded as he straightened his black silk tie.

Max strolled a little closer. His hand raised, and gingerly settled on Edward's shoulder. Marshall and Denton were at Edward's side with a pistol to either side of Max's head.

"Easy guys." Max raised his hands in submission. "Wanna call your dogs off?" Max smiled casually at Edward.

Edward nodded once, and the two men were instantly back at their posts. "I trust the dogs as you call them. You on the other hand, I'm having trouble with." Edward tilted his head to the side as he raised his brow quizzically. "Any reason for that, Max?" Edward returned the smile in kind.

"Mr. Stanton, you hired me to do a job. All I'm asking is that you let me do it." Max lifted his shoulders in a simple shrug. "We don't have to like each other, to understand each other; wouldn't you agree?" Max tilted his head this time. "Besides I only want the money." Max pulled at his ratty black t-shirt as he gave a short whistle. "I can see me sporting one of them monkey suits with a fine young thing on my arm."

Edward wasn't sure he believed Max's motives were as straight forward as all that, but so far he was all Edward had. Max was Edward's only way in, and he had proven useful on past assignments; still something about the man-made Edward want to put a bullet in his head, and never look back.

The memory faded, with Edward wishing that he had never met Max. He lay in the lonely hospital room awaiting the sentence to be passed. Ironic he thought... he had pushed for so long to make all the evidence tying him to Cecil Schooner, and subsequently Jordan Buckley-Gates disappear. Now that it had, he needed it to prove that he had not ordered the death of those children. Not that it would change what Edward was; he was still a murderer; he was still a very big figure head, bankrolling a drug and gun cartel, and he was still a man that deserved to go to prison for his crimes. All of that remained true. He was ready; he deserved his fate. It wasn't the government's punishment that kept him awake. No. He had long since made his peace with that. It was the contempt he was sure would fill the eyes of his blue-eyed-angel that would be a punishment against his very soul. Sadly, Edward could not think of one redeeming quality that would make him worthy of anything less.

36

Kirsten was so tired her bones and muscles ached from being in the confined space of the bone-prison. She needed to stretch her legs, but fear kept her a prisoner inside of her crudely fashioned cell. She wouldn't move. The tears had long since stopped falling. She was so dehydrated that her eyes burned, and her lips stuck together. The bones on the bottom of the cage pressed deep into her legs, causing them to feel dead and heavy. All of that did not matter to Kirsten, as much as being in the cage with nothing to protect her skin form the dead of night, and what she knew was lurking not far away.

She could hear the hissing and growling—the slight footfalls of the Manerky as they passed on either side of the cage. Her eyes strained against the dark, causing them to burn more as the wind whipped across them. Her head pivoted, wildly in search of hands or spears that may venture into her tiny space. Anything that she knew would inevitably break through the minute slots of the bone cage; she could feel her skin prickle at the howls and hoots, as the Manerky paraded by; sounding like nothing more than an avenging jungle come to haunt the Cadotion tribe.

She pulled more tightly into a ball. Though the action threatened to lock her leg muscles up like a vice, horror commanded it; she placed her hands over her ears, and started to gently rock. The cries and hisses; the moans and growls; the clicking and calling, and yes, the smell was going to drive her mad.

Harder and harder she rocked, praying the incessant noise would come to an end, and all at once it did. Kirsten froze. The silence was more maddening than the hoot and calls. She sat very still listening; her eyes strained even harder now against the darkness for any sign of the invaders, she knew to be passing, but still she could see nothing.

She had never seen a night so dark as this; the clouds had started to gather early that evening, turning the sky a gloomy-gray with errant streaks of sunlight that peaked through the cloud cover, turning the gray an ominous shade of blue. Even then, Kirsten knew that this would be a night as dark as death itself. She could feel the shutter spread through her body under the weight of the fear.

Kirsten froze as she felt someone bump into her cage. She scooted as close to the center of her make-shift prison as possible. She wasn't sure if one of the warriors had run into the cage by accident, or if someone was actually trying to grab her through the bone-bars. She sat in silent-terror, waiting for her unwanted fate, and then as if the beast-people had read her mind, long-cold-fingers reached into the dark, and wrapped around her mouth. She squirmed, violently against the iron grip, but in the end her struggle for freedom proved futile. She felt something press into her neck, and then the whole world went black.

37

Julie's heart seemed to protest her every step, but still she ignored the unrelenting urging, and knocked on Mavis Upchurch's door. She had called the hospital administrator, but was promptly sent to Mavis' office. Julie had not wanted to involve the woman, but her involvement with Edward was becoming more than that of a patient and care taker. It needed to stop. She needed distance; perspective.

Julie straightened her sheer mint green blouse, and assured that the black camisole beneath was keeping a safe distance above her cleavage line. She had changed her mind three times that morning, not sure what to wear.

Mavis had an air about her that wilted Julie's defenses.

"Come in." Came the haughty voice of a woman with too little time on her hands.

Julie brushed the last refrains of lent off her black dress slacks, as she straightened, and then forced herself to open the dark brown door.

A medium built woman, with short curly brown hair sat behind a dark-cherry-wood desk with a mountain of manila folders, to the left of her. She feverishly scribbled her signature at the bottom of each of the pages of the folder she was flipping through. Julie could not imagine that Mavis was really reading all of the papers that she signed.

"Have a seat." Mavis directed as she pointed the butt of a black ball point pen at a short brown leather chair. The small chair looked to be an underling, squatting in submission before the large black leather high back chair that Mavis enthrone herself in. Leaning forward, scrutinizing the pages of the folder in front of her, Mavis kept her eyes pinned to the task.

Julie sat carefully down as she lay her purse over her lap, and started to trace a finger over a silver-studded cross in the middle of the black purse.

"Well, Miss Lealand? I'm certain you had a reason for coming to see me today." Mavis arched a manicured brow as she momentarily lifted her head from her work.

Julie's mouth went dry. Her hands started to sweat as her mind searched for an excuse to leave. All of a sudden under the scrutiny of this overly busy woman, her problems seemed very trivial.

"Mavis… um… Miss Upchurch… that is… I" Julie blew out an exasperated breath as her eyes burned with tears. Too much was going on. She needed to just leave. Why was she being so petty, anyway? Ronald had been gone for five years. It was understandable that she missed him after thirty years of marriage, but lately, since Edward had come into her life, Julie found herself licking wounds she had long since thought healed.

"Miss Lealand." Mavis sat back in her chair after laying her reading glasses on the desk, and sitting her pen down. "I don't mean to trivialize your problems, but I'm a very busy woman." Mavis pointed to the stack of manila folders. "So with all due respect, could you please tell me what this is all about?"

Julie rose from her chair. She would seize the opportunity. The woman had all, but told her to leave. Julie prepared herself for the abrupt goodbye that would follow—it didn't matter. She knew she had no one to blame, but herself. She should have never come to Mavis Upchurch's office. The woman was delved the 'Ice Queen,' by the nursing staff. Here she sat in the third outfit of the day, expecting… what? Compassion; understanding? All of those were responses Julie would expect of a human being dealing with a fellow human being; all of those were beyond the robot-persona engendered by the 'Ice Queen'… emotions that lay somewhere beyond the borders of Miss Upchurch's too busy world.

"Sit down, Julie." Mavis allowed a heavy sigh. Then leaned over to the small gray intercom-box, as she massaged the bridge of her nose with the thumb and index finger of her right hand.

"Candace could you brew some coffee?" Mavis pinched the bridge of her nose with the index finger and thumb of her right hand once again, before pushing back into her chair.

"Yes, ma'am." The bubbly voice of a younger woman filled the speaker.

Julie sniffed, and then reached into her purse for a tissue. She had none. She felt so stupid—why cry? This was yet another emotion that Mavis would not understand. Even if Mavis Upchurch was equipped with the capacity to understand; how could Julie expect the woman to understand something that she could not understand about herself?

Mavis pulled a drawer open on the front of her desk, and pushed a floral print box of tissue across the desk toward Julie. Julie pulled several of the napkins from the box as she collapsed into a pool of tears.

"You know I have a one cup policy." Mavis tilted her head to the side.

Julie blew her nose. "I'm sorry."

"Don't be. Just let Candace bring me one cup of coffee before hearing news this bad. K?" Mavis laughed lightly.

Julie froze. It seemed so odd a thing to witness. The melodic sound did not match up to the crude-ambitious predator that the woman engendered.

"Oh, no. Now I've ruined my reputation for being the 'Ice Queen." Mavis rolled her eyes, as she put air quotes around the words Ice Queen.

Rolling her chair back, Mavis walked around the desk, and sat on the edge. "Julie despite what you may think of me… I would like to think that my staff would come to me if there was a problem. I guess I never gave much thought to the nick name; until now." Mavis reached over, and patted Julie's hand. "You have been with us for over twenty years. Always on time; you are never a problem. Even when your husband passed away, you refused to take time off." Mavis shook her head. "I see a lot of me, in you."

Julie peered up into the hazel eyes of the Mavis Upchurch, she had never before met.

"Some days I miss Mason so much that it feels like there is something besides oxygen in the air, because it seems too heavy to breathe." Mavis confided. Mavis pulled a picture frame from behind a three tiered paper holder. She smiled down at the image in the silver frame, and then passed it to Julie.

Julie gasped. She had expected to see the smiling face of an older man, but instead a young, handsome man with dark wavy brown hair, and radiant blue eyes stared back with a charismatic smile.

"We were so in love," Mavis said as she looked at a leafy-green plant near the office door. "That photo was taken twenty years ago; two days after his twenty third birthday." Mavis turned to Julie as a single tear slid down her cheek. "That photo was meant to keep me quiet." Mavis heaved a sad laugh as her voice took on a far-away tone.

"Mason left for a family reunion, but never made it. A woman with failing eye sight, refused to believe her time of driving had come to an end. She was headed to the pharmacy to get a prescription refilled."

"It was a closed casket funeral." Mavis returned the photo to its hiding place on her desk, as she shifted her weight and straightened her face. A knock sounded at the door.

"Come in Candace." Mavis called, while sitting back in her high back chair.

Julie sat silent as a young attractive red haired woman with impossibly huge green eyes brought in a silver tray with a black rimmed coffee pot. Two ornate blue and green cups rattled against the silver spoons protruding from their tops. Beautifully-ornate silver, serving vessels containing cream and sugar, seemed oddly misplaced in the medicinal surroundings of the white-walled office. Setting the tray down, Candace smiled, and then left the room.

Mavis crossed to the intricate pot, and prepared her cup, and then carried it back to her desk. She held out a hand to offer Julie some. Julie thought about turning the offered refreshment down, but then considered the one cup policy. Without further delay, she prepared her cup. Then, hurriedly returned to her seat.

Mavis swallowed, and then eyed Julie over the steaming white cup. "So, what's this about?" Mavis asked then took another sip of her coffee.

"Do you know the patient in room 304, Mr. Stanton?"

"Mr. Stanton." Mavis furrowed her brow. "Oh yes. Edward Stanton, the child killer."

The outer edges of Julie's vision tunneled, as her coffee cup clattered to the floor.

CHAPTER

38

Lane stayed back at the inner chamber, readying it for any of the Cadotion tribe members that may come. He also wanted to be there in case Kirsten or Aniahi were to return.

Jordan had stressed the importance of making certain the inner chamber was lit well. The room needed to shine like daylight. With that in mind, he lit several torches, and stationed each around the perimeter of the room, but that just did not seem to match the image Jordan had painted in his mind.

According to Jordan, the Manerky were nocturnal by nature. She wasn't certain of their reasoning, but the Manerky had abandoned the sunlight in order to train in total darkness. The act had caused them their sight, or at least a good part of it.

Lane had searched Aniahi's tent, and found a small spade. He knew it was there, because he and Jordan had bought Aniahi a small kit for gardening for the herbs she used in her healing remedies. He had worked hard to dig a small trench around the perimeter of the inner chamber, following the natural contours of the wall. The cave already had a slight indention, and the walls were for the most part soft, and in some place chalky, making the task not as daunting as it could have been. He then filled the trench with pitch and set it ablaze.

Lane stood back as the fire cascaded around the room, igniting all of the flammable substance in its wake. The amendment definitely fit the vision in Lane's mind.

Jordan crouched behind a large dip in the mountain wall—the natural curve of the fissure hid her from the prying eyes of the enemy. Garrison, a few feet away behind a large boulder stood just as still as she. They both patiently studied the habits of the infiltrating enemy.

Every quirk, every nuance, was being taken into consideration. It would not be enough to quietly walk among the hundreds of warriors that would be filtering through the pass; Jordan and Garrison needed to mimic their every move. These were not mere men, but trained animalistic creations that had been self-altered in order to be the best hunter they could possibly be.

Jordan watched with open intrigue as the warriors contorted their limbs to mimic different animals. One minute they were tigers on the prowl, and the next hands waving overhead, they looked like nothing more than baboons readying for the attack. Low hisses and growls escaped their throats. Clicks and bird calls filled the air as they covered ground and sky in their unpredictable murderous game of charades.

The bodies of each of the warriors were painted in angry swirls of red paint; it was the same as the archers that Jordan and Garrison had worked to eliminate on the mountain side. Their eyes a milky shade of white over a gloomy brown, stood out in the waning sunlight. Each warrior moved with precision, with an exception of a very few, but even the youngest, most inexperienced of the warriors moved with the ease of the creatures they were trying to mimic. If not for them standing in such close proximity to the older more experienced warriors, Jordan might never have seen the inadequacies of the inexperienced.

She felt a part of her hope dwindle as she took in the mass of warriors; there were hundreds. How could she and Garrison ever expect to tear down such a force as this? She didn't know how, but she knew they must. Her children's very existence depended on their success, but as Jordan watched the precision of the army of warriors she could not imagine how. She was beginning to think that grabbing her family and as many of the tribesman as possible, and rushing to the shores and fleeing the enemy grasp would be their only hope.

Garrison sat wide-eyed, scanning the enemy swarm; the cold realization of what they faced ran through his veins. He quickly turned to Jordan. She too looked overwhelmed by the daunting task set before them.

The cloud cover was complete as the last refrain of straining sunlight started to die out behind the cloud's ominous darkness. Both Garrison and Jordan had taken precautions to ensure that if they were to bump into one of the warriors in the dark they would go undetected. Mud claimed from the river's edge was painted, carefully over their bodies. Copious amounts of the viscous substance would mask their smell.

Though for the most part, the Manerky troupes moved like a well-oiled-machine; Garrison had noticed some flaws in the parade of savages: some of the younger warriors tended to fall short when mimicking the ritualistic-gestures meant to capture the essence of a specific animal being mimicked. That may be their only saving grace. Garrison had no clue what the penalty would be for the inexperienced warriors; maybe death. He hoped not, because it was the younger warriors' shortcomings that he was hoping would mask the flaws in his and Jordan's attempt at fitting in.

Jordan watched as Kirsten rocked helplessly in the cage made of bones. How terrible must it be for the young girl to have lost her family, and now this?

Kirsten's hair was in a ratted clump on top of her head as if she had been dragged to the cage, and tossed in. Jordan wanted to reject the image, but she knew these beings held very little value for human life. Even the way they carried themselves seemed to suggest that they were not human, but some breed of animal not quite beast, but certainly not low enough to be man. Each member of the Manerky tribe was skilled in the aggressive behavior of animals on the hunt.

As Jordan viewed the parade of warriors, she was struck by how dehumanized they were. There was a chill in the air, yet none of the tribe wore anything to protect against the coming winter. Their heads were shaved bald, some of them had thin spindly shards of white-bone-looking-prominences sticking out from either side of their face, just below their cheeks, and to the side of their noses; it gave them a cat-like appearance. Some of the warriors had jagged teeth that seemed to have been filed down into a serrated edge, like a shark. Every part of their anatomy whether added or subtracted, was done so in an effort to make them a more efficient hunter.

Jordan didn't want to imagine what the teeth would be used for, or any other part of the deadly-looking menaces for that matter. She just wanted to put an end to this nightmare. Her heart drummed as she thought of her children coming face to face with the man-beasts. She was desperate to end this. She could not allow that to happen.

The final shards of sunlight dimmed, as the thick clouds closed in like a scroll rolling together. At first, Jordan's eyes searched the darkness, but then she closed them as she searched for the calm center of her being. With a quick prayer, she surged into the task before her with all of her being; she knew this.

Jordan and Garrison both had spent two weeks in a pitch black room; learning to trust their other four senses. Daily, at alternating times someone had entered that dark world. Each time the person's intent, friend or foe, would have to be ascertained through instinct.

Jordan learned to use her sense of smell first. If she attacked someone with a plate of food she would lose the next day's meals.

The counselor wore a sweet smelling perfume; before she had come to that realization, Jordan had lunged for the counselor. She was given seven lashes with a bullwhip for the offense.

The two weeks of darkness, had been the hardest part of her training, and the most hated, but Jordan had gained very valuable abilities that had saved her life on more than one occasion. She prayed that this time would prove no different.

Garrison ghosted through the ranks of the Manerky, avoiding contact at all cost. He listened as his brain slowly began compartmentalizing the different sounds. Light footfalls brushing the valley floor, moved passed as he weaved in and out toward the low whimpering. It was the sound of Kirsten, begging with inferior need; the Manerky paid her pitiful cries no heed as they went about preparing for their murderous task.

Garrison listened as his mind caught another sound. The gentle whoosh of air, as a fallen warrior fell to the hands of an unknown enemy. The snapping, like a dead animal being pulled from the icy ground—it was the sound of a neck, as Jordan ran through the center of the parade of warriors, flanking Garrison. She was running interference as he made his way determinedly to the cage where Kirsten begged for her life.

Every now and again, Garrison, too sank the cold steel of his knife into the neck or temple of a passing warrior; careful to place the warrior gently on the ground; in the rows he knew to be void of the marching killers.

Garrison knew, as did Jordan their time was running short. All too soon, the Manerky would know that strangers walked among them.

Jordan held her breath as a warrior brushed passed her, and suddenly stopped short. She moved slightly to the right, trying to avoid contact with the enemy again. She could tell by the rigid jolt of the warrior's body that he had felt a subtle difference in Jordan's physique. Something about her body did not register quite right for the enemy tribesman.

Jordan had braided her hair, and pinned it tightly to the back of her head, so that it would not hang loose. She didn't want any of the Manerky to feel her hair, and recognize the difference. She had not thought much of her physical attributes, beyond her hair, that would cause alarm for the enemy. Now, as the enemy's arm brushed passed, and came in contact with her chest, Jordan knew that she had forgotten a vital part of her anatomy that set her apart in a very distinct way.

Jordan waited for the sounds of shrieking, or hissing, anything that an animal would do to announce an invasion into their world. Her breath still froze, she waited in the darkness unsure of the threat to come.

39

There was no war cry, no scream of warning, just an intent to kill, and then action that would make it happen. Cynthia lunged at Max with the letter opener, the moment he turned from John. At the same moment, in the corner of her eye, her brain only half recognized John doing the same.

Cynthia plunged the letter opener deep into Max's back, and then reached for the chair she had been sitting in. An explosion ripped through the silence, and Cynthia turned to see Max drop.

Blood oozed down John's hand as shock filled first his eyes, and then his entire face. Cynthia smiled at the fallen Max; she was exuberant. All of the marks gone wrong, but it was this moment, this chapter in the book of her life that had mattered most, and she had thankfully gotten it right.

Cynthia's mind seemed to catch up with the moment, her eyes sought the wall behind John. There had been a gun shot, but there was no damage to the wall. As if in answer to the unspoken question, John staggered to a knee. Blood filled the right chest area of his white-dress-shirt. Cynthia gasped. Her hands flew, reflexively in front of her, as she raced forward.

Anguished screams splintered her consciousness, before she realized they were her own. She reached into her pocket, and claimed her cell phone. Her hands shook so violently that it made the screen blur. Finally, able to dial the number, she placed the phone on the floor next to John, after turning the speaker on. She pulled a cloth from the table, and pressed it with the palm of her hand into the saturated wound.

Cynthia leaned over John, and whispered through tears. "I love you." Her breath caught as though the air was heavier than she remembered. She ignored the feeling.

"My life has been better, complete because of you." Cynthia choked. "You are God showing mercy on me; you are a gift." She traced the smooth features of her husband's too young face. "I don't want you to go, but if you have to I will see you when my chores are through." Cynthia reminded John of their favorite country song, 'I'll be loving you.' She laid down beside him, and held pressure to the wound. Her eyes closed as she gently caressed his hair, with her other hand.

"Not my will, but thine, Lord." Cynthia whispered through tears clogging her throat.

"I can only imagine." Cynthia started John's favorite contemporary gospel song by Mercy Me; it had always given him strength. She prayed in the darkest corner of her mind, where she held out hope that God would allow her to keep this wonderful gift, that this time would be no different.

Police filled the house. Cynthia was only faintly aware that they had arrived. She was pulled from John's still-body, so paramedics could do their job. She didn't know if it would help. John was so pale, and the paramedic had said something about diminished breath sounds, and a sucking chest wound.

Cynthia stopped listening. She couldn't bear it. She glanced over at Max as the medic checked his vitals. It was then that the truth had been revealed. It was not Cynthia, but John that had delivered the fatal blow. The crystal shard was still lodged deep in Max's carotid artery. The huge puddle of blood under his body, was all the evidence that she needed: Max was dead, and John had saved her life.

Cynthia stood numbly by, as the paramedics worked, feverishly to save John's life. She felt so selfish. What would John be coming back to? She had no right to thrust this life upon him, and yet she could not let him go.

"Give me a Vaseline-gauze. I need two large bore IV's." The young blonde paramedic with brown eyes, and dark rimmed glasses called, while he ripped John's shirt open.

"Bag him. Do it in the bus! Load and go, kid." The much older medic with salt and pepper hair, and too much in the mid-section amended as he walked to the head of the stretcher.

Cynthia breathed a little easier when the senior medic took control of the scene. She understood the younger medic's desire to learn, or even practice those skills that he had already obtained, but she was relieved to see that it wouldn't be on John.

By the time they arrived at the hospital, John had a tube down his throat that ended at a large blue bag; the lead medic was pumping the bag with his right hand every few seconds. He also had a needle protruding from both his right and left arm, and there was a patch of gauze with some sort of a jelly substance in the middle of it that was taped down over the gunshot wound; only three sides were taped. Cynthia thought it a very crude method for stabilizing such an obviously life threatening wound, but John was a lot less blue.

Cynthia felt as though the ground was moving beneath her feet. How could this be happening? She had left Black Heart behind, and yet it was reaching up like the hand of death; come to rip out her very reason for being.

She rushed behind the medics as they raced John through the emergency room doors. She absently watched as the silver doors bellowed open, welcoming in yet another moment of gore. She pressed forward, but was stopped short by an older nurse that encouraged her to allow the staff in the room to do their job. Cynthia looked at her hands. They were trembling, but worse still the evidence of her husband's horrific truth left them stained in crimson splotches.

40

"Can you believe it?" Sandra, a young nurse with brown hair, and bold green eyes asked as she fluffed Edward's pillow. "Lord, I knew New York was something else, but New Jersey? It kind of makes you wonder." The heavy set blonde with blue eyes, and too much make up countered while she massacred a piece of gum.

"Yeah, and that John guy was flown in here." the blonde confided.

"Shh!" Sandra warned.

"What Eddie? Oh, Eddie's good people. Besides, he probably doesn't even know the Benton's." Misty, the blonde waved a hand to dismiss Sandra's concerns.

Edward didn't' like the way Misty called him Eddie, but he was more concerned about what he could find out from the rehabilitation nurse, than what she was calling him.

"Say, what happened?" Edward smiled sheepishly. He watched as Sandra cast a weary glance at Misty, and then Misty shrugged.

"This John guy got shot. He was flown in from Morristown, New Jersey. We're the closest trauma unit." Misty seemed to puff up with pride. "Said the guy's in a bad way, but he's in good hands. Dr. Monroe is the best there is." Misty boasted.

"Here we go." Sandra rolled her eyes. "You're just in love with the guy. He walks on water, according to this one." Sandra held a hand over her mouth, as if telling some juicy gossip, while pointing her thumb over her shoulder at Misty.

"Hush, honey. She's just jealous, because Dr. Monroe asked me to dance at the company Christmas party last year." Misty smiled so big, Edward thought her cheeks might pop.

The loud thwack of elastic snapping filled the room as Sandra yanked the glove off of her left hand. "My dance cart's all full, honey." Sandra gloated, while hoisting her left hand forward. A large princess ring sparkled in the florescent lighting.

"Oh, my God!" Misty shrieked, then darted around the bed, and spent the next ten minutes swooning over the large diamond on Sandra's left ring finger.

By the time Misty and Sandra left Edward's room, he knew everything about Sandra's wedding: flower arrangements, dress sizes for the entire wedding party, and where they would go for the honeymoon, but he knew next to nothing about John Benton's shooting.

Edward couldn't imagine who would want John Benton dead, but he had a sneaking suspicion that Max was somehow tied up in it.

Edward again pushed back his fear of the impending images, as he flipped on the small television. He searched the channels for nearly fifteen minutes, before finding a newscast about the New Jersey shooting.

"Trouble just keeps piling up for Morristown, New Jersey." A short blonde woman with red lipstick was standing outside of the New York trauma unit.

"Yet another fiasco unfolds with... yep... you guessed it... our friends at Black Heart, and The Truth." The reporter shook her head, when a photo of Max flashed onto the screen.

"Sources say this man, who has been identified as simply Max was found dead at the Benton's home in Morristown New Jersey. According to Cynthia Benton, wife of John Benton, now in critical condition; Max broke into the couple's Morristown home, and held them at gunpoint. The standoff ended in a struggle that claimed the life of Max, and left John Benton in critical condition." The reporter went on to say there was nothing further at this time.

Edward flipped off the television. So that's it, he thought. All is lost. Max is dead, and with him any proof that Edward had not been responsible for the deaths of the child agents had perished alongside him.

C H A P T E R

41

A bright light like nothing Nick had ever seen billowed from the inner chamber. Sweat immediately beaded on his forehead and upper lip. His breath came in heavy pulls, as he carried Tristan further into the heat and light.

The room was lined with three torches per wall. The center of the cave floor was adorned in a large metal cooking pot, sitting atop a group of pikes that were wedged out; the side of the wedges snaked up the pot holding it in place. A fire licked the air above. The walls had a hollow groove hewn out that connected in the four corners of the chamber. Fire blazed from the hollow trenches.

Nick hurriedly ran to a pallet of fur, and checked the placement to make certain it was a goodly distance from the many blazing fires that had been set. Satisfied that it was, Nick laid Tristan's sleeping form on the pallet. He then hurried over to Penny who was doing the same. His side ached from the weight of Tristan's body, but bending to place him on the pallets was worse. Nick breathed through the flashes of pain, as he turned to Penny.

Judging by the scowl of disapproval on Penny's face, her opinion was the same concerning their smoldering accommodations. But he was relieved that she did not seem to be aware of the wealth of pain that he was truly in.

"What's going on?" Nick finally broke the silence.

Penny grabbed a torch in either hand, and started out of the inner chamber to the tunnel exiting the chamber to the right.

"Aunt Jordan knows," Penny mumbled.

"Knows what? How to barbeque us?" Nick grumbled.

"Look, there's a perfectly good explanation for all of this." Penny waved her hands around to indicate the fire-engulfed room. "And I'll be glad to explain it, but for now grab two of those torches, and put them down that tunnel a few feet." Penny indicated the middle tunnel as she disappeared into the tunnel to the right.

Nick watched, as the darkness was vanquished by the torches in each of her hands. The cave wall was illuminated with an eerie-ethereal-glow around Penny as she went.

After a few minutes of fighting with a hole, already dug out for the torch, Nick was able to bury the second torch. He tried desperately to ignore the pain streaking through his side. In an attempt to place his thoughts elsewhere, he allowed his mind to drift. He absently wondered where everyone was. He would have thought that at least Kirsten and Aniahi would stay behind, while Lane and Jordan cleared the village of the enemy tribe, but the chamber had been void of anyone; not that he could blame them. Nothing could survive in that heat.

When he finally made it back to the inner chamber, Penny had already claimed two more of the blazing torches. He found her fast at work in the far left tunnel.

"Grab two more, and place them in the tunnel we came in, okay?" Penny cast Nick a simple smile, as she continued to thrust the last torch into the hole. The loose dirt was crumbling back into the hole, making the task more difficult; just as it had done with Nick in the tunnel to the right.

Nick moved to her side, and started to twist the torch like a screw into the hole.

"There." Nick smiled, as he moved his arms away from the torch, and brushed into Penny by accident.

It felt so good having Penny here; yet Nick wished she were any place else on earth. He couldn't fathom anything happening to her. His hand rose automatically, in compliance with the terrible thought. His fingers snaked into her hair; his body seemed to have a mind of it's on, as he moved unbidden to the feel of her so close.

His eyes drank in the site of her: emerald eyes, gazed up at him, as if mesmerized by an awakened need she did not yet understand. Their eyes met then, as every fear, every unspoken need poured into the drought of their unquenched desire.

Nick broke the kiss first. His body was tingling with tiny fires that had been ignited throughout his nerve endings. It was always hard for him to stop, but he never wanted to force anything on Penny; enough had been forced upon them both, without his male-hormones adding to it. But as Nick pulled back, Penny tightened the grip she had on his hair, and deepened the kiss.

Nick's heart slammed into his chest, alarms sounded in his head that this was not the right time. How many times had he and Penny talked about the basis of their relationship? How many times had she equated their time together to the characters of that movie, Speed?

Nick's mind screamed that their relationship was on the precipice of something; but what?

He pulled away then, and in Penny's eyes he could see the same fear.

"I'll get the torches." Nick said in a voice husky with desire.

He turned back for a moment. "In time, we will see." He smiled. "I believe there is more to us than just two people seeking refuge in a storm." He turned then, and started for the other two torches.

Penny's heart pounded in her chest as she stood frozen to the spot. She wanted to scream. Something was wrong with her. What woman wouldn't cut her chest open, and throw her heart, without reservations, at Nick's feet: he was handsome, sweet, understanding, and unfortunately very intuitive. Penny kicked a piece of clay away from her foot.

"Don't beat yourself up kid." Lane's voice broke through the silence.

"How long have you been there?" Penny scowled.

"Long enough." Lane flashed an innocent smile.

"Wait, what are you doing here? Oh Lord, your Aunt Jordan is going to freak!" Lane was moving now, as he gently took Penny's arm, and ushered her back to the inner chamber.

Penny pulled her arm away. "I'm okay, believe me." She smiled. "Besides I know a lot about our new friends." Penny gestured toward the village.

"How?"

"Doesn't matter. School paper," Penny shook her head. "The point is that I do, and I need to talk to Aunt Jordan. Where is she?"

A shadow fell over Lane's blue eyes, as he nodded in the same direction that Penny had pointed.

"She and Garrison went to find Kirsten. She's missing."

Penny nodded.

"Nick and I brought the children. They are in the fire pit." Penny cast a disapproving glare at Lane.

"Sorry, Jordan said make it look like daylight." Lane confessed.

Penny softened her look, as she gave her uncle's arm an affectionate squeeze. "I understand, but seriously the smallest amount of light hurts their eyes; you don't have to torch the place literally." Penny laughed.

"Got it." Lane nodded.

"So, what's back there?" Penny asked, as she started to move toward the inner chamber.

"Another chamber." Lane sniffed. "I found Aniahi."

42

Julie left the DON (Director of Nurses) office, and decided to make a quick run through the E.R., as shocked as she was to hear about Edward Stanton being the HOD for Black Heart, a CIA funded organization—she had to admit it made sense. But a child killer? Something about that did not sit well with the reaction that Edward had had to Amber Noel. It was as though she had pulled a viper out of her purse, and laid it on the bed beside the man.

People led by fear did not go out looking to kill the source of that fear—that was hate—the reaction Edward displayed was clearly fear... if not hesitation, or something akin to it. Julie was afraid of spiders. She wasn't about to go into an area heavily populated with spiders, and kill them. She knew plenty of people that would share her sentiment concerning the eight legged pests, but what would have to happen to make a grown man cringe at the mere sight of a baby?

Julie wasn't sure, but she was determined to find out, and she knew exactly who to ask.

She was no child. She was a grown up, a woman of God. She had learned a long time ago that God placed people in her life for a reason.

Edward Stanton may not be meant to spend the rest of his life at her side, but God meant for her to make sure that he did know who He was! One way or the other, though she may not reap the fruits of her labor, Julie would make sure Edward Stanton, former HOD for Black Heart, supposed child-killer, knew exactly who her God was!

With that, Julie slammed the palm of her hand into the square-silver button to open the doors to the emergency department.

Julie rounded the corner, and saw the nurses' desk. The faster she walked the more each step felt infused with the righteous direction of the Holy Spirit. No matter what may come, she knew with all of her being that this was her path.

Janice Turner sat behind the wrap-around-mahogany desk; with her glasses perched on the end of her nose. She looked to Julie like nothing more than a wise-old-owl. Her gaunt-pointy little nose lifted in righteous-indignation, as she cast a withering glance in Julie's direction. She shook her head causing her spray of salt and pepper curls to bounce, playfully atop her bone-thin shoulders.

"Don't start with me. You, old bat." Julie laughed, as she pointed a manicured nail at Janice.

"Every time I see you; it's what do you know Janice. You need to find you another informant." Janice stepped away from the desk, as she stapled a file. "I have work to do."

"Yeah, sure you have work to do; Facebook." Julie ran around the nurses' station, and grabbed Janice by a bony-arm. "I'll make you some homemade apple pie."

"Not hungry." Janice sighed, as she rubbed her flat belly.

"Janice!" Julie eyed her frustrating friend.

"Okay... Okay." Janice laughed. "Buy me lunch, and I'll spill the beans."

"I thought you weren't hungry." Julie raised her brow, but then shook her head, deciding not to rock the proverbial boat.

"Okay!" Julie clapped her hands three really quick times.

"And I want that pie." Janice pointed a bony-finger, as she raised a brow, she peered, threateningly over the rim of her glasses.

Julie grabbed Janice's blue smock, and flattened it over her tummy.

"How in the world do you stay so skinny?" Julie shook her head, then clucked her tongue.

"Metabolism," Janice smirked. "Don't hate. It has its draw-backs," Janice said, while tightening her blue smock over her flat chest.

As Julie pulled the bag of apples form the refrigerator, she couldn't help but think about all Janice had told her.

Janice had gone on, and on about a man named Max being hired by Edward Stanton to track Jordan Buckley-Gates... Julie remembered that name being in the news, though she couldn't imagine why she had not remembered seeing the name associated with Edward Stanton's.

Apparently, Edward had a grudge against Jordan's grandfather, Cecil Schooner, because he killed Edward's girlfriend, and one true love, Amorous Dawson.

Max had gone rogue, and started to manage things in a way that would leave Edward holding the proverbial bag; but why?

Janice had overheard John Benton's wife, Cynthia Benton talking to one of the police officers. Cynthia was giving her statement. Cynthia had told it all. Max had broken into their home, and held the couple at gunpoint. A struggle ensued, and Max was killed. John Benton was struggling for his life in the ICU (Intensive Care Unit).

Julie would bake Janice her apple pie, and deliver it to the E.R. Afterward, she planned to make a trip to the ICU. Julie knew the visiting hours. If she got there in time, she was bound to run into Mrs. Benton. People in crisis liked to talk.

Julie laughed, as she walked up the corridor toward the ICU; she would never forget Janice's reaction, as the other nurses swarmed in like vultures on road kill.

Julie sat the pie down with the plates, forks, and napkins she had brought. She winked at Janice, and kept walking.

"You're the devil." Janice grouched.

"Learned from the best. Enjoy 'your' pie." Julie emphasized the word your, as she tossed a comical glance over her shoulder, and disappeared out the double-doors.

As Julie walked through the white-washed walls of the hospital halls, she felt in some way treacherous. She didn't want to misrepresent herself, or lie to Cynthia Benton, but if she came right out and said that she was there on Edward's behalf—even though it was his spiritual behalf—Julie just knew that Cynthia would shut down.

Still, Julie knew that God was Truth, and He could not operate in deception—lies. Julie would have no other recourse, but to lay her chips on the table, and let them fall where they may. (I was born and come into the world to testify to the truth. All who love the truth recognize that what I say is true. John 18:37, I am the way, the truth, and the life John 14:6).

Edward Stanton had a long-dark-road ahead of him, and it would be even-darker without Christ's holy light to show the way.

Julie was determined to do what she knew God's will for her life to be; Edward needed light to find his way through a very dark situation; Julie prayed that she could be the vessel for that light.

43

Cynthia pulled the thin-white-cotton blanket up around her shoulders, in an attempt to ward off the chill. Her fingers felt like ice. The hospital was so cold. She had just been evicted from the ICU for the second time that afternoon. ICU visiting hours were ridiculous. She couldn't stand it when she was away from John.

Tears slipped from Cynthia's eyes, as she thought of John in the hospital bed connected to all those tubes. She felt so utterly helpless and alone. The idea of John leaving her here in this world to brave it alone was unthinkable.

She bowed her head, as the weight of that possibility crashed down upon her. She prayed hard for John's condition. Though it looked bleak, she had witnessed miracles in the face of insurmountable odds. She knew that God could do anything. She knew, also that Faith was the key that unlocked God's power, and poured His blessings in the form of miracles on His people.

Cynthia didn't know what God's will, concerning John would be. She wanted to be brave, and walk in the courage that she knew would be given to her if God were to take him home, but her heart was heavy with grief. The moment she thought to pray for strength, to make it if John were to pass from this world to the next, her heart and mind seemed to reject the idea. It was as if God was telling her not to give up. He was demanding her belief; nothing less than her complete and total commitment to the knowledge that He would see John through.

She searched her mind and heart; she took inventory of her deepest beliefs—did she truly believe that God would show up, and heal John wholly, completely? She thought of the mission trips she had been on: holding hands with other missionaries, praying for the healing of a baby born with a hole in its heart, or without the basic necessities of digestion; a mother malnourished to the point of death, trying to give birth all the while gasping for her last breath, but determined to bring the new life of her child into the world; a father working in the fields without the strength required to walk across the floor, but determined to make a better life for his family. Every occasion, Cynthia had prayed with complete resolve that the miracle she asked for would come.

Why now? In the face of her husband lying on the cusp of death, could she not just know? Cynthia leaned over, and put her head in her hands.

"Lord, please give me the Faith that I need to believe that you can heal John." She tried so hard to remain strong as she prayed. She didn't want to stress the baby, but there was something so humbling; so good about being real with God that it shook her to her core. This is where she went for the answers. This is how she made it through her hardest days; her best days; through all of her days.

She gave in completely to the truth of what she felt: the sadness, the doubt, the shame, and the fear... she laid every unchecked emotion out for God to see; though she knew that these were nothing she could hide, she knew there were things she could hold on to; things that could corrupt the spirit, and destroy the very fabric of a Christian's Faith; those human emotions so easily triggered, she would gladly throw before God's feet, and allow Him full disclosure. He would take them. She didn't want them, she didn't need them, and they certainly would not help her pray for John's healing.

Cynthia was so caught up in her commitment to seek God's face that at first she did not sense the lady sit down in the chair to the left of her. It wasn't until she felt the hand on her back, and heard the soft prayer being said on her behalf that Cynthia looked up into the powder-blue eyes, and the gently aging face of a woman with soft blond hair. Cynthia noted the veil of white hair shrouding the woman's beautiful countenance. She almost seemed angelic as her face and eyes glowed with the love of Christ.

Cynthia felt a pull like nothing she had ever experienced before… she opened her mouth to say something; anything, but then closed it again as she fell into the woman's outstretched arms, and began sobbing.

Julie felt no hesitation… she knew that God had sent her to this woman, and for reasons she could not explain, she knew that this woman was John Benton's wife, Cynthia.

Julie had come here seeking answers on Edward Stanton's behalf, instead she had found the truth. She was here for a greater purpose. God had sent her to be with Cynthia as she walked through the valley of death—holding on to her husband's hand—begging for his life.

Julie had done the same with her own husband. In the end, for reasons she still did not know God had taken Ronald home to be with Him. Julie might have been angry with God, if it had not been His presence that was holding her to this world. Her children needed her; her husband needed to know he was leaving behind their mother, a woman capable of holding things together in his absence. Julie could not imagine life without God. He was her everything, and though she had not understood His reasons, He was her life raft; her connection to sanity; He was her all and all.

It had taken Julie almost two years to feel like the air was not full of led. It had taken the birth of her grandchildren to plant her feet firmly on solid ground… she had to be here; her children needed her, but most of all she needed to guide their hand as they struggled to raise their own children. She needed to help Katie learn to be comfortable as a mother with the demands of a child as young as Amber Noel.

Julie could feel the pain, and uncertainty of that time, and she knew that that was the path that Cynthia Benton traveled now.

Julie gently tightened the embrace as she willed all of her strength to be passed to Cynthia. In that moment, Julie knew that no matter the outcome—Cynthia would be changed forever by this moment: the way that she looked at life, the way that she thought of John, the way that she treated him; every detail—if he survived—of their lives would be forever changed by these moments spent in despair; praying for his life. Julie knew, also that she and Cynthia would be bound forever by the all-consuming reality that God is the only way to make it through a grief born of this kind of loss.

The years seemed to drain away as Julie allowed her heart to once again dive into that long-dormant anguish that had claimed so much of her existence. It was there that she would find the way to bring her new friend out of the waste lands of death's valley, and into the sheltering arms of their Risen Savior.

44

All of the life seemed to drain from his body, as Lane allowed one last look in the direction of the other chamber. Why had she done it? Why would she hide away, and languish, alone?

Aniahi had seemed fine when she and Kirsten had laid down, before he and Jordan left to rid the mountain side of the enemy. Lane racked his mind for any sign; anything that he may have missed that would have told him what Aniahi, had not… that she was dying. There was nothing. Aniahi was healthy; she was strong.

Lane could only imagine that Aniahi had left the cave not long after he and Jordan. There would be only one thing precious enough to pull Aniahi from the sanctity of the inner-chamber: the children.

Lane imagined Aniahi running across the valley floor, trying to stay low so the archers would not see her, but someone had seen her; someone had run her through with a spear. Aniahi had made her way into the other chamber, a place that even Lane had never ventured; there she had breathed her last. She had died like a dirty secret.

Lane felt so guilty. Didn't he know that Aniahi would go after Amelia and Tristan?

He staggered to a wall, and fell against the clay surface. He felt so heavy. He wanted time to mourn her loss. Didn't a life as selfless—as devoted to others as hers had been deserve to be championed in some way? How could this fierce medicine woman; his grandmother; his mother; how could she just hide away… alone; how could she just die without the benefit of family surrounding her?

Aniahi had rallied for so many, but in the end not one had stood by, as she took her last breath.

Lane gasped for air as the finality of that truth closed around his heart. He leaned over, and placed his hands on his knees to relieve some of the heaviness surrounding his lungs and heart. The very feeling of loss was so real; so tangible that it felt as though it would snatch the very life from him. Memories of his childhood guided by Aniahi's learned hand flashed before his eyes.

Lane was twelve again hearing the news that his adopted parents would never be coming home. Aniahi had scooped him into her arms, and in that moment she had become all things to him. This woman that was not related to him in any other way, but circumstance had shifted willingly into a place of authority, love, and yes home. She had in that instant become his mother, his grandmother, his village healer, and the only place on earth a young boy that knew so much loss could want to be. Aniahi was home.

Lane's mind ventured further into the past, to the time when he had first met Aniahi. New to the village, he clung to his mother's side. This new world stood out in stark contrast to that of the small apartment they had left behind in the states. His mother and father had adopted him at birth after the death of his birth mother. The Gates had tucked him into their busy lives with as much love, as they had time to give. Missionaries to The Truth allotted them little time to care and attend to the needs of a small child, but they felt the hand of God guiding them in the decision to adopt Lane.

The call to move to the Cadotion village had come two weeks after Lane's fourth birthday. Lane had vivid memories of the ancient-looking village. Bird calls and indigenous plant life had been a generous part of his life: The Garden, where Lane had been raised was filled with exotic plants and birds that sung their happy-warnings to all that ventured, too far into their claimed territory—but as Lane grew up in the midst of the village, his young mind filled with new sounds that had never before been a part of the wild-beauty that filled the exotic serenity of The Garden: growls, screams that sounded as if they were born of warning rather than desperation filled the surrounding mountains. Tents of tanned animal hide lined the valley floor, and children played off to the side, as though nothing were amiss. Yet in the deepest part of his young mind he knew to heed the warnings, issued by the animals that filled the snowcapped mountains surrounding the crude village.

Lane clung fiercely to his mother's leg. He sensed a calm in his parents that he had grown accustom to, but did not fully understand. He watched as a woman approached: her dark-tanned face filled with so much wisdom, seemed to have its own gravitational pull that drew him in. Peeking out from behind his mother's legs, Lane measured the woman with open intrigue. Her eyes were the color of dark honey, her raven black hair was pulled back into a web of intricate braids that were tied at the nape of her neck, and exited in three larger braids that flowed to her waist. Pastel robes played on the breeze as she bent low, and held her arms out to him. Lane moved automatically to the beckoning arms of the enchanting stranger. From that day to this, he had always found peace in their depths. Aniahi had been that woman. Lane had been drawn to her by a supernatural force that would not make itself known until several years later.

God had brought Lane and his parents, purposefully to the Cadotion village that day to teach them about the Christian faith. He had supernaturally readied all who were created for that very task. As Lane's parents passed from this earth to the heavenly realm, Aniahi had stepped willingly into the role of mother and teacher to Lane. She had readied him for his return to the states. She had made all of the necessary arrangements. She had contacted The Truth. She had bid her dear grandson; son; student, farewell as she watched him board the plane with the agent from The Truth; Aniahi had suffered in silence never allowing her self-assured learned mask to fade from sight. She had watched as Lane lifted into the air, and left her to return to her own world of medicine woman. He had never known then the personal sacrifice that his wonderful friend had made. It wasn't until he had had to leave Amelia, to take Jordan back to the states—she was to give birth to Tristan that he would come to understand the enormous cost to one's mental, physical and spiritual being; leaving a child behind, no matter the reason was a hefty price to pay. Worse still, he knew that he would return for his beautiful daughter. Aniahi, on the other hand, had no way of knowing. She had no way of knowing that the little boy, she had so willingly tucked into her world would return to her. For all she knew, as she stood watching him board the plane to the states, to be trained, as his parents had as a missionary for The Truth, this would be her last time seeing her student; her grandson; her son; her friend.

That time seemed a million years passed as Lane thought of the end that had beset the wonderful woman that had given so much to be all things to him. She would be so greatly missed. He had no idea how the Father would move him from this moment. He had no way to understand how God had brought him through the times of loss in the past, but He had. He needed to get a grip. His family needed him.

Lane thought of his daughter and son; they were waiting for him in the inner-chamber. They would want to know where Aniahi was. Who would teach Amelia all that she would need to know? How could she become the next medicine woman if...? Lane couldn't finish the thought. It felt so wrong; so destitute a place for his mind to venture that the very notion was immediately rejected. He thought of the village. All of those that lay dead at the hands of the enemy... he wasn't even sure if there would be a tribe left to need a medicine woman.

Plans had been made, and God had laughed.

"Do you, Lord? Do you laugh when we make plans?" Lane looked up at the clay-covered cave, but his thoughts were well beyond the mountain. He now stood in the throne room at his Master's feet, boldly daring to ask the question that was filling his entire being with sorrow.

Tears fell down Lane's cheeks, as he slid to his knees, and beseeched the One; THE ONLY ONE who knew the answers.

"Why, God? Why do you take everyone that I love?"

Lane knew that the question would seem a betrayal to most, but he had always been candid with God. He knew no other way.

"I go to prepare a place for you." God gently reminded Lane with the whispered words across his soul... (John 14:3) Lane remembered the verse so well; it was one that the minister had read at his parent's funeral. It had given him peace, as it did now in the death of a woman that had served so many purposes, been so many things to him.

"I feel alone Lord. How can I protect my family in this?" Lane begged; his head hung in his hands, pitifully.

"Nothing can separate you from me; not life nor death; not angels nor demons; not height, nor depth..." (Romans 8:38-39) Again God breathed His truth into Lane's situation. Every word was so pertinent to the unbelievable-reality of all that Lane had experienced... the mountains standing all around him, the demons in the past, as well as the present that rallied against him and his family, and the death of so many close to him; the words were like soothing balm to his ailing soul.

Lane felt good knowing that God was still there with him, but he worried that he would forget. How could he be reminded in this desolate place of such a wonderful truth?

"I have put my words in your mouth, and covered you with the shadow of my hand." (Isaiah 51:16)

Lane smiled, as he moved to his feet. "Thank you, Lord. I will not forget." Lane turned back to Aniahi's final resting place one last time, and then with the strength borrowed only from a Risen Savior; A Mighty God; he set his mind to the task of protecting his family.

45

Finally making it into the cage, Garrison pricked the stem of the small dart into Kirsten's neck. He hadn't been sure if the device would be useful. He had packed it because it was sharpened plastic, and would make it through airport security. He had only a handful of the darts.

The dart had been a prototype, and had only been tested on rats. The weapon was a spinoff of the dissolving bullet that he had shot Jordan with, to fool the paramedics into calling the coroner to have Jordan pronounced dead. The pill mimicked the signs of death. Garrison claimed her body, and took her back to The Garden. The bullet was designed to mask the heart rate, lower the body temperature a few degrees, and change the skin color to a gray pallor associated with death. The dart on the other hand was designed merely to incapacitate the enemy for a short time, until they could be taken to a secured location for questioning.

A small team of scientists, associated with The Truth, worked tirelessly day and night to make new humane ways to bring the enemy down.

Garrison had told Jordan of the dart; they had agreed that pulling a teenage girl from a cage, in the middle of the advancing enemy, in the dead of night... would probably cause some kinks in the need for quiet. Jordan and Garrison, both had been worried about using any weapon meant for the field that had only been tested on lab rats, but they had both witnessed the accuracy of the white coats at Black Heart, and they had also watched on many occasion as the trials had moved from rat to a human host. All of the tests had been successful except one. It was a chance that they would have to take. Either way, Kirsten's life was in mortal danger: whether from an insufficiently tested field weapon, or the enemy forces that stormed passed her cage, determined to take the Cadotion village. Kirsten was moments away from an early demise if a swift decision was not made to change her circumstance.

In the end, Jordan had agreed to the use of the dart. If the dart took Kirsten's life, it would be a far easier death, than the one they were sure the Manerky had in mind for the girl.

Garrison threw Kirsten's limp body over his shoulder. He could feel the even breathing of her now peacefully sleeping form. If he could somehow manage to take her safely through the Manerky, and back to the hidden sanctuary of the cave, then all would be well.

Jordan still stood quiet as she waited for the enemy tribesman to make his move. Would he attack, or would he chalk the feeling up to his imagination. She couldn't continue to wait for the warrior to make up his mind. She needed to help Garrison get Kirsten back to the cave. She was sure by now her ex-partner and friend had obtained the girl. The standoff that she was now in with the enemy warrior was starting to weigh on her patience.

Jordan listened as she heard a different sound come from the warrior that had brushed into her. The sound was not that of the clicking, or squawking of a bird, or even the grunting, and hissing of a monkey or cat. This sound was more guttural. The sound seemed fiercer, and almost as if it were a warning.

Jordan realized that the warrior had finally given into the need to follow the urging of the instinctual warning; it was a warning that she too had had in the field. It was the basic gripping alarm that buzzed in her being that said something was not right. It had saved her life, and had never steered her wrong, and it was sounding just as clearly now.

She had no other recourse, but to react. She listened to the howling-growl as it emitted from the warrior, and allowed the call to guide her hand. With all her might, she thrust the butt of her palm out and up: she felt the impact as the fleshy part of her palm met with the bony prominence of the enemy's nose. The sickening crunch of his nose bone, being shoved forcefully into his brain resonated throughout her senses, as the echoing-call of warning ceased in an abrupt moment of dead silence.

Garrison heard the warning call. He knew too that it was Jordan that had silenced the enemy's warning, but that the effort to foil the call was too little, too late. The damage had been done. The Manerky would be aware of the enemy among them. Now more than ever, he and Jordan needed to get Kirsten back to the cave. Once she was in the safety of the lighted cave, he and Jordan could make a plan for ridding the enemy from the village or escape. Garrison voted for the less heroic plan. The one that he felt would keep them all alive. But somewhere in the recesses of his awareness, he knew that Jordan would vote to stay; she would stand with her friends, the Cadotion people; she would fight for their right to live in freedom of tyranny. In that same part of his awareness, he knew that he too, would stay with her.

Garrison had no way of letting Jordan know that he was carrying Kirsten back to the cave. He could only start that way, and hope that Jordan would do the same.

Then, as if she had read his thoughts, Garrison heard Jordan make the pitiful attempt at the train whistle he had taught her. It was a call between the two of them that had many meanings, but in this moment, he knew exactly what his old partner and friend was trying to convey. She was alive, and she was headed back to the cave.

Garrison allowed a short burst of the same call to let Jordan know he understood, and had Kirsten in his care.

Jordan heard the answering call of Garrison. She side stepped the fallen enemy, and moved in the direction of the cave. She had to be careful not to be caught by any of the other warriors. Now that they knew of her and Garrison's presence among them, they would certainly be listening out for any discrepancies in the way that she and Garrison moved.

The Manerky were highly trained killers that walked in utter darkness; being able to pick up on the subtle differences, in the way that an enemy carried him or herself in their midst would be all too simple a task. With hundreds of them stalking the valley floor before her, Jordan could not run. She had to maintain her status as before; she would have to pretend to be one of them, especially now that she and Garrison had used the signal to alert each other of their intent.

Jordan froze as a hand reached up, and touched the back of her head. Her eyes searched the darkness madly, trying to see who was near her. Then she realized that she was trying, instinctively to use the wrong sense again. She eased back into the senses that she knew she could rely on in this moment of complete darkened terror. What had she felt?

The hand was big; too big to be Garrison's. Besides, Garrison would be headed to the cave. He would know that though he may want to, heading back for Jordan would mean certain death for Kirsten. Garrison was as mission minded as she. He would always make the decision that best insured the mission's success.

Jordan waited, glued to the spot for what she was sure would come. One of the enemy tribesman had caught up with her, and he would most surely end her life. She had to make a decision about what to do, and quick. Jordan dropped to the ground in a split as she felt hands reach under her arm, and pull her back up right. That was impossible. The enemy was as blind as she to the darkness. They could only rely on hearing, touch, smell, feeling. Nothing about those four senses would have been able to help the enemy see Jordan, as she sank low into the split in order to thwart the enemy behind her.

Jordan started to struggle away from the massive hands that held her fast, but then she was struck by how gentle, but final the grip was. Whoever held her was not intending to hurt her, but restrain her, but why? All of a sudden a large hand closed over Jordan's eyes... not her mouth, but her eyes. Why would the enemy cover her eyes in such complete darkness? Her eyes were of no use to her. And then, just as if a hand had waved over her scattered thoughts, and magically assembled them into a clearer picture; Jordan knew. She pressed back into the massive bulk of her husband as her body relaxed, but only a little. The enemy still stalked before her, but now she felt a little more capable.

Though Jordan's eyes were covered, she could see a red glow force its way through the massive-beige hand covering her face. In that moment, Jordan knew what Lane was doing. She heard the bitter shrieks of the enemy protest, and then she felt her body as it relaxed, and then drifted into oblivion...

186

Lane could see, though no one else could, but that did not leave him safe from all of the threats that Jordan and Garrison had faced. It merely gave him a better insight, as to what was friend and foe. He had seen Jordan while blindfolded; nothing seemed to make it passed her keen intellect. He was just happy that this time he had.

Lane gently, but firmly covered Jordan's eyes. He hoped that she would understand by the simple gesture the unyielding need to keep her eyes closed. He turned away from the rushing enemy, the animalistic cries of warning... he sought with all of his soul that place that existed inside of him—solely for his Savior. In that place, as before he knew that the power of God would come. It had happened before. Once, when he was in a place so dark that he had believed God-Himself had forgotten him. That he had been abandoned by the Almighty, to the darkest fate he had ever known. It was in that place that he had been reminded of that power, that all-consuming power that existed in all of God's children, but went untapped because they did not believe—did not ask.

Lane had been strapped to a metal bed, with hundreds of sharpened metal shards piercing, relentlessly into his skin at every point. He had lost hope. Jordan was tied in the corner, while Garrison was hanging, mercilessly—thought to be dead—from a noose in the opposite corner. The room had been set up in an old abandoned farmhouse, on the outskirts of Morristown, New Jersey. There, Tommy Hayden would do his worst.

Lane had forgotten about the power that lived within him, stored there by the God of creation. He had been helpless for the moment, as he watched with his angel vision from his makeshift torture rack, as demons from the pits of hell danced around his beautiful love, his wife. Each of the gruesome, creatures, taunted her with their every pulsating-putrid breath. Four of the grotesque creatures leaned over facing her, and though she could not see the hideous creatures through her limited human vision... Lane could see that their taunting words were hitting their mark. With every hateful-slanderous remark made by the gruesome four, Jordan slumped further to the floor, further into that place of depression, and endless night.

Lane, in a fit of desperation sought that place inside him: that place of endless power, that place that God had filled-completely with His love and power, that place that existed in every one of His children; there he felt that warm light as it radiated forth, and was soon filling his body, and then the immediate area around his body. Finally, as if it could not be contained the light forged its way further into the room, as the metal shards melted under the extreme power. Lane stepped from the table—he could feel his strength return. The battle was on, and soon the four blasphemous-creatures, sent from the bowels of hell to rob God's children of the truth, were returned from wince they had come.

Now, as Lane peered out into the stalking enemy, once again that memory resonated so strongly within his spirit. He could feel that familiar light; it grew in his being, and forced its way into the earthly realm.

He watched as the animalistic-enemy covered their eyes, and screamed out in pain. The warriors closest to the power of God's-holy-light crumbled to the ground, and soon perished under the purity of that light. Other warriors farther to the back, merely covered their eyes and made their way to the sanctity of the mountain, but even their screams were unmistakably filled with pain.

Lane wasted no time, as he scooped up Jordan, who had passed out under the force of the power that she was so close to. He was thankful for the time she would have to rest; she hadn't gotten much sleep. Lane knew that God would protect her and the baby. His only concern now was of getting her back to the hidden cave, among their friends.

CHAPTER

46

Penny watched as the two children cuddled together. Modilo and Tristan were near the same age, but Tristan seemed to be twice the boy's size. Modilo had fussed a little in his sleep. Penny thought the child was having nightmares, brought on by the cruel attack of the village. She hated to think that the young boy was reliving the horrific event, but what was more unsettling was the knowledge that the worst was yet to be seen.

Penny watched as a still groggy, Amelia mopped the child's brow with a damp cloth. The girl went about in robotic-fever-pitch motions, as she buzzed around the inner chamber collecting herbs and spices to make a tea for the child. She had explained that the brewed herbs would settle the boy's nerves, and stay the nightmares. Now, as she crouched beside the child's body pressing an herb filled poultice to the unconscious child's forehead, Penny watched in open intrigue. The six-year-old was years beyond what her age would suggest. She had spent the bulk of her young life as apprentice to the village medicine woman, Aniahi.

Penny fought back the tears that burned at her eyes. How would her cousin, this amazing young apprentice deal with such suffocating news? Would she rise to the needs of the village, or would she at last default to the tiny girl that existed behind those liquid-amber eyes? Penny looked toward the entrance. Would there be a village left to need a medicine woman? The question rang through her mind. She wanted so much to believe that all would be well, but the destruction to the village was staggering—even worse, the worst of the battle had yet to rage.

Out of the corner of her eye, Penny could see Nick. She tried to placate her mind with thoughts of the children, the village, anything; it was useless. The fear that Nick was wrong about their budding romance seemed to override everything in her world. In a completely irrational-inexplicable manner it bulldozed its way over every thought, no matter how imperative it may be to her survival. She would have to face it one day. If they survived all that was ahead, she knew she would be face to face with a foe that intimidated her more than the real and present danger presented by the Manerky; life without Nick. He was her best friend, but if the veil was lifted from their midst, would it reveal a truth that would take him from her life forever? Were they merely Pons being placed in each other's lives by the merciless hands of fate? Would that callous act be the dividing line that would forever rip the only person she had truly trusted from her life forever?

Penny turned to a noise. Garrison was rushing through the entrance holding an unconscious Kirsten in his arms. Penny grabbed a Barton, and twirled it in her hand waiting for any enemy to enter behind him.

"Lane and Jordan shouldn't be far behind." Garrison offered, as he moved to the wall near where Nick was sorting through weapons. Nick had retrieved the weapons from the chamber, in which Lane had discovered Aniahi's body. Penny watched as Garrison tenderly laid Kirsten's body on a pallet of furs set to the side of where Nick was working.

Kirsten seemed so small amid the bulk of furs. Her face, even asleep, revealed the terrors of her unending day. Her hair cast about her face, was in a disarray of blonde tangles. Muddy streaks carved evidence of her fear down her cheeks. Penny's heart pivoted, wildly in her chest at the sight that Kirsten made. She seemed to be the 'poster child' for how they all were feeling, but unable to voice.

Penny's eyes raced to Amelia, who instinctively claimed some herbs and spices from the wall of clay pots, and walked to the hearth in the middle of the chamber. She took up a long rock with a rounded blunt end, and started to mince the mixture of herbs and spices together. Penny couldn't watch her cousin anymore. The child's lack of alarm in the horrific situation was unsettling. Penny wasn't sure what she needed the girl to do, but walking around as if oblivious to the present dangers that existed in her world was definitely not what Penny felt the girl should be doing. Penny was eighteen, and she wanted to run, screaming to Garrison. She wanted to hide behind him, and demand that he keep her safe from the impending doom that seemed intent to fall upon them. But, even as she thought of the childlike action, she knew that she could not afford such a luxury, and she was glad that for the time being, Amelia was standing in the gap. She was rising to the occasion. Even if Penny could not understand the girl's lack of fear, she was in some small way thankful for the call of duty that was ever-present in its stead. She definitely respected her cousin.

Nothing was ordinary in this place. Children too large for their age, and acting out of character for given circumstances—Invading enemy tribes were in their midst: threatening and claiming the lives of those closest-most precious to them... and still in the middle of it all, as unsettling as Amelia's reaction may have been, Penny knew that her own reaction was determinedly more so out of sync with the terrific situation. For as she looked across the chamber filled with sleeping forms, being cared for by a little medicine woman trapped in the body of her six-year-old cousin, as the enemy pressed in around them... Penny could only think of what would become of her and Nick.

Jordan's last memory had been of the searing heat. The heat that felt as though it would consume her very being: not just her body, but her soul; every part of that which made her Jordan would be pulled up into the inferno. She was desperate to escape that burning; she was sure that her skin had to be dripping like hot wax from a lit candle to the ground before her, and then she felt nothing. She saw nothing. Lane's hand seemed to turn red from the heat, she knew would consume her; Jordan collapsed against Lane. She was lost to the chaotic heat—the impressive light, buried beneath the darkness.

She woke again to another light. But this light was not as bright; even through the covering of Lane's large hand, she could tell that had she looked upon the light coming from the throne of God, it would have appeared brighter than the sun in the summer sky.

Where was she? She surely could not be with the enemy tribe, for none of the Manerky could bare to be in the faintest of light. Though this light was not as bright as the light before, it was more than a mere glimmer of a lit candle. It was many candles. The chamber was filled with light… And then just as the thought had synchronized the question and answer in an instant, Jordan knew that she was in the inner chamber. Of course, she had told Lane to make the chamber as bright as possible in order to keep the Manerky at bay. She pushed her body up from the pallet of fur, and immediately remembering the burning heat started to check her arms, legs, and face for any signs of trauma. She was sure her skin had to be covered with second or even third degree burns, but as she felt for the damage she was certain was there… to her surprise she found nothing.

Jordan looked up in awe. She finally spotted Lane coming toward her.

"How do you feel?" Lane asked, while he crouched by her side, and cupped her chin in his hand.

"Confused." Jordan admitted.

Lane's face screwed up in confusion. Eyeing her with open intrigue, he sat on the pallet next to her. "Why are you confused?"

"Why am I not burned to death?" Jordan stuttered through the question, her face a mask of bewilderment, she sought his eyes for the answer. The heat had been intense.

She had stood in the tree line outside of Beulah County, as the car had exploded into the air, only a few feet from the fully involved vehicle that held the bodies of the two women and man that she had brutally murdered, and yet this heat… the heat that was coming off of Lane was more intense than that.

Confusion left Lane's face; he pushed a lock of Jordan's hair behind her ear. "Spiritual light is not the same as physical light. Though, it is more powerful, it is detrimental to the enemy, but poses no threat to those it protects. Though you cannot and should not look directly at it… like with Moses as our Father passed in the cloud on Mount Sinai. Moses could not look directly at the Creator, but God allowed him to see the tail end of His glory… (Exodus 33:18-23) even that was too much for Moses as he turned white headed in God's presence, even the back of God's powerful light is so mighty that it would kill any that looked upon it. We are sinful Jordan. We are not yet pure. We will have to take upon a spiritual body, untouched by sin of the flesh, before we are able to stand in God's presence." Lane looked deep into Jordan's eyes, and she could see that he was waiting for evidence that she fully understood his explanation.

Jordan nodded her understanding, but then looked back at Lane. "But how can God's light come through you, and you not be killed?"

"Jesus died on the cross. His blood covers our sins. I am also part angel. I must turn myself over completely to my angelic side, and pray for that forgiveness, before His light can come through me. If not, I too would be laid to waste by His overwhelming power." Lane touched her face, as his eyes searched again for understanding.

Jordan gave a simple nod, and then tried to stand. Her knees still felt a little wobbly. Instead she sat back down and allowed her gaze to filter over the room. In the corner on the other side of the chamber, Jordan saw a pallet of fur, cluttered with the bodies of Modilo and Tristan. With a gasp, she crawled with all of her strength in the direction of the pallet. Jordan was so thankful the whole way that Lane had not hindered her efforts. She needed to be near them; she needed to know that they were indeed well.

The cave floor seemed to grow with every inch that she traversed, as she pulled her body to the pallet where her boys' laid. Funny, she thought. She already thought of Modilo as hers. He was hers. He was now and forever a part of their family. She and Lane would tuck him away in their lives, and help him to forget the pain of the past. They would encourage him to look back at the good times with his mother. They would keep her alive in his thoughts. They would somehow make her memory so clear that Modilo would not know if it were memories, or stories that he had heard that made his mother so real in his mind. Her goodness, her well-deserved place in the Cadotion tribe as a council leader would be etched in his young mind forever. He would be proud of her, just as Amelia was proud of her mother's and father's memory. Though she knew that she belonged with them, to them, she was never ashamed of where she had come from. She had always been encouraged to speak liberally about her biological parents. Modilo would be no different. Jordan would remind him of the courage that his mother had shown, as she stood in the midst of the Cadotion village, thrusting her arms in the air at the approaching enemy. She had tucked him out of harm's way, but as she fell to her death her son would be exposed. Still she had done all that she could to stop the enemy, and in the end her son was saved for her efforts.

The enemy had seen Modilo's mother. Her bold attempt at stopping the oncoming threat had blinded the enemy to the existence of her son—tucked beneath her robes. It was that heroic moment that would forever be the florescent-marker highlighting his past. His mother's courage would shout to him from beyond the grave; he would know that it was her blood that ran through his veins; her strength that filled his spirit. Though she may no longer be with him in the flesh, strength like that did not die. It lived on forever in the lives that it had touched. Jordan vowed to never let him forget.

She scooped the boys, her boys into her lap. She pulled them up to her breast, and hugged them both to her heart. She took a measure of comfort from their even breathing. They were only sleeping. Relief flooded through her. She looked up at Lane in wonder.

Lane hesitated for a moment, and then started to explain, but was interrupted by someone entering the room in a white suit.

Jordan felt dizzy as the white clad form came into view. Her arms floated out as if they had a mind of their own. She reflexively placed her left hand back over the boys' heads, as she felt them start to tumble down her chest.

Penny moved to her easily. Jordan brushed her niece's hair away from her too young face. What was she doing here? She was supposed to be in New Jersey attending school. Then, as if the realization of the all too real danger that Penny was truly being subjected to had poured down on her, Jordan bolted up right.

Tristan gave a groan of protest then, he nestled deeper into his mother's chest. Jordan soothed her hand across her son's brow, and then tenderly laid him back on the pallet of soft furs. Penny scooped Modilo up, as she mirrored her aunt's motions.

Jordan felt lost. What was she going to do? It seemed that the threat to her loved ones grew with every minute. Now, she was not only charged with the safety of her husband, her children, her former best friend, Nick, Kirsten, but now her niece. Jordan felt crushed under the mounted fear for her family's safety. She wanted to scoop them all up, and head to the shore line. She wanted to push a boat into the beautiful waters of the Cadotion River, and leave the enemy to do their worst. She felt the shame of that thought wash through her senses. How could she leave the Cadotion people: so gentle; so full of love and life; so full of laughter; how could she leave them to such a fate as this? Jordan knew even, as the question ran through her mind what the answer would be... she couldn't; she wouldn't. Though her family were sprawled around the inner chamber, right here with her; though she could escape with them to the river, and get them safely away from the ensuing battle; she knew that she could never leave the very people that had taught her so much: how to love; how to laugh, and yes, how to live and be gentle with not only herself, but with others.

Jordan looked around the chamber. She had to make a plan. She had to do something. But what? She felt split into two parts... part of her needed to stay with her children; her niece; her family... she needed to know that they were safe, but the trained agent inside of her screamed at the impractical thought. She would have to leave them, and pray that God would keep them safe in her absence. She would need everyone that could fight to be at her side. They did not have the luxury of sitting in the chamber. The light would offer safe haven for only so long. At some point the Manerky were bound to regroup. The enemy would come. The Manerky would devise a plan to flush them out of the light soaked chamber, and back out into the darkened recesses of the mountain pass. Maybe worse; maybe the enemy tribe would filter her loved ones into the unknown crevices of the pitch black mountain to be slaughtered. Jordan flinched away from the unwanted vision of her family being ripped to shreds in the unforgiving darkness. She knew with certainty in that moment that it was exactly what the enemy was planning, because as she thought back to the time she had given herself over to the demon... she knew it was exactly what she would have done...

The moment that Cynthia pulled away, Julie could feel the chill of the room seeping in once more. She shivered while vigorously rubbing her hands up and down her arms to ward off the too cold temperature of the ICU-waiting room.

Julie studied Cynthia's eyes for a long while, waiting for the woman to say anything. She wanted the conversation to advance in a thousand different directions, so long as none of those directions ended with her having to confide her true reason for coming to the ICU. Julie knew now how selfish her underlying intent had been. She knew that though she did not want to admit the truth, she had secretly harbored hopes for the future; a future that would include Edward Stanton.

Julie had spent so much of her time engrossed in the life of her children, after her husband's death that she had given little thought to the growing void of loneliness in her heart. Now that void was so big that it stifled the air. It made the room feel smaller. The void was all she could think about; she had allowed that thought to surge into desperation; she had allowed that desperation to color her judgment. She would have to find a way to tell this woman that was so instilled with inner beauty that it billowed out onto everything and everyone she touched; this woman that was aching with the fear of impending loss, the truth. Julie would have to tell Cynthia that she had come to the ICU with one purpose in mind… to find a way to clear the name of the man that had sought to destroy the life of everyone that she loved. She had hoped to live a life once more fulfilled with love and hope with Edward at her side.

Julie knew those hopes were dashed the moment that the Director of Nurses had confided her ugly truth about his past. Edward was a child killer, and no measure of loneliness could ever make Julie ignore such a dark past as that. That too, made Julie feel bad. What had Christ died for? She felt like such a hypocrite. She had been the first to jump on the proverbial soap box of forgive and forget, it had been the creed that she had used to raise her children… the banner waved high in the Leland household, and now as she sat across from one of the victims, touched by Edward's cruel intentions, she could not imagine forgiving the atrocities of his too dark past, and yet deep inside she still could not imagine a future that did not include her dark love.

Shame filled Julie as she searched Cynthia's eyes. "Cynthia… I…" Julie averted her eyes to the pale white paint of the double doors that led into the ICU. Somewhere beyond one of those lonely white curtains, hooked to monitors, needles, and tubes lay the husband and father to the woman and child sitting in front of her. How could she tell her ugly-selfish truth?

Cynthia reached across to Julie; she tenderly took hold of her hand. "Please, go on." Cynthia pleaded.

"I don't know how." Julie admitted. "I have something awful to tell you, and I can't begin to know where to start." Julie dropped her head as tears slipped from her eyes. Even that caused her shame. How could she dare to allow herself this moment? Julie knew she had no right to cry. She had foolishly allowed her heart to be claimed by the enemy, and now she stood before one of his many victims expecting… what: understanding; forgiveness; freedom for Edward? What was it that Julie prayed for? What had she hoped to gain by coming here?

"I'm so ashamed of myself," Julie at last breathed the words. Finally, something that would start her on the right track. She owed this struggling mother and wife so much more than graveling at her feet. She owed her the truth, and somehow she would give it.

"Ashamed?" Cynthia again caressed Julie's arm.

Julie wanted to pull her arm away. She didn't deserve Cynthia's affection. She deserved her anger; frustration; accusations; contempt; but never her compassion or affection. Julie felt twisted inside; as though by allowing the action to continue she was robbing the young woman of affection she would not have freely given had she known the truth.

Cynthia searched Julie's eyes as her brow knit in confusion. "I don't understand what you mean. Why should you be ashamed?"

Julie wiped her eyes as she took a deep cleansing breath. No more stalling. It was time. She would lay her ugly truth out for Cynthia, and then with the grace of God she would wait, patiently for the woman to vent. She would make no excuses.

"I am a nurse here at the hospital." Julie confided.

"I wasn't aware." Cynthia cast a worried glance back at the stuffy-white entrance doors.

"He's okay… I mean as far as I know." Julie reassured. "I don't work in the ICU, so I can't say definitively, but I'm sure you would have been told something." Julie allowed a small smile.

"I work on the floor. I'm a charge nurse, but we've had a young nurse out on maternity leave. So we're shorthanded." Julie knew she was veering too far from the subject, but jumping straight into the deep end of the truth seemed cruel. She wanted to buffer the truth. She wasn't trying to soften the blow for her sake, but for the young pregnant woman waiting with large doe-brown eyes to be crushed by the truth.

"I'm really lost now." Cynthia absently rubbed her belly with one hand, and her arm with the other.

"I don't mean to confuse you." Julie smiled. "Do you need a blanket? It's kind of chilly in here?"

"No I'm fine. I just feel a little uneasy about the pace of this story," Cynthia admitted, as she allowed a humorless laugh. "I've always been the kind of girl that liked all my bad news in one gulp." Cynthia drawled.

Julie smiled at the enduring southern accent. She so missed it. She too had grown up in the south, but after marrying Ronald had moved north. She longed for the simple days of sitting on the back porch sipping lemonade with her mother; talking about nothing special. The fast pace of the city had taken her too far from her simple roots. She had hoped to move back, but as time rocked on, her children grew up, and made lives of their own, then the grandchildren started to be born, and Julie knew that she could never let anything rip her from their lives; not even sipping lemonade on a back porch.

"I apologize. It was not my intention to cause you alarm. I just wanted to explain how I come to be here with you today, without blurting it out, but if you'd rather I did it that way..." Julie shrugged as she took a deep breath and started again.

"I'm Edward Stanton's nurse." Julie waited for any sign that Cynthia was put off by the name, but the young woman seemed unmoved by the name. "You do know Mr. Stanton?" Julie prompted.

"I do." Cynthia finally admitted. "He's the one that loosed the man that almost killed my husband. I'm a former agent for Black Heart." Cynthia moved to her feet. She turned to look over her shoulder. Julie could tell that it was Cynthia that was gauging the listener's reactions now.

"You don't seem surprised." Cynthia finally accused.

"I'm not," Julie admitted. "I know all about you, and your husband. I've had the liberty of getting to know all of you through a friend of mine in the hospital, and some well put together news reports." Julie explained with a sigh.

"I wanted to tell you why I came here, or at least why I initially came here." Julie paused. She walked to the window. She needed courage. She knew that she was not alone. God would help her through the next few moments. She just had to believe.

Cynthia turned around, just as Julie started back across the room, and sat in the same chair she had been sitting before. The puzzled look on Cynthia's face made Julie all the more hesitant.

Taking a deep breath of resignation, Julie finally continued. "The real reason I came here, or was coming here today... I changed my mind, or maybe God changed my mind." Julie knew that she was babbling. She wanted this to be over.

"Julie, please calm down. You're shaking like a leaf," Cynthia said, as she too sat in the same chair she had been sitting before. "Just tell me what it is you need to say. I'm not perfect. I'm sure I've done loads of things that were selfish." Cynthia smiled, weakly through her red and puffy eyes.

"You are sweet. Here you are facing all of this alone, and I come in here..." Julie stopped. She dropped her head dejectedly. She felt so selfish, even in this. What more could life claim from this young woman? Why did she have to be in the long line of calamities that stood waiting to claim their pound of flesh?

"I came here to try to absolve Edward Stanton, but after I got here; after I saw you... well it's, as if God renewed my thinking. I didn't know Edward. I didn't know what he was capable of." Julie sniffed. "My husband has been gone a long time. I had no thought of ever being with another man. Then I was given this case, because Carrie is out on leave. I guess maybe the time that I spent as a charge nurse, not really having to interact with others, may have something to do with it." Julie pushed at a piece of lent that had thwarted her morning inspection. "I mostly report to the Director of Nurses and try to maintain some semblance of control on the floor... not an easy feat." Julie laughed once. She wanted to abandon the piece of lent, but the distraction it afforded her was soothing her splintered nerves.

Cynthia moved closer. She took Julie into her arms. So much love and understanding filtered into the simple act of human kindness that Julie knew in that moment that this woman was not in this alone; she had misjudged her new friend... Cynthia was struggling with the possible demise of her beloved husband, but just as Julie had, Cynthia counted on her Father for strength, and thankfully understanding. Julie was so thankful in that moment. She was so relieved that she was not facing a bitter woman, someone looking for the whys; someone to blame... this was a woman of God that no matter the outcome, she would do the only thing she knew to do; she would lean on God.

As this new truth washed over Julie, a renewed strength filled her senses, and she knew that she could finally tell her truth, no matter how ugly... she had fallen in love with a killer, and though she wasn't sure how demented his mind; Julie knew she was helpless to do anything about it. Her heart was lost to her forever. Though she was ready to reveal all to her new friend, she wasn't sure how ready she was to face life with this new ache. Her heart felt as though it had left with her ability to reason... she couldn't think of any reason not to walk away, but even as she conjured his handsome face, not one of those reasons seemed strong enough to break the prison walls that loving him had forged around her broken heart.

48

Kirsten fought for the surface. She could hear voices, though they seemed familiar, they were accompanied with an echo that hurt her head. Why was everything echoing? Why was she not waking up? Did she want to wake up? The last memory she had was of being in the cage, and a hand...

Kirsten screamed. Her body seemed to be connected to the primal outburst for as the outcry finally breached the forbidding fortress of her lips, she bolted up right. Her eyes desperately searched the room that she lay in. Finally, as if scales had been lifted from her eyes, she could see to her relief that she was in the inner chamber.

Lane was standing near Jordan, who was sitting on a pallet of furs caressing the heads of Modilo and Tristan. Near the hearth, as usual, Amelia collected herbs and spices. She tentatively crushed all of the ingredients into a clay pot.

So, was it over?

Kirsten searched for Aniahi. She didn't find the old medicine woman. Across the way, however, she could see Nick leaning over someone. Kirsten winced against the lighted cavern. Her head hurt so badly. The light multiplied the pain causing her to squint. She closed her eyes to gather her scattered thoughts.

"How are you feeling?" A low decidedly male voice broke into the calm of Kirsten's stolen moment.

"Hey, I didn't mean to scare you." Garrison admitted, as he moved to sit next to Kirsten.

"You didn't," Kirsten lied. She knew the untruth was useless; any idiot could see that Garrison had startled her. She had jumped nearly across the pallet in order to get away from the assumed threat. She didn't know if she would ever be the same. Would she ever find her way back to the carefree-girl she had once been? Would she ever lay under a blanket of starlight, contemplating a forever that she was only just beginning to realize she was not ready for?

Kirsten was glad that Garrison did not call her on the lie. He seemed satisfied to believe he had not offended, yet another of his friends. She hated to relax in his discomfort, but at the moment, the normality of it was the only shred of hope she could grasp onto.

Kirsten didn't know what the story was between Jordan and Garrison, but she could tell that something had strained the once close friendship… she wondered if the friendship would, or could be mended… would the two once allies be able to return to some semblance of unity, or was this rift between them so deep a divide that all was lost? Kirsten felt bad for Garrison. He was like a lone wolf surveying the prairie, of his lonely existence for somewhere to call home. Jordan had for so long been his only friend, and though he had betrayed her trust, Kirsten could not help but wonder what could be so devastating a betrayal to tear at the iron fabric of a friendship forged in the heat of battle.

Garrison was so weary. He could feel the stress of the battle they had already encountered, but the one, yet to be upon them lingered its ugly threat as well. It was more than that though. He wanted so much to make amends with Jordan, to once again feel that link that had somehow bonded them in thought and deed. How could they ever face what was before them without that trust? Before, as he and Jordan fought side by side it was like having an extension of himself. He thought it, and Jordan accomplished the task, or vice versa.

Garrison thought back to the scene on the mountain side. Jordan had thrown the knife; she had made the shot that was his to take. That simple act had told Garrison all that he needed to know… Jordan no longer trusted him. She could not act independently of Garrison, relaxing in the knowledge that he had her back. She would give into the constant, nagging, desire to fight against the foe as one; not one with him, but one person. It had taken weeks of combat, and months in the field to overcome that deeply, imbedded, natural, instinct… now, as he moved through the memories of the day, he was certain their bond of friendship, the ability to move like parts of the same whole had been forever destroyed.

Garrison could remember the exact battle that had revealed the winds of change in their alliance.

John Garret had been as evil a being as Garrison had ever known. He had escaped the clutches of the law with only five accounts of rape and murder. His victims had been kept alive for six days, as he drained them of blood, while ravaging their bodies with his evil lustful intentions. Pictures, DNA, and the last of his victims stood out, as stark evidence of his atrocities in the court room, but still John Garret would not be held accountable for his heinous crimes. Each of the jury members had been sought out, one by one; Garret's accomplice, a young woman named Stacey Carter; as vicious as she was beautiful, had sent out her deadly warning of the fate that would befall each of their loved ones, if a guilty verdict was rendered.

Stacey was sadistic in her need to see the women tortured. She crooned over the heinous acts of her lover.

Garrison could remember the video footage, depicting the young blonde dancing over the pleading girls. She looked like a wood nymph, as she pranced about laughing and demanding Garret to fulfill her inner demons' desire for unwavering lust, and demented-depraved torture to be slaked upon each of the innocents in their charge.

Chills still ran down Garrison's spine, as he recalled the victim's recount of the days spent in the merciless clutches of the serial rapist and murderer, but nothing could outweigh the debt of shame that must have been forced upon each of the young women as the other woman stood by gazing upon their naked flesh, as they were being dismantled at the hands of her depraved puppet.

Cara Styles, a young red head with ravaging blue eyes sat like a subdued rabbit in the courtroom witness stand. The tan suit that she wore draped over her too thin body. Her once fiery-unruly mass of red hair, was now pulled haphazardly back into a sloppy ponytail. The sunk in skin of her face revealed the sharp edge of her cheekbones; evidence of the abuse she received while captured by the wicked couple. Her eyes ever brimming with tears, she sniffled, as she shared the horrible nights of her captivity. She had been hooked to a bag of O- blood. The universal donor, Garret had collected bags of his own blood to replenish the women he kept, so that he could take from them at liberty. The women were hooked to an IV of saline, and were forced to consume bread and water to maintain their pitiful existence. The rapes had been horrendous, but the torture inflicted for disobedience was far worse.

An act of "deliberate defiance," as Garret and Carter referred to the women's unwilling participation in their own torture and rape, was followed by a stiff penalty. The girls were placed in a room, devoid of any light. Night calls were sounded for minutes, sometimes hours, as the girls cried out for it to stop. Finally, Garret or Carter would enter the darkness with night vision goggles in place, and proceed to tear at the girl's flesh with fabricated claws made out of fiberglass that was woven into polyester gloves. Deep scratches were imbedded into the flesh of the young girls. After being released from the terrible darkness, the young women were usually willing to endure their captor's worst intentions, as long as it did not include the dark room.

Garrison and Jordan had followed the newly released Garret back to his layer. Stacey Carter had been inadvertently killed during a mad-struggle with one of the captives that had escaped discovery by FBI agents. Secluded deep in the belly of a well, just beneath the house, Janice Bickers awaited her death, but as Carter returned to the place of her last victim, determination had replaced fear. The young captive scrambled for her captor. First clawing at her eyes, and then slamming her subdued head into the block walls of her makeshift prison. Soon Stacey Carter lay in a pool of her own blood, while Janice screamed for someone to come to her rescue.

Janice's calls of desperation had not been met with silence, as John Garret returned to the scene of the crime.

"Did you miss me sugar?" Garret called down into the deep.

Garrison and Jordan stood back in the shadows of the room that looked more like a dungeon than the basement of a home. Garrison watched, as Garret morphed from the frantic predator in need of a victim to an outraged lover tortured by the absence of a fallen love.

"What have you done?" Garret demanded.

"From my standpoint it would seem that she has saved us a bit of time." Jordan bantered back, as she and Garrison materialized from the shadows. "Wouldn't you agree with that assessment Garrison?" Jordan asked with an offhanded nod of her head.

"I couldn't have said it better myself, sugar." Garrison drawled in an attempt to mimic Garret's sugary-sweet-southern tone.

Garret looked first at Jordan, and then at Garrison. "What are you doing in my house? Get out!" Garret demanded, as he lifted a shaking hand to the dingy-faded-cream door. Blood stains flowed from ceiling to floor, evidence of the heinous acts committed beyond its borders.

"Get out?" Jordan crooned. "I don't see how we could possibly leave here without our coveted prize."

"Prize? What prize?" Garret's face screwed up in puzzlement.

Garrison's eyes danced, as he watched Jordan move slowly-seductively toward her victim. She too had watched the videos, listened to the accounts of the last two remaining victims. She too had stood beyond the borders of the bloodstained walls that testified of the unsaid tortures, lavished upon the unwitting victims… Jordan Buckley, the self-appointed bringer of justice for women everywhere, had stood in the shadow of untold anguish and depravity, and she would now, gladly take her revenge.

"Piece of crap," Garrison addressed Garret. "Meet Jordan Buckley." Garrison pointed at his partner, as she moved with murderous intent ever closer to the bewildered killer. "Jordan Buckley, Piece of crap." Garrison finished his formal introduction, as he moved back to the nearest wall, and rested his back against the cold cement.

"And?" Garret snorted. "Is that supposed to impress me?" Garret turned his attention back to a slumbering Garrison.

"Not at first, but if you live long enough to acknowledge your own end, then I'm sure impressed will be among the emotions that filter through your mind, though I'm equally sure that it will be a fleeting thought, soon replaced by fear…" Garrison stuffed his hands into his pockets, as he nodded to his partner. "As you were."

The moment that it took Garret to turn his attention back to Jordan, was the beginning of his last. A whirlwind of grace-and-deadly intent, she arced across the distance, descending from the air like an avenging angel. Jordan sliced Garrets right ear clean from his head. With a yip of pain, Garret claimed his afflicted appendage with both of his hands, as he staggered a few steps in Garrison's direction.

Garrison leaned away from the wall long enough to force Garret back in the right direction. "Get back in there, Tiger… after all it's just a woman. You seemed to have been handling yourself pretty well up until now, against the 'weaker sex'." Garrison rolled his eyes, as he placed air quotes around weaker sex.

Garrison watched as Jordan had already spun around, readying herself for the next launched attack. Her eyes were glazed over with all that she had intended for her victim. She had no doubt thought of this moment a thousand times. She had no doubt waited for her chance to quiet the tortured cries of Garret's victims, as she once and for all claimed their revenge. How ironic that his end would come in the very place that he had created to take everything from his victims: life; virtue; certainty; dignity; their ability to thrive; everything had been shed along with their blood, and left like a stain on the walls of their dungeon-graves.

Jordan would bring their captor to the clutches of death many times, and then bring him back to endure more of the sweet revenge that she had promised his victims in her mind—she watched and listened to the outrageous accounts of their last moments.

Like a cat toying with its prey, Jordan seemed to lick her proverbial claws. She twisted around, and forced her booted foot into the under surface of Garret's chin. He flew backwards straight into Garrison's arms like a rag doll. Garrison had seen enough. He had stood back and watched, as his partner had claimed every ounce of the sweet-nectar… it was his time to claim a few of the stolen moments, before they had to set the stage for the cleanup crew to erase the last moments of the depraved killer's wasted existence.

Garrison caught the stumbling Garret under his arms, as his hands automatically claimed either side of the killer's head. With a mighty twist the end came. Garret slumped forward. Garrison forced his limp form away from him. He had no desire to touch, or be near the remnants of such a vile human being.

"Sorry… got tired of you having all the fun." Garrison offered.

"No problem." Jordan breathed against the straining fabric of her slick black suit. She licked her lips. Garrison watched, as she too seemed to morph in that moment from an avenging angel to his partner. The change had been so subtle that he had not thought to question it at the time, but would later understand the true measure of what he had witnessed that day in the belly of that demonic pit.

Though Garrison and Jordan had risen from the ashes of that kill with a new understanding of how far each of them would be willing to fall in order to allow the other to be vindicated, they had also moved to a place of mutual respect. No matter what was the driving force behind the bloodshed, as long as it was in keeping with the greater good, to protect the public from individuals like John Garret and Stacey Carter, then no questions would be asked.

The unspoken oath had remained between them until the day in the forest outside of Beulah County. There Garrison had come to realize the true depth of the entity driving his partner's rage, and yet he had protected her… he would always protect her; it was his need to protect her, his need to possess her as a token; a trophy; his only friend that had driven him to the lies. It was that need that had possibly driven them apart forever. He would somehow have to help his friend and her family make it through the impending battle without the comfort of knowing that she had his back, that he had hers… that all would be well. For the first time the partners would stand alone on a battlefield, fighting the same foe; all the while not knowing who their deadliest enemy would be: The Manerky or the rift between them that had led to the distrust that would inevitably bring about their destruction.

CHAPTER

49

Penny tried to avoid Nick's insistent gaze. She knew what he wanted, and even the froes of battle, or their impending demise would not deter him from that coveted need. He would stop at nothing to fill the gap between what he felt in his heart, and what Penny was unwilling to admit to herself. He would do anything necessary to show her that their love was more than a chance moment in the middle of a bad situation. They were more than two people that had survived by clinging to the other for refuge in the storm. They were more...

Nick had insisted so many times that their connection was based in more than the need for survival. They had been put together by the very hands of fate for a more tangible reason... Nick had pushed for so long for Penny to declare her love. She knew that he deserved the declaration, but she was not sure of the nature of her feelings for him: best friend or boyfriend. She knew that he deserved more than a tender lie. He was worth every love-soaked emotion that she could conjure, during a soul-searching inventory of her true feelings; yet she was bereft to say the coveted words. Her voice was a barren, wasteland of emptiness. She had no words to explain the volcano of emotion that existed on the planes of her soul for Nick. She could not explain what she did not yet understand. There just had been no time to think things through. When she and Nick had been together the time was filled with hardship. The times that she had spent with Nick in the quiet, she only felt the need to escape the question that burned in his insistent gaze. She feared that it was the question behind that stare that brought about the deepest part of that fear.

Love was such a big emotion. She wasn't sure that she even knew what love, at least that kind of love meant. Her only inclination of true love had been forged in her mind during a visit to the hospital, as she watched her great grandmother, her GG clutch the intangible cord of life holding her husband to the earth. Her GG had knelt before her Pawpaw's bed begging God for her husband's life.

"Don't leave me here alone," GG had begged. GG had barely been able to sit or stand on her own, but she had strained against the Rheumatoid Arthritis to kneel before her beloved's death bed. The scene had been both mournful and romantic.

On the other hand, Penny had witnessed the way that her father, Garret Junior had treated her mother, Erica. His forced authority, and Erica's subdued manner had cheapened the show of love left emblazoned in her memory. Any preconceived, romantic notions she may have had were replaced with the ugly truth; love was dead. It had instead, been replaced with strict authoritarians demanding loyalty... love was a lie. It was a wasted emotion. It had no place in a world as maddening as the one they now existed.

Penny heard the crooning tune of 'Hush Little Baby.' She tried to force her eyes not to see, but in the end she lost the battle as her gaze drifted to the loving scene of her Uncle holding her aunt, as she rocked the small children laying in different stages of slumber around her lap. The moment was so peaceful; so worthy of her GG and Pawpaw that tears finally slipped from her eyes.

"I..." Penny started to speak, but the words wouldn't come.

Nick moved to pull her to him then. She collapsed in his warm embrace. Everything felt complete when she found herself here; listening to the slow thumping of his beautiful heart, as it testified to the man possessing it. This felt so good. Why would the words not come? How did she really feel? Could she love Nick? Did she love anyone?

Thump; thump; thump Nick's heart shouted to Penny to give into the truth. She did, didn't she? She loved Nick, but to what degree? What kind of love did this man before her invoke in her?

The question hung unanswered in the space between them, as Penny nestled further into the slightly muscled contours of Nick's arms. His was a slender build. His stature not quite the massive bulk of her

Uncle Lane, but somehow in his arms she felt just as safe as her Aunt seemed now in the arms of her Uncle.

Penny felt the need to attach forever to the moment, though she was unsure what the word meant, or how it applied to her and Nick's circumstance; Penny somehow knew that if she followed that thought to completion it would end at her answer. She would know for all time the depth of her true feelings.

Time stood still, as she moved deeper into his embrace, and then just as abruptly as it had started the moment had ended.

A scream ripped through the chamber, stripping the moment of all of its beauty. Nick and Penny jerked apart just in time to see Jordan place the children to the side, and move to her feet. Though it had been a gentle act, it seemed to happen in a blur.

Garrison ran passed the fire-hearth, claiming Amelia's startled-body as he went. In a blink, he had her safely tucked beside the other two children, and was on his way back to Kirsten.

Kirsten, still in a seated position, was pointing at the now darkened entrance of the cave. Her eyes moved to each of the pathways leading from the inner chamber. Every one of the entrances was no longer bathed in light.

A fine mist of clay flew passed the screaming girl and landed mere inches from the hearth in the center of the room. Growls and clicks filled the chamber, sounding like nothing more than wild animal calls.

Penny seeing Garrison's intent moved to Kristen's side, as she pulled the Barton into her hands and stood battle ready. Soon the enemy would move into their midst. Soon they would be faced with the dreaded end…

Nick felt his body go numb. He watched, his mouth agape, as Penny moved from his grasp, and posed herself in front of the younger girl. Penny twirled the Barton with ease; her gaze moved from each entrance waiting for any sign of intruders. She looked like a warrior-goddess readying for the enemy. Her dark hair was pulled back away her face revealing more of those iridescent green eyes. Her gaze filled with one-part anger, one-part fear. Though he knew underneath that unyielding stance, beat the heart of a teenager unsure of the end, her eyes burned with fury that seemed beyond her years. Both of them had been through mountains of abuse, but as he watched Penny he knew for the first time the true wealth of hostility that lived behind her own set of enemy lines. She had grown up in a world filled with so much ugly that it had fused her heart, soul, and mind in one unified quest for retribution. Nick knew in that moment the impossible void that his demand for her confession of love would force her to cross. Love was a foreign concept to this warrior-goddess. The notion made his heart sink.

Nick wanted to run from the cave, and never look back. He had given himself over to the barren land of her uninhabitable love. He would be forced to walk the deserted planes of that dark place, burning the fires of hope. His eyes slid reluctantly from his beautiful goddess to her charge.

Kirsten was a basket of nerves. She sat on the pallet of animal furs shaking her head back and forth, muttering some unintelligible words. Nick could only imagine that the traumatized girl was begging for her life. She had already been in the enemy clutches, and now as she sat awaiting her return to their unwanted grasp, she did all that she could think to do; she begged.

Moving to the space near Penny, Nick took his own stance. His axe was tied in a loose noose on the front of his belt, while his bow was fitted with an arrow ready to fly at will.

Jordan and Garrison stood like twin sentinels, their eyes locked on an entrance of their own choosing. The thing that seemed to be out of character for the outraged former friends was the back to back stance that they had adopted. It seemed to be almost second nature. Though Lane was clearly the love of Jordan's life, the moment she had morphed form loving mother and wife to the deadly fighter they all knew her to be, Jordan had automatically stepped back into the role of partner to Garrison.

Lane moved to Jordan's side like a giant guardian, ready to bring down his wrath on the first to come near his family. Nick stood awestruck, as he measured the facial expression of Penny's uncle. He saw no fear; no jealousy. The man was one, with a focused desire, to keep his family safe. Nick could see in the depths of Lane's angelic visage, his humbling blue eyes that he would always be there. He would always hold dear what Jordan held dear. Lane would always be ready to allow Jordan to be Jordan. Whatever her path, he would stand by her side, taking whatever place was left, so long as he was able to protect her; even if it meant his last breath. As Nick listened to the haunting animal calls, dying on the wind, and then moved ever closer each time they started up again, he wasn't so sure that Lane would not get to prove how willing he was to give up his last breath.

Lane watched as Jordan and Garrison, automatically moved back to back. Something so intimate and telling filled the simplicity of that response. He couldn't help but allow the inner smile snaking through his senses to play on his lips. It was happening. If God allowed the two friends to live passed this moment; Lane knew that they would forever be fused as partners and friends. He had stood by for so long trying to tenderly push Jordan in the right direction. He didn't know why Garrison had felt the need to keep Jordan in the dark about so many things, but he had come to know Garrison well. In that knowledge, Lane had come face to face with the truth; Garrison would do anything to protect Jordan. She was his only friend, his only ally, his only link to humanity. How ironic… Garrison had found a link to the world of the living through a woman that was in every sense of the world dead inside. She had lent her strength, her knowledge, her desires, everything that made her Jordan Buckley had been willingly turned over to the demon. Yet Garrison had found completion as a human being; belonging; every ingredient needed to keep him attached to this world had been discovered in what remained of Jordan's tortured soul.

Lane had allowed the moment to pass, as he too stood ready for the enemy invasion. He prayed for God to grant him, his friends, and family the strength and knowledge to defeat an enemy as formidable as the Manerky. Lane was sure that every tunnel leading from the inner chamber was packed with the enemy tribe. They had somehow vanquished the light in each of the tunnels, but would they be able to move into the sanctuary of their hiding place? Lane knew the answer to that the moment after it washed over his anguished soul. For in that moment, God had spoken to his heart.

"What can separate you from my love? If I be for you then, who can be against you?" The sweet promise of the Father had come from Romans 8, the last verses of that chapter told it all. God was an unmovable force in his life. He had proved so many times that there was nothing to fear. God had brought him out of the most vicarious of situations. He had stood the victor of the spoils so many times in the past; every time he knew that it was God alone that had moved the mountains in his midst. It was God alone that had lighted his path and ordered his steps, and in this time of uncertainty it would be God alone that would birth forth a solution. God would bring them through this and all the moments of uncertainty to come. He had only to believe. God was the Great Redeemer.

Darkness crept into the inner chamber of the cave like a masked avenger coming to claim its doomed enemies.

Jordan took only a moment to allow her eyes to drift over each of her family members. She couldn't allow the helplessness of the moment to take center stage. Her family needed her strength in this moment, not her doubts. She had to believe that God would fill in the blanks of the unknown. She had to believe that He would move them in the path of victory. He would not stand by and allow His people to be claimed by an evil enemy such as the Manerky clan.

God had a plan for her family. Plans meant that they had to survive in order to live up to the expectations of those plans, but even as the darkness crept further into the room touching everything with its icy intent, Jordan could feel her confidence waiver.

Jordan watched as Amelia coaxed the two younger children closer to the wall. She moved what was left of her concoction after Garrison's sudden launch for her safety. She had lost precious drops of the sleep medicine. The boys had slept most of the day away, not realizing anything that had befallen the others. Jordan hated to allow her daughter, her continued subduing of their senses, but it felt more merciful for them to sleep through the ugly situation, than to shush their cries in the midst of a bloody war. So, in the end Jordan had faded to the back, and allowed her daughter that was soon to be medicine woman to do what she knew to do.

Amelia blazed across the room. Lane reached for her arm, but Jordan placed a tender hand on his shoulder, as she promptly fell back into her battle-ready stance. Lane dropped his arm, helplessly to his side, and allowed his daughter to walk passed his protection to the other side of the room where Kirsten was whimpering in fear. After a few sips, all three were sound asleep.

Jordan took in every member of those fighting on her side. Penny stood a statuesque young warrior goddess, twirling her Barton with the readiness of a mountain lion waiting to pounce. Nick, at her side, was still pulling tension on the bow string. Garrison was where he had been for as long as she could remember; at her back. Jordan allowed that thought to play in her mind. Did she trust that? Could she depend on him to persevere? Yes! Jordan allowed a smile. She could trust Garrison. No matter what had happened in the past, she could trust that he would protect her; her family; with his last breath.

Lane stood by her side as always; she could feel the torrents of faith and commitment to his Creator, billowing from his massive form in waves. All of the children, including Kirsten were tucked as safely away from the battle as possible.

Jordan only had a moment to wonder if it would be enough, for as she pulled her thoughts back to the task at hand, hordes of the enemy forces moved into the inner chamber, each wearing a bandage around their heads to protect their eyes from the light.

Jordan felt the tension in Garrison's back, as he released the first of his weapons into the first of many kills. Blood exploded from the lips of the warrior, as his mouth took the shape of an O and his chest curved away from the weapon. His arms floated upward in an automatic flight response. Jordan started to twirl her Barton in one hand while releasing her blade into the first Manerky warrior that came into sight. A whoosh exited his mouth, as his face contorted in surprise. Blood filled the space around the weapon in a starburst pattern. His pupils were already dilating as his body collapsed, lifelessly to the ground.

Penny raced forward, jutting the sharpened end of her Barton into the jugular of an approaching Manerky warrior, while Nick nocked arrow after arrow, releasing them into all that dare to fill the sanctuary of the inner chamber with their evil intent. The space around the defending friends was a blur of weapons, blood and cries of death or rage.

A soft glow of light danced over Lane's body. It vibrated and pulsated like a rubber band pulled tight and snapped. Jordan didn't know what he intended. If Lane released his God-given-angel-light into the chamber, the Manerky would not be the only ones destroyed in its wake.

50

Julie had spent another hour with her new friend explaining how she had unfortunately, allowed her heart to be stolen by this awful man. But it was as Cynthia told the story of a love, many loves really that had been started in the middle of a war zone that Julie had begun to understand the wonderful truth of it all; she truly was not alone. She had God that was always true, and all that really mattered, but as she listened to Cynthia, Julie knew that she was a part of something bigger than her little circumstance.

Cynthia, too had been a trained killer. She had fallen in love with one of God's own, John Benton. Cynthia had made the move to The Truth with the help of two very special friends, Garrison and Jordan.

Julie thought back to the newscast. She remembered Jordan. She had been the Black Heart agent that had turned missionary. She, too had been targeted by the far reaching cruelty of Black Heart. Jordan had been pursued by a missionary of the Truth, Lane Gates. During his pursuit of Jordan, the two had fallen in love and were now married with two children. Cynthia had kept the details vague, but Julie could tell that there was so much more to the wonderful stories than met the eye, or ear in Julie's case.

Julie tried to feel comforted by all of the stories. She wanted to somehow fit into the jigsaw puzzle, but in the end she had to come to terms with the truth; Edward Stanton was the HOD of the company; he had orchestrated every horrible thing that had touched the lives of all of the lovers in Cynthia's story. So, how could Julie hope to paint the story of her love for Edward into the twisting and turning puzzle of the innocent lives of those united in the froes of battle? Julie knew the truth; she couldn't. As much as her heart longed for it to be so, she couldn't fit her square peg existence into the round hole circumstances of those affected by Edward's lies and deceit. Still, she had continued to listen as the younger woman spoke.

"Edward Stanton was the HOD of Black Heart, and it's true he has done some pretty horrible things to manipulate and mold the lives of the agents he was given charge over, but Edward's only crime in relation to those children was hiring Max." Cynthia continued to fill Julie in on all of the gory details of Edward's past.

Cynthia explained that she was a profiler for Black Heart. It wasn't until she had started to put the last pieces of the puzzle together, the day that she had been taken prisoner, and John had all but been killed that Cynthia had realized how in the dark Edward Stanton had been in regards to the child agents.

"So you see, while Mr. Stanton is guilty of using his agents like pawns on a chest board to take out his most hated enemy's granddaughter, Jordan Buckley Gates; he had no true knowledge of the child agents. He didn't know that they had been put into place. Well, at least not for the purposes that they were to be used. He sure as heck didn't know that Max meant to terminate each of the child agents in the field." Cynthia took a deep cleansing breath. Anger registered on her face as she visually tried to calm herself to finish the story.

"It turns out that Max was hungry for more than money. He wanted Stanton's job. He intended to frame Stanton with the deaths of the child agents so that he could move into a place of power." Cynthia pulled a document out of a large brown briefcase by her side, and handed it to Julie.

"What's this?" Julie took the document from Cynthia, but for some reason felt uneasy in doing so.

"It's okay. I have the original still safely tucked away in here." Cynthia patted the briefcase. "Amazing how I would make copies in the middle of all of this, but for some reason, before I left the house this morning I felt the need to copy." Cynthia patted Julie on the arm. "God is purposeful Julie. You were meant to come here today to clear Edward Stanton's name. You are meant to follow this path, and it won't be easy."

Cynthia stared off in the distance as if she were momentarily reminded of her own hard path. When she again faced Julie she seemed older, and her eyes were brimming with tears. "But God is with you, always even until the end." (Matthew 28:20)

Julie left the ICU-waiting room after praying with her new friend. Both of the women lifted the other up in prayer as they asked their Father to protect them in their journey, and to remind them often that they are not alone. They asked for strength to fill them, and for God to supernaturally intervene in John and Edward's lives.

Julie walked to the elevators as she thought about the truth. It was okay to love Edward. It was not forbidden. In fact, it was expected. How had she convinced herself that God's plans and her understanding of His plans were not one and the same? Julie had spent a lifetime trying to align her mind, body, and soul up with the will of God, and yet in this circumstance she had allowed her judgment to be contaminated by her own prejudice; her own preconceived ideas about right and wrong. How many times had people fell into that trap?

Julie felt ashamed. Murder was wrong. Edward was wrong. It was black and white, or so she had thought, but hadn't she done things in the past that if others had known about it they would not understand? Julie thought about that for a moment. Of course, she had. She was certain that falling in love with a known killer would topple some of her more pristine friend's list of 'Do's and Don'ts'.

Julie knew in her heart, no matter how big a label she placed on Edward's past, he too was forgiven. Forgiveness was as much Edward's as it had been hers. He had only to ask.

She pulled the file from her large black hand bag. What was in this file? What was so vital that it would prove a man like Edward Stanton innocent? Whatever was in the file, Julie had to get it back to Edward's room. She had to convince Edward to invest in his own future. She needed to make him see that the file was proof that even God loved him, even God was on his side, and even God was making a way for Edward to find his way back from his dark past. (Jeremiah 29:11 for I know the plans I have made for you, declares the Lord, plans to prosper you and not to harm you, plans to give you hope and a future.)

Julie exited the elevator as she nodded and smiled at an elderly couple holding hands. How sweet to have lived life with another. How wonderful to know so many years at your best friend, your lovers side… Julie felt a sadness fill her heart. Shouldn't that someone have been Ronald? She could feel the familiar choking sensation as it started to press in around her throat and stifle her lungs. Her time with Ronald was over. Ronald was walking the streets of gold. Her time was here. Her time was with Edward.

Julie smiled as she thought about the truth of that statement. She was here, and Edward was her friend. He was someone that she could see becoming more in her life. How wonderful it would be to again have the possibility of a future like the elderly couple.

She sighed as she pushed the document back down into her purse. That time was a long way off. All of the redeeming evidence in the world would be useless without Edward's willingness to use it. She couldn't drag him into court, she couldn't speak for him… somehow Edward had to come to terms with his own life. He needed to realize that though his mistakes may seem monstrous, they were still mistakes. Mistakes were made to be learned from. They were to be used as tools for the future; guidelines about how not to live your life.

Edward Stanton, up until this point, had made a complete mess of his life, and a lot of other people's lives. There was no denying that fact. Julie had no intentions of sweeping any of his sins under the proverbial rug, and forgetting them. To the contrary, she intended to get Edward Stanton to pull every one of those sins out of the past and look at them. She intended to have him study and accept them for what they were; mistakes. Then she intended to introduce him to the Redeemer of lives.

Edward had spent most of the morning in a fog of uncertainty. His insides were eaten up with guilt. Had he ignored the signs? Had there been some inclination? If he had just paid a little more attention to Max could he have seen the truth? All of those children were dead, all of the lives of the people he had tried to force his will upon were in shambles.

John Benton lay in the ICU fighting for his life right now, because of Edward. Though it had not been Edward's intent, it was Edward that had used Max based on his position. Max had known John. He had a way in. He would be able to infiltrate the inner-circle of friends without anyone asking questions. Edward had set the dangerous man upon them all. It was by his own hand that each of their lives had been ripped apart.

Edward had been the one to navigate Tommy into position. He had set the depraved mind of Jordan's nephew on them all. For what: revenge? What did Edward have to show for every misdeed committed out of anger for his long ago nemesis, Cecil Schooner? Nothing. He had nothing, and now he would have the ache, a constant reminder of the most profound loss he had ever felt: more than losing his beloved Amorous; more than the loss of a love that would never be with Julie; he had lost the chance to live forever with the knowledge that he too was not alone. He would never know the source of the brilliant light that shown from his beautiful Julie and touched all that she came in contact with. Edward knew that he had squandered a lifetime of last chances. He had given it all up, traded it in for a ghost. He had lived his life by a code not worth the price he would have to pay.

He wanted so desperately to seek forgiveness from Julie's God, but he knew all too well that he was unworthy. It had taken only one look into the huge trusting eyes of Amber Noel to know the truth. Shame had filled his heart so profoundly that day. Edward could not stand to look in the eyes of one so innocent. He was a monster, worse; he was the one controlling the monster. He was the unspeakable man behind the curtain that had plundered through the lives of those that had had the misfortune of crossing his path. He, Edward Stanton was the unforgivable-blemish that scarred the face of humanity.

Julie pushed her way into Edward's room. Thankfully the nurses' desk had been empty. She didn't feel much like idle chat. She wanted to get back to Edward. The document that she was holding proved that Max had acted on his own. Edward definitely would have to pay for his crimes against the Black Heart operatives, but he was no child killer.

Julie felt lighter as she approached Edward's bed. The dim light of the overhead cast a harsh light on one half of Edward's face. She almost left the room in that moment. The shadows on the wall cast by the flickering bulb danced their wicked response to Julie's already elevated heart rate. The eerie silence coupled with the dancing shadows disarmed every ounce of resolve that Julie had gained on the way to Edward's room.

As Edward stared back from the shadows for the first time she could see the agent. What it must be to have this man lurking in the shadows, waiting to end her life. Julie shivered at the thought. But as Julie's mind began painting a picture of espionage and mayhem, her heart searched his eyes. There in the depths of their soulful brown pools lived not the heart of a killer, but of a broken man. The unrelenting sorrow in his tortured visage nearly toppled Julie's hopes.

She knew that if God had brought her to this place, He would somehow bring her through it. But how? How was she to make Edward believe in his own right to forgiveness? The document in her hand was good, but it only proved what she was sure Edward was already aware of. Still, it had to be some consolation that there was proof of his innocence; at least as far as the child agents, and John Benton's near death experience was concerned. Julie had sifted through the file that Cynthia pieced together. The evidence was staggering. Max had been recruited by Edward for Intel, nothing more. Max had acted of his own volition when he recruited the child agents. He had further acted of his own free will when attacking the Benton's. There was even a taped conversation of Edward and Max.

Julie had stopped in the nurse's lounge to listen to the tape. She needed to know. Her heart had raced as the recording began. There was traffic rushing to and fro in the background. Julie moved to the door, she latched the lock, and then sat as the voices began to fill the line. Edward had pleaded with Max to release the child agents, but Max had taunted the man. The menace in the monster's voice was still fresh in Julie's thoughts.

Julie listened to the entire conversation. Max had admitted to everything. But why and how had the conversation been recorded? Julie could only imagine one thing. Edward had possibly recorded the conversation hoping that he would get enough evidence to clear his name, but he had been taken from his office on the stretcher, before he could retrieve the evidence. Cynthia's friend had pulled the file along with the other two files. Cynthia hadn't realized the file was about Max. The file had another name. Maybe Edward had used the name as a decoy. Maybe the name was just another way that Edward had of keeping the evidence out of the wrong hands.

Cynthia had pieced together too much of the truth. She could prove Edward Stanton's innocence. Max could not allow Cynthia to tear down every wall he had put into place to protect him from that truth.

Julie wanted so much to make Edward believe in his own worth, but the closer she got to his bed, she could see that it would not be easy. For the first time, as Julie stood over this man that had stolen her unwilling heart, she could see the true debt of guilt living behind his eyes. Edward seemed so small, so lost to the truth. The enemy had spent so much time with this man that she loved against her will. She would have to be just as determined.

Edward stared out from the mountain of guilt that had been creeping in for the better part of the morning. How could he face Julie? He wanted her to leave. He wanted her to stay. He wanted everything, and deserved nothing.

51

The firelight flickered haphazardly—signaling its threat to extinguish the only light afforded them in the small inner chamber. Jordan's breath caught as she thought of the children just inches from where she stood. How long before the clicking calls of the fallen warrior's comrades become more than just a promise of intrusion? How long before their already unstable world tilted into something worse? In the depths of her soul, Jordan couldn't imagine anything worse than what her family had already experienced. The inner chamber was awash of dead warriors, and yet, more were about to spill into their stolen sanctuary. How much more could they be expected to endure, and yet just as she had been promised she was still here: on her feet; enduring the unthinkable; strong with her friends by her side, awaiting the enemy... Jordan knew the answer. She and all those that she loved were mere inches from discovering the end of the strength God knew them to have. They were all mere moments from answering the age old question; how much more can I take? How much more would God put on her shoulders, on the shoulders of those she loved? How much more could she take? Only God knew the answer, and Jordan prayed even as she stood awaiting the answer that she would endure to the end. She prayed that all those that she loved would live to tell the story. She prayed...

Almost as if it were the answer to the question she had been afraid to ask the clicking grew louder as the small chamber entrances seemed to vomit out droves of the enemy. Every porthole leading from the outside world in turn coughed up its on portion of the Manerky forces.

Each warrior the image of a spectral-demon came to claim the souls of her loved ones. Jordan noticed that the new foe was no longer wearing eye covering; their white eyes stood out more than ever against the backdrop of their singed eyelids. The holy light that had emanated from Lane had finalized what the vile-agents of darkness had begun long ago; the Manerky warriors were indeed blind now. No amount of light would send them fleeing in fear. Now, the world was darkness. No matter where the warriors ventured they were in their element. The bald heads were covered with dark runes. Though Jordan was unsure of the meaning, the tattoos were so dark and filled with so much hate that the meaning seemed to rise from the surface of each warrior's flesh as if it had been shouted; death! Crouching low to the cave floor each of the Manerky tribe members took on characteristics of an animal of some kind. The arms and legs of some draped low and gangly like a monkey, while still others seemed to smoothly grace the clay floor like a snake as it tested the ground with its wavy sideways manipulations. Yet other members of the enemy tribe stalked forward with the ease of a lion on the prowl. Though each member had adopted a different fighting style to destroy the enemy, Jordan could see that no decision was written in stone. The warriors adapted easily to the adversity. As they witnessed a fallen comrade, they merely adjusted so as not to make the same mistake.

Jordan turned to see Penny and Nick as they stood back to back both with their own weapon at hand. Penny had just thrust the end of her Barton into the jugular of an approaching Manerky warrior. The white dead eyes remained undeterred as the Manerky crumbled to a knee and blood exploded from his mouth of grotesquely shaped teeth. Droplets stained the ground and sprayed across Penny's nose and cheeks. Her mouth turned up in an angry sneer as she thrust the Barton yet deeper. A shiver traveled Jordan's spine as she witnessed what it must have been to watch herself as she was possessed by the demon in the past. Nick was releasing his arrows with all the speed he could muster. Desperation filled his young features, and Jordan knew in that moment that it was the need to protect her niece that was driving the young man on.

Lane still pulsated with the radiant glow of holy light, and in the back of Jordan's mind she wondered would any of them be able to withstand that light. Though the Manerky had lost their sight, she knew that the light that Lane was producing was not of this world. No amount of darkness would be enough to hide the enemy away. She had no time to contemplate the end. She needed to focus. Her family needed her to focus.

Moving the Barton in a circling arc, Jordan forced her way into the midst of the horde. She knew just as she had thought to bring the fight to the enemy, and away from the children, Garrison and Lane would do the same. She and Lane had only been in one battle as partners.

Jordan thought back to the time on the airplane. She and Lane had left their daughter with the medicine woman to return to the states. Jordan needed to be around specialists that could monitor the birth of their son closely. The accounts of the women that had been taken by Nephilim in the past were not good. There was no evidence that any of the mothers had survived the enormous birth weight of a Nephilim.

During the flight, a large man that turned out to be a descendent of the fallen angels just as Lane, had started to highjack the plane. Lane had thought to disarm the situation without alerting Jordan to the danger. Unfortunately, for Lane, Jordan had come to know of the problem. Waking up after Lane had left her side, Jordan had stumbled on an elderly woman trying to get as far away from two people intending to fight. Jordan assured the woman that she would be right behind her, but instead she had turned to the bi-fold-door separating the two passenger compartments.

Jordan opened the door and peered just inside. Her blood filled with ice as her eyes took in the two massive men filling the aisle. Her mind could scarcely accommodate the thoughts flooding through it. Lane stood twirling two sticks looking every bit the fearless warrior, but what was threatening to stifle her life's breath was the sheer bulk of Lane's opponent. The man had to be eight feet tall. His angry mass of black hair fell to just below his shoulders, his eyes were dark pools, sunk back in his reddened face, and his massive arms protruded through a tight-fitting white tank-top commonly known as the 'wife beater.' Anger mixed with fear and mounted becoming a raging volcano of desperation. Jordan started forward as she felt the tiny nudge from inside her bulging abdomen.

Lane was desperate to end this. His worse fears had come to fruition. Jordan was exactly where he had been praying that she would not be: right in the middle of the problem. She was awake, and she knew.

"Jordan, please go," he was almost begging. The giant's eyes darted in Jordan's direction.

"Oh… not at all Jordan, by all means stay. You can play with me after I kill your husband." The man's deep bass voice rose filling the compartment with vibrations.

"I wouldn't miss this for the world," Jordan purred coolly. "I think I'll stick around. Besides, I'd like to see my husband dismember you." She claimed as she rubbed her stomach tenderly and then slid into the nearest seat as if she were merely choosing a desirable viewpoint at a theatre. "As you were…" She prompted while she examined her fingernails in an overt attempt at appearing bored.

Lane cast Jordan a confused glance as he turned his attention back to his adversary. He definitely would be having a long conversation with his wife, provided he survived this experience. As Lane turned his attention back, the man was giving Jordan an appreciative once over. The giant then pulled his fist back into a battle-ready stance.

"Maybe, I'll keep her for myself. She's got brass… got to get rid of the kid though." The man spat mockingly. "No use for kids." He growled as he shook his head. Lane growled angrily as he thrust the stick in his right hand forward slamming it with brute force into the man's mouth. Blood splattered, painting Lane's shirt. A few rogue droplets sprayed a couple of passengers just a few seats up from where the two men were fighting. The couple's puzzled glares were all that was offered for the viscous disturbance of their usually quiet lives. The giant's face contorted into a sadistic mass as an ugly grin lined his blood-soaked lips, he swiped the back of his oversized hand across his mouth as again he offered an appreciative smile.

Lane swung his left arm again aiming for the man's smug-grotesque face. With thundering force, the man hurled his right arm up countering Lane's effort. Then with ease seeming uncommon to his massive size he struck out with his other arm slamming hard, his knuckles met with the flesh of Lane's face, just above his right eye. Lane staggered a few paces as he crumbled to one knee. The man pushed forward grabbing a fistful of Lane's hair, and hauling him mercilessly to his feet. An errant groan escaped Lane's lips, betraying him, and allowing Jordan insight as to how much the blow had overcome his senses and how close he had come to giving into the darkness that had shrouded his vision.

Jordan held at bay the gasp that struggled to free itself from the core of her being. She could not allow the giant of a man to feed off of her fear. For she recognized the demon that was calling the shots… of course, she did. How could she not? She too had falsely believed it to be an old friend, the only constant in a darkened existence. She too had fallen prey to its murderous intentions, almost losing not only what was left of her own humanity, but Lane as well. Now, here again behind the dark-dead eyes of the massive enemy crouching ready to claim all that was dear to her; was the same dark presence; Hate.

Jordan sat waiting as hope drained from her soul, threatening to thrust her anguished heart into oblivion. She could not allow her fear to betray her in the canvas of her face. She knew that any show of fear would only serve as kindling to the raging fire that no doubt burned behind the dead eyes of the large man. Jordan silently prayed to the Creator of all for a way out, an answer to the conundrum that unfolded in front of her. She obviously could not just engage in the fight. She either would have to sit idly by on an airplane that now soared thousands of feet above the ground and watch as the giant dispatched her husband, or she would have to figure out a way to help from the side lines. Looking around Jordan begged the Almighty for a clue. In her present condition hand to hand combat was out, and she did not have her six-inch blade… what could she do? It was as that question breathed across her tortured soul that her eyes landed on an egg-shell colored object at her feet. Rolling aimlessly across the floor of the airplane, after Lane had thrown it at the enemy, the cue ball had finally settled, mercifully at Jordan's feet.

Jordan took in the sight of the two men making sure that the giant was not watching her. Satisfied that she was under his radar, Jordan scooted the ball between her feet and bent her knees upward. She bent slightly to the side as she retrieved the ball and again checked the man's attention, which was mercilessly aimed at Lane. With another massive blow the man brought Lane crashing to his knees again. Raising his fists high above his head, as Lane's body swayed in a slight circle, the man was readying himself for the death blow. The giant's face contorted into a mask of euphoric bliss, obviously the sweetness of the kill already filled his veins.

Jordan seized the only opportunity afforded her. With precision and power born of answered prayers, she stepped into the aisle and thrust the ball in the enemy's direction. The cue ball and the giant's head collided with deadly force.

Lane drew on what was left of his waning strength as he thrust the pool-stick forward lodging the silver-screw-tipped end between two of the giant's ribs. An angry burst of air exploded from the man's mouth and nose. At the same moment his head was being forced backward by the force of the cue-ball Jordan had flung. As the man's body crumbled into a pile of flesh and bone at Lane's feet, Lane turned a bewildered look in Jordan's direction. Jordan crumbled to the seat, as a weak smile filled her face.

"Thank you," Lane mouthed

"Thank God," Jordan amended.

As the shadows of the past pressed back into the corners of Jordan's mind, she stepped further into the midst of the enemy forces. Lane had been a worthy opponent to his adversary that day on the plane; just as he would be now.

Garrison would be just as he had always been, a threat to any foe in every sense of the word. Jordan too would bring the fight straight to the enemies' front door, but in the recesses of her mind she could not help but worry about the children. Not one of them had ever experienced anything as dark as this. Though Amelia had given each of them another round of her sleep aid, Jordan couldn't help but wonder how much of the events taking place were drifting into the dreams of her sweet angels, twisting their happy thoughts into the dark-demented scenes that could exist only in her nightmares.

Penny's arms felt like rubber as she thrust the Barton out again and again trying to keep the enemy at bay, but each time she met with air. The one Manerky warrior that she had impaled in the jugular had been her last. Though they had not been able to get near enough to her to launch their own attack, Penny knew that the way things were panning out they may not have long to wait. Her body screamed for her to stop, to lie down and allow them to claim their pound of flesh. She had already scanned the room. The alliance was looking strong and ready at first, but as the battle raged on Penny could see that her friends and family was equally tired. Nick was running out of arrows, and had already claimed a hand full of clay to fling instead of losing the last of his arrows into the enemy's midst. He had managed to down two of the tribe, but no more.

Garrison was breathing as if through a straw. He too was tired. Penny could hear the desperation in every breath from across the chamber. Jordan thrust her Barton and danced like a firefly amidst the enemy, but for all of her brutal-grace she had claimed but only three warriors. The numbers were staggering. Time was short, and Penny was starting to see the truth behind the enemy tactics. Wearing them down had been the plan from the start. The Manerky would wait patiently as their brothers at arms fell in battle. The outside forces would patiently stand in the background, waiting for the moment to present itself. They would learn from the mistakes of their predecessors, and in the end they would step forward through the ashes of those mistakes and claim the prize. They would have their pound of flesh literally.

Lane stood in the midst of the flailing arms and arcing weapons. He was no longer among those that filled the inner-chamber fighting for their right to remain among the living. Though his body still glowed as evidence of his existence in the earthly realm, his mind, heart and soul were unified in the effort to approach the Thrown of Grace; to bring the Master into this place of darkness. For though he had wielded the light of God so many times—he was unsure of his ability to protect those he loved. Jordan and the children may very well survive the encounter, but to what cost? Would Jordan be blinded? Though she was a Blood-Washed-Christian Jordan was as Lane not without blame. Jordan had done her share of wrong even after her encounter with Christ and subsequent salvation. Lane too had struggled, but due to his close walk with Christ, and the many beacons in his life in the form of people, places and things: his adopted parents, the Cadotion village, and of course The Truth… Lane had been purposefully guided by the Almighty so that he would stay close to the purpose set for his life. Lane had more closely kept to his calling because of God's constant intervening. For that Lane was thankful, but more importantly he was able to use the holy tools of battle such as the Creator's light.

Lane would have to commit. He could no longer stand on the precipice between worlds—doubt and belief, struggling for center stage. God knew how to bless His children—He knew how to protect His children. Lane would beseech the Almighty for answers and rest in the knowledge that God's way was higher than his way—just as Heaven was higher than earth. (Isaiah 55:9) Faith without works is dead. (James 2:14-26) God expected feet to be put to prayer. Lane knew that God would expect complete obedience and complete trust.

52

Shadows danced across the wall filling the hospital room with an otherworldly eeriness that threatened to send Cynthia running from the ICU. She felt so cold and distant as she approached the sterile environment that was now her husband's world. Everything within her screamed that this was not real. This was a dream; a nightmare. This was not her life. She was really at home watching a Lifetime movie about a woman that had lost everything in an instant, and had fallen asleep; she was dreaming. She would wake up on her couch surrounded by the memoirs testifying to her husband's love for her, and she would know that all was well.

Faith seemed such a foreign concept. She needed to have faith. She needed to get as far away from the feelings that bombarded her mind, and threatened to topple her to the ground, as possible. God was powerful, and his power was not dependent on how she felt. Regardless of her feelings that ALL CONSUMING POWER was the same.

Cynthia thought about Mary as she stood at the front of the church two Sundays ago, and reminded the congregation of that truth. She had attended Rocky Mount as often as possible; as often as her mission life with The Truth would allow. That Sunday, it had been raining like the end of the world was upon them. Cynthia had almost given into the excuses; she had almost stayed at home, and watched her favorite movies, but instead she had grabbed her bible and drove the thirty miles to the church. Finding their land in New Jersey had not been complete until she and John had located the church. It was then that all of her concerns about the haunted farm being so close to their property had seemed misplaced, even humorous.

The church was perfect. The members were more like family than members of a community meeting three times a week. She felt the familiar spirit of home and sanctuary every time she crossed the threshold into the congregational. That Sunday had been no different. The young music leader's wife had stood before the church as always and poured her heart out for all to see. The words said that day had not crossed her mind until now.

As Cynthia dared to draw closer to the clay form filling the space that should be her thriving husband she understood with stark acuity what Mary had meant. In that moment, she did not feel that God would save her husband, just as Mary did not feel that God would bring her sister to a saving knowledge of his Son, Christ-Jesus. Cynthia could not muster the good feelings, the proof within her senses that she believed that God would spare her husband's earthly form that He would allow John to remain here with her for a time longer. In that moment, though she believed with all her being that Heaven was real, Cynthia felt it too far away. She felt that John too was too far away to hear her desperate pleas for his return. Though the doctors had assured her that he could hear her, Cynthia did not feel like he could. She did not feel like doing anything, but laying on the bed beside her husband and crossing the unimaginable divide into Heaven with her love, her best friend, and the father of her unborn child, but down in the depths of her barren-soul Cynthia knew that her Master was calling her to arms; He was calling upon her to have faith. Though she stood before what seemed a vacant slab of human flesh, God was demanding that she have faith.

Lazarus had been in the tomb for four days. (John 1) Jesus brought Lazarus back from the dead. John was still alive as far as the medical instruments and the hospital staff would testify. Where was Cynthia's faith? Would she sit idly by as her husband suffered, with the POWER of a RISEN SAVIOR at her beckoned call and not be willing to ask; just ask for His healing power to come and make all things new?

Cynthia felt angry with herself. John deserved better. How could she not rally for him as she had for all of the children, mothers and fathers of Honduras? This was her husband and she was allowing the enemy to come in and take what was not his to have! This was Her Salvation! This was Her Life More Abundant! This was Her Faith! And God was Her Savior! Her Redeemer! He had all she needed for the asking!

Cynthia crumbled to her knees in that moment as she cried out to the Savior. She had given into the blasphemous lie long enough! She would take back what was hers!

"Lord, please forgive me for giving into the enemy's lies," Cynthia prayed as she clutched the pale-starched blanket that was covering her husband's too still body. "Father I know who you are! I know what you are capable of! It does not matter how I feel! You are POWERFUL!" Cynthia nearly shouted the word powerful as she clutched to the blanket as if it were the helm of her Savior's garment. "You can do all things, and I'm asking you in the HOLY, POWERFUL NAME OF JESUS to do everything in YOUR POWER to heal my husband!" Cynthia threw out her declaration of truth, her demand for healing, her plea for forgiveness all in one purposefully-triumphant announcement of Christ's UNIMAGINABLE POWER!

She stayed on her knees by her husband's bed for a moment longer, before moving to the nearest high-back brown leather chair, lining the white washed walls, of his small ICU patient room. She had given everything that she had. Her body was drained. All of her hopes, all of her dreams for a future with her husband were voiced. Everything lay naked for the Lord to see, not that He needed it, but she knew that it was the toll needed to cross that bridge. She had to be real. No longer could she hide from the truth. She was terrified. She had never given thought to a life without John. In order for her to give all to God she would have to look at the possibilities, and hand them willingly over to her Savior so she did. Every fear, every doubt, every moment of pause was out on the table before her Lord.

Cynthia felt as though a weight was lifted from her shoulders. John still lay in the bed next to her. His face just as ashen, the needles still in place, tubes as before ravaged his body, the machines still ticked and purred their ominous threat of what if... nothing in the physical realm had changed. All was unchanged. Cynthia smiled, nothing had changed in the physical, but nothing had stayed the same in the supernatural: she was whole again; she believed completely; she had faced the demons lurking in the corner of her mind, hoisting their taunts, and with strength that could only come from the King of Kings, the Lord of Lords she had stood face to face with those demons. She had hoisted her own taunts; her Truth: God is Mighty, and He will defeat you! You are nothing! You will be laid to waste! You are unwelcome here! One after the other Cynthia had launched the commands given to her by the Holy Spirit, and then at the height of that spiritual battle like a javelin hurled passed the finish line, Cynthia gave the command. The only thing that had ever needed to be said.

"GET BEHIND ME SATAN IN THE NAME OF JESUS!" The words rang out in the drab room. The fire behind the command made the chilly room seem somehow warmer as it ignited the nerve endings along her back and neck. With the last of the spiritual battle behind her, Cynthia collected her purse and kissed John on the head.

"I'll be back in a few hours my love." She whispered into his ear. "I Can Only Imagine." Cynthia crooned the first refrains of John's favorite song as she exited the tiny cubicle, and started for the double doors.

"What the…" A nurse was standing behind the nurses' station just about to start her rounds as Cynthia had passed by. As usual Cynthia gave a smile, but this time the smile was filled with strength.

Cynthia continued past, not paying much attention to the alarm in the tall, slender, African American woman's voice. Cynthia liked the nurse. Andy was her name. She was sweet. Not too cocky, or full of herself. Andy had been at the hospital for fourteen years, but she was still young, and her face still registered patience uncommon to those in the medical field that long. The years had not stolen that first glimmer of hope. Andy had managed to hang on to her ideals. She had not let the death of patients take from her the promise of being the best nurse. The appetite for saving lives still clung wildly to her idealistic young mind. Sure, she had seen her share of death, but God took who He would, and He allowed Andy to save those that He still had a mission for.

Andy was great. Cynthia liked her. She had a boldness in Christ, too. It clung to her every physicality like the golden hue of a rainbow. Her shoulder length draping curls, played around her dark-skin. Her lips always glossed to perfection with a dark-shade of burgundy. Everything about Andy would suggest snobbery, but in truth she was the epitome of congeniality and humility.

Cynthia placed a hand on the square-silver button marked "push" as she walked by. The white doors plumed open inviting her into the waiting room. She felt great. She would go home. Get a shower, and clean up the bits of crystal that littered their home. Sadness threatened to seep back in, but Cynthia shook off the unwanted emotion. Feelings had nothing to do with it. God was at work! God was able! She would go home and clean up. Her husband would be coming home, and he would need a clean place to come home to. She couldn't very well have him traipsing through shards of broken crystal on his way to the bathroom.

She thought of the magnificent pieces given to her by John. They were irreplaceable, but they were inanimate objects. John was irreplaceable. John was flesh and blood. She would give every intricately carved piece of art given to her in the small cabin to take away the events that had put John in the ICU. None of it mattered. She would go home. She would remove the evidence. She would replace the lamps with something more practical. Besides, she and John had a child coming. Glass and crystal was hardly something that needed to be on tables in a living room filled with children.

Cynthia smiled. Yes, the future was bright indeed.

Andy watched the monitor on the desk, but she couldn't believe her eyes. John's heart rate was rising. More than that, though, if the monitor was right… John was… Waking up? Her mind raced. Calm down Andy, she scolded. Treat the patient not the monitor. Andy dropped her head in shame. It was a good thing she hadn't shouted to Cynthia to come back. The poor woman had been through enough. Moving from the monitor, Andy turned back and eyed the frustrating equipment accusingly. She hated this part of the job. The times when hope surged through her senses, and made her feel as though the impossible were coming to fruition; still she gave herself over to the moment. It could happen.

Hope filled every step as Andy moved closer to the curtained cubicle that housed Cynthia's once thriving husband. Cynthia had confided all of the stories of John's past. The man was strong and virile; he was a tried and true warrior for Christ. Just as Andy's grandfather had been; her father too had been rock-solid in his faith; praying over Andy and her brother through every uncertainty. It was that faith that had taught Andy; it had brought her through so many tragic moments in her medical career that should have stopped her in her tracks... so many uncertain times that should have shut Andy down; made her just as cynical, cold, and dead inside as many of the other nurses in the ICU, or the other floors of the hospital had become. Not Andy. God was in control! He was the commander and chief! He called the shots! Andy just waited on the side lines for the times that her Master allowed her to rise to the occasion—the times when she could take heroic measures, and give Him all the glory in the aftermath.

Andy slid the curtain open with the usual casual movement of just another day in the ICU. She wanted to believe that this was not just one of those moments, but she was afraid to give into the excitement welling up in her spirit. She hated how superstitious she could be; some habits would die hard. One-day God would take the terrible habit from her, and Andy would walk in faith—no matter the circumstance, or possible consequences.

As Andy pushed passed the shroud of white material, she could see that this was anything, but the usual ICU day.

"Doctor!" Andy shrieked as she raced for the call button, and ripped the cord from its silver housing.

"Cynthia!" Andy called. "Cynthia!" Again Andy yelled as she claimed John's hand before it could rip the intubation-tubing from his mouth and throat. Andy knew that calling for Cynthia at a time like this was anything but professional. But she and the older woman had grown so close, and she knew how distraught Cynthia had been. Andy never stopped to think about the consequences—there were plenty of jobs—Andy's world was short on friends as true as Cynthia.

Moments later, the small room filled with the astonished faces of the medical staff.

Cynthia's mind only barely registered the urgent call coming from John's room. Turning on a heel, she raced toward the small space teaming with medical staff.

"No brain activity!" Cynthia heard a doctor say. The confused tone by which it was said almost stopped Cynthia in her tracks. She, for a moment, wanted to escape in the other direction. Her mind begged for her not to go into the room; not to allow yet another disappointment. Stay in the moment that was yours before; believe. Her heart screamed. Don't feel! Believe!

She straightened her borrowed clothes. Andy had brought them to her the day after John had been shot; sweatpants and a t-shirt. Realizing that Cynthia would never leave John's side, Andy had collected the garments, and returned to the hospital after her shift. Cynthia thought about the young nurse's sacrifice as she stayed with John long enough for Cynthia to take a quick shower. Long moments passed as Cynthia had watched what remained of John's blood escape down the drain. She had no time to crumble, though she wanted to seep into the same desolate canyon. She wanted to be liquid so she could escape through some hole; never have to look back. She no longer wanted to exist in this place. The earth seemed too big without John's wonderful smile, his dark hair and handsome features, but more than anything it was his huge heart... Cynthia had choked back the tears as she witnessed the blood from that heart drain into oblivion as if it were worth no more than the water it had mingled with as it spun like a small tornado out of site.

Cynthia moved passed the entourage of doctors and nurses. The doctor that had used the offensive tone when describing John's mental status stood inches from the bed tapping his penlight to his temple. His bloated-red face was screwed up in a curious grimace, and becoming increasingly more purple. Cynthia decided as she turned to another physician that stood with one hand on John's forehead pulling back an eyelid at a time while dancing his own penlight across John's pupils.

"Equal and reactive." the leaner of the two doctors announced with an assertive nod of his graying head.

"Twenty-three years, Mick!" the thinner physician announced. Then shook his head pathetically. "Doctor Thomas, I've been doing this twenty-three years. His pupils are reactive to light. Furthermore, they are equal in size," he said every word slowly as if speaking to an insubordinate toddler.

"No need for a spitting match, Doctor Johnson! I think we can both appreciate the anomaly of the situation!" Doctor Mick was incredulous. His eyes flashed with controlled fury as he regarded his much older colleague.

"Uhum…" A nurse cleared her throat.

Cynthia vaguely recognized it as being Andy. Still foggy on what was transpiring in front of her, Cynthia stumbled-numbly forward.

"Oh! Mrs. Benton." Doctor Thomas nodded in Cynthia's direction.

"We obviously did not see you there."

"Wha… what's happening?" Cynthia stuttered as again something deep in her spirit seemed to push her feet forward—in a shaky-autopilot motion.

"Well, it's too soon to tell, Mrs. Benton…" Doctor Thomas was trying to explain.

"The hell it is!" The other doctor, Doctor Johnson, Cynthia acknowledged as her head snapped to attention. Now she was frustrated; an automatic response to the use of unneeded profanity. She hated that about herself. It made witnessing difficult. She wanted to be relaxed around those that may not share her ideals. She had come a long way in Christ, though she was nowhere near perfect. The simple act just made her seem… judgmental.

"I need answers. Preferably ones without so much colorful language." Cynthia winced as she cleared her throat. She had unwittingly given into the character flaw. She cast a downward glance, and then moved closer to John's bed. She absently rubbed his feet as she lifted her eyes. "Sorry," Cynthia admitted.

She realized then as doctor Johnson pointed automatically to John that she had not once looked in John's direction. Her heart would not allow her to. She was hiding from the onslaught of yet more pain. She knew that God would heal her husband, but moments after her prayer…

Cynthia finally took in her husband. The room felt as though it were spinning out of control. John's eyes were fluttering wildly. His hands lay rigidly by his side where they were being held in place to keep him from pulling at the foreign object—the intubation-tube—from his throat. Cynthia watched as desperation filled his features. Long moments passed as she too felt as though her ability to breathe was being impeded. Her hands flew protectively to her throat, and then straightened as her fingers latched on to the bed for stability. Was she going to pass out? She shook her head. No, she had to stay alert. John needed her. He would need her. Again, Cynthia shook her head as the edges of her vision tunneled. She swayed, and then she felt the cool hands of someone as they captured her arms, and guided her to the safety of a nearby chair.

"Calm down, Cynthia," Andy crooned as she watched her new friend teeter wildly. Andy moved Cynthia to the high-leather-back chair in the corner of the room. Cynthia needed to sit down. A cold compress was thrust at Andy. Allowing a small smile of thanks, Andy claimed the cloth, and pressed it tenderly to the back of Cynthia's neck. Sweat beaded on her brow as she turned a sickening shade of green.

Andy moved to the bedside cabinet—the collection of medical instruments was pushed as far to the corner as possible to give the patients, and their family's room to move around the small enclosure.

Andy pulled both doors open with a quick jerk. She claimed an emesis-bag from the third shelf. The small blue bag meant to collect vomit was collapsed into a neat circular-square pile. Andy brought it quickly to Cynthia's side as she smoothly placed the bag under Cynthia's chin while putting her other hand on the now warm rag at the back of Cynthia's neck.

Slowly, the room seemed to right itself as Cynthia again tried to look passed the crew of medical personnel working on her now agitated husband.

"Calm down, Mr. Benton. We're going to remove the tube," Doctor Johnson soothed breathlessly.

Cynthia watched as John struggled to remove the tube. She studied John's body language. He seemed more intent on sitting up, or getting out of the bed than removing the tube. Cynthia moved slowly to her feet. She waited for the nausea or dizziness to return. Thankfully neither ailment did.

"Cynthia." Andy grabbed for her arm, but Cynthia waved her concerns off with a gentle push of her hand. As soon as Andy uttered Cynthia's name, John was a volcano of movement.

"I'm here, John." Cynthia assured as she raced forward, and pushed passed the still struggling doctors and nurses.

John visually relaxed, but then his eyes grew wide again.

Tears filled Cynthia's eyes as she caressed the swell in her abdomen. "We're okay, honey." She promised as she moved to the side of the bed, and claimed John's hand. She gently kissed his hand as tears spilled from her eyes, and washed down his arm. She pulled John's hand closer, and placed it over her stomach. His fingers splayed protectively over her middle. His hand moved slightly as his middle finger and ring finger disappeared behind his palm. His index finger and thumb became an L. Cynthia watched as John's pinkie finger extended out; the sign for I love you.

"We love you, too." Cynthia choked.

Tears streamed down John's face as at last he lay back his head, and nodded for the doctors to continue.

Cynthia rubbed John's hand slowly as the doctor removed the tube after telling John to cough. She loved this man with every ounce of her being, and yet up next to the mountain of love her husband was exhibiting: the tube still securely in place; still making its unrelenting demands that his lungs receive oxygen in their time; the tube was still firmly in place—still in his throat, a foreign body, obstructing his ability to swallow; to breathe of his own volition… her love seemed hollow in comparison. Cynthia smiled back at this man that God had chosen for her—this unique being of profound strength was hers; God had not made that decision once, but twice; John Benton was Cynthia's to have and hold forever.

53

Time moved on in its unrelenting pace as Julie waited for Edward to wake. He had been sleeping most of the morning. The moment she had entered his room, she had seen in his eyes the guilt that had taken hold of his soul. He had spent a lifetime believing a lie. Cecil Schooner had only been protecting his own life. Edward knew that given the same circumstance he too would have disposed of Amorous. His heart would not allow him to see the logic. His love for her had run so deep. His need for her in his life had been as the need for oxygen. She was an obsession. Julie felt a tinge of jealously as Edward had confided in her the truth of his past. She wanted to be a strong woman, a loving friend, a trusted counselor, but in truth she was a mere woman in love with a man that had devoted his existence to another. Julie sighed, even jealously was a short lived emotion as she watched Edward now.

She was concerned that his sudden affinity for rest was more than a tired patient recovering; Edward was suffering from depression. How could she blame him? Wouldn't she feel the same, given his circumstance?

He had done many things that would be questionable. He was no innocent man. Julie knew that better than most; she had spent the day before listening to accusations from the Director of Nurses that would put any man in the electric chair, and then the proof that would absolve that same man of most of those manufactured crimes had come the following morning. Edward had done plenty to taint his own existence. He was in no need of help from the likes of Max.

Julie turned the overhead light off. The shadows had danced their eerie taunts long enough. The ominous distortions were trying her nerves. She needed to pray—to think positive thoughts. Cynthia Benton had confided so much to her that morning. She now held proof in her hand that would clear Edward of all charges concerning the child-agents, and John Benton's attempted murder. The manipulation of the agent's lives or the many criminals killed in the name of keeping law and order, would not hold much sway with a jury. Julie realized more than ever that the real judge, the jury that mattered now was the demons in the corner of Edward's mind; the whispers of guilt taunting him every waking hour, and yes, even his sleep would be filled with their relentless accusations. Never stopping their onslaught of lies, the enemy would press in from every side. Julie would have to be just as relentless in her efforts to remind her friend of his worth. She would pray for angels to camp out around his bedside, remain ever vigilant for enemy attacks. She would even have her new friend to agree with her in prayer.

A chill ran up Julie's spine. She had prayed for John that morning as she had Edward. God was going to move. Julie had always been tuned into miracles being worked in the lives of those people she had prayed for; a wonderful gift imparted to her from the Holy Spirit.

John Benton was definitely on the verge of a breakthrough.

She smiled. "Please God…" She breathed. "Edward too," she allowed a quick peak in his direction.

Something had to give. Edward needed to learn to forgive himself. People made mistakes. No matter what walk of life—people were people—just humans trying to make it through life. God had provided the only way to make it through—the only way to navigate the obstacles in life: Jesus.

Julie stood by Edward's bed, studying his handsome features. How would she ever convince this man to see himself as she did; more importantly, as God saw him?

All the forgiveness in the world would do no good, unless Edward could forgive himself. For if he deemed himself unworthy of such forgiveness, he would never ask.

This was harder, Julie reasoned. This trying to help someone move beyond self-loath, to a place of forgiveness; it was harder than letting go of a lost loved one.

Julie did not want to compare her deceased husband to Edward, but Ronald was all she had known. She had spent a lifetime at his side; that lifetime had never seemed enough. She had wanted more; years sprawled out with the two of them loving each other—all the while watching their children and grandchildren find their own way in life. All of that was lost to her—that had been a hurdle that seemed insurmountable. Yet this seemed bigger still.

Edward was closed off; in a place of torment—a hell all his own— created from walls of self-hate—walls built from the years he had spent believing Cecil Schooner had wronged him; years that Edward had given over to making Cecil and his decedents pay; Time spent in vein. Edward had believed with every ounce of his being that Cecil Schooner had stolen Amorous—he had ended her life, and claimed any chance at happiness he and Amorous might have had. That belief had grown into a mountain of hate that had bordered the ends of Edward's universe, and shut him off from life. Edward had realized that truth. He had almost left behind any opportunity to receive forgiveness, love, and life from a risen Savior. Almost.

Julie smoothed the covers down on Edward's bed, and adjusted his pillow.

"It's not too late for you," she whispered. "That's why you are here." Julie studied the smooth plains of Edward's face. Though time had etched fine lines in his features, and anger had carved tiny grooves along the sides of his warm-deep-pink lips. Julie could see how handsome he had been—he still was.

Amorous must have been lost in the canvas of ruggedly-handsome features. Her heart never stood a chance.

Julie had no doubt, for as she stood drinking in this older version of Amorous' once great love, she was lost as well.

Julie's heart splintered as she reached a shaky hand to his head. The powdered-gray misting his temples added a distinguished nuance to his features. She should not take this liberty with her heart. She knew by the stuttering in her chest that touching Edward's handsome face would send her already lost heart into oblivion.

Her hand shook all the more as it drew closer still. Why was she doing this? Hadn't her heart, his heart been through enough? Yet even as her mind shot the warning flair to her over indulgent heart, her fingers threaded possessively through his dark hair.

He was not hers.

She wanted to back away, and yet in the depths of her soul she knew that was a lie. With all of her being she wanted to taste his lips, to know what it was to be shrouded in those muscular arms—not huge muscles, but slight definition that hinted at the power this man possessed.

As Julie's mind brought every magnificent detail into focus, she realized a moment too late that her lips had found his. Shock filled her senses as Edward's hand captured her head, and held her prisoner to his unyielding kiss. Moments passed as she forgot who she was, who he was, what he was capable of.

In that moment, Julie was no longer a widow, a mother, a grandmother. She was no longer a broken-heart on the precipice of a great leap. She was now swept away in the torrent of a love that she could not afford to lose herself to. Her mind vanquished all thoughts of the right thing to do as Edward moved his upper body to a seated position, and pulled her further into his forbidden embrace.

Edward's mind raced. His body reacted in ways it had not in years. This woman that he held in his arms was beautiful, intelligent, and kind... he couldn't think past that. She was kind. She was a Christian woman with ideals, and a belief system that someone like him would never be able to understand. Here he was, yet again proving what a monster he truly was. Would he take her here? Would he treat her as nothing more than a passing thought? His mind grasped at the fleeting judgments; the perfectly sound reasons to not possess her, while his heart pumped the hormones insistently into his system. With each pump, his thoughts became cloudier. This needed to stop. Julie was worth more. She was a mother, a grandmother, she was a friend to so many...

Edward loosened his grip as his hands fell unwillingly to his side. The simple gesture was treason to his heart, an assassination of his soul—departing from her embrace, his lips falling away from hers was a bitter poison burning its unrelenting promise of death through his senses.

Time stood still in that moment. Julie's eyes blazed with desire as her breath sputtered unevenly. So long had it been since she had known such passion. Her face reddened. What must she look like to Edward? And hadn't it been he who had broken their forbidden tryst? Her cheeks filled with a deeper red as she touched her hand to her swollen lips. Edward hadn't shaved in a few days, and the stubble around his lips had burned her skin. The chapped sensation, evident as her hand petted the offended skin, no doubt a mirror of her pouting heart. What must she look like indeed?

Julie turned to her purse. She wanted to leave his room. She couldn't stand to look in the deep brown of his eyes; she was too lost already; falling in their depths would do nothing to help her now. Her heart still raced as she backed automatically from the bedside. Inches from her escape, she placed the ruffled manila envelope on the nightstand. Her hand shook more violently as she moved it away from the package of proof.

Julie looked to her purse on the high-leather back chair. It was mere feet away, and then she could walk out of this room, and his life forever. She would never have to look into his achingly handsome face again. She would never have to face the embarrassing truth that she had thrown herself at him like some school girl with a wild crush. Just feet away from this hell that she had so willingly poured herself into, and yet it seemed miles.

Julie turned to her bag as she felt his hand capture hers. "I'm sorry." Came his baritone voice. The crescendo of sound sent chills skittering up her spine.

"It was me." Julie's eyes batted back the tears that threatened to fall. "I…I…" She had no words. She sniffed against the traitorous tears that gathered in her sinuses and throat. Not now. She begged. Please not now. She hated her traitorous-tender heart in this moment more than ever. She had acted as a teenager. She had gambled with her heart, and she had lost. This man that had known so much, this agent, leader, and yes killer… her heart jolted in her chest as she imagined, for an instant his hands around her throat. He could. But just as quickly the image faded as her heart—traitor that it was—shifted the horrific-daydream back to the embrace.

Julie pulled gently trying to tug her hand free of his.

"Don't." Came his gentle demand. The bed creaked, and then he was there. He was standing next to her.

She turned to him. She had meant to push him back to the bed, but as her hand touched the warm valley of his, achingly-perfect-chest she was in his arms again.

This time it was Julie that broke the embrace. Her eyes misted with tears as she shook her head pitifully. "I need to go." She more begged than stated. "I brought the proof that you need."

Edward touched his finger to her lips. He leaned in and kissed the tears from her eyes. "I'm not innocent." He whispered into her hair.

Julie nodded as her face screwed up in anguish. "You are of this." She reasoned. "Edward, I know…" Julie was stopped as Edward again claimed her lips with his.

At last pulling away, Edward looked deep into her eyes. In his gaze she could see him for the first time: she saw the agent; she saw the cold blooded killer; she saw the man that had hated another for a lifetime; she saw a man that had wasted it all on a phantom, and then she saw who that man had become… for the first time, Julie could see Edward Stanton, the man on the verge of redemption.

Julie leaned her head to his chest. Her head tilted back as she kissed the bandage covering the jagged wound that had almost ended his life. What must I do to push him over the edge? Her heart begged God for the answer.

Him too God… Please. Julie's spirit groaned the words that could not be spoken as she swayed against Edward in the cold-dark room.

CHAPTER

54

Penny was still struggling to stay on her feet when she heard the explosion of air burst from someone behind her. Her mind denied the truth, but no amount of denial would change what was. Nick was in trouble. Though she wasn't sure how badly he had been hurt, the sound of concussed wind leaving his mouth was enough to crumble her hiding place.

Nick was desperate to fight through the cloud of Manerky. Even now in the midst of the truth his desire was as strong as ever to protect Penny. But the enemy kept coming, kept pushing in. The impossible numbers billowing in through each of the entrances was staggering.

His mind raced through every detail that his grandfather had given. Kick, chop, block… Every defense possible. He tried to deposit the pain in his side into some chamber of his mind, where he would visit it later. Desperation filled his heart as his peripheral filled with the site of Penny swatting at the enemy with her single weapon. Yet as he watched, and as he fought to be at her side, he was only pushed further away.

His body grew tired. His senses were dulling. No one would come to rescue them from the storm that the Manerky had rained down upon them. It was fight or die. Nick loosened the axe from the tie around his belt, and swung it wildly at any of the warriors venturing too close to his strike zone. It was as he chanced another sideways glance at Penny that the fateful blow had come.

At first, there was no pain just shock. Then, as if his mind had moved out of its slow motion trance, and caught up to his body, the pain slammed into his senses. Air whooshed out of his lungs. His body snapped backward, and then he slowly righted himself. He didn't have to look down to see the horrid gash that covered the left side of his body.

As Nick's arm lifted in another violent swing, the Manerky-warrior brought his hand filled with gnarled fingernails down. Blood oozed from the offended tissue. The long tearing gash followed along the contour of his left side, opening the existing wound even further. The enemy-warrior had snagged one of his thick-jagged-grotesquely angled nails into Nick's side. The gaping hole left behind throbbed with every heartbeat. If the pain before had felt crippling, this would lead to his early demise. Every breath brought with it renewed anguish that bordered on tortured-insanity.

Nick's right arm flew automatically to the wound. The moment of weakness had opened him up for another attack. He watched, helpless to stop the assault, as another Manerky bolted in from a crouched position. A sizzling hiss escaped his throat as his mouth opened to reveal the razor edge of filed teeth.

Lane was at the Father now, and he had leant his will over completely to that of the Father. He knew now more than ever before that God would protect His children. He knew best.

Lane relaxed in that knowledge as he sought his Master's wisdom.

At first, he was lost to the low buzzing, but as the sound crescendo into a cacophony of unrelenting horror, Lane became completely aware of the foreign sound. Crickets, frogs, birds, bats… the Manerky had mimicked the animals as they lavished their horrible punishments on their enemy; God would use the real thing.

All around the cave, the boisterous complaints of the animals echoed off of the walls, until the unrelenting taunts became a vicious assault on the Manerky's senses.

The warriors' hands flew protectively to their ears. As they tried to flee from the cave they began bumping into each other. Confusion filled the inner chamber.

"Now!" Lane shouted above the shrieking animal calls. His voice banged around the walls of the cave, becoming its own weapon.

Jordan snapped to attention as she heard Lane's cry for action. Though the animal calls were indeed offensive, she was not solely reliant on her hearing; as were the Manerky. The enemies were indeed stressed by the bellowing noises coming from the many animals sounding their instigated threats.

Wonder filled Jordan as she tried to think of a time she had heard so many calls in one place, and then she was reminded; the Garden. She knew then that Lane had indeed reached his Master. God was at work.

A renewed strength filled Jordan as she watched her friends and family all around tear through the Manerky ranks.

The warriors waiting for their comrades at arms to fall were already making good their escape. Jordan rolled to the side, grabbing a bow and arrows from the pile of weapons looted in the village. She righted her stance. Coming up on one knee with practiced ease, she released the first of several arrows into the fleeing warriors. One by one, as arrows cascaded down on the horrified enemy forces, they too began their frantic scramble for safety.

Ignited by the periled cries of the enemy, Jordan lunged forward, Barton in hand.

Garrison moved through the Manerky with the grace and ease of the seasoned agent he had once been. Jordan allowed an appreciative smile in his direction. The years of neglect to his abilities faded away as her once stealthy partner emerged from the ashes, and moved like a shadow on the wall.

Casing the cave for possible unchecked threats to her companions, Jordan's gaze at last settled on Nick and Penny. Penny was poised in front of her fallen friend, daring any of the enemy to come near to him. Jordan turned to Nick. His left side was ripped open. The material of his black t-shirt was ripped, and hanging open to expose the gruesomely assaulted flesh. The wound still seeped blood, but for the most part the blood had been stanched.

Jordan abandoned her attack on the outcropping of fleeing Manerky, and launched a new campaign of slaughter on her newly designated target.

Rage pulsed through Garrison's senses for the animalistic-barbarians. How easily they flee form adversity. They had swept into the heart of those he loved, and dared to visit their brand of savagery, but as soon as Lane had brought down the wrath of his God they would run… they felt it so easy to walk away. Garrison snorted at the concept that seemed so foreign to him.

"Where are you going?" Garrison howled with laughter as he brought his blade across the throat of a stunned Manerky. The warrior, crazed with dread had crashed into Garrison while probing for escape. Garrison seized the fleeing warrior with one arm, and brought his blade smoothly across the jugular with his free hand. A rumble of laughter boiled up, and spilled from his lips as blood sprayed from his victim's throat misting his companion.

The confused Manerky, now wearing a mask of crimson droplets, screeched with horror as Garrison plunged the blade soaked with his tribesman's blood deep into his chest.

Garrison watched as the empty-white-eyes of the frantic warrior bulged in disbelief. He would have liked nothing more than to relax in that moment—to take all afternoon killing each of them with the leisure of enjoying a glass of iced tea, but his movements had to be swift. The more of the enemy forces allowed to escape the chamber, the more could return. Garrison shook off his disappointment as he drove through the surrounding adversary.

Garrison was slicing through another warrior when he caught sight of Jordan kneeling down beside a fallen Nick. His mind half expected Amelia to rush to his aid, but then he remembered that she had taken some of the mixed herbs given for sleep. She now rested with her brother and Modilo in the corner of the room. Garrison peered over at the fire hearth in the middle of the cave, some of the spices were still intact, though most of the boiling mixture had been knocked across the cave floor in the heat of the battle. Garrison grabbed the small bowl of calming tea, and raced to Jordan's side; the whole way slicing through the enemy forces.

Realizing that God had things well at hand, Lane started to scoop up the children. He would carry them to the other chamber away from the enemy. Though most of the Manerky were in a flurry of trying to escape the horrible noises now assaulting their over-developed hearing, Lane did not want to become too comfortable with the idea that the children were safe. His heart stuttered as he thought of the enemy breaking away from the fight, and claiming the children for their depraved rituals.

He knew that the beliefs of what the Manerky were capable of were mere rumors, but he had no desire to find out how valid the stories might have been. Lane was headed back from his third trip to the chamber. Already he had Amelia, Tristan, and Modilo tucked safely on the other side of the chamber, away from where Aniahi's body lay. Lane had moved her body to a tiny cove just outside of the chamber. He didn't want the children to wake, and stumble across her remains.

A deep sadness had filled his heart as he carried his trusted friend's body away from the chamber. Though Lane knew all too well that Aniahi was no longer in this clay-shell, his heart still recognized the shell of flesh as his once beloved friend. He found strength in what he knew Aniahi would want. He knew that if she had been able to voice her concerns, Aniahi would have told him to move her body so that the children would not have to find her this way. Aniahi had loved his children just as she had loved him. She had given her life for that love.

Lane pushed passed the sadness as he moved swiftly down the tunnel leading back to the chamber where the fight was still raging.

The scream came moments after Lane had left the inner-chamber with Kirsten's sleeping form in tow. He was finishing the task of relocating the children. Kirsten would have been the last of his charge to be moved to the sleep chambers. It had only taken a few moments after God had released the phantom animal cries for Lane to realize the possible threat to the children. The room was a chaotic nightmare of the enemy forces scrambling for safety. Lane feared that the children might be trampled in the myriad of slaughter and frantic need.

Lane rushed to the dimly lit chamber, now serving as sleeping quarters for the younger members of their group. He quickly draped Kirsten's sleeping body in a small nook to the side of the entrance. No need to subject her to the peril that lay beyond.

Anxiety flushed through Lane's veins as he allowed a quick glance back at Kirsten, and then raced toward the unseen threat. The young girl could possibly be the safest of all the children, but at that moment her small frame lay in a fetal position on top of the furs she had been laying. She somehow seemed the most vulnerable. Lane ignored the need to pull her into his arm, and rush her into a more lit area. She lay in the shadows; unmoving. She was sleeping. She would remain outside of the enemy radar in her cove. It was the best chance that he could give her. The real danger was just beyond her shadow-filled sleep chamber.

Lane's heart raced as his mind filtered through the possibilities; someone or something had entered the chamber where the children were sleeping. Guilt crushed down upon him. It had been his idea, his need to rid the children of possible horror that had exposed the children to whatever harm was being visited upon them.

C H A P T E R

55

John had been growing stronger and more restless by the minute. Cynthia had reluctantly left his chattering side to go home for a few hours. She would shower and make good her promise to clean for his homecoming.

She wanted no evidence of the home invasion to be apparent upon John's return. She was so thankful for Andy's offer to sit with John for a few hours after her shift had ended. The young-idealistic nurse had already done so much, but with all of her friends away, Andy was all that she had.

Cynthia smiled at the now clean cabin. A couple of rose-colored lamps with silver praying hands etched in the forefront took the place of the ruined crystal ones. She had stopped by the Dollar store near their home for a few things she had forgotten at Wal-Mart. The lamps had been like a breath of fresh air. Though they were not the exact image of the former lighting, there was so much about the intricately sketched praying hands that had reminded her of the crystal lamps John had bought for her.

She was still admiring the new more practical living room of her and John's home when she heard the chiming tones of the doorbell. Cynthia froze for a moment. Her face turned ashen. The unrepentant intrusion into her serene world was as uncomfortable to Cynthia as if a copperhead were lying on the floor in front of her. She was probably still a little gun shy; she thought. It had not been that long ago when she answered the chirping tone with a pleasant smile, only to let Max into their home. It turned out that Max was much worse than having a snake in the floor of their home.

Cynthia disregarded the thought as she cautiously moved to the mudroom and peered out the small glass opening in the door. It was then that she felt her shoulders relax. She breathed a much needed sigh of relief, and allowed a smile for her visitors. The pastor and his wife had unexpectedly dropped by. Mark and Emily Wyatt carried a large wicker-basket of prepared foodstuffs.

Cynthia smiled brighter as the couple struggled with the large basket. She hurriedly ran across the room to prepare a place for the huge buffet.

"It's a little something the church members prepared. We wish we could do more." Emily's huge blue eyes conveyed the depth of emotion budding in her spirit. So petite was the blonde headed woman that Cynthia had often referred to her as having pixy-like qualities.

Cynthia regarded her pastor a moment. A wealth of concern existed behind his more earthy-brown eyes as well. The opposite of Emily, Mark seemed to look as though he would be more comfortable in a heavy metal concert than behind the pulpit preaching, though his sermons were all that was needed for one to know this was indeed a man of God. His shoulder length-brown-hair slightly graying feathered back, and fell in wispy waves. Whereas, Emily's blonde hair nestled more closely to her head in an adorable pixie style cut.

As Cynthia regarded her friends more closely she realized that she had not given the good news to anyone. All that knew of John's miraculous recovery were the medical staff in charge of John's case.

"Oh Lord, I'm so sorry!" Cynthia beamed. "I haven't told anyone."

The preacher and his wife glanced at each other for a moment, and then turned cautious eyes back on Cynthia.

"Told us what?" Mark finally prompted.

"John…" Cynthia chirped, but then seeing the fallen countenance of her friends her hands flew automatically to each of their shoulders.

"No, John woke up this morning!" Cynthia nearly shouted the wonderful news. Each time she thought it, said it, she felt the words pass over the wounds covering her once broken soul. So real was the soothing effects of the wonderful truth that Cynthia wanted to shout them to everyone that she came in contact with!

"Woke up?" Confusion colored Emily's expression as she again glanced uneasily at her husband. After a quick shrug for Mark, Emily again turned to Cynthia for answers.

"Please sit down." Cynthia offered as she pulled out a chair and took a seat first. "God healed John this morning. I was praying. I knew..." Cynthia breathed heavily as tears slipped unbidden form her eyes, and settled in her throat; making her words almost unintelligible.

Cynthia smiled and some of the excitement of before trickled through her senses.

"I felt the 'yes'... well it was like as I was praying; in that moment..." Cynthia struggled for a way to explain what had happened. She searched Mark and Emily's eyes for understanding. "It was as though I knew without a shadow of doubt that God was going to heal him." Cynthia's eyes shone as she looked across the room to the hand painted picture depicting hands outstretched in supplication. It was then that all of the emotions breached the walls in her soul. Her body rocked with the possibilities of what could have been. The possibilities that she had kept at bay for so long; things that she could not face; tomorrows without her love. It was all too much to imagine, and yet as she looked back at her friends she knew that all were possibilities that she would never again have to contemplate. As Cynthia peered into the eyes of her friends it was there that she could see the truth: Faith born of years of being in the ministry shone out from the lovely and different faces of her wonderful friends; a faith so tangible that Cynthia believed in that moment that she could reach out and touch it.

"John is fine. He is coming home tomorrow. His doctors want him to stay in the hospital overnight for observation." Cynthia huffed as she again took in the confused faces of Mark and Emily. "Longer really, but John wasn't having it." Cynthia gave an emphatic shake of her head while rolling her eyes theatrically. "I guess the more things change, the more they stay the same."

Mark cleared his throat after another confused or concerned glance in Emily's direction... Cynthia wasn't sure. She had given up on gauging her friend's reactions to the news.

"Do you need anything?" Again Mark cleared his throat.

Cynthia looked at her pastor for a moment. It was then that she realized that the man wasn't just confused; he was stricken with some unseen conundrum… he was trying to make sense of something that seemed to not calculate. He looked as though Cynthia had just told him that two plus two was five.

"Is something wrong?" Cynthia finally managed.

"Well, we just left the hospital yesterday morning." Mark turned to Emily again. He seemed to search for a delicate way to explain what it was he needed to confide in Cynthia.

"Go on." Cynthia prompted. She was still excited. Nothing that her preacher could say would darken her mood. She knew that faith was not an easy concept to grasp. Even the most dedicated in ministry could fall short when faced with 'the impossible'.

"Well…" Mark licked his lips. "Well, the doctor came in. Emily and I spoke with him. He said that John's condition was very grave. He said that he and the other doctor that he had been consulting with was going to approach you about taking John off of life support." Mark looked at Cynthia then as he reached across the table and gently took her hand. "He said that John had no brain activity… that he was brain dead." The color drained from Mark's face then as the words left his lips.

Cynthia could see in that moment what John had truly meant to this man. Both Mark and Emily were true shepherds to their flock. This man and woman of God had not taken their responsibilities to the church lightly. At times, Cynthia had thought them too focused. Though Cynthia had not been in the congregation long, she was a very good judge of character; a quality that made her profiling abilities all the more spot on. Cynthia could see that the idea of losing John was crushing them.

Cynthia patted Mark's hand. "I went through the same thing. It was as though I could understand that healing could come, no matter the impossibility of the situation, in the foreign countries that we went to. It was possible for Mrs. Jacobs, suffering with cancer; we prayed for her two Sundays ago… remember?" Cynthia looked to Mark for confirmation.

Mark nodded that he did.

"I understand what this must feel like to you both, but I'm telling you that John is coming home tomorrow. He was healed this morning. He was sitting up in his hospital bed, talking Andy's ears off when I left for home..." Cynthia laughed as she looked into the eyes of her friends. Realization was starting to wash over the couple.

Emily allowed a small gasp as tears washed down her pristine features. Mark turned then to her, and stood. His feet were moving the moment they were placed flat on the floor.

"Thank you, Jesus! You are able, Lord! You are Mighty! You are all things!" Mark chanted for a few minutes, before crossing the room to take Cynthia into his arms. "God is so good!" He whispered.

"All the time." Cynthia confirmed.

"And all the time..." Emily prompted.

"God is good." Mark finished.

Julie had spent the better part of the morning by Edward's bedside watching him sleep. She was still on leave. The D.O.N. (Director of Nurses) had put in the leave, not long after Julie had left her office. She had insisted that Julie take the time that she had never allowed herself: time to heal; time to truly let her husband go; time to spend with her children and grandchildren; time to find her way through her misplaced feelings for Edward Stanton, as the D.O.N. had so graciously stated, as if her idea was fact. Julie had no time to allow the woman's misgivings of her feelings for Edward to chaff her heart.

She felt as though she had wasted enough time, though sitting in Edward's room seemed the friendly thing to do, she knew that it could not possibly be the most effective use of her time.

Julie looked at the small alarm clock sitting portentously next to Edward's bed. The vibrant red of the numbers cast their jeering taunt as a reminder of all that she should be doing, but had yet to do. One forty-five the eerie red glow sneered its hateful reminder. It was early afternoon. She could call her daughter and check on Amber Noel. No. Amber Noel was thriving in her mother's arms. She and her mommy were bonding a little more every day. Besides, Julie had kept the baby a few hours the night before while Katie had gone to a movie with a friend. Things were really looking up for her daughter and granddaughter.

Julie turned to Edward. He was still asleep. She could talk to his nurse again about his sleeping habits; the possibility of him exhibiting characteristics of depression. That could prove to be good use of her time, but the more Julie thought about it—the more she realized the true source of her inability to commit to the silent vigil over her new friend; at the moment, though she was concerned with Edward's progress.

Julie took one last survey of Edward's overall stats flashing on the monitor. Everything seemed well: his oxygen saturation of his blood hemoglobin was ninety-eight percent, his heart rate was sixty-two; normal for a man his age and in his obvious physical state. Julie cleared her throat nervously.

As Edward's nurse, Julie had been privy to many details concerning Edward's anatomy, but that was business. She was a professional, the physical fitness of a patient had little bearing to her outside of her general assessment.

Edward was different. He had somehow awakened a dormant need inside of her. A raw passion that she had believed buried along with her beloved Ronald. The kiss had proved that belief false.

She was always aware of Edward whether asleep or not: the slightest change in breathing, or turning over to adjust for comfort; it mattered not. Every nuance that was Edward Stanton sent her pulse racing.

She blushed as she raced uncomfortably for the door. She wanted to bring Edward back from the brink of this oblivion he was plunging deeper into, but she didn't know how. Though in her heart, Julie felt the need to clear his name, and give Edward back his desire to live was somehow tied to her desire to visit Cynthia, until this moment, she had not fully acknowledged it.

Everything seemed new. Even the antiseptic-white of the small cubicle he was now standing was brighter. John was enthusiastic, vibrant, exhilarated; he felt electric. Though a part of his brain registered the amount of talking he had been doing, and even felt remorse for Andy. Although to her credit, she had listened to all of his incessant chatter with only a warm smile. John did enjoy the young woman's company. Her views on Christianity were astounding, but he needed to talk to Cynthia. She was due back anytime now.

John smiled gingerly at the young nurse, and walked to the window. Still his mind burned through every memory as they spilled effortlessly from his lips, and still Andy listened without falter. John turned back to the curtain. Where was Cynthia? He needed to tell her about the things that had fallen into place; the thoughts that had for so long evaded him. The things that should have meant more than they had. Moments with Max that John had just listened and thought nothing of the words, the meanings of the words; now all of it made sense.

John now new that his meeting with Max had been no accident, but it wasn't Mr. Stanton that had prompted the meeting… though Mr. Stanton had believed that it was his guidance that had led to Max finding and subsequently meeting John. John had spent many moments while in the deep sleep reviewing many of the conversations held between himself and Max. Many times Max had slipped up. He had revealed too much about his former life, but at the time John had not thought to place every tiny detail of the man's conversation under a microscope. John had been too trusting. He had allowed Max to continue on after clearing his throat, or adjusting the position of his body uncomfortably; all of the signs were there. But John had thought nothing of the awkward behavior. It was not until Max had showed up at the cabin and taken his wife hostage, had tried to kill both of them that John had realized that Max was a fraud.

One such conversation had been brought back to John's memory just before he had awakened from the deep sleep. Max had been frustrated, as he often was. John did note the ever present anxiety that was at the forefront of his thought to be friend's personality traits. John had blamed the impersonal, if not despondent flaw in Max's otherwise buoyant personality on his time spent in the military. Though John had found Max's ability to talk freely about events that would have cocooned the hardest of war vets, a bit disconcerting; he had passed it off as just another trait that was Max… It was one in a long list of wildly different nuances that created the picture that was the man that John had believed to be his most valued friend.

John thought back to that moment in the Congo. Max had left to retrieve his belongings. The night before had been hard on the villagers. John always the planner, had packed two days prior to their departure.

Max, however, had planned to wait until the night before; only to have his plans thwarted by an attack on the village.

Two vans full of insurgents pushed their way into the village; AK-47, machine guns exited every orifice of the vehicles.

John's heart thundered in his chest as though the images were somehow pulling him back into that horrific time.

Short bursts of rapid firing rifles blistered the air. As darkly tanned men clad in black pants and shirts exited the vans, shouting commands. Each of the men's faces was completely covered in black cloths that draped loosely from one side of their faces to the other. John could see only the skin of the men's arms as their muscled biceps hoisted the guns proudly in the air, and rained another blistering round of shots into the beautifully painted heavens.

"Where are supplies?" the lead insurgent shouted in broken English as he shoved his weapon into the face of one of the elders.

Several of the missionaries clustered together in a ball of nerves; tears streaming down each of their helpless-fear-stricken faces. Time was no one's friend in the shadow of death.

John looked to Max. His friend was sitting only two feet from him on the low lying hill. His feet dangling carelessly on the valley floor. Something, though it was lost on John's awareness at the time, had been off about Max's reaction. His eyes were distant, but it was the lack of reaction to the gunfire; the uninterested quality of his response that had haunted John's dreams as he lay comatose. None of it had resonated well with John. So many questions that should have occurred to him as he sat on the hill of that village had blended into the moments, and had been swept away in the chaos. What war vet would remain unmoved by the threats of a firing squad, but more importantly how could the trauma of his past leave Max unaffected by the mind-numbing explosions of the guns? Shouldn't there be some reaction: a call to duty; a scorching-unanswerable need to seek shelter; anything? But as John viewed the Max of his haunted vision it was there all along… Max knew the insurgents. He may have even ordered the hit on the village.

John watched in disgust as Max sat undaunted by the enemies' attack. There was nothing: no fight or flight; no counter to the threat; Max had sat there on the side of that hill in the village, and watched with all the vigor of a man making some inconsequential decision about his life: what would he have for supper; what socks would he wear with a favorite suit? Nothing about Max's demeanor that day would suggest that he was in any way put off by the events taking place.

Though John had been wrapped up in his own mortality at the time, the truth was as stark as a blinding ray of sunlight through a dying forest; Max was no war vet, and though John was uncertain to what degree… Max knew the insurgents.

If that were the truth, then what else had Max lied about? Driven by that question, John had burned through every moment of his time spent with Max. This time as he did so, he held up every memory to the light of scrutiny. He would take inventory of every memory, until the answer lay barren with no where to hide.

As John pushed through each of his moments with his thought of his friend, he had come back to the day after the attack on the village in the Congo. John's head snapped to attention. Max had made another one of his slips, but as usual John had paid little to no attention to the indiscretion.

"I miss brown eyes. Not as sensitive to the sunlight." Max's voice echoed from the past.

At the time, John had thought nothing of the words spoken. Brown eyes? Why would Max comment about having brown eyes? John had allowed the slip to move right past his awareness, and into the files of unintelligible Max moments: times that Max had mentioned something that made absolutely no sense to John; times that John had looked on as harmless humor. Now as John looked out the hospital window into the blue expansion his blood ran cold with understanding. Max had been recycled!

Though Max was gone, John knew that something about this realized omission would tie it all together. He needed to talk to Cynthia. He needed to have Cynthia look deeper into the files of Black Heart. It was time for a visit. John shook his head. Cynthia would never agree. He would have to find a way to make her understand. In order to make all of the pieces fit into the puzzle, he needed to talk to the one person that knew exactly where those pieces had been taken. He needed to talk to Edward Stanton.

56

Penny peered nervously down at Nick. She wanted to shield him, but she needed to fight. How could she do both? She had watched as Lane started removing the children from the combat zone. She hoped that he would soon return for Nick. If Lane could take Nick away from the frenzied inhabitants, then she could better focus on the enemy. Nick needed to be put somewhere safe; this was no place for the wounded.

Desperation mounted as Penny struggled to pull Nick closer to her. Blood still seeped from the angry-gaping wound that followed the length of his rib cage. Pandemonium had filled the chamber the moment the animal noises had begun ricocheting off of the unforgiving walls of the chamber. Manerky warriors scrambled to exits, each holding their ears while emitting pain filled screeches. The calls blended with the animal noises, building the cacophony to an unbearable crescendo that almost sent even those with vision fleeing from the cave.

Penny so caught between the decision to protect Nick or join in the fight did not see Garrison until he was casting a Manerky to the side. The fleeing warrior had almost trampled Nick in his attempt to escape the fevered confusion of the inner chamber.

Garrison lunged across the remaining distance, narrowly stopping the impending trample of Nick and Penny. A small band of Manerky warriors, intent on rushing for safety, through the right tunnel—whether they had seen Penny and Nick, Garrison could not be sure—regardless of intent, the outcome would have proven just as fatal.

The gash in Nick's side needed immediate attention. Garrison watched as Penny pushed futilely at the separated skin. The color drained from her young face. With Nick's life's blood slowly draining from the jagged tear, the two would soon be a perfect match of modeled-white death; their pallor was fast becoming the same.

Garrison took quick inventory of the inner chamber. Hordes of the Manerky had filtered out in a heated frenzy; from one tunnel or the other. Even with the diminishing numbers, dozens lay in different stages of mutilated-death.

The animal calls had all but dissipated.

Jordan, the picture of a vengeful Angel-Barton in hand, was cutting through the last of the enemy; as far as Garrison could tell there was nothing left that Jordan would not be able to handle.

Garrison turned back to Penny. Kneeling down he pulled the t-shirt he was wearing off, and tore it into long strips. He then tightly bound the fabric around Nick's chest, synching the wound as close together as possible. The makeshift tourniquet would have to do.

Penny's eyes rose to meet Garrison's. It was there that he could see what she was so desperate to hide; to deny. Garrison had tried to stay out of the heated stares, the arguments between the couple, but in so close of quarters one was bound to overhear things. Penny had done everything in her power to push the truth away, but as Garrison peered into his young friend's eyes the truth lay barren. Though Penny wanted it not to be so, she was desperately in love with Nick.

Garrison watched as she defaulted to a young girl. Her eyes showed every emotion with stark acuity: love, sadness, hope, loss, and so much more that he was unable to decipher.

Penny felt raw inside. She felt put together wrong. Her hands shook as though they were mirroring how shaky her insides felt. This was Nick, of course he would be around forever, right? He was her friend; her best friend. She needed him. Nick was a part of Penny's world. He was as important to the components of her universe as gravity, oxygen… he was the air she breathed. As if in that moment her body was giving evidence of its agreement with her mind's assessment, the air seemed to fill with some agent that her lungs could not respire. The walls seemed to close in as Penny started to struggle for every breath.

Garrison watched as Penny diminished into a hopeless puddle of humanity. Anguish colored her countenance. Her eyes that had not left

Nick's face once while Garrison bandaged the horrid wound, now bore into his soul. Garrison could see in the depths of her tormented glare was the question that he would not be able to answer: will Nick survive? Garrison wanted to scream yes. He wanted to fill her heart with all of the hope-filled lies that he could manage to conjure. But he knew that false hope was the last thing that she needed.

Sweat beaded on Nick's face as he started to shiver. Garrison scooped a pile of furs up, and placed them over the boy. The fitful dreams had already started, and Garrison knew all too well that Nick was in the valley. He was walking among the shadows of death. Time was all he had left as he roamed through the darkness. His survival was now a question that only God could answer.

Garrison wrapped the whole of his being around the errant thought. Did he truly believe that God could save Nick? There had been a time in Garrison's life that he would have laughed at the insanity that God even existed, much less that He would save a puny human. If there was a God, why would He condescend to help such an inferior life form? Garrison was sure that "God" if there was one, had better things to do than watch over lower life forms; especially problematic races like humans. It wasn't until he had been captured by Tommy Hayden that Garrison had started to realize just how not alone on this planet he truly was.

He could remember the promise he had made to God. He had told Him that if He could indeed deliver him and his friends out of such an impossible circumstance that he would definitely never be able to deny His existence. Garrison even considered adopting the Christian faith. So much had happened since that time, and Garrison was bereft to find faith in a God that would leave him so utterly alone. He felt as though he had no one. He had been excluded from his friend's lives; one by one, exiled to unhappiness. That was one thing, and though it upset Garrison, it was the least of his reasons for being angry at God. He could forgive almost anything, but why had God taken his best friend? Why had he purposefully placed Jordan on a mission that would place her and her family in such dire straits? Why had he left them to the mercy of so twisted a mind as the Manerky? Why had he seemingly done that the whole of Jordan's life? It was that tormented part of her past, her present, and what would seem her future that would forever take her out of his life. It would forever cast a shadow over their friendship; a shadow that would never allow Jordan to find it in her heart to forgive him. If she couldn't forgive him, if God's power was not strong enough to change her heart concerning someone she claimed to love, someone she claimed to value, then how could Garrison ever trust it to be all that he would need in life? How could he have faith that God's power could deliver Nick from the shadow of death, or protect the Cadotion tribe from the evil of the Manerky? How could he truly believe that God was powerful enough to fill Penny with the ability to let go, and show her true feelings for Nick; to trust that Nick was not her father, and she was not her mother? How?

Garrison was left with so many questions. He wanted to believe in God. He wanted to be filled with the hope and glowing light of Truth that filled the silhouette of every true believer, but he felt millions of miles away from that longed for destination. He had never been able to pull close enough to that place until Jordan.

Jordan felt like hope to Garrison. Often his closeness to her, and vice versa had been mistaken for more than friendship. The truth was, Garrison wished that he could have thought of her in that way, but Jordan had been so lost the first time that he had seen her in the alley; so damaged by life's cruelty; she had become a sort of pet-project. From that time forward, Jordan had become the sister that he had never had. She was the mother that had been too soon ripped from his life. She was his family. In her love, Garrison had found shelter from the storm of why's that threatened to uproot his world. Why had his life been so abruptly changed? Why had Black Heart felt like the answer, while in truth it was the chaos that had infested his already depraved existence with more of the same-dead-ugliness? Why had he given fifteen years to that ugliness?

Garrison took inventory of the small chamber. The destruction seemed a metaphor for the life, he had thus far led. He wanted—needed more. In that single understanding lay the biggest why of all: why did he not have more?

"You have not, because you ask not. Ask and ye shall receive." (Matthew 7:7-8)Ask and it shall be given you; seek and ye shall find;

knock and it shall be opened unto you. 8) For every one that asketh receiveth; and he that seeketh findeth; and to him that knocketh it shall be opened.). The words filled the chapped edges of his burdened soul. The response was so real-so tangible that Garrison nearly jumped away from the unseen host.

Never before had Garrison heard this audible voice. It somehow filled the room, and at the same time was, or seemed millions of miles away. He couldn't be sure, but he knew that it was in that place where he wanted, needed to be. Garrison searched the chamber for reactions. No one seemed to have heard the voice, though it had seemed to be a booming response to a question he had only contemplated, but never voiced. The chamber was just as it had been. None of his friends seemed to be aware of the voice that had seemed to completely fill the room.

Jordan had just slashed through the last of the three Manerky opposing her. Their bodies now lay in close proximity to one another: eyes wide in death, their white stares bore into the nothingness they had now become.

Garrison turned back to Penny. She still absently rubbed Nick's arms. Her hands pulling him to her in a cradling manner as they made their way back toward her body.

Nick lay his body just as still as before. His wound bound thanks to Garrison's efforts, but his eyes were closed while his head jerked away from some unseen threat.

Though Garrison knew that the threat that Nick was facing was not the voice that he had heard; he knew that to Nick the threat was just as real. Garrison was perplexed. He thought about the words. Something seemed familiar about the message as if he had heard it some place before.

He thought about the times that he had spent with Jordan and Lane; both were always trying to fill him with some biblical truth or another. Was that it? Had he heard the words from his friends? Lane had told Garrison that God dealt with his children where they were.

"That's why it is important for us to be filled with God's word." The words that Lane had spoken were whispered back to him from his memories. Garrison searched through the archives of his not so distant past.

He thought about the car ride on the way to the hospital to see Jordan. Garrison had been angry then, too. He had felt as though God had let Jordan down. She had spent her time in the Cadotion village bringing His word to the Cadotion tribe, but still she had ended up in the hospital, possibly blinded from the explosion. Someone inside of Black Heart had collected children. They had killed members of their family, and told the children that Jordan Buckley-Gates had been responsible for their deaths. The child agents had been poorly trained, they were never meant to survive; merely a distraction that would enable the agency to kill Jordan.

Garrison had conveyed many of his frustrations that day to Lane: why had God allowed this to happen? Why was Jordan in the hospital, possibly blind, and why hadn't God protected her? Why would God not just instantly heal her? The whys had gone on that day, until Lane had finally answered simply, "We have not, because we ask not; ask and you shall receive." Lane had said nothing more. He had given no explanation. He had left the words on the table for Garrison to contemplate. It wasn't until now that Garrison had considered the words.

He thought about the reply from the strange, but calming voice, calming. He thought about that. He hadn't felt threatened at all, just surprised. The voice had caught him off guard. Could it have been the voice of God? If it was then, did that mean if Garrison asked for Nick's healing, for their deliverance from this circumstance... would God answer his request? Would He give Garrison the desires of his heart?

Garrison turned back to Nick. Penny was still holding on to him as though she was literally pulling him back from the jaws of death, and as far as Garrison knew, she was. Something in him broke at that moment. He couldn't take the site of such helplessness and do nothing. He wanted it all to end. He wanted Nick to be well. He wanted his pseudo-niece to stop hiding her emotions, and live a life of truth, and love. He wanted true direction for her. He wanted Jordan to forgive him. He wanted to be back home with his friends, and he even wanted the Cadotion people to be safe.

"God help." Was all that Garrison could manage. He felt a release in that moment. It was as though he had been let out of some unseen prison. Tears cascaded down his face as he fell over and clung to Nick's leg. His hand snaked up, searching for Penny's hand. He felt the need to be touching everyone that he was praying for. He was so consumed by the prayer that was somehow filtering through his soul without the words manifesting themselves that he barely felt the hand on his shoulder.

Jordan assessed the chamber for more threats. Everything was quiet. Lane was still gone; she imagined that he had wanted to stay near the children. She found comfort in that; with them being away from the protection of the adults, the children would be open to many dangers.

Her mind finally eased. She called upon the senses developed as an agent. The room, and the immediate areas beyond, as far as she could tell were clear. It was as Jordan was coming to her full height that she saw the true threat; Nick's life was hanging in the balance.

Jordan could see that Penny was slowly descending into some bottomless pit of anguish. Her eyes were filled with raw emotion, her body slumped forward as her hands strained against the unseen force that was pulling Nick from her grasp. Bodies of the Manerky littered the inner chamber, frozen forever in the last moments of battle; this would forever serve as their tomb.

Penny had confided in Jordan the true desires of the Manerky. They would collect the youngest of the captives, and devour their flesh. In so doing, the Manerky believed that they would take into themselves the very essence of their youth. Shivers traveled Jordan's spine as she imagined such savagery. It was that truth that had driven Jordan to fight harder.

She would not allow the Manerky to sacrifice her children for a lie; the Direign-king of the underworld was a lie orchestrated by Satan. He was the true source of their worship. There would be no Direignbang; no underworld coming up to fill the Manerky with power. Satan would keep all the power for himself. He was the father of lies and confusion. He cared for no one.

Jordan shook her head. She no longer wanted the images of such depravity to fill her mind.

As she was approaching the young couple, Jordan finally acknowledged Garrison. There was something almost prayerful about the way he kneeled before Nick and Penny. Could Garrison be praying?

Jordan wasn't sure, but she knew whatever thoughts maybe consuming her once best friend, it was time to move beyond the past. It was time to meet her friend in this place; whether prayers, or mere well wishes, and a comforting touch for a friend, Jordan knew that at the core of Garrison she would find a good man. This was about a unifying of minds and spirits to reach a common goal; Nick's wellbeing.

Jordan placed her hand on Garrison's shoulder as she lifted her heart to the Father of truth, healing, and of everything. Long moments filled with quiet stretched out between the three people joined by one all-consuming desire; Nick's full recovery.

Distant wails of terror transformed the prayerful moments in an instant. Jordan was already moving by the time Garrison had made it to his feet.

A glance over his shoulder revealed what Garrison had hoped; Penny was no longer hanging on the precipice of loss. Her eyes now shone with renewed hope that Nick would somehow pull through. The white cap she had been wearing now lay in a heap where she had discarded it along with her doubts. Her short-shoulder-length hair bobbed carelessly as if to commemorate her new found strength. It was a new day, and with it came all the possibilities of a future with Nick at her side.

Garrison allowed a quick smile as he disappeared into the darkness behind Jordan.

57

Julie passed by several nurses' stations, most of which were empty thankfully. She rushed passed the last nurse's station, fingers crossed; she prayed that no one would stop her. She needed to talk to Cynthia, but she also needed to be in the room when Edward woke up. Whatever this rut was that he was in, it needed to stop.

Julie wanted more than anyone to clear Edward's name, but what good would it do to champion a lost cause? Edward would have to get in the fight, and when Julie was through with Mr. Stanton he would do anything to stop the barrage of terror reigning down upon him. Black Heart would seem a kitten compared to Julie Leland with a cause.

Julie smiled gleefully as she remembered the fundraisers she had headed up at the church. She loved a mission, and though her mission may not be dark like Edward was used to, her focus could be just as deadly.

So fueled with the fire of future triumph, Julie did not realize how forceful she had been in pushing the silver button labeled push. The ICU doors swung open with a harsh vigor. As she passed through the pluming doors she heard the whispered protests of some visitors in the waiting area; she had noticed in her peripheral vision. She felt her face flush red. She must look like a mad woman to her unwilling audience.

Moments later, Julie stepped beyond the seclusion of the white curtain into John's room.

"Cynthia I..." a man standing near the window turned. His gray slacks rustled as the fabric glided together. A deep green sweater with thick border around the neck added a certain suave-debonair quality to his already handsome features.

Julie turned quickly to the hospital bed. The sheets and blankets lay crumpled together. John was no longer there. A suitcase lay on top of the mess of discarded covers.

"I'm sorry. I thought this was John Benton's room." Julie admitted. Her face, she was sure, by now was a deeper shade of red.

"It is," Came a female voice from behind Julie.

Julie turned to see Cynthia's happy smile. Her new friend leaned in, and gave her a hug to match the warm smile.

"Julie." Cynthia gave a quick nod of her head as she pointed to Julie. "John." Cynthia again gave a quick nod of her head, but this time she pointed to the man by the window. "John. Julie." Cynthia completed her impromptu introduction, and then pushed her way further into the room.

"Hi, honey, sorry I'm running a little late." Cynthia smiled at John as her eyes filled with more love than Julie could believe would fill such a small space. "The preacher and his wife dropped by. It took me some doing, but I was finally able to make them believe that you had truly been healed." Cynthia laughed, obviously recalling the moments spent with the skeptical couple.

Julie stared blankly back at the sight Cynthia and John made; both thriving: their eyes mirrored the others love in turn. Though the touches were completely modest by nature, there was something very provocative about the quality of their affection for one another.

Julie could not reconcile the John that was lying in the hospital bed a day ago, to the image that he made now. Her mind sifted through the footage of John the last time she had seen him. He was the picture of death. His eyes were starting to sink back in his head; darkened circles bordered the edges. Tubes exited from different points of his lifeless body. The machines registering his vital signs seemed to be ushering in his possible demise rather than guarding against the possibility.

Cynthia stood like a woman waiting for her husband to give a speech in the inauguration: her eyes shone with true love, her hair scooped into a tight bun that accented her long neck, and added to the thought of eloquence she evoked. Tiny shimmering-diamond earrings, the shape of tear drops were the match for the necklace she wore. The jewelry complimented her knee length black dress. The ensemble elegantly announced the beauty of the woman wearing it with such modest grace that in that moment Cynthia looked like nothing more than royalty.

Julie cleared her throat. She felt unwelcome and uncomfortable as if she were standing on sacred ground. The two lovers were so lost in the other's gaze that all else had ceased to exist in that stolen moment. This was their moment. Though Julie felt privileged to be a part of it, in the same sense she felt like an unwanted intruder pushing her way into the most pristinely cherished time.

Cynthia was the first to acknowledge what had happened. Her face flushed. "I'm sorry." Cynthia offered.

"Don't be." Julie smiled as she started toward the nearest chair.

Julie placed her purse in the faded-gray chair, and then closed the remaining distance to John.

"Pleased to finally make your acquaintance, John Benton." Julie announced in a comical tone. Her eyes danced with the laughter that she was holding at bay. She could imagine how willing the two young lovers were to be alone; how badly they wanted to celebrate their second chance in the special way that God had given a man and wife.

John returned her handshake in kind. Though he was cordial something seemed off. He was antsy, or maybe preoccupied.

"Is everything alright John?" Cynthia asked as if she had pulled the question straight out of Julie's thoughts.

"Yes, but I need to talk to you." John cast a withered glance in Cynthia's direction. "I'm sorry. I know you've come to visit. This won't take long, but it is urgent. I'm afraid it can't wait." John's countenance took on a pleading demeanor as he turned to Julie.

"John." Cynthia quietly scolded.

"It's okay. I was just dropping by to ask Cynthia something. It'll hold." Julie offered. She felt so deflated, but what could she do. John obviously wanted time alone with Cynthia. Julie was so happy to see the man not only healed, but thriving; she could hardly begrudge him the simple request. "I'll be in Edward's room. As soon as possible please come see me." Julie finished. She gave a simple smile, and then turned to collect her purse.

"Wait. Julie?" John's voice took on an inquisitive edge. "Do you mean Edward Stanton? Are you Edward's Julie?"

Julie involuntarily cringed away from the question that for some reason felt like an assault; rather than a polite inquiry among friends. Was she Edward's Julie? She obviously had feelings for him, and was ready and willing to champion his cause, but to be thought of as belonging to him; like she was his wife, his intended? She wasn't sure she was ready to wave that banner; at least not for his victims to see. Julie felt so hypocritical. Did she really intend to hide who she was? Did it matter that much who Edward had been, and if it did, where did that leave her so called mission? In the hands of the incapable, Julie thought about that for a moment. How could she champion a cause that she did not believe in?

Julie squared her shoulders. "Yes, I'm Edward Stanton's friend." She proudly announced. If you could call us that after the kiss, she thought. Her face reddened, and Julie deflated a little.

"Please, you misunderstand my meaning." John protested. "I meant no disrespect. It's just what I have to talk to Cynthia about concerns you." John quickly explained. He moved from Cynthia's side, and pointed to the gray chair where Julie had placed her purse.

"Me?" Was all Julie could manage; her voice squeakier than she had intended.

"Yes." John's smile was disarming. "Trust me. I could use the back up."

Julie frowned. She couldn't imagine what John could possibly need back up for. Obviously he and Cynthia had a wonderful relationship. How could either of them ever say anything that would lead them to a place where they needed backup? As the question filtered through Julie's mind a stark awareness of the truth followed close behind. Edward. John wanted information about Edward, but why would he need her back up? Hadn't she said that she was Edward's friend? Surely a man like John Benton would understand the implications of being one's friend.

Julie felt the hairs on the back of her neck prickle. If John wanted answers, so be it, but he should be ready to give as many answers as he was willing to receive.

Julie sighed as she sat down in the offered chair. She needed to calm down. She didn't normally feel this combative. She was just on edge. The name Edward Stanton carried a certain stigma. She had better get used to it. Unless she wanted to take on the whole world, adopting a more tactful means when answering questions about Edward's dark-past would be her only option.

John studied Julie for a moment longer. He was feeling as anxious as she looked. Convincing Cynthia was already going to be problematic, and his approach with Julie was bound to make things more difficult.

John brushed his hand through his hair. He needed to relax. His every word was so energized by the frustration he felt. God please help me. John sent the silent plea before him. He would need God more now than ever. Cynthia wanted nothing to do with Edward Stanton, or anything to do with Black Heart for that matter.

Cynthia had a clear vision of what her future would look like; Black Heart was like a pock-mark on the face of that vision. Every move Cynthia had ever made had purposefully gotten her further from her time with Black Heart, or so she had hoped.

John turned his attention to Cynthia. Her warm-brown eyes shone with all of the trust she had for him. John felt as though his every move had brought her closer. He felt the shame of that thought filter through his senses. His mind quickly calculated all of the times he had put her in Black Heart's direct path. Max, John shook his head at the errant thought. Though Max had not been intentional, John had met the man, and subsequently introduced him into Cynthia's world. Now he was asking her to look through the files; maybe even talk to Edward.

All that Cynthia had done to steer clear of Black Heart, and in a single afternoon John would place her directly in the path of its former leader.

Cynthia felt the chills start to dance down her spine. She could tell by the look in John's eyes that he and Julie were more in sync than she might have believed. Julie was a friend, but she had been up front from the beginning. Cynthia knew what her goal, her agenda had been. Though Julie cared for Cynthia, she was doing all that was in her power to clear Edward's name.

Cynthia collapsed on the bed. How did she feel about this? Her mind raced through the usual possibilities of what could happen if she crossed the clear and present line; the line between the here and now, and what she was then. Though Cynthia had been the worst agent on record, and had to be recycled her time with Black Heart could never be erased. Black Heart was like a bad habit; always returning, always lurking in the shadows; waiting to take its pound of flesh. Black Heart would someday come and claim all that she had built. It would tear down the curtain, and expose her world to the ugly that it had once been.

Cynthia sat silently contemplating the overwhelming loss that could follow Black Heart's unwanted intrusion into her world. Doing profiles for the agency was one thing; it kept the big dog happy, but was she ready to walk up and slap the cage?

She absently caressed her stomach. There was more than just her, and John to think of now. She wanted a clean break from the agency. She was proud of all that Jordan, Lane and Garrison had done to end Black Heart's reign of terror. She had even worked in the shadows of that triumph making profiles.

Cynthia felt ashamed. So many people had stood tall on the shoulders of justice, and claimed their right to be free. How could she laugh in the face of those efforts? If she cowered in the shadows while they marched through the streets-burgeoning with that war then, where would that leave her family's future, her child's future?

"I'm afraid, Lord." Cynthia silently admitted.

"I'm with you always." God's promise whispered across her soul. You were not created with a spirit of fear, my child. God reminded.

Cynthia stood then. Determination colored her features. Her resolve iron-clad, she moved to John's side.

"Cynthia... I know..." John started to speak.

"Shh..." Cynthia placed her fingers over John's lips, and then lightly kissed where her fingers had been. "Let's go."

"Go where?" John's face was a mask of confusion.

"To shake the big dog's cage." Cynthia said as she pulled both John and Julie along with her.

Cynthia was surprised to feel Julie pull her hand away.

"I understand how you both must feel." Julie's eyes glistened with unshed tears. She sniffed, and then collected her purse. "But I can't be a part of this."

"This?" Cynthia turned to John. He too seemed put off by Julie's words.

"I know the two of you want, and deserve…" Julie dropped her head for a moment, and then looked into their eyes. "Your revenge, but Edward for better or worse is my friend." Julie smiled at both of them as she started toward the door.

"Julie, please." Cynthia felt awful. The words she had used must have seemed harsh to Julie. How would she have felt if it were John attacked, angry…? "I shouldn't have put it that way." Cynthia apologized. "I can't imagine what you must be going through; how you must feel." Cynthia went to Julie, and pulled her into an embrace.

"Julie, I didn't realize how harsh my words would sound to you. I was trying to be funny, but when I heard the words out loud… well, I guess I realized they weren't funny at all." Cynthia patted Julie's shoulder.

"Cynthia, I know that Edward did a lot to you and your friends." Julie sniffed. "Most of it was probably close to unforgivable. I can't imagine what it must have been like for any of you, but I truly feel as though I am being led to help Edward." Julie wiped the tears from her eyes. "To somehow bring him back from this."

Cynthia watched as Julie seemed to search for the right words. She wished that she could make it easier. Though Edward had manipulated all of their lives, and filled their every step with fear, he had paid so dearly for his transgressions. Cynthia wasn't a vengeful person. She didn't have an expected price for Edward's sins; it had already been paid just as hers had been. There was no toll expected that would be payment for crossing the bridge connecting the past and the present. Edward Stanton was just as forgiven as any other person had been. Christ had paid it all!

Cynthia imagined that this must be a lot like Jonah's reconciliation with what God wanted him to do for Nineveh. How hard must it have been for Jonah to preach the word to a land that had dealt so harshly with his people? It must have felt impossible for Jonah to reconcile himself to the hated notion… but he had. Jonah had gone to that land, and he had won the enemy to the Lord.

"Edward is my Nineveh." Cynthia smiled. Her eyes filled with sadness as tears slid down her cheeks. Her heart broke with the declaration. She felt the chasm between what she would do, and didn't want to do; the void that had been so hollow filled with a love that she was familiar with. It was that unending, unconditional grace that had filled the expanse between God and man; the love that had rent the curtain, and reunited God and His people forever. (See Jonah)

Cynthia smiled at John. She knew her husband; theirs was a closeness that transcended human understanding. John would have asked her to go see Edward had Julie not beaten him to the punch. Though Cynthia knew it was the right thing to do, she could not escape the image of Jonah sitting under the gourd that God had grown a tree out of; never before had Cynthia so closely identified with the biblical character.

58

Candles sputtered and then without warning darkness filled the chamber. Inky-blackness filled the expanse. Lane's breath caught. The darkness felt like a tangible force. It so completely erased his thoughts that Lane stumbled for a moment. His eyes searched frantically through that stretch of time before he realized what was happening.

Lane prayed quickly for God to extinguish the fear, and then in the span of a heartbeat gave himself over completely to his angel senses.

A scream erupted from the far corner of the inner chamber. Lane turned reflexively to the sound.

Amelia was crouched defensively between Modilo's and Tristan's sleeping forms. Evidently she had awakened at some point, and started to carry on with her usual duties as future medicine woman.

At first, Lane believed the scream had been a reaction to the sudden darkness, but as Lane continued on with his scrutiny of the chamber the truth soon took root, and buried its fangs into his soul.

Amelia was crouching in fear, not of darkness, but of the threat before her. Two young Manerky warriors growled and hissed as their jagged nails swept wildly before them like angry cats batting at prey.

Amelia's chest heaved with every breath as her caramel-eyes filled with tears, and then spilled onto her tiny cheeks. Her little girl hands extended out in front of her as they flailed in a desperate attempt to keep her attackers at bay. Her eyes searched the terrible darkness unseeing. Whimpers escaped her lips as her feet stayed in close contact with the boy's bodies. Even in fear, Amelia was the ever ready protector.

Aching-sorrow threaded through Lane's soul. His daughter, this amazing Cadotion warrior that had defied her six years to stand in the shoes of one so strong as Aniahi; his daughter that had faced every moment in her young life with determination, never backing away from the call of duty; his daughter that had answered every crisis with the same strength as her teacher was being overcome by a fear that Lane knew was certain to scar her forever.

Lane's breath caught as another emotion filtered through his being. One so absolute, so complete that it burned trenches like hot lava through the valleys of his soul.

A scream so primal that it seemed to come from another place erupted from Lane's lips.

The Manerky youth jerked to attention. Lane reached out before the boys could turn. His mind summoned all of his angelic strength, as he cradled a hand around each of the boy's heads. In the back of Lane's mind, he was faintly aware of the warrior's jagged claws ripping at the flesh of his hands. So lost to his rage, Lane ignored the slight annoyance of the clawing hands. He forced his hands closed with such brutal finality that the Manerky warriors' skulls were welded into one. The clacking sound of the skulls fusing danced off the walls of the chamber.

Lane dropped the Manerky to the cave floor. Blood and brain matter clung to the walls of the cave. In the recesses of his mind, he could feel the evidence of the Manerky's eradicated existence clinging loosely to his face.

The faint sound of approaching footfalls sent an alarm through Lane's mind. He turned to the approaching threat. His hand extending, his fingers wrapped automatically around the slender throat. His thumb moved up the side of the neck as he readied for the violent snap that would follow.

"Lane!" the voice was so familiar, but the rage that seared through his senses felt so complete. His mind swam a river of anger like black molasses; searching through the thick rage for the answer. Even as he clamored for the answer, the rage mounted and his grip tightened.

Jordan could hear the desperation in her own voice. She had faced many a foe, but never had she been so certain of her own death. The massive hand clamped with iron finality around her throat validated her suspicion. She squirmed to free herself from the massive grip at first, but then realized how futile her efforts were.

In an instant, she knew the too large hand belonged to her husband. She knew in some corner of her mind that she should find some measure of comfort in that truth, but as Lane's thumb moved upward terror followed its unrelenting path. The end was near.

Her scream ripped through her mind as the grip tightened. Not since her childhood had Jordan felt this much fear. Her hands frantically fault for freedom. She couldn't get a breath. Her head started to spin, and the whirring sounds of the cave started to blend together.

Jordan relaxed her hands as she gave herself over completely to her fate. Funny, she thought. Her mind drifting down a lazy river of euphoria. Of all the things she would have expected to think; to feel in her last moments; she felt love. She wanted to tell Lane that she understood. She wanted him to know that she loved him. She wanted to know that he would be able to forgive himself for her death; instead she drifted off into oblivion.

Lane's mind clawed for the surface. His hand still in its reflexive clutch, he pushed through the mountain of rage for reality. Bright light filled the chamber. His eyes squinted closed. He wanted to get away from the painful intrusion.

"No!" Another familiar voice shouted from somewhere in the distance.

Lane loosened his grip. His mind finally breaking through the darkness, he was able to see that it was Garrison. The second familiar voice, the shout of no had been from Garrison. But why would Garrison object to his use of brutality?

"Jordan! No!" Garrison screamed again. His cries were demanding, guttural. Lane felt the anguish as it colored every nuance of Garrison's broken tone.

Jordan? Lane's mind started to speed up. The slow motion of fighting through the rage; not connecting with the here and now moments ago dissipated.

Lane felt the knees of his victim buckle. He had not given the final twist. The snap had not come.

It was then as Lane was contemplating his actions that Garrison had lunged for Lane. Anger colored his features. His eyes were a black death of velvet midnight.

Lane thrust his hand out to thwart the attack. There was no time. Garrison was resolved in his efforts. Lane could see the accusations, the promise of death as they spun in volcanic fury behind Garrison's terrible gaze. Lane had no time to wonder at Garrison's actions.

"You killed her!" Garrison screamed as he connected with Lane's arm. His body flew through the air, and landed hard a few feet away. Lane had deflected the blow.

"Daddy, stop!" Amelia pleaded.

Why was Amelia pleading for him to stop? Why had Garrison lunged to attack him? Weren't they partners in this? Weren't they supposed to be killing the Manerky?

Lane felt the icy fingers of truth grip his heart as he at last forced himself to look at the enemy that wasn't an enemy.

Her head tilted back, her lips were a terrible shade of blue-death. Jordan's long neck bore the evidence of his massive grip. No life existed in her, not hers or the child she carried. Her arms were hanging loosely to her side.

Lane's mind rejected the sight as he threaded his fingers into her beautiful-dark-auburn hair. He pulled her tenderly to his face as he kissed the terrible bruises lining her neck. Reaching down, he swept her legs into his massive arms. He would take her somewhere, he would pray, he would find a way to take this back. But as he started to walk to nowhere in particular his knees buckled, and his world tilted on its axis.

"Please, don't let this be." His whisper to the Creator was barely audible. Lane was faintly aware of the tiny hand on his shoulder. He was trapped in a place of lost hope. His mind in limbo, he hung helplessly balanced between what was, and what he desperately longed to be true.

"Mommy said that we could do all things through Christ; not just daddy and Tristan, because they're half angels." Amelia's little girl voice filled the horrible tomb that would forever be haunted with Jordan's last moments.

Lane remembered the conversation that Amelia was speaking about. It had been a beautiful day in the Cadotion village. Amelia as usual was playing with Tristan.

Lane was so proud of the loving way that Amelia had with her little brother. She was always there: guiding, teaching, and playing with her brother.

Amelia was pretending to be a horrible monster. Tristan was a magnificent angel wielding his powers to kill the enemy. Tristan had been so proud of his ability to stop the bad guy.

Amelia's eyes had revealed something other than the joy exhibited by her brother that day: distance, longing, remorse… whatever the cause for the sadness in their daughter's eyes, Jordan had seen it.

Jordan's answer to that sadness had been abrupt. Like a super hero, Jordan flipped high into the air, and landed mere inches from Amelia. Amelia's eyes danced with excitement as Jordan lifted her into the air, and then just as suddenly let her go. Amelia soared a few feet above Jordan, and moments later rested safely in Jordan's embrace.

The action had been simple for an agent with Jordan's level of training, but to Amelia it seemed the stuff of heroes.

Jordan's words were the thing that had so permanently burned the memory into Lane's psyche. "We can do all things through Christ who strengthens us."

Lane smiled through the remorse flooding his soul. Their daughter wasn't speaking to him. She was speaking to her Heavenly Father, to her Creator. She was crying out for Him to give her proof. She wanted evidence that He was all that her mommy had promised. She was extending her heart, her hand, her soul to the plow of faith; she would not look back. She wanted Him to meet her there.

Lane's head lifted as the tiny fires lit through his body. He could feel God's answer as it generated warmth through his very being. He did not know how he would look into her eyes, and find forgiveness for what he had done, but he knew God would meet him there in that place; just as He had met Amelia.

Jordan's eyes fluttered wildly. Emerald pools of love shone back from her devastatingly-beautiful visage.

A sob erupted from Lane as his head fell forward. He began to praise God.

"Why are you crying, daddy?" Amelia's dainty hands held Lane's face so that he was looking her in the eyes. "Don't you know that all things are possible…"

"Through Christ who strengthens us." Jordan finished.

Lane nodded his head slowly. Tears spilled onto his cheeks as he whispered his response. "Yes, baby."

Jordan's hand was on his cheek now. Lane could not fathom the thought of looking in her translucent green eyes. The pain of what he had done was still too raw. She pulled his face to hers as she leaned in close, and touched his lips to hers.

"We're finally even." she laughed, but quickly moved into his embrace. "I love you. I forgive you. Just as you forgave me when I almost killed you."

Lane knew that Jordan was right. He would never intentionally hurt her. He had not known that it was her approaching. How could he live in the regrets of the past with so much thankfulness filling his heart?

A noise from behind brought Lane out of his thoughts. Though an angry demeanor still colored Garrison's features, he seemed somewhat calmer. His eyes searched Jordan for any sign of permanent damage.

"I'm fine, Garrison." Jordan assured.

Lane scrutinized his wife for any evidence that she may have any lasting problems. His heart lurched at the idea of his hand around her slender throat. Jordan was the picture of health: her words were pristine—no hoarse timbre, her neck had no sign of the ugly bruises, even her hair was perfectly in place. The only evidence of what had happened lived in his breaking heart.

He reached back, and claimed Amelia's hand. He tenderly pulled her into his embrace.

"Thank God, for your faith!" Lane cried. He buried his head into her tiny chest, and sobbed. He was so grateful for this second chance. He had his family. Now, he would have to figure out how to get them, and the remaining Cadotion tribe—if there were any—to safety.

CHAPTER

59

Edward had been sitting in the darkness, trying to collect his thoughts for a long time. He could have switched the overhead light on, but what was the point? The way he saw it his life had enough light revealing all of his transgressions. His face was plastered on every media outlet, every disgusting magazine... He, along with several former members of Black Heat, had made the front page news for about three weeks.

It seemed a lifetime had passed since that fateful day in his office. He felt more trapped than ever! He couldn't kill himself; he had seen firsthand the agony of being separated from God. Though he still had no clue what it meant to truly know God, Edward knew with stark acuity that not feeling God or sensing Him was worse. The moments in that dark place, searching for the pull that it had on his life. The pull to be closer to know Him, but how? Edward didn't know. He had never known, he may never know he realized, but to ever be stuck in that place with no option, no do over, Edward could not let that happen. It was the worst feeling, the worst thing he had ever experienced. It was more than his mind could fathom. He had experienced that deep void, and it had engraved his soul with its ominous truth: outer darkness, lack of God's presence was worse than anything he had ever known, or would ever know.

Edward Shivered as that time wrapped itself, relentlessly around his awareness. He felt perplexed. His life wasn't, at least for the moment, worth living; he would believe in Hell, had he not already experienced Hell; well in part. He knew, instinctively that there was more to be experienced; to suffer, in that place… but more than anything it was the thought of being without God that had kept him awake at night. No amount of suffering could ever match the sheer terror of that blackness. Though his life was unbearable, it had never seen a day as dark as those moments without God.

Edward felt as though he were a trespasser in his own life. An unwanted blemish on the face of mankind, he had no home in this world that hated him so completely. But it would seem that the hereafter would be beyond the borders of hope for him. He had no one, nothing, and it was exactly what he deserved. So if that were true, then why did his heart still long for something more, if it had no right to?

Edward was still contemplating his life when the door squeaked open. Light from the hall bled into the darkened room. He absently pushed his back further into his pillow. The action sent a shock of pain through his throat where the stitches were. He reflexively grabbed for the offended area, but soon became sidetracked by the brightness creeping in. The light was like an unwanted intruder. At least in the dark, he could hide from his sins. The light would illuminate every last transgression. He had had enough of his life being made public. He longed for anonymity, for a dark hole to escape.

"Edward?" Julie's voice penetrated his thoughts. She always sounded so hopeful. She was light and hope. He was death and destruction. But something felt off about her voice. Julie's tone was strained. Alarm pierced through the fog of depression.

"Julie?" Edward pushed the covers down. The slight movement sent another streak of pain rushing through his neck. His stomach turned slightly. His head spun a little, but he pushed himself defiantly from the hospital bed. He rushed awkwardly to her side. He still felt a little wobbly on his feet, but he couldn't let that stop him. He needed to be by her side. He felt so protective of her.

"Edward…" Julie's face was filled with emotion. Something was so familiar about her countenance. "I… Edward… I…" Julie struggled to say whatever it was she needed to say to him.

"Julie, slow down." Edward soothed. He was already pulling her to the chair. "What's the matter? Is someone hurt?" Edward knew how much Julie loved her family. Oh God! Not Amber Noel! Edward's thoughts raced like an avalanche. "How's Amber…" Edward's voice broke. Too much sorrow filled his heart to complete the sentence. He had only met the tiny baby girl once, but the love that Julie had for her granddaughter had so infused the memory… it had filled his senses so completely; he couldn't allow the thought to have its way with his heart.

Edward was awed by how much he already valued those that were important to Julie. She had become an integral part of his life; in such a short period of time, her happiness had become the air that he breathed. Even the thought of something going wrong in Julie's universe seemed to pivot his world wildly.

Edward searched Julie's eyes for answers. It was there. In the depths of those cloudy blue pools that the storm raged… he saw it then; the emotion that he was all too familiar with, guilt. For some reason, Julie was dripping in guilt. Her shoulders slumped under the weight of that guilt.

"Julie, what's this about?" Edward rubbed her arm, though he truly wanted to run from the all too familiar emotion. He had bathed in its sickening-stench; his life had become a lesson in guilt. Every aspect of his life had been exposed for all to look upon: dissect, jeer at. Edward would recognize the putrid odor of guilt anywhere. But why was Julie, this woman that was the epitome of good, light, hope. What could she ever have to feel guilty about?

"Edward I want so much to help you, and instead I seem to be sitting by," Julie's eyes shot to a noise coming from beyond the door. Someone was talking out in the hall. She seemed to grow more anxious. Her hands claimed Edward's then, as she looked directly into his eyes.

"Who is out there, Julie?" Edward tried to keep the fire out of his tone, but the question still sounded too demanding.

"Edward, I'm trying to tell you. I want to help you."

"Help me what?" Edward was moving now. He crossed the room to the door. His head was swimming more violently now. The exertion was making his heart pound in his ears. Julie pulled and tugged. She was trying to get him to go back to bed, but he didn't want to get back in the bed. Whoever stood on the opposite side of the door was obviously making Julie feel things that a woman of her serene nature should never feel.

"Edward, please. I need to explain things." Julie tugged even harder.

Edward could feel the mounted desperation of that tug. He placed his hands on either side of Julie's shoulders. "Julie, please. Whoever or whatever this is…" Edward pointed at the door. His finger trembled slightly. His head still spun. His ears started to ring, and then just as suddenly as it had begun it was over. Edward felt nothing. He saw nothing. He was floating somewhere in oblivion.

One minute Edward was trying to calm Julie down, and the next he lay in a heap on the floor. Julie stooped down. He was breathing, but his color wasn't good. Julie claimed his wrist. His pulse was weak and thready. Perspiration beaded on his forehead. The front of his shirt was soaked.

Julie pulled him away from the door. She snatched the heavy wood door open. John and Cynthia were standing just outside. Julie ignored them both.

"Nurse!" Julie screamed into the hallway.

"Julie?" Cynthia was the first to question Julie's sudden outburst.

"Edward collapsed." Julie turned back to look at Edward; his chest was still moving, barely. "Cynthia, go get a nurse. John, help me get him on the bed." Julie put her arms under Edward's armpits. He was heavier than what he appeared. John grabbed his legs. Soon, Edward was on the hospital bed.

Julie searched through a tall wooden cabinet near the window. Some oxygen tubing was there. She couldn't find a non-re-breather. Her heart lunged. What if she couldn't find a non-re-breather? Finally, just as Julie believed the search hopeless; on the third shelf a single clear mask with a translucent bag sat lonely on its perch. Anger surged through her mind. Why hadn't the medical techs refilled the cabinet?

Julie ignored the question. She rushed over to the wall, and turned the green knob on the oxygen valve. A small black ball floated, weightlessly up, an indication that air was indeed feeling the line. Fifteen liters. She quickly placed the mask over Edward's face, after feeling the bag with oxygen.

Edward was still breathing, but Julie didn't know for how long. This had all been too much for him. How could she have given into the desires of the Benton's? The couple were good people. They had been through so much, but if this had been any other patient, no matter how essential to the patient's freedom, Julie would have never agreed to the intrusion. She had allowed her feelings for Edward to cloud her medical judgment, and right now her medical experience was the only thing that he needed from her.

Her heart felt as though it was being choked. Her hands shook as she worked feverishly to gain an IV access. Her mind numbly wondered at why his IV had been removed so soon. He was scheduled to move to the rehab floor later in the day, but removal of his IV would not occur until moments before he was placed in a wheelchair to be moved from their care.

Cynthia had gone to get a nurse. Julie knew that she was too close to Edward. No medical personnel would be allowed to work on a friend or family member, but Julie did not have the luxury of passing responsibility to a colleague. She was all that Edward had. God was with Edward, but he would not ask. Edward was lost in a world of depression.

Julie had just taped the IV-tubing down on Edward's hand as two nurses filtered into the room.

"What happened?" Sandy, a tall light skinned, African American nurse asked. Her neatly manicured eyebrow lifted slightly as if to attach a modicum of accusation. The girl's beautiful-deep brown eyes bore into Julie's soul.

Julie absently flinched. She felt as though Sandy had punched her in in the gut. She had seen what had happened. Julie's unending need to rise to the occasion—mission-minded Julie that was the problem.

Julie felt an arm encircle her stomach.

"He collapsed. Julie started an IV, and put him on oxygen." Cynthia was standing by Julie's side. Her long slender finger lifted in defiance toward the oxygen mask that served as evidence. Cynthia's shoulders straightened defiantly.

Julie caught a glimpse of the agent, Cynthia once had been. No matter how inefficient her efforts may have been, Cynthia had the heat of a fighter. In that moment, Julie could understand what the agency had seen. What had prompted them to believe that this woman before her was indeed an agent.

Julie felt comforted by this new friend.

"I put him on fifteen liters O2. He was upset." Julie's mind sped up. She needed to give a report. What were his vital signs? "His pulse was weak and thready. He was breathing about four times a minute. His saturation was ninety-five percent." Julie turned to the machine. Edward's oxygen saturation had greatly increased. It was now 100 percent. Good. She turned then to Edward. He was still unconscious, but he was more pink. "His nasal and oral mucosa was blue, his nail beds were blue, and capillary refill time was over two seconds."

Julie looked at Edward's face his nose and mouth were no longer blue. That was good. But would he be okay?

"I want a twelve lead EKG." Julie heard herself say. She turned to the door. The doctor was coming into the room.

"You heard the lady." Doctor Ross said.

Julie liked him.

Doctor Ross had been with the hospital only a few years less then she had. He was knowledgeable. Julie felt comfortable with him being in charge. Doctor Ross had a wonderful bedside manner. Many of the patients at the hospital had asked if the doctor had a private practice; most had made efforts to transfer. Julie allowed a weak smile. He felt like an old friend, he was. The doctor's handsome features had earned him the fanfare of the women in town. His tall athletic physique combined with piercing blue eyes and dark brown hair left the ladies breathless. But it was his medical abilities, and tender hand that had gained Julie's respect.

Julie shook her head. Her eyes misted. Human comforts would not help Edward. Doctor Ross was a good doctor, but he was just a man. He could do no more to save Edward's life than God would allow.

Julie closed her eyes. She needed to pray. Edward couldn't die. He wasn't ready. He hadn't received Jesus as his Savior. She had failed him. Julie wasn't ready for him to die. The years with Ronald had seemed too short, but this… this was nothing at all. She had no time to know Edward. He had just come into her life. Why would God allow Edward to come into her life; allow her to feel so deeply for him, if He was only going to take Edward from her?

Losing Ronald had been different. Julie could imagine Ronald in the midst of friends and family, shrouded in white, praising their Lord. Julie knew that was true. That image gave her comfort. What comfort would she find when Edward was gone? He wasn't ready.

"God, please. He's not ready." Julie whispered the prayer. "Please, I'll do better. I promise. I'll beg him if I have to, but please don't take him. I'll teach him Lord. You said man could not know you unless they hear the word. (Romans 10:14 How then, can they call on the one they have not believed in? And how can they believe in the one of whom they have not heard? And how can they hear without someone preaching to them?) Allow me to do this Father." Julie crossed to Edward's bed. She reached down, and claimed his foot. She suddenly felt the need to be touching this man that her spirit was so desperate to save.

She continued the prayer. Her heart filled, and then spilled over. Soon she was no longer speaking. Her spirit was praying on her behalf; uttering things that she could not speak. (Romans 8:26, in the same way, the spirit helps us in our weakness. We do not know what we ought to pray for, but the spirit himself intercedes for us through wordless groans.) Julie's spirit was indeed groaning; it was weeping on her behalf. Her world felt shattered. Her spirit was seeking God's favor for Edward; for her. Her spirit was begging for his life, the life of the man she now knew that she loved.

This love felt different from what she had shared with Ronald. That was a love born of mutual respect, familiarity.

Ronald Leland had been best friend to Gordon Staples. Gordon was Julie's first boyfriend. It was a very innocent relationship. Julie felt fond of Gordon, but nothing beyond that, or so she had believed. It wasn't until Gordon had enlisted in the army that Julie had realized how fond she had become of him. Unfortunately, Julie would never have the chance to tell Gordon. He had died while crossing through a city in a convoy. Land mines.

Ronald had returned without his best friend. He had gone to Julie to comfort her; a last request made by Gordon.

Julie and Ronald were married a year later. Ronald had proposed after a kiss. The kiss had taken Ronald as much by surprise as it had Julie. The two had been talking about their time with Gordon. Always their time spent immortalizing Gordon had ended with a hug. But this night had been different. Julie had gone over the details many times. Maybe it was the moon. Maybe the warm night, or the crickets singing, maybe it was the shimmering lights as they cast a thousand twinkling lights on the water's surface; maybe all of it together had infused the night with magic.

Whatever the cause, Ronald had kissed Julie, and then proposed. Julie could feel Gordon, himself. It was as though he had brought them together, and insisted on their union.

Ronald had filled the hole in her heart. He had filled the years of their lives with happiness. Julie had loved him, but until now she had not realized that she had never been in love with him. Shame and guilt filled Julie's heart. Had she cheated Ronald, or had the loss of Gordon been so great that he too had found the same peace in her arms? Maybe she and Ronald were two souls lost in a moment that was bigger than them. Maybe that loss was too much to face alone.

She thought about her time with Ronald. There was no shame in what she had shared with him. She had given him all that she had, even her broken heart would testify to that. Julie had almost stopped living when Ronald had died. He was all that she knew. Though she had not been in love with him, she had clung to him like he was life itself; he had been her next breath. She had borne him children; she had pledged her life to him, and had kept that solemn vow until his death.

Her time with Edward had in no way diminished her feelings for Ronald. It had merely given her a gauge by which to measure her feelings. Though her feelings for Ronald were real; her feelings for Edward, she knew were immeasurable.

Julie knew in her heart that Ronald was well. He was singing with the angels; happy and whole. Edward was here fighting for life. He was clinging to the here and now with a flimsy grip. She could see in his disturbed visage that not much held him to this place; maybe the threat of the hereafter. He would not be singing with the angels. He would be cast into outer darkness. (Matthew 8:12 KJV: But the children of the kingdom shall be cast out into outer darkness: there shall be weeping and gnashing of teeth). He would be thrown into the lake of fire and burned up. The wicked that do not receive Christ will be destroyed.

(Psalm 68:2 as smoke is driven away, so drive them away; as wax melts before the fire, so let the wicked perish at the presence of God. Psalm 104:35 May sinners be consumed from the earth, and the wicked be no more. Blessed the Lord, o my soul! Mal. 4: 1 for behold the day is coming, burning like an oven, and all the proud, yes, all who do wickedly will be stubble. And the day which is coming shall burn them up, says the Lord of hosts that will leave them neither root nor branch.)

Julie couldn't bare the idea of it. She couldn't fathom Edward in a place like that; a place without the love of God. Tormented. A place where Edward would be no more.

Julie's spirit continued to beg for Edward's absolution as her mind drifted down a river so filled with love that she was drowning in remorse. Her soul clung to hope as her heart glimpsed the possible outcome, it would not survive.

CHAPTER

60

Flashes of light filtered in through the arched tunnel way. Roaring thunder, ricochet throughout the cave walls, amplifying the already menacing sound. Penny still cradled Nick's head against her chest. Her muscles ached from the effort, but to let him go felt like a crime against her heart.

She filtered through the excuses that she had chimed off, every time Nick had broached the subject of their relationship. It all seemed flippant-jargon, useless rhetoric now. None of it mattered. She had spent too much time; wasted too many opportunities to tell Nick the truth. She had lied to herself, to Nick...

Penny shuttered as another flash of light illuminated the inner chamber. Suddenly the room felt too cold, too lonely, and too dark. She turned to the tunnel leading to the left. The others had been gone for what seemed a very long time. At first, Penny had been too consumed with Nick's condition to notice the endless absence, but then... she scanned the cave walls again. A chill crawled down her spine.

She absently pulled Nick closer. His body felt hot, too hot. She ignored the visions of him laying paralyzed forever, his eyes eternally closed. Her eyes shut. She would reset the pictures, create new visions, things worth seeing: Nick thriving, smiling, and chasing her around The Garden; the blundered attempts at teaching her Karate. She laughed. The image clung to her consciousness. It felt good to leave the terrible darkness behind. Only the faint shimmer of candle light and the flicker of lightening stood between Penny and complete darkness.

She watched the cluster of candles, still burning, on top of the trio of wooden slats. Though the tower now leaned from the battle, Penny was thankful for the comfort that the light offered. But as she studied the sputtering flame she realized that comfort would be short lived. Soon she and Nick would be helplessly cast into complete darkness. There they would wait for the enemies' unrelenting answer to their helpless circumstance.

Some weakness remained, but for the most part Jordan was amazed at how good she felt. Honestly, there was nothing about her physical state that would suggest her having been in any sort of combat situation at all.

Jordan pulled Amelia's body more closely to her as she moved toward the chamber where Penny and Nick were still waiting. Modilo and Tristan were still fast asleep. Lane held Tristan while Garrison took responsibility of Modilo. The commute was slow, but steady. All three adults held tight to a torch. The light was the only thing keeping any of the Manerky, lingering in the shadows from launching another brutal attack.

Jordan's heart raced. The idea of having to defend against an attack, while caring for the children was not high on her list. Still the procession moved forward. Regardless of her desires, she knew that in order to gain freedom for all of them, keeping a forward momentum, however slow, was the only way to obtain that freedom.

Lane stopped to retrieve Kirsten. She was still asleep in the tiny cove that he had left her in. Shrouded from the prying eyes of the enemy, Kirsten had remained oblivious to any danger.

Jordan was happy for the small consolation.

The night so filled with terror had already claimed too much innocence: Amelia had witnessed her daddy not only kill the Manerky, but technically her mother as well. Now Amelia soldiered on, her tiny chin held high. She moved through the dimly lit tunnel with as much grace as a seasoned-soldier storming the banks of a foreign land. No whimper of fear escaped her mouth, no over-exaggerated grip of terror; Amelia moved with the others as though she were just as responsible for their freedom as the adults that surrounded her.

Sadness and pride mingled in Jordan's heart: as an agent she was proud of her courageous daughter, but as a mother Jordan felt a kind of remorse for her lost innocence; Amelia would forever be changed by the experience. Everything that Jordan and Lane had done to protect their children from the ugly world that sometimes surrounded them had somehow crept in; it had taken with it her precious daughter's right to be a child. To live in a kingdom of make believe, was lost to her forever. As Jordan watched this little adult that now stood where her little girl had once been, she knew that the Cadotion village would have their medicine woman. If any remained of the beautiful people, Amelia would stand tall. She would be there. She would be the answer to all of the tribes' questions about sickness. But there was more. Amelia would bring with her not only physical healing, but a healing that would far outweigh the simple needs of the broken human body; Amelia would bring to them guidance from above. In their daughter lived comfort for the broken, healing for the ailing, and eternity for the believer. Amelia would bring with her a living Savior, and Jordan knew with all of her being that Amelia would gladly share her gift that was indeed more precious than gold.

Lane's muscles tightened and loosened as he carried his son and now held the weight of Kirsten's unconscious body. She was draped easily over his left shoulder. He kept both children to the inside of the slowly moving procession. The advancing enemy would be unable to harm any of the children. Garrison held the outside flank of the group. Jordan marched on with Amelia cradled at her side. For the most part the tightly knit group seemed to keep all of the children out of harm's way. Just a few more feet stood between them and their desired destination.

Lane scoured every corner, every small nook of the tunnel system with an accusing glare. None of the dark spaces could be ignored. No assumption could be made that the Manerky were not waiting. That the enemy would not leap from the darkness. He felt almost childlike. He had so many times maneuvered through the dark tunnels; so many days and nights alike had been spent playing amongst the cave's hallowed halls. Now as he moved with the small group, the mountain had never felt more foreboding. The unseen threats screamed from their hiding places. The darkness took on a life of its own. Sparks from the torches filtered into the gloomy darkness, allowing the smallest glimpse of something in the shadows.

Lane reluctantly switched to his angel senses. He had been afraid that the ability that had been second nature his entire existence would fail him. How horrible had his actions been in the chamber where the children had been sleeping. He had lain to waste all of the teachings imparted on him by the Cadotion tribe by his parents. He had abandoned all of the holy truths of Christianity for the scorching-hot pull of rage. He had dived head first into furious-rage. It had almost cost him more than he would ever want to pay.

Lane stilled his senses for the plunge. He would allow the angel side of his being to take over. He would not be afraid. Fear is not of the Lord. He was not made with a spirit of fear. He is a son of God. Armed with those truths, Lane plunged into the deaths of his angelic-senses.

Suddenly the room was no longer dark. The shadows that had so completely claimed the outskirts of the candle light receded. There was nowhere to hide. Lane searched then not for the demonic forces that he knew to be lurking about, the demons that would be assigned to each of them; the liars sent from the pits of Hell to tell all who would listen of their failures, their incapability, their uselessness. Lane was not searching the mountain for that enemy. Now he searched for the enemy of the flesh; the human enemy that had been used and lied to; the Manerky.

He knew that there were those that would labor amongst the children of God. There were those that sought only to do their master's work. No matter how much he would want to bring a saving knowledge of Christ to some, it would not be so. (Exodus 10: God tells Moses to go to Pharaoh. God wants Moses to do all of these signs and wanders in front of Pharaoh even though He has hardened Pharaoh's heart. God wants His miracles to be seen and spoken of. Read for a better understanding. Romans 1:24, 28. 24: Therefore, God gave them over in the lusts of their hearts to impurity, so that their bodies would be dishonored among them. 28: And just as they did not see fit to acknowledge God any longer, God gave them over to a depraved mind, to do those things which are not proper)

The Manerky were so completely emerged in the teachings of the Direignbang- the belief that they would be able to dig down into the earth far enough to find the leader of the underworld-Direign, and that he would make them rulers of the earth… the Manerky believed with their whole being that this demonic leader of the underworld would give them the length of years stolen from lives that they had claimed, not just claimed, the Manerky believed that in order to take one's spirit into them that they would have to ingest the flesh of that individual.

Lane hated that Satan had so completely lied to these people. He hated that he would never be able to tell the Manerky the truth. They would die, and before them would not be the leader that they had believed obtainable by digging into the earth's surface; no, for them it would be the true leader of the underworld, of Hell; it would be Satan, and he would share his domain with no one. He would make leaders of no one. He was a liar, and the father of lies. He would be cast into the lake of fire with all of the other liars, and be burned.

Gruesome fang like protrusions exited the dark-reddish-brown mar of the warrior's gums. Smaller simulations stretched between the daunting fang-like protrusions. The Manerky warriors had filed the teeth between the outer protrusions. The result was a horrifying mass of yellowed razor sharp teeth, giving the four warriors the appearance of human-sharks with fangs. The warriors were unlike the other warriors. They seemed wiser. Something very eerie registered in their blackened irises. Evil.

Lane watched the four as they crouched low to the ground. Their unrelenting glares seemed only mildly hindered by the glowing candles. It was the Mi-no-hi-lo, the trance-walk. These warriors were far more dangerous than any of the enemy that had been faced. These were warriors that had spent years in the darkness, inflicting untold pain. They had overcome the worst that the Manerky could do. These were the product of an evil so vile…

Lane couldn't finish the thought. Suddenly the demonic beings littering the tunnel, seemed to diminish greatly. The cheerleaders of evil paled in comparison to the depraved-unholy minds staring back from darkness.

Lane knew that he had to get his family and friends to the other chamber. He couldn't tell them of the evil lurking closer than their next breath. Jordan and Garrison were so afraid that fear registered clearly in each of their eyes, but to know of the trance walkers... Lane could not do that. He simply ushered the clueless procession more firmly, at a faster pace. Only a few more feet into the next chamber. They were moments away from evil. Lane would gather them all. He would usher them to the boats. He would do what he should have done from the beginning. He would remove his family from the shores of the Cadotion River. If any of the Cadotion were left alive... he breathed uneasily. The thought brought with it a tiredness that he could not afford. He had to stay alert. He needed to get his loved ones far away from the evil. Help would come. Lane, Jordan, and Garrison would send reinforcement. The Manerky would be eradicated. This war zone was no place for children. It would be irresponsible to believe that the children's safety could be ensured while fighting with so deadly an enemy.

A low whispering growl emitted from the corner where the four trance walkers gathered. Lane knew their time was at an end. With a violent shove he pushed Garrison and Jordan the remaining distance. He tossed Tristan and Kirsten easily to a pallet of furs, and turned back to the threat.

Lane saw the despair fill Jordan's eyes as he forced the two candle-holders that had been buried into the ground into a crisscross pattern to guard the door.

"Get the children to the boats!" Lane shouted.

"Not without you!" Jordan's call was a defiant demand.

"Now, Jordan there's no time! I'll meet up with you." Lane said as he felt the first of the jagged nails cut like glass into his back. "I love you." He whispered as he at last turned to the evil that awaited him.

61

Edward had been in and out of consciousness for the better part of the day. Julie was running out of options. She had no other alternative, but to try to launch a defense on Edward's behalf. She needed to prove his innocence. But how? She had all of the key components that would absolve Edward of all of the more monstrous crimes, but the fact remained that he was still responsible for the lives of so many.

Julie thought about that. Edward was the leader of a government organization. But after the truth had gone viral, the government would be denying any affiliation with the organization, wouldn't they? She crossed the lobby floor again. She felt like a caged animal. Who or what would help prove what they really needed to know Max's motive?

Julie turned to the sound of the elevator doors opening. John and Cynthia stepped, despondently out of the silver doors. Cynthia looked grim. Her eyes were filled with fear, possibly even sorrow.

Julie rushed over to her friend. "What's wrong?"

"Our friends are in the middle of a war." Cynthia's eyes filled with tears, and then spilled over. "The Manerky tribe has attacked the Cadotion village?"

"The... who... The what?" Julie was confused. Who in the world were these tribes, and what did they have to do with clearing Edward's name?

"The Cadotion village is where our friends and their children live. They are missionaries for The Truth."

"Wait… are you talking about Jordan, the woman that has been in the news for the last week?" Julie was shocked. How much more could this woman take? Already, her life had been manipulated by Edward. Julie cringed from the thought. It still felt wrong that the man that she loved, and was trying to exonerate could be so vengeful. She was still working through her feelings; still trying to allow God to take the judgment from her heart. She thought about the young woman, Jordan. She seemed so strong, but even the strong had a breaking point.

"Yes." Cynthia's answer was weak.

Julie had been so deep in thoughts about Jordan that she had all but forgotten her question. "… Uh… I mean what's going on?"

Cynthia looked up then. Her eyes betrayed a slight irritation. "Our friends and their children are in the middle of that war zone." Cynthia explained. Her tone had lost some of its edge. Her shoulders slumped.

Julie rubbed her hand down the pink-pull-over sweater that Cynthia was wearing. Her new friend was trembling. Julie pulled her into a firm embrace. Every ounce of her love and well wishes rested in the hug. Julie prayed as she held her dear friend that her friends and their family would have favor. That no matter the circumstance, no matter how big the odds… Jordan and her family would rise from the ashes.

"Hey, thanks. I'm sorry. I saw you when I walked in. You don't look so well right now either." Cynthia rubbed Julie's arm. "How is he?"

"Not good… I don't know. He's in and out of consciousness." Julie looked up at the tiled ceiling. What was she doing? "What is it all for? What is he waking up to? More of the same?" Julie sniffed. She wanted to run from the hospital, but if she did where would that leave Edward.

"I've been thinking about that." Cynthia admitted, while moving to a row of chairs near the elevator. She pulled her bag into her lap. Julie scrutinized the large gray and black purse that looked more like a satchel than a woman's accessory.

"Remember the file that I gave you about Max?" Cynthia prompted.

"Of course I have it in my bag, but what good is it? Edward is not even awake, and even when he is he may as well be asleep for all of the concern he shows for his own life." Julie could feel the bitterness that she had fault to keep at bay all morning seeping back in.

"I know, but what if we didn't need Edward to stage a defense?" Cynthia asked as she pulled her cell phone and another file from her bag.

"I've thought of nothing else, but doesn't a defendant kind of have to be at his defense?" Julie sighed. Where was this going? She needed hope, but not false hopes. She needed leads. She needed evidence.

"Well…" Cynthia said as she sent a sly smile in John's direction. "These are documents proving the birth and death of a man." Cynthia said as she handed the birth and death certificate to Julie.

Julie was tired. Edward's life was hanging in the balance. She didn't have time for this. Death and birth certificates? What did it matter when someone was born or died? How could that prove Edward's innocence? Julie needed to get out of the hospital. She had spent so much time there, she was starting to get on her own nerves. Her attitude was horrendous.

"Julie these are the death and birth certificates of Mitch Hayes." Cynthia looked at Julie then. Her gaze deepened. "The file I gave you…"

"Yes it was of Mitch Hayes, but what does that have to do with Edward, or even Max for that matter?" Julie interrupted. She couldn't imagine where all of this was leading. The longer it took for Cynthia to explain what she meant—the more frustrated Julie felt. Julie blew out a resigned breath, as she moved to a chair next to Cynthia. She needed to relax, before she pushed away the only person in her corner. Whether she saw any use for the documents or not—Cynthia obviously had.

"Julie Mitch is Max."

"What? How can that be?" Julie felt the room spin a little. Mitch was Max. What? Did that mean that Edward was guilty after all?

Cynthia sighed. "Julie…"

"Let me." John said as he placed a tender hand on Cynthia's arm.

"Julie I knew Max, or so I thought that I knew Max." John said as his eyes took on a faraway gaze. "Max and I met in Honduras. We were on a mission trip. Well, at least I was. I found out later that Max was the inside man for a gun and drug cartel. He had gone to Honduras to make a trade with the leader of a very big crime syndicate, Victor Hayes.

"During his time in Honduras, Max had overstayed. He had gone passed his time on his visa. The Honduras government officials were about to throw Max out. However, he had heard about the multiple churches, youth groups, and missionary organizations-such as The Truth that were meeting to build new homes, and work on the water supply.

"Max hid among those groups." John exhaled hard, as he gave Cynthia a pointed stare. He dropped his head for a moment, and in that gesture, Julie could see that wherever this story started, it had ended with shame—John's shame. Cynthia felt his pain, as she looked deeper into his eyes. It was almost as if she were on this journey into the past with him.

John adjusted his weight, and then continued. "The Militia had come that day. They had killed many of the youth..." John turned to the wall. His voice trailed off, he sat down. The weight of the story was clearly too much.

"It's okay, John." Cynthia said as she went to him. Squatting in front of her husband, Cynthia pulled him into her arms. "You had no way of knowing that Max was a part of it all. He hid in your life, too."

John kissed Cynthia on the cheek, then gently pulled her into the chair beside him. Once she was seated, he turned his attention back to Julie.

"Julie it all makes sense now. Max was not just working for Victor Hayes he was his oldest son."

"Edward had been working Victor Hayes' case. He was sending an agent to neutralize Victor Hayes, to kill him Julie."

"Max went undercover, deep undercover! He had documents pulled up that proved his death, well... the death of Mitch Hayes. Max burned his life to the ground. But it goes deeper. Max worked with another agent. The agent got Max on the inside. James Ruston recruited Max.

James Ruston orchestrated a screw up so bad that the company couldn't ignore it. When Black Heart can't ignore it lives get changed Julie." John searched the room. His eyes were growing wider, more excited as all of the pieces of the puzzle fell into place.

"Edward Stanton did what he does best. He ordered the recycling of Mitch Hayes. The fallible damnation of it all is this... Edward Stanton, HOD of Black Heart has no clue who the recruits are recycled as. As insane as it may seem for the leader of a government organization not to know who his recruits are recycled into—Edward believed his being in the dark about the new identity was the only way to give the recruit a fresh start." John studied Julie for a moment. He knew this part of it was hard for some to understand. Julie seemed to grasp it easily, as she nodded for John to continue.

"He hired the son of the man he intended to have killed!" John exclaimed. His tone was high and his body was vibrating with the need to convey his story, Max's story.

"Mitch Hayes was standing right in front of Edward, and he didn't have a clue!" John slammed the words down like a gauntlet. His eyes met both Cynthia's and Julie's in turn.

Julie shot to her feet. The blood drained from her face. "Oh, my God!"

"Exactly!" John finally half shouted.

"So you see Julie? Edward had hired the son of the biggest drug and gun cartel in New York. Max had privy to things that Edward told no one. He was the hired help. Max was to be the end all do all. He was hired because of his closeness to me.

"Max was hired for Intel only. But Max had a prior agenda. He had allied himself with the enemy in order to not only save his father, but to obtain the reigns of the biggest government secret. Think about what Victor Hayes could have done with that kind of power. But his son had gone so deep undercover that even his father didn't know where, or even who he was for that matter."

"Victor Hayes still believes his son to be alive. He's still waiting for his son to call or do whatever it is that he does in order to check in with his father."

Julie turned to the doors of the ICU. This was bigger than whether Edward would take part in his own future. This was all of their lives. Everyone that was related to this… to the death of Victor Hayes' son would be annihilated.

Julie started to the ICU doors, but stopped. "I don't know what to do. I feel like I need to be in a million different places. Is my family safe? Is Edward safe? What about you and John?"

"Julie this puts us at a decidable advantage. I know that you are terrified. It's only natural, but this is what Black Heart does. This is what Edward was trained to do; did do for thirty years." Cynthia said as she moved to the doors.

"But Edward is unconscious Cynthia. He doesn't care about anything." Julie threw her hands in the air.

"Oh, but he does. He cares about what every agent that has ever killed cares about. He cares about making amends. He cares about a second chance. He may feel that he doesn't deserve it, but I assure you Julie... Edward Stanton thinks about nothing, but redemption." Cynthia was pacing as the declaration flowed with determination. Her jaw was set in a hard line, as she turned to John. Her eyes softened, and filled with love as she moved to his side. "Edward wants everything that he feels he doesn't deserve. I know I did."

Julie grabbed her bag and rushed to the ICU doors. This had to be it. If Edward was awake, she would make him listen. She would explain everything. She would do whatever it took to resurrect the former leader of Black Heart. She needed Edward Stanton former HOD of Black Heart to do what he did best... put an end to the bad guy. That was it wasn't it. That's what Edward had been for the most part. He had not been some killer destroying the lives of the innocent. He had been the answer to unpunished crime. Edward Stanton was the reaper for justice. He was the revenge for those that had nothing to cling to, but the memory of a lost loved one. He was the avenging angel that had swooped in and collected the due payment for those unpunished crimes.

Somehow the rash of explanations for his old life made her feel giddy; alive. She felt connected to something bigger than her mundane existence. Julie half skipped, as she turned back to Cynthia and John. For so long a widow washed up in her wishes, Julie suddenly felt free, excited to be no one else, but Julie. She laughed. "Come on let's go wake up my boyfriend."

62

Garrison was spinning as was Jordan the moment that the torches crossed the doorway, leading into the inner chamber where Lane had pushed them out of harm's way. Grunts and alien screams filled the space beyond. Garrison snatched at the stem of the torches, but Lane had somehow welded them into the tunnel wall. Molded supernaturally into the cave wall, the torches just simply would not budge.

Garrison turned to Jordan. She was already crawling under. Her hands scratched frantically at the floor of the cave, trying to gain momentum. Soon she was on the other side.

Garrison turned to where the children were now laying on the furs. The boys were still sound asleep, and Amelia was going about her usual efforts to make certain they were comfortable. Ever the good medicine woman, Amelia showed no fear. Her hands were busy with the task at hand, while her eyes searched for new ways to comfort her sleeping charges.

Garrison gave a quick once over to where Nick was still laying on the cave floor. His face was ashen. His body shivered every few seconds. The fever was taking hold. If something was not done, the boy would soon be dead. Garrison watched as Penny traced a trembling finger along the line of his jaw. Her eyes took on a faraway stare as she rocked her friend slowly.

"Amelia." Garrison's whisper seemed a little too loud for the somber feel of the room.

Amelia crossed to him immediately. Her chin upturned in anticipation. Command me, her amber eyes begged. Garrison felt a twinge of pain for the tiny girl. Where was her childhood? Why could she not cower in a corner like a normal six-year-old would, given similar circumstances?

"Nick is sick. He'll not make another night." Garrison leaned in close. He didn't want the bad news to make it to his young friend's awareness. Penny seemed too close to the edge without more bad news to fill the space between her and the hope that she so desperately clung to. The slightest push could send her frayed psyche into oblivion.

"I have just the thing." Amelia assured with a slight pat of her hand.

Garrison allowed an appreciative snort. Suddenly the little girl that should be cowering in the corner didn't seem so little. She was far beyond her years. She was in her element. Amelia was doing what she was born to do. She was the medicine woman for the Cadotion tribe.

Amelia walked purposefully to the farthest wall. She collected two clay pots, and then carried them back to the leaning fire pit. The firelight was waning. Soon the room would be thrust into darkness. Garrison moved quickly to the pit. Lowering his torch into the fire, sparks cascaded into the air. The chamber filled with light.

Garrison turned his attention to the outer perimeter of the chamber. There seemed to be no immediate threat. He wanted to go. He wanted to help his friends, but as Garrison watched Penny rock Nick, Amelia collecting herbs and spices to give her new patient; as he watched Modilo and Tristan sleeping on the pelt of furs, he knew that this was where Jordan would want him to be. He would protect her children. He would give his life, if need be. He would not leave their side, while Jordan fault gallantly at the side of her husband.

Garrison turned his attention to the crossed torches that blocked the path to the ensuing battle. If Jordan and Lane did not return from that battle, he would take their children back to the states. He would even have the Benton's petition for the adoption of Modilo. That was not the outcome that his heart was ready to accept. Garrison doubted he would ever be ready for such an outcome. He needed his friends to survive, but he needed to say it in his heart, in hopes that his best friend and former partner would feel the truth… he needed Jordan to know that he would be there; he would never let her down again. She could and would always be able to count on him.

As Jordan crossed into the tunnel her eyes squinted in pain. She immediately turned away from the light. She pulled a long piece of cloth that she kept in her small bag of ammo out, and wrapped it tightly around her head. She had to cover her eyes. She could not take the chance that she would be tempted to look into the holy light. She had not been able to see Lane, but Jordan knew from the exuberant light that her husband was well.

She took a moment before pushing her way into the froes of battle. She needed to acclimate her senses to her surroundings.

Grunts and screams pierced through the darkness. She could hear the guttural-animalistic calls of the Manerky warriors as they tried to throw the enemy off balance. Her mind swam on a sea of sound. She needed the life raft that would save her from the sinking gloom; she needed to know that Lane was not just sustaining, but that he was thriving. Her heart pounded in her chest, making the attempt difficult.

Jordan centered her mind, body, and spirit. Her hands sought and found the weapons at her side easily. She was aware of everyone and everything in the tunnel, just as if she were seeing it all first hand.

Shakia growled her warning, while her kittens purred peacefully, in contented slumber, both unaware of the trouble so close at hand. Jordan envied the innocence that she knew, all too well was lost to her daughter.

Lane stood three paces to the left of her. His back was still to her. The image of Lane turning on her earlier, in a fit of rage scorched through her mind. She knew that it had not been his fault, but anger had no place on a battle field. Rage had a way of causing one to make mistakes. Jordan knew that it would be a mistake on her part to assume that Lane knew of her presence. He had made a deliberate attempt to keep her and the others out of what he felt was harm's way.

Jordan stepped back slightly and continued to listen. There were now three warriors; if there had been others she had no way of knowing. One of the warriors was moving away from the others. Jordan could hear the steps. She didn't have to guess where the enemy intended to go. He would break away from the others in such a way that his enemy would believe him to be abandoning his brothers at arms. Jordan knew the truth. He was trying to instill false hope.

She readied for the attack. There was no need to move. The enemy would come for her. He would sense her and he would come.

As soon as the others were safely tucked away in the inner chamber, Lane acted fast, faster than human perception. The Manerky, seasoned warriors or not, would be unable to know his intention until it was too late.

The holy light was already searing through him, the moment he thrust the torches into place. Clay melted at his touch, forming a tight bond as it cooled around the torch stems. Whether or not the torch light remained, was of no consequence now. The light generating from Lane's body was sufficient to light the whole mountain if need be.

He turned back to the warriors. One already lay in a heap. The light had seared into his eyes, leaving nothing more than hollowed black holes with protruding bits of skin and brain matter. Lane allowed only a quick glance to surmise the wellbeing of the Manerky warrior; he was indeed dead.

The moment that the three remaining had realized the fate of their comrade a frenzy of hate and determination mounted as the three launched menacing attacks. Arms crossing before their faces they scratched angrily at Lane like wildcats. Their translucent white eyes glowed fiercely even against the luminous light that filtered from Lane.

Lane noted the dress of these warriors, unlike that of the tribal-underlings, these warriors wore intricately beaded human bones that were woven through the outer rim of their ears. Dark tattoos littered the entirety of their bodies, not just the top of their head. Lane allowed a more intense scrutiny of the pictures covering the bodies of the remaining warriors.

A swirling vortex of dark winds exited ominous faces. The eyes of each face forever frozen in fear. Each face seemed younger still than the last. Behind each of the heads were dancing warriors.

Lane again faced the three men in front of him. His mind raced with the truth. The pictures were not just art. These were actual accounts of the times that each of these evil beings had claimed the life of a child.

This was a tribute to the Direignbang; the feast of the coming Direign. These were the most decorated of the Manerky clan, the Mi-no-hi-lo trance walkers.

Lane felt the familiar flow of rage as it started to etch its way through his senses. He tried to push the anger back, but the atrocities peering back from the warrior's bodies would not be ignored.

Jordan braced herself for the coming attack. She could tell that something had changed; something about Lane's mood. Though she could not see the Manerky, she knew that something about them had thrust Lane back into the hands of rage. She searched her mind.

"Help me, Father." She quickly allowed the simple prayer to filter through her thoughts.

"I am here." Jordan felt the calming truth wash through her senses. With it she saw words starting to form. Jordan still listening for the approaching warrior, prepared for the strike that would come. At the same time, she pushed into the words that started to form into a sentence.

"Be angry and sin not! (Ephesians 4:26) Jordan's mouth was moving the moment the words came fully into view. She could feel Lane tense with the sound of her voice. She hated to say anything. She didn't want Lane to lose his focus, but whether through anger or the knowledge that she was where he had deliberately tried to keep her from being, Lane was bound to lose focus. She couldn't imagine that a word from God would be more of a risk than leaving him to the anger that was pulsating through his body.

"Jordan?" Lane whispered.

"Yes." Jordan admitted in a normal voice. "No need to whisper Lane they can hear everything."

"Why are you here?" Lane prompted. The incredulous tone of his question did not escape Jordan.

"Because you are." Jordan said flatly. It was that simple to her. Why would Lane even need to know why she was there? The answer was as plain as writing on a wall. They were one.

Lane was silent after that. Jordan heard the grunting of combat blows, the labored effort of Lane's breathing, but nothing more. She still waited for the warrior to come. Her mind started to swim with the possibilities. She couldn't take the chance of removing the cloth from her eyes. She could do nothing more than stand still, and brace for the attack.

At last Jordan heard the blows come to an end. Lane's breathing was relatively unchanged. Her attacker had never come. She strained against the dead silence for answers. Why would the warrior have changed his course?

Then as if to answer her question, Jordan heard the sound of muffled footfalls. She didn't want to make a mistake. She couldn't attack Lane, thinking that it was the warrior, but surely Lane would announce himself. Surely, he would not try to sneak up on her in such an explosive atmosphere.

Jordan pulled her weapon up close. Her stance was a simple defensive pose. Her legs spread shoulder width apart, her elbows bent with her hands tightly fisted around either end of the Barton she clutched.

Closer still, Jordan heard the steps draw near. She could almost feel the heat generating off the massive body. Jordan stifled the smile that tried to make its way across her lips. With ease she started to spin the Barton. The serious set of her jaw, a warning to her would be attacker.

The moment Lane heard Jordan's voice his mind switched to overdrive. One warrior was already dead. Still three remained. Though the three had been guarding their eyes, they had managed to land a couple of good blows. Lane's arm stung with the slice-marks made by the Manerky's grotesque fingernails.

He watched as the Manerky to the outer side was pulling away from his comrades. At first, he had believed it an attempt to escape his fate, but the moment Jordan had spoken, Lane knew exactly what the warrior's agenda was. He would silence the threat from behind.

Lane thrust a booted foot into the middle warrior. The skinny man flew across the expanse. His body crashed into the cave wall, and then melted awkwardly down the clay covered structure.

The warrior left facing Lane turned to his friend long enough to give Lane the opening he needed. Lane lunged for the man's neck, and with a loud horrific twist the Manerky's struggle silenced.

He turned his attention, then to the sneaking warrior. The moment that Lane faced the man, his back stiffened. His steps ceased. He wasted no time as he reached in, and placed one searing hand on the warrior's face. The man jerked-awkwardly back from the threat, but Lane was there. He wrapped his hands completely around the sneaking warrior's head and allowed the power to pour into the evil being. Like hot wax the man's face dripped to the floor.

Lane shook the remains of the melted flesh from his hand. He pulled the black shirt he had been wearing off, and wiped the disgusting ooze onto the fabric. His eyes searched for any other threats. Satisfied there were none, he turned to his wife.

Jordan was still standing with the Barton in hand, but now she had taken on a more deliberate defense pose. Her head tilted to the right slightly as if she were searching for any sound that would tip her off as to where the enemy might be.

Lane knew the risk, but something about seeing his beautiful, dangerous, wife standing there so intent on her would be attacker, filled Lane with something akin to desire born of mischief. The idea filtering through Lane's mind felt thrilling.

He tiptoed as quietly as possible, always aware of where his wife's weapon was. It would take her no time to dismantle the enemy. He had learned long ago to never underestimate Jordan. The closer he drew the stiffer her stance became. Then all of the sudden something seemed relaxed about her. Her head though tilted to the side, was no longer stiff. Where her arms had been rigid with the effort to keep her weapon close, they were now loosely, almost playfully spinning the Barton.

Jordan knew that it was him. Lane felt the thrill of the hunt dissipate as he moved closer, and simply moved the Barton out of the way.

"How did you know?" He asked, while removing the blindfold from her eyes.

"Don't take this the wrong way, but it's kind of hard for a six foot five giant to hide amongst pigmies, don't you think?" Jordan laughed as she raised up on her tiptoes, and brushed her lips tenderly across his.

"What about in the hospital? I was nowhere near you. Garrison was right there with me, and still you knew it was us." Lane hated that his voice sounded almost defeated, but he had believed that he had her; if only, this one time. But instead as usual his agent-wife had foiled his attempts at sneaking up on her.

"For one, we had put in a request for a certain type of food. I smelled the food. Another reason is, because quite frankly, Lane no one else has as heavy a footfall as you. Like I said it's kind of hard for a giant to hide among pigmies." Jordan laughed.

The sound was melodic. It reminded Lane of how blessed he was to have her in his life. He no longer cared about being able to sneak up on his wife. She was his wife. She was here. She was thriving, and moments earlier she had been draped over his arms-lifeless. Now as her laughter filled the tunnel and echoed back to him, Lane's heart filled with more joy than he believed he would ever be able contain.

He held her to him. His arms trembled with the effort of not crushing her, but wanting to hold her closer still. His mind was swimming with thoughts of the many blessings he had to be thankful for when a noise from behind brought his thoughts up short. Jordan too had heard the sound.

Jordan's hands were already seeking both ends of her weapon. She moved to Lane's side. Her feet again were shoulder length apart. Her eyes studying the tunnel where the noise had come from further down in the darkness.

"More of the enemy?" Jordan whispered.

"Most likely." Lane admitted; his voice sounded tired. He was tired of this foolish game. The moment they were rid of one group of the Manerky warriors, another would inevitably step in. Always they had a fresh man in, while to the contrary, Lane and his group struggled to stay on their feet. If something did not change the course of events, they would all pay the ultimate price.

Jordan didn't want to let Lane know, but she was completely spent. Her hands barely claimed the Barton. Her feet ached from the torturous hours of maneuvering the mountain side, and then the tunnels. Her body could not, would not continue with the abuse. Her poor-sweet-baby could not, possibly withstand the very taxing battles.

Jordan's gaze settled on Lane. He too looked beyond weary. His eyes had lost their usual luster. His arms seemed more droopy than usual. He had channeled his angelic powers, the power of God on more than one occasion; a lesser man would have already collapsed beneath the stress.

She listened to the faint footfalls. Still the enemy persisted. Still they came. No matter how tired she and Lane might be, it would not stop the endless pursuit. Her mind entertained the thought of giving in, but she could not. If not for her children, her husband, her niece, her friends… all that she loved; Jordan would had given in to the hunger, the ache, and the exhaustion already. But she had no other recourse, but to push ahead for those that she loved.

"Jordan, listen to me." Lane said as he placed a comforting hand on her arm. His eyes never left the tunnel. "Take everyone to the river. Get as far down stream as you can. Garrison will help you." Lane's voice had never sounded as desperate as now.

"No!" Jordan's tone had been more hiss than plea. She winced absently. Her mind half expected Lane's hurt countenance to level what was left of her waning resolve.

Suddenly while Jordan studied Lane's beautiful-tormented profile the desperation vanished from his too lovely features. All at once an exuberant smile replaced the anguish that had moments before wrecked his angelic visage.

Jordan was stunned by the out of place reaction to the approaching enemy. Had Lane caught a second wind? Was he now hoping for the fight? Had God spoken words of encouragement to him? If so she needed the words to come to her aid as well. It was then that Jordan turned to face the supposed enemy.

Laughter split the air as hordes of not the Manerky warriors, but the Cadotion villagers stepped from the darkness. Each of them was holding on to the next as they exited the darkness. Their eyes reluctantly adjusted to the faintest of light coming from the torches that Lane had welded to the wall. The darkness in the tunnel had been so complete that the procession had moved very slowly. The fear that must have accompanied such a venture…

Jordan's eyes filled with tears as she let go of Lane's hand. Her feet could not move fast enough. She raced to the people that she had been afraid to be left alone with. Each one of the Cadotion villagers, materializing out of the darkness had held a special significance in her world.

Juanino, a beautiful young village girl clung to several of the village children. She had been playing in the middle of the village, as she was accustomed to do. Only thirteen years old, Juanino had stepped up as a kind of village babysitter. The young girl loved children. She had spent many a day helping with Amelia and now Tristan. It had been her kind spirit that had granted the couples of the village stolen moments of coveted intimacy.

Jordan studied the long braids and golden eyes of Juanino. Her skin was a sun-kissed brown. Her face so perfect it had seemed that the hand of God had brushed each line to perfection, and so He had.

Jordan looked to each of the children. Her heart was breaking even before the thought was complete. "Juanino, where are their parents?" Jordan asked in the native tongue.

Juanino turned to the back of the tunnel. Her hand floated easily to a cloud of adults that were clustered in the darkness. Each moved forward. Their eyes filled with fear, until the moment their children had come into view.

"The children wanted to stay with me, and the elders." Juanino explained. "Mother and fathers weary, but they allow. It makes for better moving." Juanino tried to translate her thoughts into English.

Jordan smiled. Amelia had been working with the young girl every afternoon. She was doing well. Though some of her words didn't exactly fit for the message she was trying to convey, Jordan could usually decode the information well enough.

There were dozens still, of the Cadotion villagers. Lane had moved to the torches. With a thunderous yank the makeshift door was removed.

Jordan and Lane stood like twin sentinels guarding the Cadotion villagers' safe passage into the inner chamber where Garrison and the children were still waiting. Lane had stuck his head through the door, briefly to make certain that Garrison didn't mistake the Cadotion people for Manerky, and harm them.

Soon everyone was safely beyond the borders of darkness, and pushing out of the entrance of the tunnel into wonderful sunlight.

Lane's eyes canvassed the blanket of destruction that was now the Cadotion village. Bodies lay on the ground in different stages of gore. Mangled tents, strewn possessions mingled with dust, and village pets were crumbled in heaped reminders of the ugly that had visited upon them.

Lane's knees buckled. His hands never leaving his sides; he crumbled to the ground. Everything was lost. The village had been ripped a sunder. Nothing was left for the loving people that had so completely filled his life with joy.

The Cadotion people stumbled out into the sunlight at last. They were seeing the destruction that had beset their village. They would crumble under the loss.

He turned to see a couple standing near their tent. There was no crying, no wails of the loss that had claimed their possessions. No eyes turned down in remorse for what was lost. Instead, children played with Juanino, while the adults rallied to the task set before them. Couples smiled shyly as they shared stolen moments of passion: a smile, a touch, hug, and sometimes even a kiss would pass between the lovers as they worked to right their ruined homes.

Awe filled Lane's heart as he moved to his feet. How had he lost this? Where in his walk had he forgotten this profound show of the truth; this simplistic stone that was the foundation by which the Cadotion had built their lives?

As Lane watched each of the villagers rebuilding their lives from the ground up his heart filled with a renewed hope.

It was then that he searched for his own family. There near the base of the mountain, Jordan, the children, and their friends worked in like manner to rebuild their home. Nothing about Jordan's appearance shouted failure or loss. Nothing about the way she moved would suggest that she was ready to give up. This wonderful woman that God had entrusted to him… this woman that had feared the time that she would spend in the center of these people that embodied love, togetherness; his wife was more like the Cadotion people, than Lane had remembered to be.

Lane watched for a moment longer, taking in the beauty of it all. The shared glances, the touches, all of it… every nuance that filled the moments as the people pushed forward to their new future, all of it at its core was what it meant to be Cadotion; to be Christian.

63

Though the Cadotion village was not completely back to its original splendor, large steps had been made to put things back in order.

Garrison's impromptu visit to the American Embassy had raised a lot of attention. News casts were filled with the faces of outraged Americans.

Jordan's story had captured the hearts of viewers everywhere. Picket lines and marches alike filled the street in front of the Whitehouse, with demands for Jordan and her family's safe return to the states. So much had been wrong in America, rumors of wars and uprisings, due to political agenda, overriding need. The story had gone viral on Facebook, as well. America needed to feel good about something. The people needed to be unified on an even playing field. Jordan and her family—the story of change and hope—had been the threshold for that new ground. America had fought hard, united in the need to right someone's world, if not their own.

The Cadotion village was filled with troupes; the National Guard had been deployed in response to the cries for help. Though John had been detained in a fight for his life, the moment he had regained consciousness he had impressed upon Cynthia and Julie, Garrison's plan to rally the American embassy. Julie's church group was notified at once, as was Rocky Mount; the Benton's church family. A few more phone calls had been made, and soon the embassy as well as the White House had been overrun with e-mails, letters and picketing tax payers demanding the safe return of their fellow Americans. They would not be ignored, and united in a cause the American people had proven to be an unstoppable force.

Jordan sat cuddling Modilo and Tristan. So tired from the struggle to put things back in order, the boys draped loosely at her sides.

Amelia finally gave into the exhaustion. She sat in Lane's lap. It had taken some doing, but they were finally able to convince their daughter that she would soon return to take her rightful place as medicine woman. Jordan did not relish the thought of leaving her daughter alone; especially now that Aniahi was gone. But she knew that the Cadotion people would take care of her. Besides she and Lane still had plans to return. The other tribes would return in the summer. They deserved to know the truth. They deserved the right to choose, and with American troupes and local military forces united the Manerky were being ran down; no hiding place would stop the two forces after the horrific sights that they had been privy to in the Manerky village. The images would haunt Jordan forever.

Jordan held her head back as a rogue breeze filtered through her hair. She knew that there had never been a time in the history of the world that more resembled the end. Even the Apostle Paul would agree with the assessment. The world was evil. Ugly lived on every corner of their reality, and yet, in spite of it all, she still could not deny God's existence. She took in the masterful art of the heavens, and the V-shaped pattern of some birds flying low across the horizon—there would be no excuse—man would have no reason to not know. Even the very works of His hands testified to His existence. (Romans 1:20)

Lane sat on the opposite bench. The family road together in a large houseboat provided by the government. They floated easily down the river, headed for Denali.

Garrison had stayed behind. He wanted to make certain the Cadotion villagers were being treated fairly.

Jordan smiled. She was proud of the change in her friend. The Cadotion ways were hard to resist, but it was the true change—the spiritual change that had so profoundly filled Garrison—that had made the biggest difference. Christ had so completely transformed and renewed Garrison's thinking that his countenance glowed with evidence of His love.

Nick and Penny had been airlifted to the nearest trauma center. As soon as Nick was stable he would be moved to the New York trauma center, where John and Edward were being treated.

Kirsten was coiled up on the bench next to Lane. She awaited her meeting with Edward Stanton; she had not wavered in her resolve to seek his forgiveness.

Jordan was proud of Kirsten as well. Her bravery in spite of all the horrors in the past few days was phenomenal. The girl was acting far above what her years would suggest she might.

Jordan studied Kirsten's young face. Her long blond hair was matted with bits of clay. Smudge marks covered her cheeks and forehead. Though she slept, sleep deprivation had left its dark evidence under her frantically moving eyelids; fitful dreams still ravaged her slumber.

Shakia lay in a box under the bench where Kirsten slept. Her kittens lazily draped this way and that. Kirsten's hand never left her once feared adversary's silken-black and white fur.

Shakia nuzzled Kirsten's hand for much needed assurance from time to time, and even in her fitful dreams, Kirsten freely provided it, as she absently stroked the stressed cat's head.

Jordan was thinking about the treaty now. The Manerky's fate had at long last been sealed. They would no longer have the chance to hear the truth. Total annihilation had met them down the wrong path. Not by the hands of the many tribes that called the Kanchenjunga mountains home, but the military.

While the National Guard worked to repair, the damage caused by the Manerky attack, marines infiltrated the Manerky stronghold. Dozens of children of all ages were released into the custody of the Cadotion tribe; some of the children had belonged to the other tribes that had left for the harsh winter to come. The Denali government had been petitioned and agreed that the children would best be served among people that they more closely identified with. The Cadotion would keep the children safe, and return them to their true families upon their homecoming.

Even more children were found mutilated in the center of a circle of pikes. Atop of each pike were human skulls; hollowed holes stared out from battered sockets in different stages of decay. Ominous reminders of the torture they had endured.

Jordan found no measure of comfort in the Manerky tribes' early demise. Though they had paid for the atrocities they had committed, with their lives, it was their souls that would be lost forever. She no longer viewed the world through the once cynical eyes of a vigilante killer; she was now the child of a forgiving King that had taught her heart a new way. His way.

The Manerky, like so many, had been lied to by the enemy. Promises of a coming rule with the king of the underworld, would be replaced with death and destruction.

Jordan sniffed as she willingly took Lane's offered hand. He was always in tune to her every emotion. Sadness filled her heart; so much loss; for what?

Finally, making their way back to Denali, Jordan, Lane and the children boarded a plane for home. Shakia and her kittens were securely tucked away in with the other pets, below the passenger compartment. Though Kirsten had feared being away from her new companion, she had conceded with grace.

They had stayed a night in a hotel. Everyone needed showers, and a good night sleep before continuing the long trip back to the states.

64

Jordan turned to Kirsten as they walked down the hall toward Edward Stanton's room.

"Are you sure you want to do this?" Jordan was split down the middle; while closure was always good, Kirsten had already experienced so much.

Kirsten nodded. Her eyes betrayed the fear that she would not allow control of her mind.

"Okay. Let's go." Jordan prompted as she tucked Kirsten under her arm.

Lane walked purposefully at their side. To his credit he made sure to match his stride to that of theirs. Jordan allowed a moment of appreciation for her husband's handsome features. The tan pants and button down shirt he wore seemed out of place when compared to his fall of blondish-brown hair tucked in a neat thong at the nape of his neck. His angelic visage was colored with a stoic gaze. His ice-blue eyes set on the possible trouble to come.

Lane had called Anderson, the HOD of The Truth. He had given his report on their time in the Cadotion village. Anderson had personally taken Amelia, Tristan and Modilo to the Garden. There he would keep watch while Lane and Jordan accompanied Kirsten on her quest for forgiveness.

Shakia and her kittens had been taken back to The Garden where they would wait for their new master's return.

Kirsten's stomach felt as though it was in knots. This meeting had been on the horizon of her young existence for nearly two weeks, but no amount of preparation could have prepared her for the fear that coursed through her veins. Her bones ached from the incessant shivering. Her knees felt as though they might buckle under the pressure that she had placed on herself.

Oh, how she would give anything to show the confidence that Aniahi had in the face of certain death.

Kirsten's mind and body were one with the fear that had so completely resonated within her. The fear seemed to be more a part of her than mannerisms she had exhibited for the whole of her life: the way she walked, talked; everything that was Kirsten. More than the fear, guilt ate away at her spirit like cancer.

Kirsten had overheard Lane and Jordan earlier that morning. Edward Stanton was innocent of the child-agent fiasco. He was innocent of the deaths of the child-agents and their families. Suddenly, the fear that she had lived with for the better part of two weeks had taken a backseat to the mountain of guilt pressing down upon her; her hands were tainted with innocent blood; Edward Stanton's innocent blood.

Julie sat like a cornered rat in a room full of vipers. Never before had she witnessed so many eagle-eyed-gazes in one area. Edward was sitting near the window. His dark-intent gaze studied the streets below. The moment she had given herself over completely to the idea of Edward— the idea of them as a couple—Julie had felt light, giddy. Now she wasn't so sure. She didn't' know this Edward: his raptor gaze, his intent watchful glare that promised death from above to the streets below, left Julie anxious and undone.

Cynthia, too seemed different. She thumbed, feverishly through a stack of papers. Her unending scribbling quieted only in the moments that she pulled another paper from a new stack.

Cynthia was in her element now, making the profile, while Edward stood ready for the right course of action. This was a delicate ecosystem of checks and balances; wrongs that had to be righted. One wrong move and Victor Hayes would crush them into powder.

All at once Cynthia looked to John, and then back to the files. Her head began shaking pitifully as John leaned in and whispered something to her.

"No!" Cynthia hissed under her breath.

"No, what?" Edward calmly demanded. Irritation lined his face. He seemed frustrated to have been brought out of his thoughts so abruptly.

"No!" Cynthia's tone was still demanding, but seemed to take on more of a begging timbre.

"We're the same size. It'll work. You said yourself that Black Heart has a team that could…" John's words trailed off as Cynthia shot to her feet, and walked, hurriedly to Edward.

"Please, Mr. Stanton tell John no. Tell him this is not a good idea. Tell him he's not trained. Tell him…" Cynthia's eyes spilled over with tears. Her voiced was strained. Her head fell forward. Julie watched with open-intrigue as her new friend morphed into a begging child; an excruciating mask of pain stole over her face, as her hands pumped pitiful at her sides into tight fists. Though she had not touched Edward, Cynthia's leaning stance had been so imploring that Julie's heart twisted with pain for this young woman. How ironic that the very person she had feared most had become her champion. Julie could scarcely look away as she felt her body leaning forward. She didn't know whether to run to her friend and offer her comfort or stand her ground—to see how this man that she had fallen for against her head's attempts at interjecting common sense pleas to abandon such a mission that could only be met with turmoil and end with her broken heart—would react to the begging of a young woman that he had once pulled the strings of her life like a puppeteer.

Edward abandoned his position as Head of Department. No longer was he the studious-professional, waiting for word from an informant… the hit man waiting in position for information on his mark. His features softened into the tenderer Edward. The man that Julie had met in the hospital. The man that had been uncertain of his future. The man that had been reborn on his road to Damascus…like Paul, Edward had been broken and somehow, Julie knew—though hope seemed to be trying to abandon her at every turn—she knew that God would put him back together for His use.

"Cynthia, what is this about?" Edward asked as his arms wrapped around her visibly shaking shoulders.

No words came as Cynthia shook her head helplessly. A silent no rested pathetically on her lips as she defaulted to a puddle of tears.

Edward cast a confused glance in Julie's direction. The simple notion made Julie feel a little more at ease.

"Cynthia, you have got to calm down." John soothed as he rubbed his hand up and down her hunched back. "It's just a phone call, and a possible meeting. But there will be snipers all around."

"Snipers? Where will they come from John?" Cynthia wiped, pitifully at her eyes. "Black Heart is dead. The government denies any involvement. There is no team. There is no one." Cynthia flopped helplessly onto the bed.

"I wouldn't say that."

"Jordan!" Cynthia squealed as she raced over to her friend.

Julie turned to see the woman that had spoken. Never before had she seen such an exquisite image: emerald green eyes shown back from a tan face. Dark-auburn-hair cascaded down in wavy-curls that danced around the hourglass curve of her hips.

A young girl with brilliant-blue eyes and wavy-blond-hair stood next to the woman called Jordan. Julie absently wondered if the gates of Heaven had opened too wide, a second too long. She was sure that part of the angelic host had landed in Edward's hospital room.

The door pushed wider still as Julie's eyes flowed upward, and higher still. A very tall man with broad-shoulders, and features that seemed to have been chiseled from granite, bent low, and then straightened behind the woman and girl.

Julie's breath caught as a brilliant smile stretched across the man's angelic visage. His electric blue eyes brightened as he bent to embrace Cynthia.

"Why the long face?" His baritone voice was like butter.

Julie watched as the sweet-love filled lines of his face hardened into accusation. She followed the giant's accusing glare. Her breath caught as she realized that Edward was the focus of the man's intent scrutiny.

Julie stepped from her corner. She no longer cared about the vipers in her midst, or the number of angelic hosts popping up in Edward's hospital room. Anger burned through her senses. She was shocked at how immediate her reaction had been.

Julie lifted her chin, defiantly as she stubbornly claimed Edward's hand, and refused to let it go.

"Edward is innocent!" Julie blurted.

No one could have anticipated Kirsten's actions. Not even she had expected this. She sprinted forward. Her feet racing to the object of her need.

Tears streamed—endlessly down her cheeks—clouding her vision. She all but leaped through the last remaining steps that separated her and Mr. Stanton. Oh, how she needed this ache to be over.

If Mr. Stanton did his worst, it could not compare to the tornado of emotion ripping her apart from the inside out.

"I'm sorry." she cried pitifully as she clung to Edward. Her arms draped around his waist, and held on like twin vices. Her breaths came in jagged pulls. Her head spun as she raced through every transgression, and begged for forgiveness. This was the place, the person that could take the pain from her. No matter how long it took, or the price she would pay, Kirsten would stay until all of it was taken. She no longer wanted it.

"Would someone care to tell me what's going on?" Edward felt like he was in some kind of movie where everything was backward. Had he been paying so little attention to his life?

Julie reached for Kirsten, but she clung to Edward all the more. Edward's torso pulled forward, nearly knocking him off balance. The effort of maintaining a standing position was already a tremendous feat. The last episode had claimed so much of his strength.

"Mr. Stanton, maybe you should sit down." Jordan finally said as she moved to the hospital bed.

"Please, it's Edward. Stop calling me Mr. Stanton. I'm no longer the HOD of Black Heart." Edward complained. "I didn't like the title when I was the head of department. I certainly don't intend to entertain it now." Edward complained as his fingers fought to torque the girl's vice grip away from his body. Whatever the problem the girl's pleading and unrelenting hold were not about to let up. He frowned down at the teenage girl.

"Edward, please sit down." Jordan corrected as she pointed to the bed.

Edward allowed some of the frustration he felt for the girl's tugging at his body to show.

"Kirsten, honey… please calm down." Jordan crooned as she tenderly pulled Kirsten's trembling body away from the focus of her attention.

A pleading glance from Jordan prompted Lane to move forward. Lane reached down, and lifted the girl easily into his arms. Her crying had calmed to a gasping-sniffle.

"Mr….. I mean Edward. The thing is Kirsten was one of the child-agents…" Jordan's words came up short as Edward bounded to his feet.

"Dear God!" Edward whispered as he started for the still whimpering girl.

Jordan was moving too. Her hand caught Edward's arm as she gently tugged him back to a seated position.

"She's fine it's just this day has been a long time in coming for her." Jordan smiled weakly at the trembling girl.

"We all believed that you were the one who organized the child-agents. Black Heart was lost. It had to be stopped-destroyed. It no longer stood for what it had once stood for. There was no justice.

"Lives were being destroyed; whole families killed." Jordan turned to Kirsten.

"It's not her fault. She is brave to want to take the responsibility, for the blame upon herself. We were in the room when Garrison came up with the idea. No one tried to stop her. Anyone of us could have." Jordan shook her head as tears splashed onto her cheeks.

"It is all of us that owe Kirsten an apology. We allowed her to venture, where no adult should have gone."

"We put that voice distorter in her hand." Jordan's voice trailed off.

Edward could feel the weight of this mistake as it bore down on Jordan. The waves of guilt rolled off of her in droves. It was almost too much too bear.

Edward felt like the room was about to pivot. Had Jordan just admitted that it was Garrison, she that had tricked him? It was Kirsten, this wide eyed angel… a teenage girl that had been the ruin of the big giant; Kirsten had brought Black Heart to its knees?

"Say something. She came here because she's eaten up with guilt. We can't convince her that she's innocent in all of this." Jordan challenged as she defiantly wiped the tears from her eyes. "You can be mad at me or Garrison, but Kirsten is innocent." Jordan lifted her chin, more of the defiance registering in her beautiful features.

"Well done, young lady." Edward said with a pat on Kirsten's shoulder. "It looks like Miss Kirsten here is quite the agent. She was given a mission, and executed it perfectly." Edward stalked back to the bed. His hand rested easily on Jordan's shoulder. He could feel his former employee stiffen from the unexpected gesture.

"I'm sorry for everything I've ever done to you and your family. One day, I pray that you can believe that, and maybe even forgive me." Edward breathed as he moved back to his seat on the bed.

"Until then," Edward cleared his throat. "We have a mission." he turned to Kirsten, whom was now standing beside Lane. Puffiness filled her young face. Her breathing still somewhat labored from the stress that had plagued her body. Her eyes bore into Edward, and in them he saw the heart of an agent.

"If Miss Kirsten would take a seat, I'd like to hear her take on the situation." Edward watched as the young girl boldly left the security of Lane's side. She moved with measured strides to the bed.

Edward's eyes sparkled with the possibilities. The heart of an agent indeed. Though the days of stalking his prey may be at an end, in this his last mission, Edward would impart a legacy. He would entrust his most sacred of secrets to young Kirsten. Never again would this young woman cower in doubt. For hers would be the certainty of a seasoned agent. She would dawn the horizon of her existence with nothing less than complete assurance.

65

Victor Hayes sat in the back of his stretch limo, waiting for Mike Harrison—or was it Mark—the man's name mattered very little to big time business tycoon, Victor Hayes. What did matter, however, was the wait. Mike or Mark was making Victor late for a very important meeting.

Victor eyed the leather upholstery. The familiar surroundings, too familiar—Victor mused—were starting to bore him; along with every other drab nuance that was an unfortunately, permanent fixture in his overstated lifestyle.

He no longer counted his many assets, or the people sharing them, for that matter, as blessings. His wife, Gina had long since stopped cowering under his command. Allie and Roy, his younger two children were living near each other on the East Coast, but hours from his parental-influence. They had left New York for the scenic beaches of California.

Allie no longer accepted his phone calls. If she were an employee, Victor would have had her killed.

He sighed as he plucked a piece of lint from his suede-three-piece-suit. The fabric, like that of the limousine seats, felt familiar and good. He ran his palm across the collar. Its silken fabric stood out against the suede backdrop of his jacket. It was the finer things, he admitted with an appreciative grin.

He pulled a cigar from the inside pocket of his jacket. The sweet, pungent odor of tobacco arrested his senses, taking him back to the good-ole-days: days of bowling with friends. The slick-shiny-real-wood-floors, with their fresh coat of wax, and the sounds of heavy balls hammering into that lanes. The mumbling vibrations as that ball careened toward the pins.

"Strike!" Victor said as his eyes sparkled, and his cheeks filled with crimson. Those were the days. Freedom. Oh how he loved the simplistic time, before his life had turned on him. Before the pursuit of something more had turned him into a corporate puppet. Every wonderful-simple moment of his life had been crippled and distorted into a pursuit for money. More was a concept that had replaced everything: menial and monumental alike, in his imperfect world.

Though he was the head of the biggest crime syndicate in New York that was only skin deep. It was the behind the scenes lifestyle that was crushing his spirit: his wife's constant Botox and surgeries to improve her appearance had led to a plastic face that he no longer recognized; Victor wasn't sure, most days if she was shocked, scared to death or excited, but whatever the case, she had long since started to look more alien than human. His children ignored him, and had moved away to escape his constant meddling in their lives, or so that was the picture that they had painted.

Victor tucked the cigar back into his pocket. The only person he could count on was himself. He had believed his oldest son trustworthy, but now it would seem that even he had abandoned dear old dad.

It had been three weeks since Victor had last spoken with his son Mitch. His son had confided in him, some very disturbing news. Apparently, he made the top-most-wanted list of Black Heart. Fortunately, his son was in a position of trust with the HOD, of Black Heart, Edward Stanton.

Mitch had put into place some very incriminating circumstances. Edward Stanton would be left holding the bag, while Mitch moved into a position of authority; Stanton's office. Once Mitch was in that office, he would relinquish the reigns to Victor.

Victor was becoming impatient an irritated. Waiting for a call from his son or a meeting, anything… was becoming a true test in patience; something he sorely lacked.

The last time Victor had spoken to his son was three weeks earlier. His son had told him to watch the news. Victor had watched, in amazement as all of Mitch's hard work had come to fruition. Black Heart would be Victor's for the taking.

Victor's face screwed up into a mask of discontentment. He was frustrated. Where was his driver? He would have the man's head. He eyed the double-plated-mirror-tint glass that bordered the driver and passenger compartments. Contempt filled his heated glare. He would have to leave the limo. He had no alternative. He was sure that the man wasn't in the driver's seat. He had already pushed the intercom button, and even tried beating on the glass several times.

He rubbed his hands, fruitlessly down his coat; making certain to touch every pocket. He had left his cell phone on his desk, which normally would not have been a problem.

Janice, his receptionist would hold all of his calls, and in case of an emergency his driver had a list of the more crucial contacts. Today, however his driver had taken a leave of absence.

Victor was getting increasingly irritated. Mitch could call at any time. Victor forced a frustrated sigh as he at last resigned himself to the task. Leaving the safety of the limo was not a good idea. The bullet proof windows allowed for a modicum of protection, but to leave that fortress, however small was not smart. Those who truly wanted Victor dead were not limited by bullets; he quietly admitted to himself. However, it was some protection as opposed to the nothing that he would have, upon leaving the limo.

He had made many enemies, none so daunting as Black Heart. Though that enemy had been neutralized, to assume there would be no attempts on his life by that enemy was a mistake he may not live to regret.

As the door pushed wider, he was struck by the silence. He expected to hear the incoherent-rambling of pedestrians as they pushed passed one another, on their way to whatever menial appointment, filled their meaningless lives. But what he witnessed was nothing. No cars, no buildings, no people; it was the absolute lack of anything, even remotely related to a city setting that had him thunderstruck.

Victor's head swiveled all about taking in the barren land that he now occupied. Sudden regret filled his senses for having left the air-conditioned comfort of the limo. Never before had he so instantly and profoundly understood the error of a decision as this.

He had adamantly objected to all of his wife's concerns. She had told him, but he had discarded her every attempt to persuade him to remove the tent on the windows of the limo. The view of the outside world had been impeached by the two-way-mirror tint; no one could see in, but more detrimental—as he could now see—was that he could not see out.

The limo had always been a serene area for him to get away from the hustled-city life. No matter the time traveled, and Victor spent many hours in the confined space of the lavish-over stated vehicle—the trip was filled with time to think, reflect, or simply rest. No matter the worries that plagued those of the outside world, the limo was a neutral—hidden world, unaffected by those worries.

As each ruined aspect of the desolate plane came into view, Victor was helplessly aware of his mistake. His limited view of the outside world, had left him as exposed as the yellowing-dead-grass had been to the sun's unrelenting rays.

He stepped away from the car, as he began examining the rugged land that was stretched out before him. Everything about the place screamed that nothing existed in its desolate terrain. No vultures circled the sky, no trees offered their protection from the scorching sun. The grass seemed so brittle that it would snap under the slightest touch.

Victor absently closed the door of the limo, and stepped further into the dry-life stealing heat. A clicking sound emanated from the limo, and then the motor hummed to life. Shock colored the sweat-covered planes of his reddened face. A desperate grab left him empty handed as the limo drove out of reach.

Panic pricked like a thousand alarms sounding inside of his mind. Victor had never before felt more exposed. He watched as the limo moved further away. He turned around. No one, nothing was there with him, just the long dead images of ravaged foliage were left to share his fate.

Something occurred to Victor as he considered the forgotten images; they were not the only thing that had been forgotten. Try as he might, he could not remember waking that morning; going to sleep the night before. Nor could he remember leaving his office. It wasn't until he had searched for his phone to notify the head of his bodyguards of the trouble that he was in that Victor had realized his phone was missing.

His mind had blindly put the pieces of the puzzle together. But as he stood, abandoned in the scorching heat he realized a forgotten phone was the least of his worries.

John Benton thought Victor Hayes would never step out of the limo. The moment he heard the door shut, his foot was pressing the gas. The limo lurched forward, awkwardly as John stretched up, and slammed the shifter into drive. He wasted no time speeding away from Victor. Just being in the limo with the New York-crime boss- sedated or not, was too close for John.

John had only a small part in Edward's well laid out plan to take Victor Hayes out, but that part had secretly brought John mountains of discomfort. He felt bad that his nerves were frayed during such a minute portion of the plan, especially when the others were in the hot-seat.

Cynthia had done her part as profiler. She would sit on the sidelines connecting Victor Hayes to every possible source: everyone that the man had ever had dealings with would be picked apart, until the perfect person was identified; this person would be the source the one person that Victor Hayes trusted explicitly. Unfortunately, the source had turned out to be his dead son, Mitch Hayes, better known as Max.

Edward had decided to infiltrate Victor's iron fortress through another avenue; a kink in Victor's armor.

Victor owned Hayes Industries. The company was truly an elaborate ruse—a smoke screen covering up the true source of Victor's billions, a smuggling operation. But it was Victor's true love that left him the most vulnerable to enemy attacks.

Hayes Industries was housed in a high-rise. Thirty floors of clueless clerical workers labored away; day in and day out selling smuggled goods, such as bags, clothes, jewelry; anything was subject to make the inventory. Sales did not matter. It was the basement that was filled with untold amounts of cocaine, marijuana, all kinds of illicit drugs, and guns of every caliber; this was the true source of Victor's wealth.

John watched as the unending nothingness gave way to a line of cars, the rendezvous point. Lane stalked across the flat planes of the vacant lot just outside the city. His bulky-angelic form seemed somehow at home in the desolate-plane; as if he were an avenging angel awaiting command.

John couldn't believe the brutal heat. The perfect end to a monsoon spring. The perfect touch for what lay ahead for Victor Hayes. The former drug lord would believe himself to be in the belly of the Sahara Desert, but in truth he was mere hours from the city. Far enough away from the skyline, the heated planes were a dried up oasis of death.

Edward Stanton knew of the place. Earlier mob bosses had buried the bodies of their enemies in the forgotten land. Black Heart had dealt just as finally with that criminal element. Now Victor Hayes would walk the barren land of lost lives to his own death.

John peered back through the mirage of unrelenting heat waves. How ironic. Victor had done his share to fill the land of death, and now he would share the fate of those he had abandoned to its unforgiving landscape.

Three hours earlier

Jordan studied her look in the mirror. She barely recognized herself. It had been so long since she had donned such a slinky dress. Her eyes sparkled through the eyeliner and mascara that outlined the bold emerald green of her irises.

She touched the barely visible bump at the base of her stomach. She hated to act and dress in the way that she was now. It filled her memory with a time not so far in the past. A time when she had stalked the night in search of prey.

She was a mother, a wife, but more importantly she was now a new creature in Christ. She had repented of her past transgressions—turned from those sins—she was no longer bound by the desire to do those things that had once indwelled her with false happiness.

Her life was truly fulfilled, truly happy. Jordan allowed the truth of who she was; the new Jordan to filter through her consciousness. The image before her was the lie. It was a necessary evil; one that would procure the future for her children that they so richly deserved.

She touched the fall of auburn curls cascading over her right breast, and resting neatly at her abdomen.

"Miss Deloache, sorry to have kept you waiting." A deep male voice abruptly interrupted Jordan's thoughts.

"Please, call me Roxanne." Jordan batted her eye lashes as she gave Victor Hayes the appropriate alias.

She stepped away from the antique floor to ceiling mirror. Long before she had decided to check her look, she had been admiring the intricately carved engravings around the boarder of the lavish piece.

"Early nineteenth century France. It took some doing, but I'm proud to say I was finally able to obtain this exquisite artifact form a collector on the boarder of Paris." Victor explained as his bloated hand caressed the fine markings that surrounded the manila wood.

Jordan reminded herself not to recoil in disgust, as Victor's meaty hands then claimed her more slender ones. She resisted the urge to retaliate against the offensive gesture. Moving to the mirror's edge, Jordan caressed a stylish swirl that bent low into a series of lines. Each line exited the most center portion of the starburst like swirl, and then began another series of swirls.

"I've never seen anything like it. I was glad you called. I did not think that you would." Jordan turned back to meet Victor's unrelenting gaze. "You're a very busy man, and hard to reach." She allowed a seductive tilt of her head. As she moved back within Victor's reach. "But I think you'll be satisfied that you returned my call."

Jordan moved even closer to Victor as she swept a lock of hair back over her shoulder. "As a collector myself, I can certainly appreciate the need to devour all things beautiful."

She turned back to the beautifully adorned mirror. Her back stiffened, and then relaxed as she felt Victor's large hands claim her shoulders.

"I do love all things beautiful, Roxanne." Victor breathed as his fleshy hand caressed the curve of her neck, and slipped his fingers under the edge of the simple gold chain lying there.

The simple confession felt more like a warning than conversation filler. Still, Jordan refused to give into the instinctive warning flair that ignited throughout her. She pressed into her intended prey. She had been here before. There was nothing to worry about. This was a day in the life of the former woman she had been.

She slid her fingers through Victor's as she gently pried them away from her waist and turned to meet his intent gaze.

"Then, you will absolutely adore what I have to show you." Jordan smiled as she pushed closer into his fleshy arms. Her fingers glided easily down the curve of his chin. "I'm going to show you something that you will never forget." She purred.

The moment transported her in her mind back to another time. A time in the woods outside of her old family home, where she had first met Lane. She had used much the same tactics on him. Just as she pressed into Victor now, and purred her delectable lie, Jordan had done the same to Lane.

Lane had carried Jordan's limp body back to his cabin in the woods. It was a makeshift home; a place for him to hide out while staking out the object of his mission, her. Lane had been quite the gentlemen. He had passed all of her tests of seduction, and had even called her on her lack of discipline as a fighter.

Jordan watched Victor Hayes. The bloated, petted-overindulged-picture of ruined man, stare back at her, and it was all that she could do not to run him through with the first sharpened object at her disposal.

Victor's fingerprints were stained in blood all over the streets of New York. New York's nightlife owed every dark facet to this man's efforts. He had pulled the proverbial rug out from under the decent-hard-working men and women of the grand city. The efforts made to make New York a better place had all been squandered, one blood-soaked-dollar at a time. He was a picture of the rottenness disease that left its putrid stain on the face of her children's future.

Jordan's face distorted into a mask of angry-contempt. Her hands shook, as her breath fell into a more labored pattern. Sweat beaded at the back of her neck. The slinky dress she wore felt as though the material was becoming too tight. The gold chain around her neck was choking her.

"If you'll excuse me. I need to use the ladies' room." Jordan announced as she moved toward the door.

The door was open. She could see the illuminated- restroom-sign, glowing its red redemption. A few more steps between her and distance—freedom from his evil stench. She needed space to think.

Her breath caught as a whoosh of air exploded from the split between the door frame. The door mercilessly slammed home and Victor's massive body pressed up against her. His breath tickled the back of her neck. The smell of stale coffee and donuts prickled her senses.

"Not so fast Roxanne. Or should I just lay aside the pretense; call it like I see it? What do you say Jordan? Sound like a winner?" Victor pushed closer still. His sweaty cheek pinned her face to the door. Salty flesh accosted her senses, as the hard wood of the door bit into her face.

The air in the room felt like led. Hard-thick-led that Jordan was forcing into her lungs. Her mind raced for a solution. How did he know who she was?

"Don't be so surprised, Jordan. A man like me doesn't become this successful by ignoring his instincts." He moved away from the door, but his eyes never stopped their ravenous sweep of her body.

Jordan relaxed for the first time since she had entered the room. It felt surprisingly good to shed the pretense of Roxanne Deloache. She was now and would always be Jordan Buckley-Gates. No matter how far she moved away from Black Heart, it would always burn within her. Every minute detail that she had learned, every nuance of being a deadly predator would be a memory away. At any moment, she could default to the person she had once been.

Pretending to be someone she wasn't could be a helpful tool. However, Jordan much more preferred her own identity when dealing with the enemy. Her mind didn't have to hold on to each tiny detail of the person that she pretended to be, every nuance of the character: the walk, the accent, the background. None of it mattered as the vale slipped away and Jordan stepped from the shadows. Victor Hayes knew who she was. Why disappoint New York's biggest crime boss?

Being herself felt comfortable, like shedding a confining outfit after a long day's work. It was the cotton comfort of her pajamas, as they slid up her stressed skin; a day of laying on the couch in front of old movies. This was Jordan. She no longer had to guard the gates of that forbidden warehouse. The gates that locked away all of the horrors and treasures alike that made her Jordan. In one fateful rip the doors swung wide, as Jordan spun on a heel.

Victor's eyes danced. His face filled with anticipation. No alarm— no dread of what if colored his features. Expectant hope registered like a beacon calling ships in the night to a moonlit lighthouse. The hunger for a break from his normal-mundane life navigated her like a vessel to its port. He desired this. He needed it, craved the thrill.

Jordan's skin prickled. All of the sudden, it wasn't so great to be her. She longed to pull the façade back in place. For she knew that it wasn't the outer man that had driven her senses to the brink of madness. No, if she were being honest with herself, she knew that it meant nothing. The thing that pierced her heart, and shoved her headlong into oblivion was that she recognized him. She recognized the evil within that drove the man to do the awful things that he did. She felt naked before this evil she had so willingly given her life to. The self-indulgent wickedness that craved vengeance, needed more, and sacrificed all to have it. The same evil that had possessed her nephew, had possessed her and now wrapped its gruesome tendrils around Victor Hayes.

The fear of becoming her former self was far more substantial than the fear of facing the man. Victor Hayes knowing her true identity was of little consequence. But the idea that she had once shared this same hungry-evil-need to control everything. She had once believed that she was the center of everything. She had believed that she was the only way. She had deemed herself the answer—the messiah to all. She had dethroned the Creator and stepped up to manipulate those in her life; pressured them to fall in line. It had been her way or no way. She had been the sun to her planet, but her rays had been so relentless, so unforgiving to the life of others that she had sucked them dry of any humanity. Like a vampire rushing to its next kill, she had left them for dead in the deadly wake of her relentless need for more.

Though Victor's agenda might be different from that of Jordan's, the end result was the same. He had alienated everyone. He had believed himself the only way, and he had pushed for all to fall in line. Those that refused, he would crush under his heal.

Jordan tensed for a moment in the uncertainty of what she might become. The dark menace called to her from its unsuspecting host. The eyes of Victor Hayes laughed jovially as if everything were in his protective grasp; as if he alone had orchestrated the entire moment.

Jordan knew better. She knew that the thing that peered out from the man was the true captain. Hate was the true keeper of the wheel. Hate guarded every thought, pushed every button. The demon would stand at the ready, and would claim the spoils of the battle. Victor Hayes would cease to exist. The beast within would step through, as he lay aside the camouflaged controls—the façade of servitude—he would step through and claim what was left of the man. He would rip the human vessel to shreds as he forced his own will.

Jordan found the calm of her center. It was there that she could feel the Holy Spirit beckoning to her. The still small voice of God as He gently reminded her that she was His. No longer did she have to cower in the corner, awaiting her fate. Her fate had been sealed! She would fall in line with the rest of God's warriors when the end of time came. She was no longer food for the depraved minds of demons. She was the daughter of a King, the King!

Jordan remembered her reason for coming. She moved closer to Victor. His eyes stopped there dancing as all of the sudden recognition filled his once gloating visage. Her lips turned up as the dark certainty of the demon's smug persona faded away, and Victor's face was left with a simple dumbfounded grimace.

"So you ready to go?" Jordan asked. Her hand had already dropped the syringe back into her pocket undetected. The Rohypnol… the medication had been tweaked by a friend of Cynthia and John's at the hospital to make certain that the dose was the correct dose for Victor. There could be many outcomes of the medicine: drowsiness, dizziness, excitability, and others. Jordan prayed for only two; memory loss and compliance.

Victor simply laughed as he moved for the door and followed her. Led like a dopy dog, eager to please its owner, Victor followed her lead. They moved past the receptionists.

"Mr. Hayes, do you need me to hold your calls?" The irritating blonde asked. Her burgundy lips turned up in a nervous twitch. So eager to please.

Jordan watched as Victor turned a dumbfounded look to the woman and stepped into the elevator.

"Yes, please. Hold his calls. He isn't feeling very well. His wife asked me to come pick him up. He won't be in for a few days." Jordan explained as the silver doors closed in front of her. Her heart stuttered through a few beats as she waited for the woman to concede.

"Yes, ma'am." Was the woman's only reply as the elevator descended? Jordan was only a few more yards from the front door of the building. Vast windows arched at the top, and were filled with stain glassed images; giving the immense room the feel of a cathedral.

A few more shouts of false concern, alarmed throughout her mind, before Jordan, mercifully stepped into the bright sunlight. She smiled simply as the driver stepped from the limo and opened the door.

"Good morning Mrs. Deloache, Mr. Hayes." John smiled to Jordan as he closed the door and moved to the driver's seat.

CHAPTER

66

The sun was just starting to blister the horizon. The sky fading from a dark purple to a lighter shade of what almost appeared to be pink, brightened with every new addition. It made no difference, the color of the sky, being outside was a welcomed change to the eight by ten hospital room that Nick had been in for the last few weeks. He watched as an elderly couple ambled slowly toward the entrance to the hospital. There seemed to be no clear way to ascertain where one ended and the other began. Every step, however, measured was filled with the strength of the bond that their years together had forged.

Vehicles circled a loop where his wheelchair was stationed. Each time one would move forward it would pull to a subtle stop. The driver would emerge from the vehicle, and move to the passenger side to open the front or rear door. A patient accompanied by a nurse pushing them in a wheelchair, not unlike Nick's would lock the wheels of the chair, and proceed to help the patient from the chair and into whatever door had been opened.

Nick shifted his weight, as he watched the last of the procession roll away. His body was still tired. His mind still hazy from all of the days of sleeping. He felt as though there was a vice in place around his skull. For all of the haze, there was one thing that Nick was absolutely clear on; his decision to let Penny go. He had already spent too much time trying to push his will upon her. It was time to respect her wishes and move on. If his near death experience had taught him anything, it was how truly short life could be.

Penny had made her intentions and feelings toward him very clear. His lost puppy act had moved way past pathetic. It was time to move on. He would talk to Lane and Jordan about returning to the Cadotion village to rebuild. With all of the tragedies that had befallen the tribe, a lot of help would be needed to set things to right. Garrison was already on board. He had remained with the tribe. It seemed that every former member of Black Heart had been bitten by the bug. Nick knew that something very fundamental to human nature lived in their need to help the people; maybe it was the loss of life, or the belief that with every life righted their life too was being lifted from the ashes—maybe redemption could be theirs after all. Each of the former agents had in some way touched the lives of others; unfortunately, a large part of that had been negative by nature.

Rebuilding the Cadotion village felt like giving back, making amends for all of the wrong. But at the core of it was the feeling of serenity. He craved the oneness that had so completely filled him. In the village, he still thought of Penny. He still longed to be with her, to bend her will to match that of his own, but all of his troubles were dulled by the beauty… the daily need for survival—something happened the moment that he stepped through that mountain pass. Though Nick may never be able to explain it; it would always be a part of him, and to deny it would be a crime against his soul.

The moment that Nick had made up his mind to let Penny go, it was as if an understanding had fallen over him. As though the lie that he had been telling himself about the future he had with her had been blocking the truth about who he was really meant to be. The Cadotion people were an integral part of who he was. He was more certain of that than he was of his next breath. Lane had explained that Penny was meant to be a part of that future, but that Nick had finally embraced God's purpose for his life. In so doing, Nick had put God's will at the center of his world. His eyes were finally on the most important thing in life; his mission. Penny was a part of his future, but maybe not in the way that Nick had hoped. Either way, it was up to Nick to follow after what God had purposed for his life. Any part that Penny may have in that future would be revealed only in his obedience to God's will for his life.

Nick felt that Lane's explanation, as plausible as it may sound, even for someone that wasn't completely sold out to the Christian faith, seemed a bit far reaching. Though Nick had no way of knowing what his 'mission in life' might be, there was no denying that he felt a sense of responsibility to the people. Having been there as the Manerky snatched everything good from their land had infused a sense of priority within him. The notion that he was to be part of the healing process, part of the tribe itself had so integrated within his being that it accompanied his every thought.

Nick pushed back in the wheelchair. The plastic fabric felt hot and sweaty, but the nurse refused to let him stand on his own. He had been doing well in physical therapy, but the nursing staff had been adamant that he wasn't ready. The swimming of his head and the tired feeling in his body kept him from challenging their decision about what was best for his welfare. The doctor had assured him that everything would return to normal. His body had suffered a lot of abuse. The blood loss from the vicious cut down his side alone, would have been enough to kill him, but the added infection from the grotesque-misshapen-disease-infested fingernails of the Manerky warrior had filled Nick's body. The fight for his life had left him tired and disoriented.

He adjusted the blanket that was between him and the wheelchair. The slight fabric of the thin white cover did little to ward off the stickiness of the vinyl seat. He wanted to leave the hospital. Everything about the place felt just as uncomfortable as the sweaty wheelchair. He needed to be out in the open. If he closed his eyes he could just feel the cool breeze that pushed gently through the mountain pass. A satisfied moan escaped his lips. The gentle caress of the wind was like soothing fingers on his skin.

Penny stood frozen on the sidewalk a few paces away as she watched Nick. He still seemed so frail. His body had suffered some emaciation during his stay at the hospital. He had refused most of the nourishment that the medical staff had offered, during the worst of the infection. She had even gone to his favorite fast food place to grab a burger and some fries; still he had refused.

She had stood by in a frantic state of helplessness as Nick descended into darkness. His body was clammy and hot. Sweat had poured off of his brow as his head frantically twitched from one side to the other. His eyes darted about, trapped in a horrible dream state; in that place, between realities. Though she called to him, she could not reach him.

She pushed the terrible thoughts away. He was back now. She had to focus only on the positive. He was only a few feet away; his strength was returning. Every day he became a little stronger, even the light was returning to his dark eyes. Penny watched with open intrigue. Her breath caught. Though his body was slightly thinner, something so massive, so majestic seemed to fill his countenance, as his head moved against the gentle sway of the wind.

Suddenly, she was filled with an inexplicable jealousy of the wind; it could touch him so easily. Nick welcomed its touch, while he seemed to shy away from hers more and more every day. She was desperate to slow down only one part of his healing process, the part that she was sure would separate them forever—leaving her behind to sift through the memories of their long-forgotten past. For as he grew stronger in his body, his resolve to move on grew as well. He hadn't said anything, but Penny could see it, she could feel him pulling away from her. No longer did he reach for her, no longer did she catch him smiling and looking away. So many times, he had touched her, but her mind had been too bogged down with what the touch meant to him, to enjoy what it meant to her. She had allowed the plot of a movie to dictate the real world—her world. She crossed the curve and made her way purposefully to him. Never once did she think about the consequences of her decision, her actions. She was being guided now by something stronger than her own will. She was being pushed forward by the unstoppable force of her love for Nick.

Penny's hand was on his face and then touching his neck. The nurse was a few feet away. She had averted her eyes in order to give them some semblance of privacy. Penny was grateful, but at the moment she wasn't sure if a sea of eyes would have stopped her intentions.

Nick's eyes were still closed. His face still registered that far away contentment, as though he was worlds away from the tragedy that had beset them all. She was still moving toward him, when his eyes at last popped open.

"Hi." Nick sounded shocked to see her so close to his face.

She ignored the simple gesture as she dove right in to claim her prize. Her lips found his and her mind filled with a rush of sweet gratification. No questions berated her mind; no uncertainty of what might come from this tomorrow. She was all relaxed. She was all in. She was completely sure of one thing, what this kiss meant to her. Nothing else mattered.

Nick was shocked. The kiss had been more than unexpected. Though it felt good, it also felt like a violation of his will. He was sure that he had everything figured out. The kiss was clouding that truth. As much as he still loved Penny, he wasn't ready to fall back into that place of confusion. Loving her had brought nothing but confusion. He was tired of it. He wanted serenity. He needed peace. Love was not meant to be this hard. Penny had never been sure about her feelings for him. She had always pushed him away. Each time she would deepen a kiss, it would drive Nick over the edge. Every time he felt closer to what he was sure his heart could not live without, then moments after gouging holes in his defenses, Penny would pull away and retreat into the usual proverbial fetal position of uncertainty. Nick was tired of it all. He had tried. He had pushed for her love, her affection for so long. She had made it clear what she had wanted. Now it was time for him to move on, to claim what he wanted: serenity, peace, love; true love… he needed more than the tortured conflict of a teenage romance gone bad.

Nick opened his eyes, as he gently pushed her back.

"Penny, I can't." He wanted to look in any direction, but the one that shown the ache in her emerald green eyes.

"I'm sorry. Did I hurt you?" Her eyes told of the humiliation that she felt for the rejection.

He had not meant to hurt her, but his heart was too shattered to allow anymore rejection. Penny deserved more, but so did he. His every moment up until this had been filled with ploys to gain her heart, her hand in marriage. She had been his every goal, his every waking desire. He had allowed his desire to color what was truly best for him—for her.

Nick shook his head. This had been a long time in coming. It was better to end it quickly. Nothing could be gained, but more pain by dragging it out. "I'm fine, physically." Nick quickly amended.

"I don't understand." Pain was quickly being replaced by fear. Her face was a tortured mask of anguish.

"We need to talk, but here…" Nick gestured to the meandering visitors. "I don't think that this is the best place." The thought was incomplete. Though his mind raced for the right words, there were none. He was killing a dream, vanquishing an era of his existence. His words would set her free. Maybe someday they would set him free as well, but as he looked into the eyes of the one that he had so completely believed would be his future, he was suddenly unsure. Would he ever be able to let her memory go? Would he spend the rest of his life in regret? Shame filled his being, as his mind sifted through the possibilities of snares. Had he set a better trap, would he be able to hold onto her now? In that moment, he knew the earth-shattering truth. No, she was not his to keep. He had given his heart away and it would be returned destroyed. He had no one to blame, but himself. Penny had made her intentions clear from the beginning, yet he had thrown his heart at her anyway. For that he would pay the price. But as he looked into her eyes, he knew that he could never again hold her prisoner to his desires.

All of a sudden the cool-crisp breeze felt too cold. There seemed to be too many eyes watching her as she stood in front of Nick. Penny turned to the nurse that had averted her eyes. Even the lack of attention felt like an intrusion. She deserved this, she knew that, but for so many to be a part of her humiliation… Even the thought felt too much to bear. Penny turned and ran to her car. Her legs felt so heavy. She had waited too long. Nick was done. And so he should be. What had she expected—that he would wait forever while she waded through the cobwebs of uncertainty? He had just as much baggage. He had just as much in his past that should conceivably hold him back, yet he had known from the start what he wanted.

She had gambled with the time that she had. She had stood by and allowed him to slip away from her; treated him like a second-class citizen. He had stood in the shadow of his desire for her love for far too long. Time had promised a forever that was not hers to keep. It laughed at her now, as it ripped him from he embrace.

She was faintly aware of his voice as she climbed into the car and wiped the tears from her eyes. She never allowed a backward glance. Even in this she was too cowardly. She owed him so much more. She owed him standing there, while he berated her with facts. She should remain strong—shoulders squared taking everything that he said in, but instead she squealed tires out of the hospital parking lot and headed for a safe haven that no longer existed.

CHAPTER

67

Fires still burned at the east end of the mountain pass, but the landscape had started to look a little more like home. Garrison tried not to notice the barreling smoke, pluming far above the mountain side into the beautiful blue sky; it was the endless burning of the dead that had fallen in the raid. A huge ravine had been dug just outside the west mountain pass to place the bodies of fallen tribesman; there those that had lost a loved one could dispose of their remains while mourning their passing. The putrid smell of burning flesh floated on the air; an acidic aroma combined with a smell like burning feathers that turned every breath into a chore. The dark line of smoke etched its way up, a sinister reminder of the days, months, and years that would be faced without loved ones; it would be a long and arduous road. Time would seem as though it were standing still, but it would eventually march on; all things eventually passed; this would be no different. But, Garrison knew that for all of the time that did pass he would never be able to forget the smell of burning flesh. Its pungent odor would remain in his memory stores for as long as he lived.

Garrison smiled as he thought about the people of the Cadotion village. They were a strong and determined people. Ugly had been a part of their history. The Manerky had tried to destroy them in the past, but God had sustained them. The people would pull out of this. God would see to it. He had been in every detail of their lives. It amazed him to see how much God actually showed up. How much He actually paid attention to His children. As the scales fell from Garrison's eyes he was able to see more and more the times that the Savior had stood in the gap and protected not only him, but all of those that he loved. Each person has a mission for Christ, and when that mission is complete, not before, they will go home to be with the Lord. Sometimes the enemy would put obstacles in God's children's path; these obstacles, Garrison had learned could cause disease, poverty, hate, and even death. He looked around the village. His heart longed for something that could erase the ugly of the last few weeks.

He watched as a little girl ambled, awkwardly toward her mother. Sahalia (translated: song of my soul) was all that remained of her family. Mahalia, (translated: piece of my soul) reached down and scooped up the toddling child as though she was the air that her lungs needed after a long jog.

The Manerky had claimed every member of her family, including Aniahi, the medicine woman. Mahalia had been the only child of Aniahi's sister. Garrison wondered why the responsibility of medicine woman had not followed the bloodline, but Lane had explained that the ability did not travel in the blood. Garrison knew what Lane meant, it just seemed odd. In his own family pressure had been placed on men and women alike to carry on the legacy of those before them. It seemed a breath of fresh air to be removed from such imprisoning ties. Though he still missed his family very much, he would never miss the label placed on him as the only son of a business tycoon. He would never miss the mapped out future that would overshadow any plans he might have had for his own life.

As Garrison watched Mahalia, he was keenly aware that more than her bloodline captivated his attention. She had lost everyone: her husband, her mother, her father… yet she stood tall, a beacon of strength. He had no way of knowing whether she favored others in her family, but Mahalia was the image of Aniahi: her strength, her purpose, and her ferocious intent for living; every nuance that had been present in the medicine woman was represented in the statuesque tribeswoman before him. Her eyes glowed with the promise given to her by the presence of the little girl in her arms. Hope was alive in her touch. She was not looking back. She pressed forward, grateful for the life she had been spared.

The graceful curve of her body, met with the long strands of her braids that danced elegantly about her hips. Golden eyes, full of curiosity and love scanned her surroundings as she playfully dipped her child and hoisted her back into an upright position. Mahalia was the epitome of motherhood and yet in the same instance she remained every bit the image God had designed her to be. Every curve, braid, the seductive arch of her neck, and the gleaming white of her teeth that shown through the delicate pink of her lips; elicited a response. His body and mind unified in the need to hold her, touch her, know her... It was as though, the one he had waited a lifetime for had stepped out of nothing, and his heart longed to claim her. He would not be complete until their worlds collided in the rapture of forever.

"Hey." Jordan's voice pulled Garrison from his thoughts.

"Oh, hey." Garrison cleared his throat as he reached for Tristan. He suddenly felt the need to not be standing alone under Jordan's scrutiny.

"She's beautiful." Jordan's voice held no accusation, though her eyes searched, ever the agent, for a flaw in the perfect picture that Mahalia and her child made.

"I was just watching the girl play." Garrison lied.

"I hope not." Jordan said with a playful look of distain.

"What's that supposed to mean?" Garrison knit his brow as he forced his eyes away from the woman and child.

"Just saying... no grown man should be looking at a child the way you were looking at that woman." Jordan punched Garrison in the shoulder playfully as she claimed her son. "Come on, Tristan. Uncle Garrison needs a time out for telling stories." Jordan teased as she pulled Tristan to her and scrunched up her nose.

"Uncle Gaywison needs time out?" Tristan questioned in his little mocking bird fashion.

"Don't tell him that." Garrison scolded. His eyes were tired and his neck muscles were beginning to feel the strain from trying not to turn back to the woman.

"Well... tell the troof, then you won't have to go into time out." Tristan chirped.

Jordan placed her free hand over her mouth and stifled a laugh. "Oh my! You really do have it bad."

"Jordan!" Garrison growled.

"Oh don't be such a weenie. Just go over there. For crying out loud! Would you look at yourself? You are a former agent. You have…" Jordan stopped mid-sentence. Garrison could tell that she was considering Tristan. He had become quite the little mocking bird. Everything they said had to be thought about. "Well, you know what I mean. Just go over there."

"Yes, mom." Garrison frowned as he ruffled Tristan's hair.

Garrison had considered Jordan's teasing for a long moment, before turning to walk away. Who was he kidding? He was a washed up agent for a company that had been a lie. He had worked harder than anyone to conceal that lie. He was the prime recruiter for the company. The beautiful woman and child before him deserved so much more than what he had to offer. Besides it had been too soon after the death of her husband, for Mahalia to think about a relationship of any kind, especially one with the opposite sex. Though Jordan had explained that most of the marriages in the village were made based on the attributes of two people, and not the love that had been forged between their souls. Garrison couldn't conceive of being with someone for the rest of his life simply because they accented his natural abilities as a human being.

The tribe had been this way about everything; no matter how complex or menial the task. The Cadotion viewed the world as their time to show themselves to the great spirits as the best they could be. Moving into the next life, could only be a positive experience if the tribe member had led the best life that they could while on the earth. Therefore, every decision was thought out carefully. All things in a Cadotion's world were meant to bring them to that all important 'best self'. Mahalia had probably not loved her husband. Jordan had explained that he had been carefully selected to accent the attributes in her life. She was a descendent of the great leaders, and though she was not a medicine woman, she would one day take her place among the tribal council leaders. Her mate could be no less than a mirror of the great leader she would someday become.

Garrison felt his heart drop as the reality of how unsatisfactory he would seem to Mahalia. No matter how much his heart wanted her, his mind reminded him of the harsh truth; it would never be. She would select her next husband, in the same way that she had her first; with careful consideration of her standing in the village. Garrison would never do.

CHAPTER

68

Edward had waited a long time for the nurse to return with a wheelchair. His heart fluttered. He felt as though he were waiting for another kind of chair: the electric chair. Though no handcuffs had been placed on his wrists, he was remanded to the custody of local law enforcement. He was unable to be transported to the station, and would have to spend out the remainder of his time in the infirmary of the local prison.

The judge had decreed that though Edward did not propose a potential threat for being a flight risk, in his current debilitated state the hospital could not assume the responsibility of such a volatile criminal element recovering among the civilian population. Edward would not be able to live among the residents in a federal penitentiary; his training created a potential for risk wherever he might go.

Edward knew in his heart that he would never harm anyone again. He felt the remorse for his past transgressions with a new fervor every day. The mountain of guilt was tearing away at his humanity. He welcomed the punishment he would receive. Though he knew that he had not granted permission for the child agents to be trained and used in the field to lower Jordan's defenses, subsequently leading to her death; Edward understood that it was his lack of concern for what means his hired hand was willing to use to bring about the desired outcome that had led him to this moment. He had turned a blind eye, and now he would pay for it, as it should be. He would offer no defense on his behalf.

Julie had been by everyday hoping to change his mind, but nothing she could do would change the facts: Edward was a cold-blooded killer.

He had done everything in his power to manipulate those in his charge. Lives had been changed and lost, courses of history rearranged because of him. Though he had kept many of the agents in his charge alive by recycling them, it had been his command that had brought the death of so many. Who had he believed himself to be: some replication of God? He had sat in his office, on his Mahogany-thrown and hoisted each command with little regard for those that it affected. Now, he too would sit by and wait as his fate met the order of the person in charge. He would be the one sentenced—his life changed forever by the whim of another. He fully accepted and planned to honor any decision made, though he prayed to a God that he knew would never listen that his sentence would not be death. He could not return to that horrible place, and he did not know how to find this all-knowing Supreme Being. He was lost.

He had tried to get Julie to move on. Even Jordan and her family were adding to the pile of petitioners to the cause that was Edward Stanton. Did they not understand how unworthy a cause he truly was? Was the world so filled with evil that his crimes paled in comparison? Did they feel his flag was the only one worth being hoisted for freedom? Edward thought not. He knew not. He deserved his fate, and it was time for his small community of supporters to allow what would be to be.

Julie studied the white-washed walls of the prison visitation area. Every visit she had made had been alone. No other prisoners accompanied them. No one waited for their loved one to join them. The warden had been very gracious in his tolerance for inmate visitation. She eyed the two guards dressed in blue Dicky slacks and shirts. Their hands were at their sides in a stern line. Their feet were together and their heads faced forward.

The door plumed open as it seemed to vomit out Edward's dejected form. He was dressed mundanely in prison issue orange pajamas, or at least that's what they appeared to be to Julie. His face was a mask of indifference.

Julie was tired of this new Edward. She could just choke him or shake him into submission. What did it take to make the man pick up a bucket and filter water from his own sinking ship?

"I've had it with you!" The words were a betrayal of her inner emotions. Things that vortexed inside of her, raging for release. Things that she had kept tightly tucked away. It was her silence that had bought her placement at Edward's side. In the beginning she had nagged him as much as any other person to join the fight for his freedom, but after seeing the others be subsequently removed she had learned how golden silence truly was. Now, she was certain it was too high a price. If she was going to lose him, it would be on her own terms; she would go down fighting, even if he refused to.

One of the guards cast a stern look in Edward's direction, as if to say, "Don't even try it buddy!"

Edward shifted his weight as he cast an aggravated glance in her direction. She could see that her outburst had been duly noted, and was in no way appreciated by Edward or his guards.

"I neither want nor need your sympathy. We've been over this. I am guilty and I need to pay for my crimes." Edward breathed.

"Yours and everybody else's!" She hissed. Julie adjusted her mint green sweater as she cast a sweet smile in the direction of the guard that had sent the warning glare earlier.

"What?" Edward adjusted his body so that he was now fully facing her. His eyes were that of the steely agent. His no nonsense persona fully invoked to ward off any attempts, she had made to get him to rise to the occasion.

"Nothing." Julie relented.

"Look, I know that you mean well. You all mean well, but this is my life; my decision. I made some mistakes. Societal rule dictates that I should pay a debt. I intend to do that." Edward lifted his hands, and then allowed them to dejectedly fall back to his lap. "I can at least live up to that much of what and who it means—meant to be an agent." He amended. "I was supposed to be taking down bad guys that the government allowed to slip through the cracks. Instead, somewhere along the way I became what I was trying to rid the world of."

Julie was angry now. "Oh why don't you come off that cross already?" This time she met his steely gaze head on. She was not backing down! His decisions affected her life, too. Everything that Edward Stanton did or did not do from here on out would dictate her fate. She would live with or without the man that she loved based on his actions.

"Julie, I'm not in the mood for this. I am here in the infirmary trying to work to start my way back to some semblance of the health I once had. I actually want to be alive. I have learned that I do not want to be anywhere that God is not. Though I do not yet fully understand what that means... I do however, understand that I did this. All of this, and I deserve to pay for it." Edward turned to the wall as he allowed a frustrated sigh. "What is so hard to understand about all of that?"

Julie pushed at the tears dripping down her cheeks as her lip started to quiver. "The part that takes you away from me." She finally allowed the words to come. It wasn't that she couldn't admit them to herself. It was just the pain that admitting them was so great. Her stomach felt as though she had been kicked in it. The air escaped forcefully from her lungs, and the outside of her vision became dark. She needed air.

As if an unseen force had catapulted her from the chair, Julie jumped to her feet, and raced for the door. She eyed the guard nearest to the door intently, waiting for him to open it. She loved Edward with all of her heart, but at the moment she could not put enough distance between herself, the man he had become and the man she knew he could be.

Lately, dreams had plagued her every sleeping moments. She had fought to keep her mind away from the undesirable outcome on the course Edward had charted for himself: the electric chair, the syringe of death, or even life in prison would be the only future that Edward could hope for. His actions would exile her to a life without him. If he were put in prison, they would both be destined to live out the remainder of their lives alone.

Julie understood all too well what it meant to take responsibility for one's actions. She knew that the notion was commendable. It was admirable, but Edward didn't just want to accept responsibility for his actions, he wanted to load up the sins of others as well. He had no redeemable quality. He deserved death. He believed himself to be the worst kind of monster. The truth was, there was a room full of people that would attest to the times that his actions had clearly charted another course and not only saved their lives, but had placed them closer to the future that God had intended for them.

Julie ran down the hall toward the outside of the prison. Her vision was so blurry. She thought that it would be like looking through a window at her future, it appeared just as murky. At the moment, without Edward to share her life, she could not see any future worth having. Sadness spiraled through her senses draining her of any desire to put one foot in front of the other. All the oxygen seemed to be drained instantly from the room. Her feet dredged closer to her car, the day she had bought it, it represented happiness—life. Now though, it was simply a red vehicle that held the key to her escape. She climbed in and sobbed. Her head slowly tilted forward. She ignored the meandering crowd that was headed to and from the hospital. Her mind gave way to the torrent of sorrow, as she laid her head on the steering wheel, and allowed misery to wrap her in its unrelenting grasp.

69

Time stood still as he continued to watch Sahalia play with her mother's hair. One tiny hand twisted the black strands while the other patted her claimed treasure. Her bright-golden eyes twinkled as the sunlight filtered through the mountain pass and lapped luxuriously at her face, and made lazy-twinkling-shimmering lights all around the ground beyond.

Mahalia bounced the tiny girl. Her hands ran lovingly across her back, and then circled back to the nape of her neck. Garrison could see that though every amount of affection possible was placed in each tender stride of the mother's hand, her mind was clearly somewhere beyond the moment.

"Hi." Garrison called as he moved to the mother and child.

"Obiahon." Mahalia called back in her native tongue.

Garrison felt his shoulders instantly tense. "Wonderful. She probably did not speak English." He thought. He had only just gotten to the Cadotion village. Many times he had thought to visit; after all, his best friend had raved on and on about the people in such a way that made him feel as though he had known the tribe his entire life. But something had always stopped him. He had been too busy, and truth be known—he had no desire to visit outside the states. His heart had always been for America. If he could not find it in the good ole U. S. of A. he had no desire for it.

The thought twisted his heart now, like a knife being thrust into all four chambers at once. This golden-eyed-beauty with skin the color of darkened mahogany had instantly marred his beliefs. He had not lived until he had breathed the same air as she. The love that she mindlessly put into every caress was more than most people put into a purposeful hug. He felt at once envious and thankful to be allowed to witness the beauty of the moment. This moment lost in time, would forever be a part of what had thrust him head and heart—long into captivity—he would forever be lost to her. He knew it. He felt it. Here he was in her world, lost to her charms, her loving touch her aura, and none of it was meant for him. She was a moment in someone else's time. She didn't even speak his language, nor did he speak hers...

"Hello." The word came like a soothing balm to his aching soul. It was manna meant for the angels, and yet he stood here tasting it; enjoying the sweet savor of nectar meant solely for the gods.

For a moment, Garrison stood spellbound. His mind rejected and yet grabbed tightly onto the offered olive branch. He felt foolish. Words escaped him. His eyes stilled on her as if she were a picture captured for his gaze alone.

"Hi...Hello." Garrison fumbled with the words, as his mind stumbled through the archives of acceptable greetings. "I'm Garrison."

Too much. Garrison's mind warned. It's too much. She probably needs one word sentences something more basic. He again struggled with a proper, more understandable way to express himself.

Laughter that sounded like a heavenly quartet drifted on the wind. His mind only just registered that it was coming from somewhere behind. Frustration set in as he realized it had been Jordan. Lifting his hand awkwardly behind him Garrison waved his interfering friend off with a sharp-snap of his right hand.

"Mahalia, is it?" Garrison asked in a slower cadence. He tried desperately to not sound like someone shouting at an elderly-hard-of-hearing patient, or worse yet a child that could only understand slow speech.

"Mahalia. Yes. You are Garrison. A friend to Lane and Jordan. My Aunt Aniahi has told me many things about you." The timbre of Mahalia's words accompanied with confident body language, assured Garrison that the woman standing before him was as intelligent as she was beautiful.

"You speak English?" The words seemed a little less intelligent than he would have wanted. Garrison inwardly cringed at his simple declaration.

"Very well, actually." Her words, though arrogant were met with a humble tilt of her head and a gentle smile. Garrison was sure that in no way did the woman standing before him think herself superior to him, or anyone else for that matter. There was something so simple about her demeanor. Her pastel robes, according to tribal tradition even spoke of humility. Someone of her obvious standing in the tribe would be able to wear more proud-decorative colors. Yet her pastel blues and pinks drifted on the wind, belying her obvious status—her claim to greatness swept away with her choice in garments; yet something so monumentally courageous—so epic-powerful-unrelentingly graceful—something about the persona that was Mahalia spoke of the woman that lived inside her, in a way that was undeniable. No amount of wrong garment selections or quiet tilts of her head could hide her obvious strength. In that moment, as the realization swept over him Garrison felt humbled. He was bereft for a comment. What he would not give for one clever thing to say.

"I spent a few years in America. I wanted to know what was out there, beyond the borders of the Cadotion village." Mahalia offered. Her eyes glancing briefly at her daughter, as she ambled toward the other children in the middle of the village to play, and then back to Garrison. "I love my people very much, but I am somewhat of a dreamer. I suppose." She offered a melancholy smile, before continuing. "Lane's family entering our world brought a lot of wonder to the tribe. I was no different than my fellow tribesmen, smitten with the young American couple and their beautiful son. Lane and I played continuously. He was easily, my best friend." Mahalia cast a proud smile toward Lane, where he now stood talking to one of the village elders. Jordan not far away, hid curious glances. Garrison knew all too well that the third degree that he would be under later would be both thorough and long.

"I wasn't aware that you were friends with Lane and Jordan." Garrison offered the simple comment in hopes that Mahalia's story would flourish. He wanted so much to know this woman. His mind raced at the mere thought of her. Her simple beauty seemed to somehow incapacitate his senses. He was hers for as long as she wished it to be so.

"I've only just met Jordan. She has been a part of the village, but until last year, has not truly gotten to know my people. She is a good person. I can tell. I would like to know her truly, someday." Mahalia gestured toward Jordan, and then returned her attention to Garrison. He watched, as her contemplation drew inward, and waited however, impatiently for her story to unfold.

"Lane talked a lot about his second home in America. When we were children, we would sit for long moments on the river's edge as I hung on his every word. I learned many words in English in those days, but it was not until I visited America, and lived there for a time that I truly began to understand the language more fully."

Garrison thought about her accent. It was obviously very thick. He would no doubt be able to ascertain that she was indeed from a foreign country if he had met her in the States, but her use of the English language was, quite simply masterful.

"How did you learn to speak English so well?" His obvious appreciation for her skill brought a brief coloring of pride to her countenance that was just as quickly pushed away.

"I attended college in New York. I was only there for a couple of semesters, but that was all I needed. I only wanted to learn the skillful use of language. I took a Humanities class, Creative Writing and some Basic Math. I did my best to keep up, though I had no true major, well not one that I wanted to pursue. I had my motives of learning to speak the English language skillfully, so that I could maneuver easily around the city. I loved visiting the museums." Mahalia, cast a far off gaze across the horizon and Garrison could tell that she was briefly reliving those moments she had spent in the U. S.

How he would love to take her and Sahalia back to his world. He could share it with them in a way that Mahalia had only just begun to imagine. Her time in New York had been like a rough draft of the greatest novel ever written compared to what he could show her. He would stop at nothing to lay his world at her feet.

"The Metropolitan Museum of Art was one of my favorites. I would love to go back." Mahalia claimed wistfully. "I want so much to show that part of the world to Sahalia, but at the same time this place houses such a beauty that can never be replaced. I can never find this kind of love-community anywhere else in the world. New York was so fast." The last words were almost shouted as a declaration. Laughter erupted from Mahalia. Her eyes danced, as she waved her hands out.

"People rush there. They are going somewhere they do not ever quite reach."

Garrison allowed a chuckle of agreement. How well he knew. His eyes rested for a moment on the village. Though things had been like a war zone for a day or two, they were starting to calm down. The smell of burning flesh was even starting to seem a little less unbearable. The blue-and-white-cloud-speckled horizon whispered of better days to come. He couldn't want for anything more. Though he would follow her anywhere, show her his world—the world, anything really that she wanted, a bigger part of him wanted for her to want this—to stay here in the Cadotion village; hidden from the hustle and bustle of the world beyond. He could feel the desire for more fading with every breath he took—each pull of simple-fresh air vanquished his need for anything more. He only wanted to share her world, to learn of the Cadotion ways. He wanted to live every moment at her side. He wanted to help her raise her daughter, and yes, to bring many more children into the world that shared their mother's beauty and her zest for life. Maybe his uncanny ability to survive in the face of adversity would not be a bad trait to inherit. Garrison wanted so much to believe that he would be enough for her. He wanted to believe it, but he knew that he was a former killer. He had nothing, but ugly to mar her world. His was a different story, one of death and destruction, while she stood with the sun on her back, silhouetting her like a golden reminder of the line of royalty that she would soon be joining. She was a village elder, though she had not yet taken her place, she would. It was her birth right. Her duty and he had nothing to offer. He had nothing to bring to such a prestigious table that was obviously set for only the worthiest of the Cadotion descendants.

70

Penny hadn't made it far. She stopped the car a block away. She could still see the hospital, but knew from his vantage point, Nick would not be able to see her. Sobs racked her body. She had never felt so much loss. Something inside of her felt so at odds with her own existence. She had spent a lifetime keeping the world at arm's length; waiting for the other shoe to drop. It was inevitable, she knew… the world would let her down. It was only a matter of time. Her strategy, though not purposely orchestrated, had been simple push them away first. She ducked and dodged her way through love, sidestepping every attempt made by others at getting close to her.

Nick, for so long had met with that same scrutiny. This man-child that had swooped down into her dark world, and had overlooked his own dark truth to bring light and hope to her tainted world—for every moment that he had spent trying to infuse each day with happiness, she had called his bluff. She had countered each beautifully-simplistic plea for her love, with a slap of her hand. She had swatted him away for the last time.

She knew the truth all along. She had been too broken, too damaged for Nick. For anyone, really. Her life, a picture of waste forged on the underbelly of disgrace, she had grown up in a putrid-pit of hell. Her mother, not what she had seemed…Penny now knew that she had sat there, a trembling mass of human-refuse, cowering in the corner of her own ugly existence. Erica had allowed all of it. The angry words, the beatings, all of it. Every moment still haunted her dreams, and she knew that no haircut or school… not even the love of an extraordinary boy could stop the shadows of her past from darkening her future.

Her father was a disgrace to what it meant to be human. An opportunistic cancer, killing the two of them a little at a time. Penny knew now that, though Junior Buckley, her father was dead, he was still holding all of the cards at the table of her life. She still recognized, or at least she believed she had recognized him in everyone that crossed her path. Mistrust had settled around her like a cloak. With its steadfast presence she had erected walls to keep people out, and to keep her dirty secrets in. Her vile skeletons, stood like grotesque-scarecrows, batting away the joy in her life.

Penny refused to look at the door of the hospital. Though Nick had long since disappeared into a cab and gone back to his life—a life that no longer included her—if it ever had, she couldn't bear to see the memory of him in the wheelchair. The frail image that remained, burned so brightly in her mind's eye. But the coolness that had settled between them was more than she could stand, more than the aftermath of the war in Denali—the remains of a love that she had never given a chance haunted her with more fervor than the shell that stood in the place of a once strapping young man…a young man that had longed to share his life with her.

Tears fell from her eyes and splashed onto the steering wheel. Her hands trembled, as each breath became harder and harder to take. She watched as the dragonflies blurred into blotchy ink spots. Penny pitifully pushed at the wetted material of her steering wheel. The covering had been a gift to herself for getting accepted into the community college. Her secret hope. She loved to watch the colorful creatures dance around. Sometimes stopping to light on the edge of the pool, a small baby blue dragonfly would watch as she swam laps around the pool at school. The interest that the small insignificant creature showed in her, somehow made her feel important. She felt validated in some way. As if the cosmos was taking time out to say that it knew she existed. It knew all of the ugly things that had transpired during the course of her existence, but hang in there because someone out here knows. Something or someone greater than she had taken if only a small interest—still an interest in her mundane existence.

She wanted so much to believe that her life could be different; that her truth could be more. She wanted to adopt her Aunt Jordan's new way of thinking. She had attended church with the Benton's and had even gone to a few of the bible study groups that had been forming around campus. She was desperate. She needed so much to believe in something. She wanted to believe in her worth. She wanted to believe that someone could love her like Mr. and Mrs. Benton had said that God did. But why would He? Why would a Heavenly Father be any different than her earthly father?

She believed that all of the pieces no matter how ugly were in just the right hole. No one wanted her and no one loved her. Everyone in her life simply tolerated her; maybe even felt sorry for her. Either way, it was the same. At some point each of them would grow tired of the charade. Each of them would eventually move on; Nick would be no different. She sniffed as she again dabbed blindly at the soaked fabric. A sad smile barely lifted the corners of her mouth. Was she destined to be left with her nosey dragonfly?

Penny couldn't help but ponder why she felt so disturbed by the idea of Nick being one of those people. She loved her Aunt Jordan, and even seemed to thrive in her presence. She felt the same way about the Bentons. She couldn't lie to herself anymore. She was more than comfortable around Garrison. She confided things to him that she had told no one, and yet he stayed. Her house of cards was starting to crumble, and she had no excuse that could hold sway... no good reason why each of the people that would soon grow tired of her had spent years by her side. Each of them had went well out of their way to ensure she be happy; have a future. Each of them had done more than tolerate her.

She swallowed hard. The truth was right in front of her the entire time, and she had been too lost in self-pity, too dedicated too self-loath, too devoted to her own exile from human contact that she had thrown away every chance that she had at happiness. Every moment that Nick had spent being tender, kind, and patient had been assassinated by her skepticism, her constant speculation about what they really shared. It had been like a rose growing in concrete—her stony heart, too hard to allow the roots to take hold. She had squandered her chances, gambled with her future and she had lost. Nick was lost to her forever.

She dropped her head to the steering wheel as the remorse for her dead future with Nick closed in around her heart, a tamponade of regret choking off every beat.

The days had passed slowly since her breakdown in the hospital parking lot. Penny had called Cynthia.

"Let me take you to lunch." Cynthia had encouraged.

Penny hated to admit it, but she had agreed to the outing reluctantly.

Cynthia had confessed many things about her own life. She had even told Penny that she, too had felt unworthy of John's love, based on events that had been no fault of her own, and untrue all together. She had believed that she had been caught up in a night of stolen passion with a boy she had just met, and known nothing about. John had been that boy. He, on the other hand, had believed that he had lost time due to his growing drug addiction, and had taken advantage of the girl that he had spent the night talking to. A girl that he had wanted to get to know—possibly pursue a future with. Both had been wrong about that night. Their drinks had been laced with drugs. They had both talked throughout the night, until the moment when Cynthia had fallen down the stairs, and landed at the bottom. She had awoken the next morning to disheveled clothing, her body feeling put together wrong, and she was lying in a pool of her own vomit. John on the other hand had opened his eyes to see the same picture, only he had believed that he had committed a crime against this beautiful-idealistic-young-woman that he had only just met. This amazing young woman that he had lost forever due to drugs. He had slinked away into the corner of the room, and watched as she walked out of his life. It was later that the two of them had discovered that through a series of events, out of their control God had brought them back into each other's lives. As good as it had been, the lies of the past had come back to haunt them. It had reached years into their future, and had almost ripped their happiness up by the roots. Almost.

Penny had taken in every nuance of Cynthia's story. She had the gist of it. Two people had met, subsequently fallen for each other, and both had believed a different version of a night's events—both had been a lie. Years later, life had brought the same two people back together—life had regurgitated that faithful night's events—it had nearly uprooted their happiness due to a lie.

She wanted things to be different. She had resigned herself to a life without Nick, but she was determined to be more purposeful, present in her other relationships. His loss had helped to breathe new life into her. In a way, losing Nick had taught her to hold on more tightly to those that she loved, rather than push them away. Some of the walls had even started to crumble. She felt more alive than ever, and yet, something she knew would always be missing from the canvas of her life.

Penny had grown tired of the sadness. She needed to step outside of herself. She needed to be invested in something that was bigger than her little world. She wanted to have a new experience. She thought about the Cadotion village. So much would need to be done to get the people back on track. She had taken a semester off to regain focus. She needed time to heal. Her grades were slipping due to time she had spent daydreaming or worse yet, losing time all together. She had no clue what had been on her mind during those moments. She had just stopped trying to stay in the moment. She had started to give herself over, completely to the nothing. Finally, tired of the status quo, Penny had made her way to the office. She had only been in Trigonometry for two weeks, withdrawal at this point would not affect her grade point average, nor would she owe for the time spent in the class. She hadn't been enrolled in any other classes because she hated the subject so much that she knew that all of her concentration would be needed to get through the dreaded subject matter.

Penny sat on the airplane. This was the right decision. She needed something outside of her own problems to focus on. She would go to the shores of the Cadotion village, and without the battle she could allow the magic of her aunt's beloved home to work its magic on her broken heart.

71

Nick rubbed his still too thin wrists. Rehab had been grueling; things that he had taken for granted before had become nearly impossible: walking across the floor without assistance, picking up a cup of water—he could feel the frustrating shake of his limbs as they protested against the weight of the smallest object. Six weeks, they had told him. It would take them six weeks to get him back to some semblance of his former self.

He was determined, though his legs and arms burned with every repetition of the weight machines, and the muscles in his side screamed their protest he pushed passed it. The trauma physician had explained that the muscles in his side had not only been torn by the grotesque claw-like fingernails of the tribesman, but they had also suffered a great deal of atrophy from weeks of being immobile—he had lay in a coma-like state, not moving any of his limbs. The rehab nurse and Penny had done a lot of vigorous rubbing and makeshift exercises; lifting his legs and arms. However well-meaning the intentions of each woman, it did not produce the same results. His muscles while moving did increase the workload of the heart to push the blood flow uphill, as opposed to the straight forward effort that occurred with his legs and arms lying flat on the bed, the muscle fatigue that was paramount to building muscle was lacking.

The winds caressing his body felt like a promise of new beginnings. He breathed in the lilac fragrance that danced on the morning breeze. It was welcome. Finally, after days of the putrid burning flesh smell, he could at long last smell the aromas that he had become accustomed to: Scents that he now identified with the Cadotion village. No matter where his journey took him in life, Lilac would forever transport him back to the shores of the Kanchenjunga Mountains, to a lazy river that snaked around the majestic sentinels that looked down over a small pass; the home of the Cadotion villagers.

As wonderful as the wind's promise felt, Nick could not completely shake thoughts of Penny. The smoldering-green-eyed beauty that had blazed a trail through the center of his world, and left him aching from a love that was never fully realized, never truly given a chance. His heart hurt far more than any physical pain he would have to push through to reclaim his life. The ache that burned through the center of his being was so oppressing that breathing at times seemed to be the most daunting of tasks. Sometimes looking at the beauty of the village left him feeling desolate. The pain doubled as he stood taking in the awe-inspiring tranquility, yet he was bereft to find the will to look away. He longed for a love that was greater than the sum of its human counterparts. He wished for a future that would never; could never exist. He was drowning in remorse for a death of a love that had never truly lived.

He pushed at a clump of clay beneath his booted foot. He had too much to do; the list of chores he had made for himself was daunting, yet he knew that keeping busy would be his only means of survival. Sitting idly by as the memories of what almost was, but never fully brought to fruition was too painful to witness. He would keep his mind full, and build his muscles in the process. He could already feel the strength returning to his legs and arms. He knew that he had a long road to recovery in front of him, but moving the debris of falling tents to the outskirts of the mountain pass to be destroyed in the fire pit, along with gathering wood and sap for the rebuild was doing its part to transform his withered existence back to his former man.

The National Guard had left behind a group of volunteers to help with the rebuild. A chainsaw growled its whiny protest against a tree trunk. Sparks and sawdust flew wildly out from the point of contact. Nick rubbed his temple before he gathered a log into his arms. Twisting it around to lay in the bend of his elbow like a small child, he pulled another couple of small logs to rest on top of it.

"Never remember it being so loud out here."

Nick startled at the familiar voice. He turned to see short bobbed brown hair and emerald green eyes. He blinked his eyes frantically. How much more could he take? This had to stop. His mind was cruel to play such a harsh trick on his heart. He was already overwhelmed with rehab. His heart ached all the time, and it felt as though his soul had been sheered in half. Wasn't it enough? Now his mind had to conjure up apparitions? He felt his knees buckle. His arms went limp and the wood clattered awkwardly to the ground. His breath sped up and his heart stuttered, as he staggered forward. His eyes closed in for a moment so that a tunnel of blackness stood between him and the ghost. Just as he was about to collide to the ground an arm scooped underneath his own arm and dragged him back to his full height.

"Hey…whoa…" The apparition called to him. "Are you okay, Nick?"

Nick shook his head wildly, trying to ward off the darkness. This could not be. Was she truly here? The arm holding him up, and the body pressed to his side felt real.

"Nick?"

"Penny?" The name was a life raft thrown to a drowning man. He held on to it, as hope rocketed within his heart, and then crashed on the desolate floor of his soul. What if she were here? It would be more of the same. He would pursue her—push passed her obvious attempts at avoiding his efforts to fuse their paths. She had made her desires crystal clear; there would be no future that included them as one. He would walk alone, destined to grieve her loss for eternity.

Nick allowed a weak smile, and then straightened his tunic. He moved back a little as he pulled his arm from hers and started to bend to gather the fallen logs. Penny closed the distance. She pulled his face to hers and covered his mouth with her own. Her hands laced into his hair. She moaned, and the sound of pleasure mingled with the vibrations against his lips. The tantalizing strokes of her tongue, thrust Nick's heart over the edge. His soul abandoned his body and soared above them, dancing to the thrumming of his rapidly beating heart. His mind scowled at the procession, entirely disgusted at the complete lack of self-preservation. Finally, breaking through the stronghold set in place, created by the lie that his heart and soul had erected in moments—his mind screamed out the ugly truth. She doesn't love you, fool! She merely feels sorry for you. You almost died. She is your friend, nothing more.

Nick pushed at Penny. Finally, he could pull from her grasp; it was such a daunting task now. Weeks earlier he could have thrown her over his shoulder and hauled her to any portion of the village that he had wanted her to be... now, a mere push was like climbing the steepest mountain side.

"Penny, I can't do this with you. I get it. You feel sorry for me. I almost died. You may even feel somewhat indebted to me, after all I did get hurt during a moment that I was trying to protect you, but we both know that if you had been faced with the same decision you would have of gladly chosen the same path as I did. I am your friend, and you would do anything..." He was still in the middle of explaining when Penny launched her body at his.

Normally, he would have caught her in mid-flight, but today he barely had enough strength to carry his own weight. They stumbled backwards a few steps, and then gravity won the struggle as their bodies landed ungracefully on the ground.

Penny was desperate to break through the wall of lies that surrounded Nick's heart; lies that she had fed him for months of combat training, and the most beautiful summer she had ever experienced. The moment that their bodies pommeled the ground, she wasted no time. Climbing on top of him, she settled her bottom on his lower abdomen, careful not to touch his side. Though she was sure a lot of healing had taken place, she knew too that it could still be tender. She watched his facial expressions, suspiciously for signs of pain. Finally, satisfied that he looked more shocked than hurt, she covered his body gently with her own, and looked directly into his eyes.

"Would I do that to you, if I felt sorry for you? I am sorry that you were hurt Nick, and it broke my heart to see you like that, but such is battle. We both knew going into all this that death, dismemberment or loss of each other was a possibility. I'm not a child Nick. And I am not so out of touch with my feelings that I would assume that I loved you simply because you were mortally wounded. Not anymore!" Penny waited for a moment. She wanted to give him room to contemplate his answer, but she could see the wall being erected over his heart again.

Without another thought she lowered her lips to his again, and ignored the futile pushing of his hands against her shoulders.

"I know it's not fair for me to ignore your wishes to push me away." Penny breathed. "After all, you did pursue me for nearly a year, and I stupidly pushed you away because I didn't trust love. I didn't trust people. I had been too hurt by them Nick, but I won't give in!" Penny hoisted the declaration, as she again caressed his lips with her own. "I won't walk away." She again breathed against his slightly parted lips. "I will not allow you to do to me what I did to you. I know that's not fair. I get it, but you see Nicholas Stephens you are stuck with me! I don't work without you. Nothing about my life, my future, nothing about me, makes sense without you, so even if you say no until the day I take my last breath; even if you push me away on my death bed, I will be fighting with all I am to be with you because that is the only way that I make sense."

Penny squealed as her body flipped to the ground, and Nick now sat on her lower abdomen. She almost felt betrayed. For once it felt good to have the upper hand—not that she wished any of this to be happening to anyone that she loved, especially Nick… she just couldn't help but to appreciate the obvious leverage that she had over him; at least for now.

"So, you are saying that you are going to push yourself on me, and hold me down like this until you take your last breath?" His eyes were hard to read. They almost seemed on the verge of dancing, and yet there was an air of contempt that blazed out through their deep brown pools.

She felt her heart prepare for the first of many swan dives that it would take to the deepest canyon of her soul. Tears threatened to burn at the backs of her eyes. She sniffed and shook her head slightly. Nope! She owed this fight so much more! She would not win his love back with cowardly attempts. Tears were not going to help her case. She had put him through more hurt than a river of tears could ever wash away. She would try to be brave. She would borrow from Nick's playbook. It had worked… eventually. Even as she felt the crack in her soul grow wider still, she knew her heart would never stop praying for a miracle.

"Yes!" She declared as her voice slightly cracked. In truth, she felt overwhelmed. Her emotions were raw and undeterminable. So many feelings swam through her senses that she could scarcely sift through them all. She couldn't decide what she felt more: afraid, sad, happy... Examining each emotion as it came into focus, she soon realized that none offered true clarity.

Nick stood from the crouched position above Penny. Her eyes watched with increasing curiosity, he offered her a hand. She took it with some reluctance. What did this mean? He was ending their playful interaction, but why? Was this the end? Her mind raced through every unwanted possibility: he was through with her. She had every opportunity to make a life with him, and she had squandered every one of them. She was destined to walk alone, wishing for just one more time to be at his side. She would forever hope for him to hold her; to pull her to him. She longed, even now to have the small token of his love, the small ring upon her finger—the promise of forever that she had so easily thrown away. Why had she been so stupid? So careless?

As she came to her feet, Nick turned his back to her. Penny's heart dropped again to the bottom of her soul. This time shards of regret pierced each chamber, and the ache of loss closed in around her being. She lost the battle to the tears, as they fell with complete abandon down her cheeks. Her throat started to congest with tears. Her breaths came in ragged pulls. She wanted to run from this unwanted fate, but there was nowhere for her to go. Even as he delivered the death blow to her spirit, he would be her safe-haven, her home. This is where she wished—longed to be. She would take even the smallest of scraps, if it would allow her to exist in his presence. The thought made her feel pathetic. She knew that she was. Her thoughts were pathetic; the reality of what she was willing to endure to be a part of his world was incomprehensible. Yet she could not make herself walk away. She could not move from the spot. She waited for whatever words, physical act... that would bring about her end. And in that end, she knew that she would plead her case. She had nowhere to go.

"Penny... I can't..." Nick started to speak, but Penny could hear the tears in his voice. She tried to strengthen her resolve to stand and listen to the words that she was sure would crush her soul, but there was nothing left in her. It was taking all that she had to just stand.

"Nick." She couldn't finish. She wanted to say that she understood why he no longer wanted her. She wanted to beg for his forgiveness, and throw herself at him in one last futile attempt at keeping one foot in the door of his life. She knew, though that it would do no good. He was done. She had pushed him too far.

Nick turned then. His hand was extended, palm flat, facing up in the space between them. The small ring lying in the center of his hand like a grand crown or an ominous omen, she could not tell. She could only wait, as her breath caught and she stood awaiting his next words.

Nick reached out and claimed her left hand. He lifted her ring finger and slid the ring past her knuckle.

He then dropped to one knee. His eyes moved to hers. "I don't want a promise of a future with you. I want everything. I want you. I want us to be forever. I want every day of your life to be at my side, not a promise; a reality. I want us to be real. I want us to be everything for each other that we have missed: everything that our parents could not be. Everything that we have always wished for, but was afraid to believe in. I want to know that you are mine. I want you to know that I am yours. I want our every tomorrow to be filled with laughter, tears, anything, if it is us, living each moment…"

Penny was sure her heart was going to fly from her chest. She raced into Nick's arms and crushed her lips to his silencing his words. She needed no more words. She only wanted to begin their life; their reality.

72

The bed felt so good after an evening of working in the flower beds with Cynthia. It was grueling work, but Kirsten enjoyed the normalcy. Staying with the Benton's was a good fit. Though she missed her parents with every heartbeat, she felt safe with John and Cynthia. They had tucked her into their lives, and had even made room for Shakira.

Kirsten rolled to her side. She was about to reach for the former black and white menace turned cuddly kitty over night, when the cat flipped upside down, and crumbled forward into a pile of fur. Her paws wrapped easily around the hand that Kirsten offered. A chuckle escaped her lips, as she offered her other hand to the now spoiled cat. Shakira's golden eyes rolled back in her head as she luxuriated in the coveted affection.

Kirsten thought of the three kittens, now with families of their own. Cynthia had placed a picture on Facebook of the cuddly crew, and surprisingly enough all three kittens had been placed in great homes in record time. It felt decidedly good to have brought about closure to at least Shakira and her kittens.

Still lost in contemplation, Kirsten squealed when the door to her room opened.

"Oh honey, I'm very sorry." Cynthia offered. Her face was a mask of regret. "I did knock." She offered.

Kirsten noticed the pink laundry basket brimming with folded clothes. "No. Not at all. Come on in. I was just thinking about Shakira's kittens. You know, how happy I am that they have great homes…but at the same time…" Kirsten shrugged.

Cynthia crossed the room. Placing the basket of folded garments in a simple brown leather chair in front of small corner desk. The room was cozy. Not a lot filled the small space, but it was enough. She had a bed and computer in her room. No television, but it really didn't matter. She did not generally invest a lot of time in television. The Benton's had explained that they did have a few rules, though simple they would expect them to be followed. Kirsten was welcome to stay as long as she needed as long as she agreed to abide by their rules. No television until after homework was completed, no television after eight o'clock p.m., and bedtime was by nine thirty p.m. All meals were always eaten at the kitchen table. Family forums were held once weekly, and every member would be expected to bring one complaint and two compliments about each member of the family including oneself. No one would be allowed to complain about any member of the household outside of the forum. Any suggestions for a better way to do things in the home were placed in the suggestion box on the wall of the mudroom. Family night is every Friday night at five o'clock. Time away from family night had to be requested two days in advance, and must be of the utmost importance, as family was above all else except God. Every Sunday was church, morning and night.

Kirsten thought that some of the rules were possibly a bit silly, but could see how they could strengthen family ties with communication. She wished that her own family, though wonderful had of been more wrapped up in each other. She felt loved, but she sometimes felt a little too alone. She more times than not, was allowed to just live her own life, at her own discretion. It seemed to be a very big responsibility. She had to admit that she felt a sense of comfort knowing that she would have the Benton's so close, she would be able to count on them, and though they were clearly setting boundaries for her, she would still have a voice.

"What's wrong Kirsten? Are you worried that the people may not take care of the kittens?"

"Maybe. No. I don't know." She shrugged again. "I guess I am happy they have homes, but a part of me just misses them." Kirsten looked over at the now purring cat. Her eyes had drifted into slumber, and her front paws twitched slightly. She pointed toward Shakira. "Do you think she misses them?"

Cynthia looked toward the cat, and then back at Kirsten. "You know honey, I think she may be aware of them, as in they were a part of her, and she did what she needed to ensure their survival…but I don't think that animals feel quite the same way about their young as humans." Cynthia rolled her eyes slightly. "Well, most humans." She amended. "It's not that Shakira doesn't love them; it's more that she is geared toward the survival of her species. She will continue to produce life as long as she is able, and with each new litter of kittens she will do everything in her power to ensure their readiness for the world. However, when it is time for the kittens to become cats… adults, she will push them away. Push them toward their new life." As Cynthia thought of the words 'each new litter' she made a mental note to call the vet.

Kirsten watched as Cynthia absently rubbed her hand across her swollen abdomen. "Speaking of babies…When is he or she making his grand appearance?"

"Any day now." Cynthia rolled her eyes again. "The sooner the better!" She griped.

"That bad, huh?" Kirsten mentally cringed away from the thought of her own body being hijacked by a tiny human and distorted into an aching mass of discomfort.

"No. Not really. It's different that's for sure. I do hate the forgetfulness." Cynthia allowed a humorous huff. "It is definitely not something that I would ever want to do alone." She looked toward the door, and Kirsten could tell that she was thinking of John.

"I don't want to do it at all!" Kirsten blurted. Her face screwed up in a dissatisfied frown.

"Well… I hope that you will continue with that mindset at least until you are thirty and married." Cynthia laughed as she playfully poked Kirsten in the side.

"No worries there." Kirsten leaped from the bed and started to pull clothes from the basket and place them in the cherry-wood chest of drawers that lined the wall to the right of her bed. She absently noted the pastel pinks and blues of a small carousel. She loved the happy tune tiny music that crooned from the base.

"Want some help?" Cynthia asked as she stepped over to the basket and started to reach for a red t-shirt.

Kirsten patted the shirt back down in place. "I'll manage. Maybe you should try and rest for a while. You look tired."

"I suppose I could take a nap. I didn't sleep well last night. My back was aching. It has been doing that for two days now. The doctor says it is normal. I am having Braxton Hicks." Cynthia rubbed her lower back as she made her way to the door.

"Yep! I can't wait to never do that!" Kirsten scoffed.

"Right at this moment, I can't say I blame you kid." Cynthia breathed through gritted teeth.

73

Julie was moments away from snapping. Her mind had blown right past all the reasons for keeping cool. The niceties had long since fallen away, and she was on a roll with her new-found freedom of speech as applied to Edward. She had never wanted to belt anyone so much in all her life. She had prayed that the time spent dealing with Victor Hayes would snap him out of the funk that he had been in—but here he sat in his wheelchair waiting for his turn on the parallel bars with little to no will to live.

He was still brooding over her interference in his freedom. His quest for self-destruction had been thwarted by a phone call to the judge that had liberated Jordan from a death sentence. Now Lane and Jordan were back in the Cadotion village and she was here with the self-appointed monster that deserved, in his not so humble opinion, death or at the very least life behind bars.

She was so tired of the perpetual bad mood that he was in, but short of leaving she had no other alternative, but to listen to his constant negativity. It was either that or just walk away. She knew that she could never do that. Even if her heart had not been fully invested in Edward Stanton her soul definitely was. She was tied to him in every way that would or could ever matter. God had charged her with speaking truth into his life. Unfortunately, at some point she knew that she would have to dust her heals. She knew that the word was clear on these matters. She was never to throw the meat meant for the children to the dogs, or cast her pearls before the swine, (Matthew 7:6, 15:26) in other words if Edward would not receive her, then she would be forced to walk away because God would not abide with his stubborn refusal of His love forever.

She moved to Edward's side. Her hand reached for his, and pulled each of his hands to her shoulders, as she assisted him with standing. Each step was labored. He had a long way to go on this, his road to recovery. She wanted to be there, to see him make it through to the end, but she could not imagine what it was all for—if he refused to get excited about his own existence what did it matter if he could walk? What would he be walking to?

"Hi, mom."

Julie turned to the sound of her daughter's voice. Amber Noel was as bouncy as always. Her crystal blue eyes as bright as the sky melted Cynthia's heart each time she peered into their depths. A tingle of goodness generated through every fiber of her being every time she was near her sweet granddaughter.

"Hey, Memaw's baby girl!" Julie squeaked. "Look at that beautiful smile!" Julie pulled the baby, now two months old into her arms, after settling Edward back in his chair. She looked at Katie. "Hey, baby. Is everything okay?"

Julie didn't like the dark circles under Katie's eyes. Though these days definitely found her daughter a lot happier, Julie knew that Katie was balancing a good bit on her shoulders.

"Oh yeah, I just needed to ask you if you could watch Amber Noel tonight. I hate to ask, but I have been asked to come in early at work, and I have a paper due in Microbiology." Katie explained. She had a look of horror on her face.

"Of course, I can!" Julie turned to Edward. "I mean if Mr. Edward wouldn't mind watching some Christmas movies with us girls tonight." Julie smiled at her granddaughter as the sweetest grin filled her cherub face. Her rounded cheeks filled with dimples and a rosy-red that brightened her blue eyes even more.

Edward looked at his hands as he tried to avert his eyes from Amber Noel's. He cleared his throat. "Not like I'm doing anything else."

"Did you hear that Memaw's beauty? Mr. Edward is going to watch movies with us. What do you think about that?" Julie's eyes danced with the excitement that she felt for this sweet-precious creature that had so fully filled her life with happiness, wonder and promise. Her mouth spread with a huge-toothy grin.

Amber Noel let out a high-pitched squeal and reached for Julie's teeth.

In that moment, Julie saw something that she had not seen in weeks on Edward's face, a smile that was full of hope. A warm blush filled his face, as he shifted uncomfortably in his chair. Julie thought his reaction to her granddaughter showed a lot of promise, and then she smiled inwardly—she was not above using low-balled tactics such as the cuteness of a certain little heart-stealer namely, Amber-Noel.

Julie bounced her gleeful-squealing granddaughter making certain to elicit as much joy as possible. The moment that Edward appeared at the height of his discomfort, she strolled over and deposited the ball of joy in his unsuspecting arms.

"Well I... Um... no... this is not a good idea. I wouldn't." As Edward struggled for the proper argument, Amber-Noel let out the loudest squeal and reached for the stubble on his chin. Her meaty fist closed around a rogue strand and gave a hardy yank. "Yow!" Edward protested before bursting into shocked laughter.

"Quite the little fighter, aren't you!" He declared appreciatively, while fisting his right hand, and feigning an upper cut to her drool-filled chin. Another squeal rose from the happy baby, and then distorted into a rolling growl, as she made a motor type sound. Her tongue sprinted through her cherry lips, blowing spit bubbles. Her eyes lit up, an even brighter shade of blue as she again reached for Edward's chin. Dodging Amber-Noel's attempts to pull his beard, yet again, he bobbed his head to the side, and then sticking out his own tongue blew spit bubbles as well.

"I can see he will be quite the role model." Katie drawled dryly, with an absent roll of her eyes.

"Oh, let them play honey. Pooka seems to like him." Julie laughed as she pushed a lock of Katie's hair back over her shoulder.

"Ugh...Mom, why even bother giving her a name? It's not like you use it, or anyone else for that matter." Katie blew out a long sigh. It seemed so mournful as if she had been holding it in for a long while.

"Honey." Julie managed as she pulled Katie into her arms. "Does it really bother you that much that I gave your baby a nickname?" Julie doubted the truth of her statement, but she didn't want to take the idea off of the table. After all, she had given a nickname to her oldest son's child, only to have his wife become angry, and demand that the nickname she had pre-approved be used for the child. In truth, it had frustrated Julie that she could not give the nickname that she had chosen for her grandson; it was a way of bonding; a rite of passage for every child born. The grandfather and grandmother had always nicknamed the grandchildren not long after birth, as a way of branding them as their own. Her then daughter-in-law's objections had somehow hollowed the experience of grandmother in her grandson's life. It had taken a certain amount of joy from Julie. She had been made to feel inadequate in every way possible by Jenny. Not long after Justin's second birthday, Jenny had announced her involvement with another man and had long since went on with her life, leaving both Heath and Jonathan behind. Julie had wasted no time picking back up with the nickname that she had initially wanted to call her sweet grandson. Ning Ning suited Jonathon. It spoke to his love for the video of the 'What the Squirrel Say'.

"No, mom. I've already told you it is fine." Katie blew out another frustrated sigh, before flopping back in a nearby metal back chair.

"Katie..." Julie stopped mid-comment as she moved back to Edward's side.

"Is she bothering you?" Julie raised one manicured brow as she reached for Amber-Noel.

Edward's only response was a slight push of her hand in the opposite direction of the baby.

"Okay. I'll be over here talking to mommy, if either of you need me." Julie offered as she reluctantly strolled back to her daughter. She faintly acknowledged Edward's crooning voice, as he spoke to her granddaughter, "Tell Memaw to go away, we are just fine." Another gleeful squeal split the air moments later. The declaration of happiness, served well in convincing Julie that the two were indeed doing well together.

"Honey, what is all of this about?" Julie reached over and claimed one of her daughter's fitful hands. She had been nonstop wringing them ever since Julie had claimed Amber-Noel.

"Mom." Another sigh, this time deeper.

"Okay Katie, you are scaring me. What is this all about?" Julie's face was a mask of torment. Her nerves were set on edge now. Red flags were going up all over her mind. She could only think of one thing that would cause her daughter this much stress, and it was not midterms, or a paper in Microbiology.

"Do you remember the guy that I have been telling you about? The one that hangs out at the library. He is in my English literature class." Katie started to bounce her legs.

Julie pushed her open hand down over her daughter's fitful legs, in an attempt to stop the bouncing. "Yes, honey. You said he talks to you, and had helped you with your last paper." Julie looked over her shoulder once again at her still squealing granddaughter, though her nerves were on edge with all of the suspense surrounding Katie's unfolding tell, she couldn't help, but to feel a small sense of pride and she supposed joy as well. The manner in which her granddaughter was interacting with Edward was all that she needed to see. She knew that somehow, in this small moment, God was conveying a truth; Edward Stanton was going to be alright. He was in this moment, experiencing the best rehab of all; her Pooka. She knew all too well, from personal experience that there was no way to remain sad. Nothing but happiness could survive, in the presence of such unbridled joy.

Julie turned back to her daughter, her legs had stopped bouncing and she had visually straightened her stature in the small metal chair that offered little comfort.

"Mom." She turned to Julie and captured her eyes with her own. Julie fell into her daughter's hazel glare. "I...his name is Bobby, and he wants to take me out on a date. I really like him, but I'm afraid." Katie turned to her daughter, as shame colored her face.

Julie felt an instant red-hot rage fill her senses. She knew what her daughter was thinking. She had seen the glares, and heard the whispers at church. She loved her church home, but some of the elder crowd could sometimes be a bit judgmental, and a lot proud of their forty plus year marriages, combined with their seemingly pristine lives, unpocked by sinful indiscretions. Well at least any sinful thing as horrible as having a child out of wedlock. The absurdity of anyone thinking their lives perfect, simply because they had been married for half their lifetime, popped out a couple of kids and remained faithful to the same church body for decades toppled Julie's understanding. She too had been married to the same man for years. Their separation had come through his death. She had given birth to their children and had raised them to the best of her ability. She had remained true to the same body of believers for three decades, her father had preached in that church. Yet not one of those attributes would hold up in the courts of God as good enough for her to inherit the kingdom of Heaven.

She could not judge others, but she was certainly one of the best fruit inspectors, and from what she could see many of the holier-than-thou-club that nestled together, had little to brag about as applied to good-ole-fashioned kindness. Not many of the elders or young socialites for that matter would be winning very many humanitarian awards for their treatment of others. As far as Julie could see, they seemed to be best at making the new-comers to the church feel inadequate. More often than not, she had witnessed what would be good future additions to the church, hard workers walk out. Julie had talked with Cynthia and had learned of her church, Rocky Mount. She had heard so many things that had made her feel sad and shameful for her own church. This situation that was budding with her daughter, the self-doubt and shame she knew was a product of the way that she and other young and old people had been received by the too-perfect-for-you crowd. Julie was raring to go. She already had her speech ready for the following Sunday and had gained access to the pulpit. Pastor John had gladly conceded. He and a few others, including his sweet wife had been working to make a change in the church since his acceptance of the position. Julie had spent long hours on her knees asking God to remove any unproductive feelings of anger that would translate in a way that may keep the church body from receiving the word that she had for them.

"Katie, I know where all of this is coming from. You are a good girl that made a mistake. However, your daughter is not a mistake!" Julie tried to calm her tone. She sucked in a deep cleansing breath, and tried to relax before continuing. She noted that she had a long way to go, before addressing the church on Sunday. She would definitely not be able to think of her granddaughter while giving the speech. It was bad enough, thinking about someone hurting her daughter, but if she allowed herself to think on her granddaughter concerning the matter for a moment too long, her anger became an inferno.

Another deep breath, and Julie tried to start again. "I know that you have received a very negative reception from some of the seniors in the church, not to mention the young adult groups that met and married their high school sweet hearts—have had the blessing of a great marriage and even better walk with Christ, but..." Julie searched for words that were truth, without judgment. "Honey, everyone makes mistakes. Some people have a hard time admitting their mistakes, but no trouble at all noting and pointing out other's mistakes. The truth is, that is a sin. Whether they would admit it or not, that is judging. So whether that person has ever done what it is that you have done, they have opened themselves up to being judged with the same measure by which they have judged you." Julie looked around the room. She spotted two pens on a shelf. One was long and slender, while the other was plumper and had a flashy silver writing engraved into the prominent blue background. Julie collected the two pens, and then moved quickly back to her daughter's side.

"Katie, what most people do not realize is that God is listening, and every word will be taken into account. Therefore, when someone says something mean about your person...when they insinuate that you are not what you should be..." Julie stopped mid-sentence as she decided just to use the visual aid that she had claimed in order to make her point clearer.

"Do you see these two pens?" Julie asked while looking from first one pen and then to the other. Finally, she gave a pointed look at her daughter.

"Yes. I see them." Katie swallowed an obvious lump in her throat as she batted at tears, not yet fallen from her eyes.

"Julie lifted the slimmer of the two pens into the air. "Let's suppose that I went around saying that everyone had to look exactly like this long, slim, gray pen, and if they did not look exactly like this pen then they would all not make it to Heaven."

Katie's face screwed up into a mask of confusion.

"I don't quite understand what these two pens have to do with the ladies' rotten attitudes at church." Katie admitted with yet another resigned sigh.

Julie just turned in her chair for a moment to glance back at the baby. She was being still enthralled with Edward.

Satisfied that Edward was indeed capable of handling her rambunctious granddaughter, and intrigued at where the ability could have possibly come from—Edward had no siblings or children for that matter… yet he cared for Amber-Noel like a pro—Julie turned back to her daughter and resigned herself to the demonstration.

"Just listen, honey." Julie pleaded. "So I am going around town making everyone feel just awful because I am demanding that they all look exactly like this slim pen, which by the way isn't as nice as this blue and silver awesome-pen." Julie allowed a moment of appreciation before continuing. "You notice that though I demand that everyone look and act exactly like the skinnier, duller pen. Though I, in fact, look like this artful and easier to hold fatter pen."

"Mom!" Katie rolled her eyes and allowed a quick exasperated laugh. "Focus… gees you and your pens."

"Yeah, I kind of do have a thing for nice pens." Julie chuckled. "Okay. So I make my demands, I make everyone feel awful, and lots of people won't even try, because they feel that they will never live up to the unreasonable expectations that I have set for them, and refuse to follow." Julie looked deep into her daughter's eyes. "One day, I die." She allowed a moment for her daughter's obvious discomfort for her imaginary demise.

Julie gave her daughter a once over. Although, she did look a little pale the color had started to return to her young face. She felt so bad for her daughter, she had so obviously not given any thought to life without her mother. Julie patted her hand, and tucked a loose strand of hair behind her right ear. If she were being truthful she did not like to think about a time where she could not run to the rescue for her children; especially this, her baby. Things had always been just a little harder for Katie. Everyday a struggle, every decision made with extreme duress, due to all of the decisions in the past that had ended in disaster.

"Hopefully, that time will not be for a very long time, sweetie." Julie smiled. "Now back to my story. "I am standing before God, and he points to the slender gray pen, and then to a long list of names. He goes on to explain that the names are those that will never accept His Son as their Savior, because I made them feel inadequate, not enough. Worse yet, God pulls the blue pen out, and then points at me. He pulls me in front of a mirror. I look at the pen in His hand, and then back at my image in the mirror. I realize for the first time that the entire time the things that I noticed about others was always the things that I hated about myself. I turn to God. The feeling of guilt is so heavy. I cannot seem to get my breath. The air is just too thick." Julie can see that Katie is really listening now, and more so than before she actually seems to understand, or at least some of what Julie is trying to explain is starting to shed a little light on the issues that are going on at church. She breathes a little easier, as she allows a simple smile, and then lifts both of the pens into the air. She looks directly at Katie. She is now enacting the role of God, while she makes her daughter take the role as her facing the Almighty. "For all of your years, you stood as judge over my creation. You made them feel unworthy of My love. You told them that they had to look exactly like this pen, but no one could actually live up to the demands that you made that's why I sent My Son to die for their and your sins. Unfortunately, that was not enough for you, and you made sure that it was not enough for others as well. You were not even able to live up to the image that you created in your mind, an image that was created from your own self loathe. You took the things about you that you hated most, and culminated them into this pen. You created an unreasonable-unobtainable goal for my creation that even I knew was not possible, which is why I sent the comforter, the Holy Spirit. You made it so my creation would not listen to me. Your lies separated them and you from me forever. You do not even look or act like the image that you have deemed the price one has to pay in order to be good enough to obtain My love, My redemption. You have pushed Me to the side and made yourself God. Unfortunately, you will take your place with those that you have condemned, in the lake of fire. Depart from me, you worker of iniquity, for I never knew you!"

Katie looked away for a moment. She batted at the tears now streaming down her face. A sniffle escaped from her heartbroken visage. As Julie reached to her daughter, she heard the deep rumble from behind of Edward. She turned to see that Amber-Noel had fallen asleep, and Edward was listening. His eyes were misted with unshed tears, and his cheeks were red with the obvious distress he had been feeling.

"Oh. I didn't know that you were listening." Julie walked over, and reached for her granddaughter. Edward lifted the chubby-body of her beautiful granddaughter easily. She could see that the rehab had been good for him.

"I've never heard anything quite like that." Edward admitted with an exaggerated sniff. Julie placed Amber-Noel in her pumpkin-seat, and draped a light blanket over her lower body. A half smile curved her lips and lit her face with angelic beauty.

"No?" Julie asked, while walking to the reception window. She placed the two pens back on the flattened-egg-shell surface of the counter top. Allowing another appreciative glance, she turned to a box of tissues. Collecting several, she strolled back to first Katie, and then Edward. She positioned herself so that she could be near Amber-Noel and still have access to Katie. She felt the need to be with all three of them at once, though she wasn't sure who needed her the most.

Julie decided that she would just allow the demonstration to stand for a while; sometimes there just was no need for words. She looked down at her slumbering granddaughter, and again thanked God for her presence in her life. She then made a mental note to call her son and ask for her grandson for the weekend.

Katie was the first to move. She walked slowly to her mom, and bent down so that she could face her more easily. "Mom..." Katie dropped her head for a moment. When she again looked up, there was a peace on her face. A bright smile lit up her young face, and for the first time in a very long season of sadness and guilt, she could see her daughter; her Katie: young, happy, energetic, the world at her feet—she was there. Julie smiled as she touched her face again, and leaned down to place a light kiss on her forehead.

"I love you my sweet baby girl." The words were, but a whisper, yet the truth laced within every word could fill the world.

"There is no one like you mom!" Katie hoisted her own declaration, as her face filled with joy and conviction. Julie could see no doubt registering in her daughter's eyes. She meant every word.

"No one." Julie heard Edward's breathy concurrence.

"You two need to stop, before you make me cry." Julie sniffed. She straightened Katie's shirt as though she were once again six years old with bouncy blond pigtails and a face-full of freckles. Where had the time gone? Her baby was now a mother, a good mother. She was strong and determined. Yet she had somehow lost her way in the debris of unwanted opinions and unsolicited judgments. She had forgotten to be happy. She had forgotten to love each day, and be joyful in all things. She had forgotten the person that God had claimed her to be, and she was no longer living her life in expectant hope of His promises. She no longer believed that God knew the plans that He had for her. (Jeremiah 29:11)

Julie said a silent prayer that God would use this time to change all of that. She prayed that not only her daughter, but all of her children and grandchildren would live their lives each day in expectant hope of God's goodness. She prayed that Edward too would learn to walk in the promises of God, and that all of the hurt and doubt would leave him.

Julie collected Amber-Noel's things. She turned back for a moment to ensure Edward that she would be back in a moment. She allowed her granddaughter to continue her slumber under Edward's watchful gaze. He watched as she disappeared around the rounded wall. Her arms and hands full of baby paraphernalia.

He felt something different was taking place in his heart. Something akin to preparing soil for coming seeds to be planted. He felt green, as if he were alive for the first time in his life. His heart felt lighter, he looked at the sleeping baby as she again smiled. Obviously her dreams were filled with happiness. "I can just imagine what you must be dreaming about pretty baby." Edward admitted with a smile. His hand pushed at a tear as it rolled down his cheek. The example that Julie had given, using the pens had been like a call to his soul. His inner-man moved from the darkened perch, on the deepest canyon of his soul. He felt himself being drawn to her words, as if God had tapped him on the shoulder and told him to pay close attention. Though he had not been one to set precedence too high to reach for others; he had indeed done that for himself. In everyone around him, he could find some redeeming quality, but none existed within himself as far as he had been concerned. He thought of himself as a vile man. He deserved nothing less than God and man's judgment and wrath. He had never given himself a chance. He was a vengeful, intolerant man that had chased after the man that had destroyed his only happiness; he had killed his Amorous. He knew now that she had never been meant for him. He had been in that alley, searching for more. Dissatisfied with his boring life, he had sold his mundane existence for wild adventure and the life of a death-dealer. He had never been meant for that life, and she had never been meant for him, nor he for her.

Edward looked around the medicinal white of the rehab room. It was a reminder of a mundane existence that he had once sold for a nothingness so great that it had nearly blotted out his existence, and for so long had miraged the true happiness that had always been his; he had always been, but a step away from his truth. He had never gone too far, or done too much for God to forgive him. He had always been worthy, not because of what he had done, but because of the preparations that God had made from the beginning of time—God had known that he would never be able to live up to the standards that man or even God had set into place. He knew, and He had prepared a way. He had sent His Only Son, Jesus Christ to die on the cross for his sins, and then He went a step further…He had sent the Holy Spirit to comfort man in His absence; a constant presence, reminding man of his goodness and worth; guiding man away from sin and into the arms of God.

Edward admired the peaceful smile on Amber-Noel's face as he vowed to soak up every truth that would lead him to a saving knowledge of Christ.

"Are you two ready?" Julie chirped as she rounded the corner, and brightened the room a little more with her charismatic smile.

"Absolutely!" Edward called out from his hospital chair. He was ready: he was ready for life everlasting, a renewed mind and heart, he was ready for peace that was beyond his understanding, and he was ready to embark on a mundane life of joy and laughter with the radiant beauties before him. He knew now that Julie would be his, to have and hold, and as a bonus he would tuck Amber-Noel, a ball of living joy into his life and heart.

He would teach her to be careful and how to defend herself, while she taught him not to take himself quite so seriously—her grandmother would teach them all about the Creator of everything. She would teach them to embrace His word and live according to His statutes. Edward felt the smile that he had seen on Amber-Noel's angelic visage as it made its way through part of his soul. He felt it bursting and spreading as it soothed old aches, and quieted dormant concerns. It was infecting every part of him with its sweet savor.

Long after they were driving to Julie's home, he had started to embrace the new future that he now knew had been hand selected and orchestrated by God; his very steps had been ordered to this place. He had no clue what that truly meant, but to embrace it was a joy like he had never known.

CHAPTER

74

The plane ride was more relaxing than Jordan had ever imagined that it would be. She sat next to the window and gazed into the thick-fluffy clouds. A sense of awe filled her spirit and burst over into her heart. She could feel God's arms as they wrapped around her. She felt His love more and more in her life now; maybe it was the entrance of Lane into her broken-darkened existence, maybe it was her daughter, Amelia, with all of her sparkly-little-girl qualities—the voice of imagination whispering its golden promises across her once lethargic soul; maybe it was the tiny heart of her son beating beneath her own heart, in a place that was said by the doctors that he could never exist, Tristen was a miracle made possible by God after healing her broken being: mind, body and soul; maybe it was the Cadotion village with all of their love and loyalty; or the new life budding under her heart in that now healed place that existed as a portal between worlds, delivering the sweet souls from Heaven to Earth—Jordan was not sure what the reason, she could even argue that it had been her moment of death—Lane had accidently ended her life during a heated battle with the Manerky...whatever the cause, she had never been so grateful. As they traveled on a blanket of clouds toward the states, tears slipped from her eyes and down her cheeks, a silent mourning and joy colliding on the walls of her soul. Her mind a lazy river of thought: she would miss Aniahi, her confident, medicine woman, mother, grandmother, mother-in-law and friend; she would miss her beautiful daughter, as she would now be stepping into the place of medicine woman, years too soon—though she would have her parents for a time, Jordan knew that the moment would dawn on the horizon of her life far too soon, separating her from her childhood, guiding her to the woman that was awaiting her, the tribe that awaited her trusted wisdom. It somehow seemed too much, and yet, somewhere deep in her heart, Jordan knew that her six-year-old daughter with her achingly small shoulders, was more prepared than most to take on the responsibility thrust into her hands. Aniahi was meant to stay by her side. She was meant to have years spread out before her to teach, groom and prepare Amelia…life had chosen differently; evil had reached its ugly hands into their happy world and claimed its pound of flesh.

Jordan sucked in a deep breath. The sadness was becoming too much. She wanted to remember only the good times that she had had with Aniahi, but she knew it would not happen that way. For a time, she would feel ache so strong that it would fill the air with iron. She would feel the gravity of her loss, monumental weight pushing down on her life, as every moment that Aniahi had championed for her would be felt in droves…her loss would be apparent in every aspect of their lives, for she had been paramount to their very existence. It would take time, but eventually as she was now able to do with her mother's memory she would be able to celebrate the moments of her life that had enriched her, changed her and prepared her to be the woman that she had become.

Jordan felt Lane's hand slip around her shoulders. A gentle tug told her that he wanted to comfort her. Tristen was strapped in the seat between them, so she just leaned her head, awkwardly into it, and accepted his affections willingly. His touch always brought her comfort.

"Amelia is with her Uncle Garrison, and Mahalia has offered to check in with them. She will be continuing as much of the training to be the medicine woman as she can remember." Lane offered with a sad smile.

Jordan touched his hand, caressing his wedding band for a moment. She offered a resigned smile as she caressed her protruding tummy. She knew that he was right. She was worrying about nothing. She turned her emerald gaze back to the clouds, and for a moment gave herself over to their weightlessness. She allowed her mind to drift along their billowing surface, and imagined that she could run across the tops. Her hand smoothing through the smoke texture. Soon her eyes closed. Her mind drifted to another time.

Her mother was there with her, sitting amid the white-fluffiness. Her voice warm and inviting like the freshly baked Banana bread that used to cool on the baking rack at her grandmother's house. Jordan laid her head in her mother's lap, finally giving up on deciphering her words—better she just soaked up her mother's nearness, while she had the time. The dream felt so real. She could feel the smooth silkiness of her mother's skin and smell the inviting aroma of her White Diamond perfume. She sucked in several deep breaths, trying to fill her nostrils and her mind with the very essence of her mother; how she missed her. She could feel her mother's fingers gliding though her hair as she lifted a strand and inspected it for tangles, and lay it down to lift yet another. Jordan closed her eyes in the dream for a moment, and when she again opened them she was lying on the banks of the Cadotion river. The Kangchenjunga Mountains ghosted in the back of her awareness as she now drew closer to Aniahi's inviting smile. Her hand flowed on the breeze in front of her showcasing the beauty all around. Jordan only half-heartedly acknowledged the glorious landscape, her heart was too set on the contours of her dead friend's beautiful visage. She noticed every nuance of her now younger, but easily recognizable face. She also noted that the scar that had once been over her right eye was no longer there. She saw no sign of the ravages of time that had once told a story of wisdom on her lovely face. She had no silver dusting her head, it was now the coal-black that it had once been in her youth. Jordan vaguely wondered if this would be true of everyone in Heaven, this forever young, thirty-three-year-old appearance... that boasted of the most beautiful time in a human's lifespan. She had often heard her mother comment that she would love her thirties.

Her mother would caress her face, during her early twenties, and repeat the same thing each time, "You just think you are beautiful now, Jordan." But she didn't. She had never been one to be conceded. She did not think herself ugly, but had certainly not stood in the mirror congratulating herself on her stunning-good-looks. "One day, when you are in your thirties...mhhhh... you will see." Her mother would sigh as she spoke, and seem to fall back into the past. Her face was at once, a mask of regret and contentment.

Jordan looked deep into the golden butterscotch hue of Aniahi's eyes. She wanted to get lost there and listen as this woman of incredible wisdom spoke to her soul. She enjoyed their talks so much. The sadness was overwhelming; the wait would seem so long before she could talk to her friend again. She wanted to keep the moment unrushed, to breathe it in, but she sensed that her time with Aniahi here in this moment—wherever she was, would be limited and possibly the only time that she would have. She had so much to say, and yet more than anything she just wanted to exist here with her friend. She wanted to enjoy the way that she could sit with Aniahi and breathe. She never felt the need to entertain, or to be entertained. It was a simplicity that flushed the hurried state of the world away. She was so thankful for the time, and yet saddened for too little of it.

Aniahi smoothed back a lock of hair behind Jordan's right ear, in much the same way her mother had. She then placed her hands around Jordan's shoulders and pulled her into a deep hug. The scent of Lavender immediately arrested her senses. It was the scent that Aniahi had bathed in. Both calming and cleansing, the flower was among the medicine woman's most coveted spices.

Jordan stayed there in her arms for long moments, before drifting lazily across the sands of time. Her mind collected every variable of information, every offered nuance of her lost loved ones; even Modilo's mother stood waving to her from an enormous tent. Her pastel robes floating on the breeze, as she mouthed thank you. Jordan knew in an instant that it was for making certain that her son was safe and cared for. Jordan at last emerged from her dream-like state. Her eyes lashes batted fiercely as if trying to beat the images back into the not so distant past.

She turned her head and saw the slow deliberate smile on Lane's lips. Her mind swam dizzily further back into reality as she took in his angelic face. His chiseled-in-stone, godlike features beckoned to her to join him in the here and now. As much as she longed to walk among those taken too soon from their lives, she was drawn to him—her heart would always be for him. He was her home. He would forever be the place that God had created for her to rest, her soft place to fall; Lane was God's loving embrace and promise that He was there. He was a beautiful reflection of God's love for her.

Lane took turns with Julie, Kirsten, John and Edward dancing in front of the nursery window. Each was comparing the two babies sitting side by side in similar glass-encased cribs with lamps shining down onto the tiny little girls. Lane marbled at the tiny stature of his daughter, Destiny Aniahi Gates. A mop of blonde hair ensconced her angelic face. Her eyes were the same color emerald as Jordan's. She was the image of Tristen, except her hair was blonde like Lane's, where Tristan's was the deep Auburn of Jordan's. Also, Tristen's eyes were as blue as a spring sky just like Lane's, while Destiny's eyes were the same electric emerald as Jordan's. Her size was dwarfed, compared to that of Tristen's at her age, as well. She would obviously not take after Lane in size. Lane blinked back tears of joy, as he turned his attention to the bed immediately to her right.

Cadence Selah Denton was the picture of her mother, Cynthia. The name given the small brunette with tiny curls delicately playing around her face was a combination of their love for music and the Lord. Selah means to lift in praise. Cadence is the rhythm or tempo of music.

John tapped the glass as he mouthed the words, "My song."

Lane smiled at his friend for a moment, and then turned his attention to Julie and Edward. He noticed their hands were intertwined between them as they passed sheepish smiles of pleasure. He imagined that their happiness was as much about the beautiful girls as it was the new life that they walked toward. The couple would waste no time. They had already talked to the church and would have a small wedding with just their closest friends and family members. They had decided on not having a wedding party, and would go with the traditional vows. It was all tradition anyway. They just wanted to get onto the business of living.

Lane felt the joy of their love as it boiled over and seemed to embrace all those around them. It felt good to have so many people in his and Jordan's life that had the same values. He stood gazing at his daughter for a moment longer, and then tenderly touched a shoulder on each of his friends, before turning to walk back to the room that he knew Jordan to be. She would be resting.

As Lane stepped into the dim lit room, he breathed a deep sigh of relief. So many things had happened to spoil each moment of happiness. He had no way of knowing if or when life would turn, but he knew enough about God to trust Him in every moment. Still a place deep within his soul, rejoiced in the moments like this…Jordan lay on the bed with her Auburn hair scattered in tangled heaps. The red-blotchy patches had started to retreat and the warm hue of her sun kissed tan skin shown through with radiant life. Her arms were swept protectively around their son, Tristen. His dark-Auburn locks swept to his shoulder, surrounding his cherub face. His nose turned to his mother, as a smile lifted his heart-shaped lips in a satisfied smile, and then fell back to an O-shape. He nestled further into her arms. No doubt he was smelling her, sensing her closeness. The time that she had been away from him to give birth to Destiny had obviously been just enough to stir his need for reassurance. Lane watched as Jordan scooted absent-mindedly closer to their little boy, and scooped him tighter into her embrace.

"Nothing could be better than this life that you have given me, Father." Lane offered the reverent prayer, before lying back into the plush-leather-dark-manila colored cot against the wall opposite the door.

CHAPTER

75

S now was just beginning to decline its glistening-reign over the mountain tops. Only scant traces of winter remained in the crisp March air. Spring would soon be dressing the Cadotion village with her luxurious splendor. The smell of Lilac was already present. Small birds soared on the breeze, calling their happy cheers for the new life to come.

Jordan watched as the river lapped against the shore, beckoning to the children to enter its cool promise, and enjoy the hidden treasures buried beneath the sands; the shimmering-glassy surface of different colored rocks ghosted into view. Temptation called to the young-adventurous minds—treasure hunts would soon fill the air with the children's excited chants and laughter, as they ran up to the shore, boasting of their looted treasure, and hoisting it proudly in the air for all to admire.

"Mama, Obiahon." Amelia touched Jordan's arm. She was so tall now. At sixteen her legs swept across the ground in a graceful dance. Her hair was darker now, and much longer. Braided in the traditional elder fashion, it was a crown of declaration; shouting to the wisdom and place that she held among the tribe.

Jordan appraised the upsweep, and waterfall like layers that cascaded down, each level becoming thinner. Baby's breath adorned the sweeping edges, adding a bedazzlement of grace. Loose braids danced along her hips, with every turn of her head. Her eyes still the same golden-amber, now belied the woman she had become: strong and fierce, yet gentle and calm. Her daughter was no longer an apprentice spending her days trying to take in all that Aniahi, and eventually Mahalia had to impart. Amelia was now the acting medicine woman. She stood alone, key-holder to years of knowledge. Soon she would take an apprentice under her own wing. She, like Aniahi, would spend long hours passing the secrets of the medicine woman on to the next generation. So important was the task. Jordan could now see that. The world that her daughter lived in, as beautiful as it may be, was one of uncertainty. Her time was not known, her days, just as all humans was but a vapor—yet to hold so many secrets that could save lives in such a primitive place...

Jordan sighed. It was so hard to think of her little girl, as the capable young woman she had become. It seemed just days earlier she had been toddling down the aisle between the wooden benches to take her place as the apprentice to the medicine woman. Jordan had been so unsure of placing such strenuous expectations on one so young, but now as she looked upon the stoic-vision that was her daughter—she knew. The answer was clear. There was no one more right for the trusted place among the people.

"Hello, honey." Jordan squeezed her daughter's offered hand. "How are you holding up? I know yesterday was very trying." Jordan searched Amelia's eyes for any sign that she was not accepting the loss of the hunter as God's will.

"I'm good, mama. I know that it was the will of God." Amelia's simple smile turned brighter, lighting her entire face. "His son is awake and strong."

"That's wonderful!" Jordan offered. Joy filtered through her body, a feeling she had become accustomed to.

The hunting party had been ambushed by a pride: a lion and his four lionesses had been scouting the same area. Sohi and his son, Goarash had been together at the time. Four other hunters had moved on to gather the hunting supplies, and load the large Sambar deer. The huge animal was the largest that the hunters had seen, and would make a great start on the food supplies needed for the upcoming spring celebration.

Jordan had been helping to tan leather with some of the younger children and younger women when the hunters entered the village with shouts of praise. She could hardly believe her eyes. The massive animal that they dragged on a board behind their horses was the image of the deer that she had seen in America. It had all the necessary attributes that spoke of an animal in the deer family, but the sheer bulk and massive amount of fur... she guessed the animal to weigh near a thousand pounds. She had never seen the likes of the Sambar. As the hunters danced around their prize, she could see that the deer, head to toe was at least a couple inches taller than she, at five foot nine, she was taller than the average woman, yet this animal dwarfed her. Horns burst forth out of its massive head, thirteen points—she marveled at the beauty and felt saddened by the years its many points had testified of, and the years thwarted, due to the circle of life. She knew though that this was the way. She had killed animals to survive while traveling through the woods, on many of the missions she had undertaken, to take out a mark.

Jordan shivered as she thought of those lives wasted at her hand.

The life of Sohi was over. The lion's revenge for his stolen prize had been swift. The villagers had rushed in, investigating the terror-stricken cries of the teenage boy, Goarash. Massive amounts of blood escaped the three long gashes in Sohi's neck. Truly, he had been gone, before his body had been lain on Amelia's table. Though his eyes seemed to flutter in disbelief of his undesired end, it had only been the reframes of nerves twitching. Before the hunters could get to the mortally wounded hunter and his son, Goarash had rushed to save his father. He had thrust a spear deep in the angry lion's side. A wild sweep of his paw had left an ugly mark on the side of the boy's face. The others had come just in time to ward any further attacks. Loud hoops and the firing of the only gun, a twelve-gauge given to the leader of the hunting party—a gift from Garrison, in truth he did not like being in the woods with such large game, carrying only spears and crudely made weapons—had scared the lionesses off and wounded the lion enough that he would not continue in the fight.

Jordan was proud that Goarash had survived. She would be sure to check on him later. Maybe one of weapons she had been working on would be a good gift for the fallen warrior. The Cadotion people were a practical people. They knew well that death was as much a part of life as being born. Though Goarash would miss his father greatly and there would be a time of mourning, he would be expected to take his place back amongst the other hunters soon.

Amelia moved away after another gentle squeeze from Jordan's hand, leaving Jordan to again take in the landscape and all those that filled it.

Garrison and Mahalia chased their toddling daughter, Cadotia Americus; named for the two worlds that had collided to create her in love. Sahalia stood at hand. She adopted a ready stance, a weary smile morphed into a bout of giggles as she headed off her sister's attempts at escape.

Jordan turned her attention to Garrison for a moment. Their eyes met; a satisfied smile filled his face. Her best friend was genuinely happy, and for the first time, it felt as though fate had not left him behind. He had taken his place in the world. He had even earned a place at Mahalia's side as an elder. Attending many of the hunts, he and Lane had proven worthy contributors to the Cadotion way of life. Many times, it was Garrison alone that had brought back food enough to fill the hungry bellies during winter.

She felt a sense of completion and peace, knowing that when she was gone from the village that her friend would thrive. She knew also that Amelia would always have her Uncle Garrison and Aunt Mahalia for support. The thought of leaving their daughter when the time came, had always been a pock-mark on the face of their future. But Jordan knew, as did Lane that one day God would call them to a mission-field somewhere else. Their time in the Cadotion village was coming to an end. It felt good to know that those that she loved would be together, enjoying the tribe and all the love and wonder that it had to offer. Yet at the same time to have a stronger connection with someone that had been a more tangible part of their forever—she remembered all too well how intimidating it could feel, to be amongst those that you did not necessarily know—no matter the good intentions and love that the people had for Amelia, and no matter that she shared their same tan skin and the beautiful golden hue of the Cadotion eye color—it could feel like you were drowning in a sea of faces that had no true connection to your inner most being. Garrison had been a part of Amelia's forever. He had spent time up front and accounted for. Though he shared no blood, or even similar attributes as her daughter, Garrison had shared space and time. He had tried to be a part of each of her children's world. Even Penny, her niece had benefit on many occasion from his long talks and trusted companionship.

Jordan allowed her gaze to move on across the faces of those that she loved. It felt good to see John and Cynthia finally coming to the village. They had always been a serene couple, but something about the enchantment of the mountain range and the people that lived in its majestic pass lifted a person to a higher state of euphoria. It was a blissful state that kissed every nerve ending. It filled your entire soul with bliss and spilled over onto those around you.

Kirsten was now attending her first year of college. Due to her time in the village being captured by the Manerky, she was not yet ready to venture back into the mountain passes. She had assured Jordan that she would keep an open mind about the village, but just needed some time to pass between that dreaded time.

Cadence and Destiny squealed with feigned horror as Tristen chased them. Now thirteen, he was the image of Lane. His huge Nephilim body was already beginning to dwarf that of his sister, Destiny's and Cadence's small statures.

Jordan couldn't help but allow a huff of laughter to escape, as her giant of a son tried to mimic his father's catlike reflexes and graceful stride. As beautiful as her boy might be, his attempts were no match for that of his father's. She knew that it was years of training that he lacked. She wondered if Lane, had too, once been awkward. Had his height and bulk made grace seem more like barbaric stumble?

Lane had pushed himself to be the best for the mission that he would one day undertake. Jordan, once the darkest of Black Heart agents, had an even darker heart. Lane would find her and bring her back, not to the compound, to be recycled, or worse still, erased from existence; he would bring her to a place of understanding—a place where she would meet the Creator of the universe, and come to a saving knowledge of His sacrifice, love, grace and mercy. She would be filled with His truth and changed forever.

Standing here in the wake of that memory, she felt a sense of pride for all that she had left behind, and all that she had gained. She still missed her mother and Aniahi at times, but she knew without doubt that she would one day be with them again on the shores of another body of water: The Crystal Sea.

Giant arms circled her body and pulled her to the unyielding mass of a muscled wall. Jordan laid her head back on Lane's chest, and allowed her mind to be swept up in the current of thoughts. Heaven was but a heartbeat away; not so far, she pondered. Her mother and Aniahi would be waiting for them there, but until then…she allowed an exaggerated sigh—this was theirs to enjoy.

A high-pitched squeal pulled Jordan from this blissful haven of her thoughts. She turned just in time to see Nick rushing down the river bank with Penny over his shoulder. Her arms sought purchase around the slight definition of his muscled arms. His lean, but powerful legs strained, only slightly underneath her long-lean frame. Her hair, much longer, bounced, in a careless-dark-auburn flood of waves. Another squeal escaped her throat, as her eyes rose to meet Jordan's. Emerald green, the shade of her own beckoned to Jordan from her niece's exquisite countenance.

"Aunt Jordan, help!"

"Oh, no ma'am! You got yourself into that mess. I'm sure you can get yourself out just fine." Jordan laughed with a slight noncommittal wave of her hand.

"Well, that's rude." Lane complained.

"Rude?" Jordan's brow furrowed as she turned to see what Lane was talking about. A self-satisfied grin started to grow more pronounced on his still-too-chiseled-in-stone features. She had long-since stopped worrying about her aging face, compared to that of his angelic visage that seemed breathtakingly frozen in time. Though he did age, it was much slower than that of humans. Now forty-three, most people thought that she was truly thirty-five, while Lane looked to be twenty-eight at the most, though he was in fact three years her senior. She had gotten dirty looks from women in the grocery store. It had proven to be a source of irritation for the longest time, but she had soon learned to embrace the difference, and had at times picked on her cherub-faced spouse in moments of would be unwanted scrutiny. Making remarks such as, 'come to mama' or 'cougar on the prow' had been a very satisfying way to get even with Lane. He had retired some of his gloating and the onlookers had lost interest quickly, not having the desired effect on the couple that had 'broken the rules' was somehow not as satisfying, if they weren't horrified by the jeers and stares of disapproval.

"Yes. Rude." Lane admonished.

Jordan felt the flex of his arms. She knew a moment too late what his plan for her would be.

"No! Lane!" Jordan growled. She tried desperately to attach ferocity to her words, so that she sounded threatening. She knew where this was going.

"Your niece asked for your help." Lane growled back. "Yet you dismiss her pleas for help." He admonished while scooping Jordan's body above his head. Her arms and legs searched frantically for something that would stay her execution—something that would hold at bay her unwanted fate.

Lane scooped her, effortlessly above his massive shoulder. "Here you are a trained agent, with abilities…beyond capable of addressing her issue. Instead you remain unmoved by her cries for help?" A playful tenor lifted his voice.

"Former agent. I'm a missionary now remember?" Jordan offered up the useless explanation for her inaction.

"Missionary. Yes!" Lane huffed. "Exactly! Aren't you Godly-types supposed to be…oh, I don't know helpful?" His voice was now belying the hilarity in which he regarded her predicament, and the obvious ineffectual attempts her scrambling for freedom was having on his hold.

"You were a missionary first, angel boy! You go help her!" Jordan declared with one last grab for freedom, before she felt her body flip effortlessly forward.

The instant feeling of cold skidded through her nerve endings. Her breath caught, and she was instantly moving for the shore. The day was warm for near spring, and the winter had not been so bitter cold as the year before. Still the water was cold, not freezing, but cold enough that she and as she could see, Penny knew without a doubt that they wanted to be anywhere but in its depths.

"Woo!" Lane complained as he joined his drenched mate.

Jordan turned to see Penny scrambling for the shore. Her lips were shivering in protest. Lane moved closer to Jordan and wrapped his arms around her. Wrapped in his warmth, the coolness of the water was no longer a concern.

"Go stand by the fire and get warm. Get those cold robes off." Jordan called behind Penny.

"You know she is twenty-seven, right?" Lane asked as he rubbed his nose against her cheek.

"Yeah…tell me about it." Jordan sighed.

"You want to get out?" His hands were rubbing her back, the chill of the water completely at bay now.

She watched quietly for a moment without answering. All the children had rushed back to the camp. She could hear the calls of laughter as they, no doubt joined in the dancing—celebration for spring had already begun. "No. I'm good." She sighed happily, as she moved further into his embrace. This was her home, here in his arms would always be her portion; her piece of Heaven on earth.

From the beatings of her father and brother, her mother's inaction to save her from a disgraceful childhood, to Black Heart and its unleashing of death that had dipped her dreams in the shadowy-darkness of nightmares…worse still, when those nightmares had seemed to climb from the recesses of her fear-filled soul to the pages of her life—coloring her world with the demonic host of hell come to the world of the living, making even the possession she had experienced pale in comparison… as she watched the horrific faces of the Manerky parade their campaign of death and destruction through the midst of the Cadotion village. She had for far too long been given to an anger that burned away at the last of her humanity. Her life had for so long been a practice in patience, not learned—tests failed. Lane had been a happy turning point in her life. He was her home; her peace. A brilliant example of God's grace shining down on her. Lane would always be God showing mercy on her. She looked deep into his eyes, and it was there, as always that she could see the years behind, the day before them, and the years to come. An eternity of hope stretched out before them, as God's answered prayers swept through their lives and colored each knew horizon with His love and hope… His promise of forever shown back from her husband's sky blue eyes, a testimony of love that existed only in the heart of a Savior.

God had been saving her from the beginning. She could see that now. Though the waters of her life had been too murky at times to see clear that truth—she could see His grace so clear. He had set in place every moment planning for her rescue. Like a conquering hero, He had met her in the depths of her sin, in the darkest moments of her life—He had been there, waiting for the moment when she would at last reach out to Him. Though she had not seen His offered hand at the time, as she looked back across the sands of time, she could see only one set of footprints. She could see the moments that He had carried her to the next moment because she had been too weak to stand. Every moment had been sweeping her down the current of her treacherous existence to the banks of the Cadotion river, and into the arms that would forever still the waters of her troubled soul.

A FEW WORDS FROM
THE AUTHOR

Words cannot convey the depth of emotion that I am feeling as I come to the end of this journey. Black Heart has been a healing process. It is through the created lives of each of the characters that my own demons have been exorcised.

God has made every step of this journey with me, offering a wisdom that I did not possess. It is important that each of you know here, now that I am not a writer. I did not go to school as most accomplished authors have. I dropped out in the tenth grade, and by the grace of God was allowed a great opportunity: college.

To understand the full debt of gratitude that I felt, and yes, the bewildering concern as well that I felt about God's desire for me to write—I will need to take you all back.

Two small children, at the time depended on me for everything, though I knew I had nothing but the love in my heart to give; I knew that it would not be enough. Love as admirable an emotion, and needed a commodity as it is, does not fill hungry bellies. Therefore, I knew obtaining a GED was a must!

I worked many minimum wage jobs: McDonald's, Krystal's, ect... I also spent time in mills. No direction, I moved from job to job, hoping to make ends meet; barely understanding what that concept meant. I started work at Lanier Healthcare, and was filtered through a six-week course for CAN, Certified Nursing Assistant.

During the nineties I think my life had fallen to its lowest point. I won't drag the details of my then horrible existence around. It is God's grace that I wish to shine light on, not the ugliness of that time. As I was saying, it was the lowest point of my life, but it would soon turn around.

I started pulling twenty-four hour shifts at Lanett and Fire EMS as a volunteer firefighter. God being the loving and good Father that He is, would soon honor my sacrifice. I was offered the ability to go to college, which I jumped at. EMT-Basic, and then Paramedic technologies. I passed both with flying colors, but through an unfortunate event at National Registry for EMT's I was unable to pass the Medical Oral exam, portion of the battery of tests for Paramedic EMT. I had, however passed all requirements for Basic-EMT, and began my new career as an EMT. The next six years were a practice in knowledge and self-esteem. I felt like a new woman. I loved myself, and felt as though I was making a difference, but even then I had no true understanding of God's affections for me; His love was a foreign concept.

In high school, I had my first brush with what it meant to truly love the written world, but it had been a fleeting admiration that had been kept solely to reading. My understanding of literature was a limited as my understanding of God's grace.

After years of EMS, the career vomited me out into a heap of uncertainty; a wreck in Atlanta, Georgia on I-85 ended a six-year career, after a man in a black sedan pulled a 'swoop and squat', on a rainy-congested highway. I said my goodbyes, but never truly let it go. Maybe I felt let down; abandoned. Whatever emotion that ebbed the hurt and anger inside of me, it left no room for reconciliation. I walked through the motions of expected Christianity; a belief system passed down from my grandparents and my parents that I mimicked well.

I was working at a collision center, how ironic, I went from being the hope of those in the collision, to being the person at the welcome desk after the collision. I felt empty. Useless. Then one day as I sat, staring out of the large picture windows into the streets of the bustling Opelika highway, I felt a nudging to write. Though at the time I had no clue that those moments of free thought and inspiration, would lead to a trilogy—I felt even then God was doing something. Not to make me rich and famous, but to use me in a manner that exceeded my abilities. God was taking me, a high-school dropout, with limited education that by the way had nothing to do with literature—he was using an unlikely host to deliver a powerful message! He is God! He is able! Like Jordan and all of her family and friends, there is nothing that is too bad, no sin that you have committed that would classify you as too broken for our Savior's blood to cover; to present you clean, a new creature, worthy of the Father's love.

As the words filled the pages, and the characters became more real to me, I began to realize just how much of me was in each of the characters. The more I listened to God's voice as He prompted me what I should write, the more I began to understand how much He truly loved me. I understood how many times He had been there lifting me out of the gutters of life. I could finally comprehend the fullness of His affection for me. His affection for you. Everything that He has ever done has been to bring us closer to Him, to make our lives more, fuller. He loves us so much that He sent His ONLY Son to die for our sins! We mean that much to Him!

His word is guide-book of lives lived, experiences had that can teach us all what not to do on our journey. I hope as you read the Black Heart Trilogy that you can pull from the made of experiences of the characters that God so graciously gave to me, but I know that your life will be richly blessed by the true events of the lives lived and shared on the pages of God's Holy Word!

Thank you all for allowing me this precious time to share my heart and thoughts with you. Thank you for taking this journey with me. My thoughts and prayers are with you all. Until we meet in our Father's house, keep up the good fight, be strong in the Lord and never forget you are His love; His everything!

www.ingramcontent.com/pod-product-compliance
Lightning Source LLC
Chambersburg PA
CBHW031611180726
48284CB00005B/1495